THE DALLANCY BEQUEST

Recent Titles by Tessa Barclay from Severn House

A BETTER CLASS OF PERSON
FAREWELL PERFORMANCE
A HANDFUL OF DUST
A LOVELY ILLUSION
THE SILVER LINING
STARTING OVER
A TRUE LIKENESS

THE DALLANCY BEQUEST

Tessa Barclay

This first world edition published in Great Britain 2005 by
SEVERN HOUSE PUBLISHERS LTD of
9–15 High Street, Sutton, Surrey SM1 1DF.
This first world edition published in the USA 2005 by
SEVERN HOUSE PUBLISHERS INC of
595 Madison Avenue, New York, N.Y. 10022.

British Library Cataloguing in Publication Data

Barclay,   Tessa
    The Dallancy bequest
    1.   Women genealogists - Fiction
    2.   Genealogy - Fiction
    3.   Love stories
    I.   Title
    823.9'14 [F]

    ISBN 0-7278-6181-6 (cased)
    ISBN 0-7278-9134-0 (paper)

Typeset by Palimpsest Book Production Ltd.,
Polmont, Stirlingshire, Scotland.
Printed and bound in Great Britain by
MPG Books Ltd., Bodmin, Cornwall.

One

L aura Wainwright had always had a weakness for a beautiful voice. The voice she heard on the telephone now was
just the kind to make her feel soothed and pleased and attracted
– it made her think of brown velvet, of rich cream. Moreover
it had what she thought of as an American accent. She said,
'Yes, this is Lauron Family Research, how can I help you?'

'Ah . . . Yeah . . . You do research on relatives, ancestors,
that kind of thing?'

'Yes indeed, that's our business. Is there something I can
help you with?'

'Yeah, well . . . maybe . . . It's kind of tenuous, you know.
I thought I might come to you because you're based near
Oxford and that's where I'm staying for the moment. And I
just have the notion that the family originally came from
somewhere not so far off, kind of in this area, you see, though
I could be talking through the top of my head because really
it's all just . . . you know . . . sort of hearsay.'

Laura smiled to herself. She'd heard this kind of prologue
to many of the research jobs she and her father had under-
taken.

The name of the firm was derived from their two names,
Laura and Ronald. Genealogical research had not by any means
been Laura's aim when she was taking English Literature at
university, but family events had made it happen. The break-
up of her parents' marriage and her father's subsequent long
bout of depression had meant that she had both to earn a living
and stay close to him. So now here she was, partner in a little
firm that took on yet more family problems, but thankfully
those of strangers.

She said now, in the brisk yet friendly fashion she'd evolved
for dealing with hesitant clients, 'Would it be a good idea to

1

start with your name? I'm Laura Wainwright, one of the researchers. And you are ... ?'

'Of course – what a fool – may name's Crandel, Neil Crandel.'

'And your address?'

'I'm staying at the Sceptre, just outside Oxford. It's a hotel.'

'Yes. I know it.' My word. The Sceptre was one of those magnificent country houses that had been carefully developed into a holiday centre, and its prices were beyond anything Laura could afford. Had she landed a client who'd turn out to be an American tycoon?

'How long are you staying in England, Mr Crandel?'

'Oh, for a bit. Indeterminate, is that the word? See, my dad died recently, and I got knocked about in an accident, so I'm kind of convalescing, if you understand me, and I thought that, instead of just hanging around at home getting cabin fever, I'd take a trip. Do something Dad wanted to do, make a try at tracing our forebears but not from so far away. Dad had done some stuff through a friend at home, you see, but it had kind of trickled into the creek.'

She was so taken up with enjoying the rise and fall of that gorgeous voice that she almost failed to take in the sense of his words. But she pulled herself to attention. 'Your father had done some research?'

'Not personally, at least not much. No, he paid a pal to do it, but I guess you know how it is, at a certain point in the past it seems to fade off and get fuzzy.'

She named a couple of well-known genealogists of the United States. 'One of those?'

'N-no, it was a guy Dad knew who was into that stuff – Linus Perkins, he had a stand of timber a bit north of us, did it as a hobby.'

'North of you where?'

'North of Wenaskowa.'

'Wenaskowa – that's ... er ... Arizona?' she hazarded, thinking of the Western films she'd seen.

The response was a deep chuckle. 'Arizona? Ms Wainwright, your geography is way off. Arizona is one of the American states.'

'And Wenaskowa isn't in an American state?'

'Good grindstones, it's in Alberta! And Alberta's in—'

'Canada,' they ended in chorus.

There was a momentary pause then he said, 'I'm sorry. I take it for granted that you know where my home ground is, just because it's been the big factor in my own life. The word for that is parochial, I think – am I right?'

'Not at all, probably if I were abroad I'd expect people to know Brinbank is in Oxfordshire.'

'No, you wouldn't, you've got a wider outlook than your own cabbage patch, I can tell that by your voice. Say now, do you think you'd be interested in doing some work on the stuff my dad started? He'd got back as far as a great-great-great-grandparent called Crandel who emigrated to Canada in around 1861 or maybe 1862, then did a slow move westward from Quebec until he put down roots in Alberta.'

'Do you happen to have the information with you, Mr Crandel? Any mementoes, photographs, legal documents?'

'Sure. I could send them to you if you like.'

She thought it would be better to meet. She wanted to see the owner of that slow, easy voice. 'You say you're at the Sceptre?'

'Yeah, could I invite you to drop in on me there? So you could see the stuff? Or I could come see you – I've got a rental car, I quite enjoy driving along your twisty little roads and peeping over the hedges at your countryside.'

She laughed. 'You'd only see a few miles of countryside but if you'd like to come here, it would be handier for looking at documents – we've got viewers and magnifying lenses . . .'

'That makes sense.' She could hear he was pleased. 'How do I get to you?'

'Got a pencil?' She gave him instructions for the fourteen-mile trip, hearing him chuckle to himself at some of the village names. 'When would you like to come?'

'Well, how's about today? I'm here on my own, you know, nothing to do but please myself. Or is today inconvenient? Because if so, tomorrow's fine with me, or the day after . . .'

'Today would be good,' she said, guessing at a certain lone-liness in the background. 'I could give you afternoon tea.'

'Afternoon tea!' He laughed at the words. 'With *scones*?'

'Absolutely.'

'It's a date. What time is "afternoon tea" with you? At the hotel it's four o'clock.'

'Then I'll expect you at four, Mr Crandel. And don't forget, bring all your research papers and anything else from your family's past.'

'Yeah, it's all together here in a folder. And, say, we ought to talk about fees. I got your firm from a history magazine but it doesn't mention fees.'

'I'll give you one of our brochures when you come. Until this afternoon, then.'

'See you then. So long.'

Her father was out at a neighbour's house doing some gardening. When he came home muddy and tired at lunchtime she decided not to mention that they were to have a visitor. His reaction to news of any kind was difficult to foretell – sometimes he'd be relatively interested, sometimes he'd be cross. She waited until he'd washed and changed and put in his hearing aids before she felt it was a good moment to tell him about Neil Crandel.

'I thought at first he was an American and might be tremendously well off, but instead he's a Canadian from some place out in the wilds of Alberta.'

'Alberta,' Ronald mused. 'That's . . . where? Out on the western side, up against the Rockies?'

'I've no idea,' she confessed. 'I'm going to look it up when I've got the food in the oven.'

She was a fair cook, moderately enthusiastic. She'd prepared a casserole on the previous evening which she now put in to heat up, with the dessert course, which was already baking. The vegetables went in the microwave. That done, she found an atlas and tried to find Wenaskowa but had no success.

Well, you wouldn't find Brinbank, in an atlas either, she told herself with a shrug. But Alberta proved to be on the eastern side of the Rockies, as her father had suggested, which seemed to indicate it was an agricultural state or perhaps went in for lumber. Pine trees on mountain sides . . . 'A stand of timber to the north,' Crandel had said. She could picture it – quite like something in a Western film after all, only it would be one of those where the wagon trains trekked up and down mountain passes.

'If he knows about trees perhaps he can tell me what's wrong with the rhododendron in Kim's garden,' Ronald said. 'It's being attacked by something but I don't know what. She's going to lose it soon if something isn't done.'

'A rhododendron's a shrub, not a tree,' Laura objected.

'That thing in Kim's back garden's as big as a tree. She says she thinks I ought to prune it but I'd need special ladders to get up to it.'

'Perhaps she should get someone in with proper equipment.' She would have liked to add that Kim could well afford a proper gardener, instead of relying on the inexpert attention of Ronald Wainwright. She spooned lamb stew on to a plate for him with rather unnecessary vigour. She wasn't really very pleased at the amount of time and energy her father spent on helping Kim Groves.

Then she reproved herself. She must stop thinking unkind thoughts about Kim. Just because she was taller and slimmer and more outgoing than Laura, that didn't mean she was a bad person. All the same, a successful solicitor ought to be able to afford paid help in her garden. No need to be calling on Laura's father, who spent far too much of his time . . .

There she went again. Her father had a perfect right to spend his spare time where and how he wanted. But she'd like it better if he didn't spring to attention every time Kim crooked her little finger.

Ronald had taken a long time to recover from his divorce. He'd gone into a severe depression, which had been threatening even before the break-up. He'd been losing his hearing over a period of years but had refused to acknowledge the fact.

History teacher at a high-priced private school for boys, he'd been unaware at first that the moment he turned to the blackboard loud whispers and muffled laughter would break out. Naturally the boys extended their misbehaviour until even when they were face to face the class was out of control. Ronald was called before the head for a reprimand. He made efforts to improve his classroom methods. Nothing worked. He lost his temper with his pupils, began to be known as Stalin because he gave out so many bad marks.

This was when the first signs of a depression began to appear.

5

Laura, at university, would receive near-hysterical phone calls from her mother. 'He's locked himself in his study with a bottle of brandy, Laura! What shall I do?'

'You've got to get him to a doctor, Mama!'

Easier said than done. It took almost a year. The doctor diagnosed his psychological problem at once but noticed also that his patient had great trouble hearing him when he turned back to his desk to write notes. He gave him a hearing test in his surgery, made a hospital appointment for him, and then for months a long downward slide took place: Ronald failed to keep hospital appointments, resisted the diagnosis of his hearing problem, lost his temper with his wife, his class, his headmaster, his friends and neighbours, and became perhaps the unhappiest man in the county.

Laura could only be helpful when she was home on vacation, and even then only from the periphery because she had to have holiday jobs to help pay her university expenses. During the summer breaks she worked as a guide in a stately home, conducting tourists through the rooms, answering their questions. It was here that her interest in genealogy was born. She found that to meet the demands of the visitors she had to know more than just who had been the maker of the bureau in the main drawing room: who had ordered it, and why, and was that his portrait on the opposite wall, and why was he wearing that long robe, and how long had he been a judge? And so on and so on.

During Laura's last year at university her mother gave up the struggle to keep her marriage going. It came out that she'd been turning for comfort to a man she'd meet at a neighbour's party. She left to join him in Singapore, where he'd taken the post of manager of a big hotel chain.

Laura did her best to look after Ronald, who went into a lethargic state of what seemed to be complete indifference. He accepted the divorce without comment, accepted the dismissal from his school as inevitable, seemed ready to slide down into some final despond. Yet some spark of determination still existed. Within a year he began to respond to the medication that countered the depression, so that he was persuaded to do something about his deafness.

His appearance improved. He shaved his lean cheeks, had

his thinning brown hair barbered, put a little more weight on his lanky frame.

Meanwhile, to be able to stay at home with him and yet bring in a little money, Laura had accepted a job helping with the computer research of a genealogist. When at last her father was back on an even keel he was able, with his knowledge of English history, to help her with background information. Before long it was obvious that as a partnership they were good at the work, and thus Lauron Family Research was born.

It had brought them a reasonable income. If sometimes Laura felt that she was moored in a backwater, she put the thought aside. She enjoyed the work, she was able to take some care of her father, and, though the society around them was a bit limited, they had good friends and neighbours.

Except for Kim Groves, she found herself adding. At once she checked herself. She'd made a vow not to think badly of Kim. Yet when she studied her father, wolfing down lamb stew so as to get back to Kim's neglected garden, she felt she had some justification. Kim was clever and good looking and fit, and what was more, well-off. She was perfectly capable of seeing to the garden herself, and doing all the odd jobs in her house. Or, if not, she could pay a handyman.

But no. She preferred to call on Ronald Wainwright. Because the minute she bought the nearby house and took up residence he'd fallen under her spell – and she knew it.

Laura sighed to herself and offered a second helping to her father. 'There's apple pie for dessert,' she said. 'Leave some space.'

'Don't worry about that.' He added vegetables to his refilled plate. 'So you're giving this backwoodsman afternoon tea.'

'Yes, with *scones*.' She smiled at the recollection.

'Good lord, not going to bake specially for him?'

'No, I did them when I baked the pie. He probably won't guess they're not fresh out of the oven.'

'Think he's going to turn up in a checked shirt and one of those hats with a brim and ear flaps?'

'Like in the Monty Python sketch?' She laughed. 'Who knows. But he sounded nice.'

'And he wants what?'

'Research on his family tree before his first Canadian

7

ancestor – I think that would be at least a great-great-great-grandfather, mid-Victorian. He seemed to think he came from somewhere in this area, but that's probably oral folklore.'

'You don't need me to stay to meet him?' Ronald glanced at his watch. 'Or I could come back, seeing it's only one thirty now. That would give me a couple of hours on Kim's rose garden.'

It was March, and the bushes in the old-fashioned rose garden needed to be pruned. But, Laura said to herself, there are roses in *our* garden that need pruning. And I'm not going to do them, because if I do Papa will only tell me I've done it wrong.

'It's okay, I'll handle our new client. If we need to have a brain storming session that'll be the time to call you in.'

The truth was, her father wasn't good with clients. He got impatient with them. Although he was better than in the past, his temper was still unpredictable.

She brought the apple pie to the table. Her father watched her put a wedge on a plate for him. 'You're not having any?'

'I've had enough to eat.'

'Slimming again?' He shook his head at her. 'I don't know why you worry about it. You were meant to be curvy, you were curvy as a child.'

She smiled but made no reply. No use trying to explain that it was a matter of fashion. She wasn't very tall; curves that might have seemed pleasing on a long-legged blonde were merely plump on a brown-haired, grey-eyed shortie.

When she'd cleared up the after-lunch debris, there were still two hours to go before her new client arrived. She'd had no fresh air and exercise today and exercise was an important element of the anti-curve campaign. So she decided to walk to the village, which was somewhat less than a mile away. It was the day for the mobile library, so she'd change her books and buy a few groceries.

It was a blue-sky day, March at its best. Homeward bound and loaded with her books and goodies, she admired the cherry blossom. She found herself quoting Housman's poem 'Loveliest of Trees', and then laughed at herself for being so clichéd. But clichés existed because they fitted the moment and this was a moment of pleasure. Life was good: a history

8

book she'd asked for had been waiting for her and on the shelves she'd found an Anne Tylor she hadn't read. Moreover, Stubbs the provision merchant had had a delivery of Italian specialities, so for dinner tonight there would be pasta with ricotta sauce.

Swinging round into her gateway with all these good things in her rucksack, she was taken aback to see a strange car in the drive. Her client? A glance at her watch showed her three thirty – he was early. And here she was, tramping up to him in her old slacks and chunky walking shoes, her hair in a mess from the breeze.

He was standing at the door, his back to her, clearly awaiting an answer after ringing. It was a broad back and he was tall. He seemed to be canted at a slight angle, but this was explained as she got a better view – he was leaning on a stick and a large manila envelope was tucked under his arm. Sturdily built, clad in a leather jacket and Dockers. A lumberjack in reality?

At the sound of her footfall he turned. 'Ms Wainwright?'

'Yes, I'm sorry I was out—'

'My fault, I know I'm early but I didn't know how much time to allow in case I got lost.'

The voice was just as engaging as on the telephone. He was smiling, holding out a broad, capable-looking hand. They shook.

She led him indoors, took his jacket, ushered him into the living room. He said, 'Gee!' This was because of the oak beams that ran across the ceiling, and the fireplace with its big inglenook. Most people were impressed with Old Brin House, a seventeenth-century ploughman's cottage converted and extended by owners over the years.

'I guess this is really old,' he ventured, brown eyes wandering over everything. 'Our place back home was looked on as pretty historic but it only goes back about a hundred years.'

'That was . . . what . . . a farm?' she asked, shepherding him to an armchair.

'Oh, no, Dad and I raised trees.'

'I beg your pardon?'

'We had a tree nursery. You know, if somebody wanted a Japanese maple, we supplied it.'

9

She couldn't suppress a smile. Not a chopper-down of trees, a grower of them. Rather hastily, to cover her amusement, she said, 'If you'll just excuse me a minute, I've a few groceries in my holdall; I need to put them away. And I'll put the kettle on.' She gave him one of the firm's brochures. 'That'll give you an idea of our scope and our prices, Mr Crandel. They're quite high, our rates, but we do have a lot of resources. However, if you think it's going to cost too much, no hard feelings, we'll just call it off.'

'Do I still get the scones if I call it off?' he enquired.

Laughing, she went out. In the kitchen she put her purchases in the cupboards and hung her backpack on its hook. The books went on the dresser to be examined next time she had a meal alone. The plate of scones went into the microwave to warm while the kettle boiled. She whisked them out, buttered them quickly, and in a few minutes she was re-entering the living room with the tray of tea things

Neil Crandel was examining the bookshelves, his walking stick hooked over the back of the armchair.. 'You've read all these?' he enquired, waving a hand at the display.

'Yes, I'm a bookworm. Do you read a lot?'

He shook his head. 'Only what I have to. Outdoors, that's my world.' He turned his glance on the tray she was setting down. The good smell of the scones was in the room. He sniffed appreciatively. 'That takes me back a few years. My mother used to bake.'

'But not any more?'

'No, she passed away about seven years ago, viral pneumonia, a big shock. Dad and I just ate things that came in packets after that, mostly. Or we drove into Wenaskowa for a steak.' He gave a grin. 'I guess you'd say we just pigged it.'

He accepted the teacup Laura was holding out, to set it on a little table by the armchair. When he moved his limp was noticeable and when he sat down he stifled a sigh of relief.

'I hope that's how you take your tea. Milk in first in this household,' she said. He looked mystified so she added, 'There's a long-standing argument – should the milk go in before or after you pour.'

'Not in Alberta,' he countered.

She decided she liked him. He was as nice as his voice.

10

She guessed him to be in his early thirties. There were lines in his broad face that came both from life in the open air and anxieties.

'Are you on your own in England?' she asked. 'Or . . . with a companion?'

'There isn't really anybody,' he sighed. 'Now Dad's gone . . . He had a brother whom I scarcely remember, he went south, settled in New Mexico, I got in touch but he didn't come to the funeral.' He shrugged. 'Sure, it would have been a long way to come, but I'd have thought . . . So since there seemed nobody else to hang with, I decided to follow up Dad's exploration into family ties.'

No mention of a wife, she remarked inwardly, then chided herself. Really, that was no way to be thinking. He was a business client, that's all.

'Did your father talk a lot about his research?'

'I don't know if you could call it research. He asked old Linus to look things up on some computer program he'd bought and sure enough there was some stuff about land deeds in the state archives and the electoral rolls?' He ended on a questioning note.

'Yes, those would be primary sources.' She offered the plate of scones.

'You baked these?'

'Yes I did.'

He took a bite. 'Well, if your genealogy is as good as your baking, I'd say I've made a good choice.'

She allowed herself to enjoy his approval, even if her cookery was the main reason.

She didn't expect anyone to fall for her out of overwhelming passion. In general men treated her as if she were some sort of good-hearted sister, although Richard had been different. Richard had been intense, serious, forceful: his entire world had seemed to consist of study and his love for Laura.

Yet after the graduation ceremony they'd parted, vowing of course to get together soon and work out their future. They'd gone their separate ways, the flame had somehow dwindled, and Richard was now in an embassy in some distant land, or so she thought, because she never heard from him any more.

Neil Crandel could hardly be more unlike Richard. He had

11

a slow, easy manner. Something about him implied a relaxed outlook on life, perhaps even a lack of ambition – but that was assuming too much from a few minutes' acquaintance. He certainly wasn't a go-getting townie. Everything about him bespoke a life lived in the country, and it made her feel friendly towards him because her own life was in many ways a response to the fields and meadows among which the old house nestled.

He talked in response to her questions about his work back home. The tree nursery had been very important not only because it was the family source of income, but because he and his father had clearly loved trees. He gave her some idea of their work, naming the species in popular demand, and when she looked baffled at the botanical names, translated them for her.

'*Chamaecyparis*? You don't know that? It's usually called false cypress – one of those little guys that folk like to dot in the middle of their lawn – the dwarf varieties, I mean. The Japanese horizontal type, Hinoki – we did a big sale on those. And then of course, because gardens in my part of the world are kind of big, we did a good business in tall trees. The Roble beech – I don't think you get it much in Europe, it comes from Chile, you see—' He broke off, embarrassed. 'Gee, what a bore! As if you care!'

'But I was enjoying it,' she assured him. And it was true. His enthusiasm was infectious. 'All the same, perhaps you ought to let me see what you've been able to bring in the way of family papers . . . ? That's if you've had enough tea.'

He surveyed the remaining scones on the plate. 'I see I've eaten four,' he remarked, trying to look ashamed. 'You'll have to forgive me. Dad and I used to wolf food down in big quantities, but we'd tell each other that was because we were big fellers and did heavy work. No excuse now I'm living a life of leisure.'

He took the manila envelope from the little table at the side of his chair. 'Here's what Dad got from Linus, and a few bits of the kind of stuff that I found in dresser drawers and bureaux. And in the cardboard box there's a kind of an heirloom. See what you think.'

She accepted the envelope, tipped it, and let the contents slip out on to the coffee table between them. There was a collection of birthday cards and party invitations, theatre programmes and household bills, all together in a polythene bag. There were three transparent plastic folders, each holding perhaps five sheets of paper. There were four photographs in traditional cardboard jackets, somewhat worn. There was a thin cardboard gift box of the kind once used for presenting linen handkerchiefs.

She gave her attention first to the folders. These contained printouts derived from a computer program with which she was familiar. They covered specific timespans of the nineteenth and twentieth centuries, concentrating on Canadian records. As she examined them Neil gave her a commentary.

'It seems clear that the first Crandel landed in Montreal. It was a major seaport even then. You'll see that the first actual mention of him is 1865 but he seems to have arrived earlier. You see he's mentioned in the newspaper in a list of people on the move. "M. Crandel, resident of this city these last three years and now leaving to work on the new La Source Fruit Farm." That was west of Montreal. Dad found that out but of course the place is gone now, swallowed up by the suburbs.'

'That happens. Did he start moving with the intention of going to Alberta, do you think?'

'Who knows? It's likely that he was looking for a spot where he could acquire some land. That seems to have been the aim of a lot of the immigrants. From what I've gathered, they just kept moving until they found a place to settle. But the journey wasn't always straightforward.'

'There was a railway by then, surely?'

'Oh, sure, but folk had to earn their living as they moved west. I'd think the family stopped in various settlements along the way.' He got to his feet, picked up the photographs, and after examining them held one out to her. 'See, that's the kind of place they probably pulled up at. Maybe the old guy in the picture offered employment to the men of the family. For all I know, one of those guys might be my great-granddad or a great-uncle.'

The faded photograph showed three men sitting on a bench in front of a strange small building. She frowned at it.

'The cabin's pretty typical, I gather,' he explained. 'At first it was wood-built, but maybe after a winter or two they put brick cladding on the outside. The background's a bit hazy – I guess the camera wouldn't have been too great. But I think that's prairie out there – not a tree to be seen – so whoever they were they were mebbe in Ontario, still on their way. They hadn't got as far as Saskatchewan, Saskatchewan isn't flat like that. But that's all just guesswork.'

The men in their best clothes looked shyly out of the picture. They were wearing trousers tucked into heavy boots that laced high above their ankles, waistcoats and hats. One had a shirt with a stand-up collar. The other two, somewhat younger, looked as if their shirts were home-made. The eldest was holding something in his hand, a book that might have been the Bible or a prayer book, which might imply that he was a visiting preacher.

Laura had seen many, many photographs like this. The people in them always seemed to her to be appealing for her attention, telling her that they had been real, been important, had influenced the lives of others, had borne children and left their imprint on the world. It was this feeling of rapport with the denizens of the past that made her good at her work.

She put the photo aside. The next printout took the research past the turn of the century, into the twentieth. Etian Crandel was named in a reproduction of a newsprint clipping, describing him as a horse-breaker who'd won a prize at a fair at Shirredo.

'Shirredo?' she enquired.

'That's Manitoba. The family moved north, it seems. I suppose they went because Etian was offered work. Then you'll see that next he's gone south a bit to Island Lake—'

'Still called Etian,' she put in. 'I thought at first it was a misprint for Ethan?'

'Yeah, it's odd, but folk had funny names. I thought perhaps it was something out of the Bible, or he might have been named after a place, but I couldn't find it anywhere on a map,' he said. 'What d'you think?'

'Etian . . . Could it be someone's version of Etienne?'

'What's that – some place you know of?'

'It's French. They'd been living in Quebec earlier on, perhaps it was a name that came from back there.'

He gave her an admiring glance. 'I never thought of anything like that, Ms Wainwright. You catch on to things real quick.'

'Call me Laura,' she said. 'If we're going to be poring over old photos and papers together, we can't go on being distant.'

'Works for me,' he said.

For over an hour they went through the documents, photocopies of birth and marriage certificates beginning to appear as the family settled at last in Alberta: the memorabilia of family life.

At length she turned to the thin cardboard box. She saw how intently he watched as she opened it, and guessed that this had some particular value to him.

Inside the box, carefully folded and resting on a pad of tissue paper, was a piece of lace. Very beautiful, its intricate pattern somewhat disarranged by the folds but still holding its charm, the cotton a little discoloured by the passage of time – a work of art from days long gone by.

'That's some kind of a collar when you open it out,' Neil said. 'I've had it out once, just to look at it, but I was afraid of doing it some kind of damage so I folded it up again and put it back. I haven't disturbed it since. What do you think?'

'It's what was called a "bertha",' she said. 'A Victorian fashion, originating somewhere around 1850. I think they were made to be more or less detachable, but they went round the neckline and then came down either to meet at the waist or to fold and perhaps tie.'

'Bertha? But that's a girl's name.'

'Mind what you're saying!' she said with a chuckle. 'It's named after the mother of the great Charlemagne, who in her day wore something like this for reasons of modesty.'

'Charlemagne, eh? Does that mean I'm related to a king?'

'Only by lace.'

They broke out into laughter, pleased with themselves for their quick wit. Sobering, she held the collar out across her palms. 'This is very fine.'

'Very fine?'

'Made by hand, of course – by a very special lace-maker, perhaps to order. Expensive.'

'Expensive?'

'Oh, certainly. Lace of this kind was only worn by the well-off. Peasant girls sometimes had lace for a "best dress", but that would be a piece made by themselves, or by a learner.

This collar took a long time to make and something as skilled as this would have cost a lot of money.'

'Let me get this straight, Laura. You're saying this was owned by someone who had a lot of money?'

'Absolutely. Your ancestress back in the Victorian era must have been a rich lady, Neil.'

'A lady?'

'Oh yes.'

'But . . . hold the phone . . . what's she doing emigrating to Canada and going with her husband as a worker on a fruit farm?'

She nodded in acceptance of the mystery. 'That's what we have to find out, my friend,' she said.

Two

He gave her an enquiring glance. 'How're you going to find out?'

Holding up the lace collar, she said with some satisfaction, 'This is going to help me begin. That's if you'll leave it with me.' She began folding it so as to return it to its box.

'Of course, take the lot, I brought it so you could use it how you wanted to. But I don't get it. How's that piece going to help?'

'I have a friend who knows all about lace. You see, every district in England where lace was made had its own patterns. Christine will know where the bertha was made.'

'So what? How does it help to know where the lace was made?'

'Things like that were often made to order. Even if not, a handsome piece would be handled by a middleman, a sort of tradesman who travelled around visiting the rich households, taking their orders or offering them special merchandise. So if Christine can identify where this was made – and I'm pretty

16

sure she can – I'll know whereabouts it was sold, and I can look up the vendor's records—'

'Records? You know where to find his records?'

'More or less. They're likely to be in the local archives. You know, in those days everybody kept ledgers, where every-thing was painstakingly written in by hand—'

'But a pedlar? Would a guy selling things from door to door keep a ledger?'

'Oh, dear me, you've got the wrong impression! This wasn't handled by a mere pedlar. This was expensive stuff, offered by a respected tradesman who went around with his own horse and cart, with his name painted along the side and a welcome waiting wherever he went.'

'My!' He seemed lost for words. 'That's *clever*! I can see that was a lucky pin I used when I picked your name out of that magazine!'

She was closing the box on the lace bertha when she heard a car in the drive. A glance out of the window showed her it was Kim. She got up hastily so as to meet her at the door but too late – the door was always unlocked when anyone was at home, so Kim was already in the hall.

'Laura, your father's got his mobile switched off again,' she complained as she swept past her into the living room. There she paused in surprise at the visitor. 'Oh – I'm sorry—'

Neil was struggling to his feet. Laura murmured an intro-duction and Kim immediately lost interest. She regarded anything to do with family history as a bore and a waste of time. 'How d'you do?' she said, but turned back at once to Laura. 'I've been trying to ring him all the way home but he's not answering. I wanted to know whether I should hire a power saw so he could deal with that sickly tree, because of course I could have stopped off at the garden centre and got one.'

'What kind of tree?' asked Neil.

Kim looked at him in exasperation. 'A rhododendron. Why?'

Laura rather hoped he would tell her a rhododendron was a bush, not a tree, but instead he asked, 'How tall?'

Kim sketched a graceful arch with one hand. 'I'd say . . . about twenty feet?'

'Oh, she's a tough old gal then. You've had her a long time.'

'I inherited the confounded thing when I bought the house

two years ago. But you see,' she said, beginning to think this was someone who might help her with the problem, 'I've been concentrating on the house. Now that I've got that more or less up to standard – and I think I have, haven't I, Laura?'

'Oh yes. The house is lovely,' Laura agreed. She knew this from having been invited to Kim's Sunday brunches as each stage of the refurbishment was reached. Everybody was escorted round to admire what had been achieved, so she could have told Neil how much the restoration of the ceiling mouldings had cost and where Kim had found the fireplace to supplant the cracked marble surround in the dining room. She could also have told Neil that she'd watched the garden going back to the jungle with each succeeding season.

'So this rhodo's been neglected for two years?' he enquired.

'Well . . . neglected . . .' She was a little offended. A frown was forming on her brow. She brushed at her black hair, which as always looked as if she'd just come from the hairdresser.

Kim always dressed in business suits for her day at the solicitors' office. So here she was in a charcoal silk-and-wool two-piece and a cream silk blouse, worn with black tights and stiletto heels. Nothing could have been more designed to make Laura feel like some bedraggled pigeon alongside a glossy lapwing.

What made it worse was that Neil seemed to be appreciating her appearance very much. She felt a pang of disappointment. She'd thought he was someone special but he was like all the rest – ready to fall under Kim's spell as soon as she crooked a finger.

'My father's been helping Kim get the garden together,' she volunteered. 'But of course he's only an amateur. Neil's an expert.' Why was she saying this? Why help Kim see a good reason to add him to her list of devotees?

But of course he'd tell her all that himself anyway. And he followed up her opening by saying, 'Could I take a look? I might be able to tell what's wrong with her.'

Kim laughed. 'A rhododendron is female?' she asked.

'Sure. All blossom trees are girls. All the rest are guys, although some of those cute Japanese maples might be babes.'

Kim gave him a puzzled glance that seemed to say, What kind of an expert are you? But aloud she said, 'If you wouldn't mind dropping by some time?'

'Love to. In fact, I could come now, if you like? Laura and I have just about finished our talk.' He broke off to ascertain this was so, and she nodded.

'Yes, if you'll leave it with me for a few days, I'll be in touch. At the Sceptre, yes?'

'Yes, I'll be there for the foreseeable future.'

It was easy to see that Kim was impressed by this information. A man who was staying at the Sceptre was her kind of person, no matter that he talked nonsense about trees.

'You'll find Papa at your place. As to the mobile, he's probably got his hands dirty and doesn't want to fetch it out of his pocket.' More likely he'd taken out his hearing aids. He always said there was no use wasting the batteries when there was no one there to listen to. But she wasn't going to explain that to Kim because Ronald hated having anyone reminded of his deafness.

There followed a discussion as to whether Neil should go in Kim's car or follow her in his own. Kim's house was on the edge of Brinbank village, so Laura suggested he should go with Kim and walk back for his car – and couldn't hide from herself the thought that it was because she wanted to see him again.

But no – it seemed foolish to get to Brinbank and then turn back on his tracks, because her house was on the way to Oxford. So Kim drove off in her Volvo with Neil following in his rented Honda.

Laura was left at the old ramshackle gate, gazing after them chagrined.

Her father came home as the dusk of late-March was setting in. He was tired but cheerful. 'That chap,' he began as he settled down to a pre-dinner drink, 'that new client – turns out he knows all about trees!'

'Yes, so I gathered.'

'Oh, of course, he'd tell you that over afternoon tea. Well, he was a godsend. I thought I'd be lopping bits off that rhododendron and couldn't think how to get at it, but he walked around it for a few minutes and stuck a gardening fork in the soil and said it was dying of thirst.'

'But it rained quite hard yesterday—'

'Yes, but the whole of March has been as a dry as a bone – remember, you were worrying our daffodils wouldn't last

19

long. Yesterday was the first real rain for about six weeks. But, anyhow, this chap says that rhododendrons have shallow roots and that old thing of Kim's is on a knoll so it wasn't getting any moisture at all.'

Laura waited to hear the rest. It was unusual for her father to be so talkative or to be so approving of a newcomer. 'So I said, "It's not got a disease?" and he said, "It hasn't been watered in months?" So of course I had to admit that nothing had been done to the garden for ages and Kim asked, should we prune off the ends of the branches, and *he* said, "Run a hose out and give her a twenty-four-hour soak and she'll recover but you won't get any blossom this year." So that's a relief, because Kim was talking about hiring a band saw or something, and I don't know how to handle a thing like that.'

She'd thought he might see Neil as an intruder, almost a rival. Quite the contrary, he mentioned him more than once during the evening.

'Quite a character, isn't he? Talked about that blasted bush as if it was a person! How did it go about his research? We taking it on?'

'Yes, I thought I could get an intro to it by enquiring about a piece of lace he brought. It's in the envelope with his other mementoes. Would you like to take a look?'

'No, no, I'll let you deal with that, you're the expert on English costume. Besides, there's still a tremendous amount to be done in Kim's garden.'

'But, Papa, you've got replies from Ireland that you should deal with, on the Donovan case.'

'Oh, that's all Internet stuff, I can do that on my head. No, I must get on with Kim's place because spring is rushing towards us and if I don't sort out what to save and what to cut down, the garden will still be a sight all summer.'

'Please don't take on too much. You know how your shoulder plays up if you cart things around a lot.'

'No, that chap Neil Crandel's offered to lend a hand. He'll be a great help. He seems to know his stuff.' And on that note of approval Ronald signified that the discussion was over by reaching for the television remote.

Next day Laura drove into Oxford to speak to Christine, a friend from university days who now acted as consultant to film and television producers when they needed advice about period costume. She studied the piece of lace that Laura offered.

'My word! That's a very special thing. Looks to me like something a husband would give his wife on the birth of a son, or as a wedding present.'

'Can you say where it was made?'

'Oh, certainly. It's English bobbin lace, and comes from Buckinghamshire or Northamptonshire. Let me see.' She went to her bookshelves to select a thick volume. She put the book on a table and began to flick over the pages. 'There,' she said, putting a finger on a black-and-white photograph showing a piece of parchment with a design. 'There's the pattern. You see here – it's drawn on parchment, copied from some well-known theme but, in this piece you've brought, with some added variations of the lace-maker. She'd have the pattern in her cottage, you know, and after she copied the main version she'd draw in a few little embellishments – look, that sort of curled-leaf effect she's used – and then she'd pin the pattern on the pillow and she'd prepare her bobbins – I think there were a lot of bobbins for this design, perhaps eight or nine hundred.'

'Good heavens!'

'It would have taken quite a long time to make. Certainly a special piece, which she'd work on over a period, going to it fresh every morning, and then when she got tired she'd put it aside in its linen wrapper so as to turn her attention to more workaday stuff. Judging by the thread, I'd say it was probably made between 1850 and 1860 or thereabouts.'

'You are so clever, Christine! And that fits in with what I was half expecting, because my client tells me he thinks the family originally came from roughly this area.'

'That doesn't follow. Fine lace was taken all over England to be sold.'

'You gave me the impression that this piece might have been made to order, though?'

'Well . . . yes . . . It wouldn't have been made on spec.'

'So isn't it likely it would have been ordered from someone who travelled around the big houses—'

'Oh, quite, I quite agree, it was probably made in an area about fifty miles from here, and it's likely to have been ordered and sold within that area too.'

'How about the merchant? Any clues as to who was trading in lace and ribbons during those years?'

'Hang on, I'll look.' She turned to the index of the volume, muttering to herself as she did so. 'Ellen Potter's salesman – no, he was further north . . . Rose Carman – she won a prize with a pattern like this – no, she died before this was made. But she might have taught someone . . . who traded for Rose? Highsmith . . . Yes, and didn't Telson travel around Towcester?' She found a piece of paper and began scribbling. Laura waited quietly. She knew better than to interrupt her friend when she was on the track of something.

In the end her friend handed her a list of five names. 'You know we don't always have the exact dates when these men were in business. One of those is a haberdasher who had a shop in Buckingham, the rest peddled lace and French ribbon among the landed gentry and so on. If you don't find your man among that lot, come back and I'll see if I can think up anyone else.'

'Great! I think I can get at the archives tomorrow.' After writing out a cheque for her services and getting a receipt, she hugged her and left.

The search for the Crandel ancestors wasn't the only case that she was engaged on. She spent the rest of the day catching up with correspondence and doing some work at the computer. The following day, Thursday, she drove to the town of Buckingham to spend some time among the records of the tradesmen who used to do business there.

At her lunch break she sat on a bench by the Ouse, enjoying the sunshine and eating her sandwich – a virtuous sandwich of wholemeal bread and salad. Her thoughts wandered to the names she'd looked up in the rolls of the town's Victorian tradesmen. How proud they would have been to know that they still had importance a century and a half later. But she wished they'd kept better records. *To Mrs Arkaway, Dressmkr, four lengths of three ins. Fern Dsn., 2 Guineas, Paid in 2 portions of 1 Guinea each, Sept and Oct 4th.* How long was a 'length'? What was Fern design?

Well, neither applied to the piece she was trying to track down. So far she'd spent over two hours, and it might well be she'd have to go to some other source and start all over again.

She threw the remains of her sandwich to the ducks and

went back to work. And there, standing out on the ledger page of one Thos. Jedderall, Supplier of Fine Lace and Imported Ribbons, she found it.

To the account of G. E. Dallancy Esq., of Peridal Manor, One Lace Bertha to the measure of One and a half yds. made to Special Order for the wedding of his daughter Marianne, by Lucy Childers in her pattern of Rose among Lilies, 18 Guineas with in addition 5 Guineas for the Exclusive Attention of the Lace-maker at the work. Then on the next line: *Account rendered on delivery, 23 Guineas.*

Success! Now she knew who had bought the lace. G. E. Dallancy Esquire. The title esquire used to mean someone next below the title of knight, but by the Victorian era was used as a form of polite address to a man you thought was your superior. But being the owner or tenant of Peridal Manor probably meant he had money, and the fact that he paid promptly implied he was an upright man. And for whom had he bought this special piece of lace?

None other than his daughter Marianne. A memory flickered at the back of her mind.

When the Crandels moved originally from Montreal to make their long trek across to western Canada, the newspapers had mentioned M. Crandel. She had taken it for granted that in Quebec, M. Crandel meant Monsieur Crandel. But what if it meant Marianne? And, if it did, why was she mentioned as if she were the head of the family? Where was her husband?

So the next thing was to find out whether someone in the Dallancy family in England married a man called Crandel.

Neil's question came back to her: if she was from a rich family that could order expensive lace, what was she doing as the wife of a farm worker in Quebec?

Well, sufficient to the day is the work thereof, she misquoted to herself, and drove home feeling tolerably satisfied.

Her father had had to cater for himself today. She found the usual debris in the kitchen – the butter left out of the fridge, crumbs all over the table, a mug with cold coffee in it, a plastic container in which she'd stored cold chicken. She cleared up without annoyance: her father was not and never had been domesticated.

She made herself some tea and thought about what she'd

23

learned today. Taking her drink into the living room, she got out the photocopies that Neil Crandel had supplied. An important one was a deed of ownership, showing that Etian Cardell, only son of widow Marian Crandel, had settled with his mother in Alberta on a small piece of land in 1880.

A widow. That seemed to uphold the idea that the 'M. Crandel' mentioned in the Montreal newspaper clipping was Marian Crandel and not some Monsieur Crandel. The newspaper, after all, was printed in English for the English immigrants living in the city.

Had there ever been a Monsieur Crandel? Or had she arrived alone, penniless except for a few personal belongings including the piece of lace? Now that she thought about it, the newspaper announcement was odd. In speaking of a woman, surely it would have been more polite to call her Mrs Crandel. It was almost as if the journalist had been uncertain about her marital status.

Well, whatever the circumstances, lace was something a woman would pack. Small, weighing next to nothing, but worth money if it ever happened that she needed to sell it.

Etian Crandel was spoken of as being the settler on the land in 1880. He was the man of the family, the head of the household. She thought he would have to have been at least seventeen or eighteen to be taken seriously as a landholder. So if in 1880 he was signing deeds, he'd been born around 1862.

Had his mother sailed to Canada with a baby in her arms? And a husband by her side? Had the husband deserted her once the hardships of immigrant life bore down on him?

She'd got this far when she heard a car coming into the drive. She looked out of the window to see Neil Crandel's Honda nosing through the gateway.

She jumped up, scattering documents all over the carpet. Flustered, she got down on her knees to gather them up. And this was how she was engaged when Neil and her father walked in on her.

'Saying your prayers?' Ronald enquired, grinning down at her.

Neil began helping to gather up the papers. One glance told him they were those he'd given her two days ago. 'You've been slaving over a hot land grant.' He helped her up. 'Your father said you were in Buckingham today.'

'Yes, quite productive.' She patted at her hair, though why, she couldn't have explained because nothing had happened to it – it was the papers that were now a muddled heap on the coffee table.

'Tea!' cried Ronald, gesturing at her cup. 'Is there a cup for us?'

'No, I only had a teabag—'

'Off you go and make fresh. And if you've got a cake or anything, that would go down well. Us two have been hard at work.'

Neil looked a little surprised at the orders being handed out, though he said nothing. But as Laura went off to carry out instructions, he followed. 'No need for the full performance with scones and a china teapot,' he said. 'I don't expect treatment like that every time I drop by.'

'How exactly do you come to be here? Papa said you'd been working.'

'Yeah, he rang me at the Sceptre. He'd done something a bit silly with his secateurs and wanted to know if he'd killed a plant in Kim's garden. So I decided to go and have a look.'

'Oh, but that's too bad!' she exclaimed. 'Papa shouldn't be calling on you to rush up and correct his mistakes—'

'It's okay, no problem – after all, what am I doing all day? Hanging around entertaining myself in the intervals between seeing the physio.'

'Oh dear! Is it all right, having you tramp about in a garden? I know Kim's garden is full of things to trip over or get tangled in.'

'You're not kidding! That place is going to take for ever to sort out.' He laughed. 'It'd send me crazy, driving out to work every morning with all those weeds and messed-up plants needing attention.'

They were going through the preparations for tea-making as they talked. Laura found it very pleasant to have someone helping her. He took mugs off hooks, set them on a tray that he found by opening a cupboard or two. She poured the boiling water into an old brown pot, supplied milk and sugar, set biscuits on a plate, and led the way back to the living room. She noticed as she went that Neil had to touch the passage wall now and again to steady himself, and hoped that he hadn't overtired himself in Kim's garden.

'Only biscuits?' her father complained as she set down the tray. 'I thought I smelled a cake baking last night?'

'That's for dessert tonight.'

'But I only had a skimpy sandwich for lunch!'

Neil shook his head at him. 'Now behave, Ron. I saw you munching a chocolate bar while we were working.'

Her father had the grace to look shamefaced. 'Well, a man gets hungry wrestling with those roots and things. Anyhow, what do you think? Did I wreck those penstemons?'

'I'm no expert on garden plants, pal, especially in England. The climate here's a lot different than in Alberta. But roots generally don't mind what you do to the bits above the surface. I think they'll survive.'

'That's a relief.' He popped a home-made shortbread biscuit into his mouth.

'What about you, Laura?' Neil asked. 'Did you do much wrestling with anything today?'

'It was quite productive. I think I found out who made your lace and who it was sold to.'

'You didn't!'

'That's not bad, Laura,' her father approved. 'You've only been on the case for two days.'

He was generally very sparing with his praise, so she flushed with pleasure. She couldn't help thinking that Neil Crandel had a good effect on him. Often when he came home from a session with Kim Groves's terrain, he'd be cross and frustrated, chiefly because he wanted to do well and earn Kim's smiles. Today, although he seemed to have had problems, he didn't appear to be perturbed about it. Even being denied the cake hadn't damaged his good mood.

'So don't keep me hanging in suspense,' Neil said with mock indignation. 'What did you find out?'

She gave him a summary of her findings and what her thoughts about them had been.

'So-o . . . You think this rich young lady married a guy who wanted to go out to be a poor pioneer?'

'Could be, couldn't it?'

'That would be neat, if you're right. It's kind of romantic.'

26

'I hate to break up this daydream, but isn't it more likely that the lace was stolen by a maid? Who then went off to marry her working-class young man?' Ronald remarked.

'Oh.'

'Or *he* stole it – the man. Perhaps he was a farmhand on their estate or something.'

'A man wouldn't steal lace, Papa. He'd steal a piece of silver, or a gold watch or something.'

'Well, that's true, I suppose.'

'Oh, come on, folks,' Neil urged. 'Let's give them both the benefit of the doubt. She left all her wealth and comfort behind to marry a poor man, and they sailed off to make their fortune in the New World.'

'With a piece of lace given to her by her father, G. E. Dallancy, as a wedding present? Come on, man,' grunted Ronald, 'if he knew she was going to marry a colonist he'd have given her a purse full of sovereigns.'

'He's right, Neil. Parents of rich girls wouldn't let them marry a man like that—'

'Well, maybe she eloped with him.'

'That could be,' Laura agreed, having already had that thought herself. 'An expensive piece of lace would be easy to take if she had to avoid suspicion. I mean, if she was running away she wouldn't have been able to pack a trunk – she'd practically have to go in what she was wearing.'

'That's the stuff! I like it better and better. This makes her sound like a first class great-great-great-person. I'm going to back that version.'

Ronald was laughing. 'You'd be no use as a researcher, my lad. You can't let yourself get carried away by romantic notions.'

'But you can't deny that it could have happened that way. There she was, in Montreal, going to a job as a farm hand on a fruit farm.'

'Well, of course I can deny it. How do we know they didn't set out for Liverpool with trunks and hatboxes full of stuff, and then have it stolen when they landed in Montreal? A great many emigrants lost everything they had like that, or they were cheated by crooks offering them gold mines, or silver mines, or something of the sort.'

27

'You're just a meanie,' Neil said. And to Laura's surprise her father was laughing again.

'Well, anyway, I'm going to look at the census reports for that area tomorrow,' she said, 'to verify that G. E. Dallancy had a daughter who got married around the right date.'

'How does that work?'

'She'd be on the 1851 census as a spinster, and then hopefully on the 1861 as a married woman.'

'So where do you have to go to look at the census? Back to Buckingham?

'No, no, I can do it on the computer. We've got the 1841, '51 and '61 census for Buckinghamshire on disk.'

'Good Lord!'

'They're just tools,' Ronald said in a comfortable tone. 'A carpenter would have a good saw and chisels, we have some of the records we use a lot on the computer. We have access to others by subscribing to search sites. But we do a lot of work for people who hire us because we live near where they want the research done – we've got the census for Oxfordshire and Bedfordshire and so on. But there *are* things you can't just look up on computer, of course, so there can be quite a lot of legwork.'

'And quite a lot of perception,' Neil observed. 'Thinking things out, I mean. Kind of reasoning out who would take a piece of lace abroad.'

'Well, yes. Laura's good at that sort of thing,' said Ronald.

A compliment from her father! Almost unheard of. She smiled and offered him the plate of biscuits. Ronald took another shortbread and crunched thoughtfully. 'So we'll do the census tomorrow,' he murmured.

'You're not going to dig and delve in Kim's garden?'

'No, I think I'll give it a rest for a day or so,' he said. 'My nerves need to recover after the mistakes I made today.'

'Well, I don't know if we made any actual *mistakes*,' Neil volunteered, 'but, thinking back, seems to me those roots were pretty congested. Two years at least, eh? Nothing done to them. Perhaps you ought to go back and divide them up a bit.'

'Using what? A guillotine?'

'Oh, come on, Ronnie. Stick in a couple of forks back to back, give a heave on one and then the other, bound to work in the end.'

28

'Not tomorrow. I won't have got my nerves calmed down by tomorrow. The day after, and you've got to come and help me do it.'

'We-ell ... Not Saturday, I've got something on for Saturday.'

'And not Sunday,' Laura put in, 'because that's when Kit has her brunch party, and I don't think she'd want two muddy-looking men heaving things about in her garden.'

'Oh. Right ... Monday, then, my lad. If you come on Monday, I promise to have a go at those confounded clumps.'

'It's a date.'

'Oh, Papa, honestly, you can't keep on dragging Neil into your gardening problems.'

'I'm not dragging. He's volunteering – aren't you, Neil?'

'Yes, sir, I'm a captive volunteer.' He gave a mock salute.

'No, it's not fair, Papa—'

'We'll pay him to volunteer—'

'Slave wages, I bet!'

'No, no, my dear, I'm going to offer him some of your home cooking. How about it, Neil? As a reward for *volunteering* I invite you to share our dinner tonight.'

'Papa!'

'I accept your terms,' Neil said promptly.

Laura gave her father a glance of exasperation. He hadn't even asked if there was enough for three. But the exasperation faded immediately.

Neil was going to stay for dinner. How very . . . unexpected. And pleasant.

Three

Laura served the meal in the big kitchen. It proved to be a success, much to her relief and thanks to food stored in her freezer. The cake that she'd denied to her father at tea-time provided an ample dessert – two layers of sponge sandwiching cherries picked last autumn from their own tree and preserved in a puree with honey.

To go with the meal her father opened a bottle of Sauternes: he was disappointed when Neil stuck to mineral water. 'Come on now, lad, there's only just one glass left,' he coaxed towards the end of the meal. 'It'll go nicely with your pudding.'

'No, thanks, Ron, really, I mustn't. I'm taking these painkillers because my ankle aches a bit, and I'm not supposed to drink.'

'Poor old Neil,' Ronald said, with a wine-induced sympathy. 'Did in your ankle, did you? Easily done.'

Laura seemed to recall some mention of having to see a physiotherapist, so began anxious enquiries. But Neil shrugged it off. 'You know how it is,' he said. 'Messing about with machinery on a hillside . . .'

'So that's where you're going on Saturday, to see a physiotherapist?'

'Yes, to a guy recommended by the orthopaedic surgeon. The two of them are in London so I go up by train. But the appointments are fairly frequent at the moment, three times a week – a bit of a drag. Still, that leaves me plenty of time to mooch around, looking at the landscape.'

'In Oxfordshire?'

'Oh, yeah, and I've been to the Cotswolds, and I enjoy going where there are trees worth looking at – though of course they'll be more interesting when they get their leaves on. That's neat, you know, how English trees get those kind of shy-looking buds on . . .'

'You don't have trees with leaf buds in Alberta?' she asked in amazement.

'Oh, sure, some, but not this early in the year.'

'How do you know where to go to see "trees worth looking at"?'

'Aha! Us tree-growers have our ways! Like the freemasons, or the Fellowship of the Ring.'

Ronald grew bored with a conversation in which he hadn't played much part. He rose, saying, 'We'll go in the living room, Laura, it's more comfortable. Use that Machu Picchu coffee, will you?'

He led the way out of the kitchen.. However, Neil lingered. There was an almost apologetic smile on his angular face, as if he felt he had to redress the autocratic style of her father. 'Anything I can do?'

'Cups and saucers and sugar and milk.'

'How about just mugs?'

'No, Papa doesn't approve of mugs at proper mealtimes.'

'Oh, right.' He picked china off the shelves of the kitchen dresser. Laura made the coffee as directed by her father. When its aroma began to permeate the kitchen Neil said, 'Smells great. Your father's a bit particular about his coffee, then?'

'Well . . . I suppose he is. About a lot of things. He's . . . He wasn't too well for quite a while and he got . . .'

'Picky,' Neil supplied.

'Yes, I think that might be the word.'

'My dad was the same. Not about food, but about . . . little things . . . unimportant things. After Ma went, his temper seemed to go a bit tetchy . . .'

They completed the arrangement of the coffee tray then stood for a moment studying it.

'While we were at work this afternoon Ron told me a bit about himself. About splitting up . . . That was hard, I could tell.' He looked for spoons in the cutlery drawer. 'I had to cope with something sort of similar when Dad changed,' he went on. 'But I decided to treat it as just something that happened, that's all – like the weather turning to rain, or my hockey team losing a game.'

She smiled. 'Yes, that's what it's like.' She hesitated then added, 'You're good for Papa. I haven't seen him in such a good humour for months.' She added inwardly, And you're the only person he's ever allowed to call him Ron.

'Oh, it's my natural charm—'

'No, I mean it. A lot of people would have brushed him off when he appealed for help over that stupid garden.'

He gave a slight nod then picked up the coffee tray. She wondered if she ought to stop him, remembering his slow way of moving, but she repressed the thought. They made their careful way to the living room.

Ronald was dozing in his armchair. A good meal and most of a bottle of wine after a hard day's work had taken their

31

toll. Neil grinned and put a finger to his lips. They sat down together on the sofa and Laura began to pour the coffee.

'I'm sorry. He'll came back to life in a minute,' she said in a low voice. 'This often happens.'

'That's okay, it's nice to be treated like one of the family.'

She handed him his cup, then began: 'I wonder . . . it just occurred to me . . . I mean, you must find it a bit lonely now you're here in a strange land?'

'No, of course not. I mean, England's my ancestral home. I like to go around, taking it in.'

'But you do it on your own.'

'That's true. But, say, I knew I'd be on my own once I got here. I'm not complaining.'

'You could always drop in to see us any time you want company. Normally . . .' She hesitated. 'Normally I don't give out invitations like that because Papa can be quite abrasive with strangers. But you and he seem to have hit it off.' She gave a little laugh and added, 'Besides, he needs you to tell him what to do in Kim's wilderness.'

'Oh, I see! It's a plot to get free advice.'

'That's it. But seriously, Neil, any time you feel like having a cup of coffee and a chat, just open the front door. If it's locked it would mean no one's at home, but otherwise just walk in.'

'That's . . . that's real nice of you, Laura. I'd like that. Could I turn up tomorrow some time, to hear what you found out about this girl who got the lace as a wedding present?'

'Of course. Some time in the afternoon would be best. It might take me a while, moving from one link to another, but let's say – well, in time for afternoon tea!'

They laughed, and Ronald awoke, blinking and trying to look as if he'd been wide awake all the time.

Next morning Laura settled down to a tracking session. She found the family living at Peridal Manor in the 1851 census – the family and its servants. She felt a thrill of achievement when she read the full name of G. E. Dallancy – it was given as George Etian. Marian Crandel had named her son Etian. The name was so unusual that it couldn't be coincidence. To her it seemed almost certain that Marian Crandel had been the Marianne Dallancy listed in the census.

32

Marianne had disappeared by the 1861 census report. That meant, simply, that she had removed from her father's house. In the case of a spinster, the usual reason for that was marriage. She put in the disk for the parish records of Buckinghamshire and after some problems tracked down the listing for the church that served Peridal. It seemed Peridal was little more than a hamlet and so was part of another parish.

She found the marriage of Marianne Dallancy. Marianne had not married a man called Crandel.

It gave her something of a shock. She stared at the name. Sir John Higston, of Ramhurst in the county of Buckingham. She was still staring at her computer screen when her father put his head round the door, demanding lunch.

With reluctance she rose. Yet what was the point of sitting there in bafflement? She'd found what she was looking for, the marriage of Marianne Dallancy. What came next, if anything, needed thought.

Her father was full of irritation as he sat down at the kitchen table. 'Cold meat and salad? Is this the best you can do?'

'There's some apple pie for dessert—'

'Just because you're on a permanent diet doesn't mean I have to suffer too,' he surged on. 'Salad! That's not the kind of food for a hungry man.'

'Would you like some soup, then? As a starter?'

'Not out of a tin, if that's what you're suggesting!'

'No, no, it's some I started yesterday, for dinner tonight.'

'All right, I'll have that first, then.'

She judged that the replies from his elderly correspondents in Ireland had not produced the information he'd hoped for about the branch of the Donovan family that had engaged him. This proved to be the case. He grumbled through the soup and for part of the main course, but began to feel better as the meal drew towards apple pie and ice-cream.

'It's extraordinary, really,' he complained. 'They know this stuff but they don't seem to be able to set it down in a letter.'

'You can't telephone them?'

'They're not on the telephone. They seem to live at the farther end of some little western peninsula. Well, I'll try getting in touch with their local priest. He might be able to help them write a sensible letter.' He watched as she collected his plate

33

to clear the way for his pudding. Then he said, 'How d'you get on with Neil's family foundations?'

'Like you, I've hit an obstacle. Marianne Dallancy didn't marry anyone called Crandel. She seems to have caught a local bigwig for a husband – he's a Sir John Higston.'

'Well!' He cut into the apple with his fork then paused to shrug. 'We meet this sort of thing all the time. It's no big deal. Someone else took that lace collar to Canada.'

She sighed, sitting down to keep him company while he ate. 'But the coincidences are too great, Papa. The woman in Alberta is called Marian. I'd take a bet that's a local version of Marianne. And she called her son Etian. George Etian Dallancy – she called the boy after her father.'

'Ha!' said Ronald. 'How do you know she wasn't some poor lass that he seduced – George Etian, I mean – then sent off with his by-blow to the colonies with a piece of lace to sell if she ran out of money?'

'Papa! Talk sense! The lace was bought as a wedding present for Marianne Dallancy. Are you seriously suggesting he could get it away from her to give to his cast-off lover?'

'Why not? The head of a family could do more or less what he liked in those days. If he said to his daughter, "Hand over that lace," she'd have to do it. Not like today, when women get their own way most of the time.'

She disregarded the acid comment about women in general. He was apt to come out with things like that when he was irritated. 'But . . . A man who'd take the trouble to order a thing like that, well in advance of the wedding . . . He sounds as if he was a good-hearted sort.' Ronald was shaking his head so she added, 'And, anyway, surely it would have been easier to give her actual money? That would have avoided all the tears and protests if Marianne had been told she had to let him take away her lace bertha.'

'Yes . . . Well . . . There's something in that.' He ate for a while in silent consideration then went on. 'All the same, it seems clear to me that Marianne Dallancy and the Marian who ended up in Alberta are two different people.'

'I don't think so. I think it was Marianne Dallancy who became Marian Crandel with a son called after his grand-father.'

He frowned at her. 'You'd have a hard job proving that.'

After the meal he went with reluctance back to his own task. She stacked the dishwasher then went to her computer. She began the time-consuming work that might trace the facts she needed. A look at the next census – that of 1861 – provided the news that Marianne Dallancy was no longer a member of the household at Peridal Manor. But neither was she a member of the household of Sir John Higston at Ramshurst.

'She went to Canada,' Laura muttered to herself. 'I *know* she did.'

But, if that were true, it opened up a possibility that might not be entirely to the liking of their client.

He arrived in late afternoon, knocking politely on the front door before coming in. 'Anybody home?' he called.

She came to the top of the stairs. 'Just go into the living room, Neil. I'll be down when I've logged off.'

When she joined him he was sitting forward in his armchair, massaging his damaged ankle. His usually tidy brown hair was tangled by the strong April breeze and she thought he looked tired. 'What have you been up to?'

'An acquaintance took me on a tour of the Oxford colleges.' He sounded rueful. 'I'd no idea it was going to be like a trek around Africa.'

'Just sit there and relax. I'll get the tea.' As she was going into the kitchen her father came downstairs, happy to be released from chores concerning the Donovans. She heard him greet Neil with enthusiasm and soon the murmur of voices told her they were chatting. When she joined them with the afternoon tea, Ronald turned to examine the goodies.

'Oh, little almond cakes! That's nice!' He took the plate, offered it to Neil, then popped a cake into his mouth.

'I've just been hearing about Neil's walk around the colleges,' she told him. 'A friend took him on a tour.'

'You've got friends in Oxford, then?'

'An Internet friend. There's a sort of fraternity among people who're interested in trees. Seems there's all kinds of inter-esting things in college gardens.'

'I didn't know that.' Laura altered her mental picture of his former life, as a worker on an isolated holding with his father. She'd thought of it as being somewhat cut off, he and his father alone on this holding near the little town – what was its name? Wenaskowa. But he had a group of learned friends by way of the Internet. She'd thought of him as lonely and forlorn here in England, but perhaps he had a network of acquaintances.

He was describing the trees of the college gardens when she gave her attention to the conversation again . . . 'Magnificent Paulownia,' he was saying. 'Not in leaf, yet, of course, but lots of blooms – been there since about 1800, so Martin said.'

'I've never heard of it,' Ronald said. 'Polonia? Like *polonaise*, meaning it comes from Poland?'

'No, no.' He spelled it out. 'I think it's called after the guy who first brought it back from China in seventeen hundred and something.'

'And it's rare?'

'Not especially – in Europe, I mean. But it's rare around where I live. You know, Wenaskowa's pretty far north, and it's high – on the outskirts of the Rockies. What we have growing in the landscape is mostly pine, on the hill slopes. Of course, Dad and I grew tender things, but we grew them in special conditions and treated them like babies.' He broke off, embarrassed. 'Was I giving a lecture? Sorry.'

'No, no, it's interesting,' said Ronald. 'Trees – I've never paid much heed to them except if they produce apples or plums. That's more Laura's kind of thing. She's always bothering about the environment.'

'Well, she's right. The way the world's going, we'll have cut down most of the rainforests before we reach the half century.' Once again, he pulled himself up. He busied himself with his cup of tea.

Laura said, 'You speak of it all in the past tense. You keep saying you *grew* things. Have you given it up?'

'No-o. Well, yes. I'm in the process of selling up. After Dad died . . . I was in hospital quite a while, you know, and though Billy kept it going – Billy was one of our work crew . . . Well, it was only an interim measure, and I had this feeling that with Dad gone I didn't quite know where I belonged, kind of. So I thought I'd come over here and carry on what Dad had begun, about the family and all that, and there was this good orthopaedic specialist that my doctor recommended . . .' He stared at them. 'Why am I doing all the talking?'

'It's because Laura has some results to discuss with you, and she's sorting it all out in her mind before she begins.'

'Results? About Marian?' He was eager to hear the news.

She nodded. She began with, 'You know I'd traced the owner of the lace as being Marianne Dallancy. I found her in the 1851 census, aged seven years.'

'That means she was – what – about seventeen or eighteen when she left for Canada with her husband.'

Laura cleared her throat. 'She didn't leave for Canada with her husband, Neil. She married in the parish church of Peridal, and the bridegroom was a Sir John Higston.'

'What?'

'So my opinion is,' her father put in, 'that the woman who appears in your documents as settling in Alberta in 1880 was probably some maidservant or village girl who managed to get hold of the lace because she needed something to fund her passage to the New World.'

'You're saying my great-great-great-grandma was a thief?'

'No,' Laura said with emphasis. 'That's Papa's suggestion but I think he's wrong. Whoever took that lace with her didn't sell it to pay for her passage. She *kept* it. I think the Marian Crandel who arrived in Quebec was Marianne Dallancy. I mean, Lady Higston.'

'Wait a minute. I don't get it.'

'It's one of Laura's fairy tales,' Ronald said in a scornful tone. 'She weaves them sometimes, around the people she's researching.'

'It's just a theory,' she admitted. 'But I think it could be right. I think . . . I think your great-great-great-grandmama went off to Canada with a man called Crandel. Marianne Dallancy disappears from her home and her normal surroundings before the 1861 census. A few years later Marian Crandel is settling with her son Etian in Alberta. Etian was the middle name of George Dallancy of Peridal. Logic seems to me to demand that Marian Crandel and Marianne Dallancy are one and the same person.'

Neil sat in silence, his broad brow wrinkled in thought.

'Laura's yarn, if you believe her, seems to be that Marianne didn't like being Lady Higston, fell in love with another man, and ran away,' Ronald elucidated. 'Hence the lace. She and I agreed when we were discussing it before, a piece of lace would be an excellent item to have with you if you were leaving by stealth. If she was running away, she could have actually worn the collar on her dress that day.'

Laura waited, anxious for Neil's reaction. She could tell he was taken totally aback by what was being suggested. Experience told her that this could be a sticky moment. Clients could be hurt or angered by what their researchers unearthed: she'd had one client who actually turned violent.

But not so in this case. 'Good for her!' he exclaimed all at once.

She gave a laugh of relief. 'I thought you might be upset!'

'Upset? Not me! I think it's great. A spunky kid! What? Giving up being a ladyship and setting off for the unknown with nothing but what she stood up in? That's my kind of gal!' He took one of Laura's little cakes, tossed it in the air, caught it triumphantly, and took a bite. 'Marianne became Marian, a commoner. And she never sold the lace, she kept it, so that means she and her husband made good.'

'No.'

'I beg your pardon?' He gave her an anxious glance.

'You're forgetting, my boy, the husband vanishes from the scene,' Ronald pointed out, with rather too much candour. 'And she couldn't have *married* Crandel unless she was willing to commit bigamy.'

'Oh!'

'Things are seldom as straightforward as you think when you get into genealogy,' Laura comforted. 'It's certainly true that she was a very brave girl.' She thought to herself that perhaps Marianne had been rash rather than brave, or perhaps desperate to get out of a bad marriage. Nevertheless, the decision to emigrate with little or no money was in many ways admirable, speaking of a spirit willing to face hardship and perhaps poverty.

'So . . . What are you saying? There wasn't a man called Crandel?'

'Oh, it's probable that he existed. It's not exactly a usual name, after all. Not a totally outlandish name, but it's not like

Smith or Jones for instance. So I think there must have been a man called Crandel, and . . . if you want me to . . . I can try to find out something about him.'

'Well, sure. I mean . . . Do I take it that he's my great-great-great-grandpa?'

Laura gave a little shrug of uncertainty. 'There's no way of knowing at present. Marian's son might have been the child of Sir John Higston.' She said this with some hesitation because it was an extremely delicate issue.

'That's not so likely,' objected Ronald. 'She wouldn't have run away if she was pregnant by her husband. At least *I* don't think so. I mean, in those days there was so much disgrace attached to adultery that she'd never have brought it out into the open, not if she could avoid it. She ran because she was expecting a baby and there was some reason Sir John would know it *wasn't* his. And as I don't suppose a woman in her position would exactly sleep around, she was pretty sure the baby was Crandel's.' He was nodding at his own thought processes. They were rather insensitive but they were reasonable.

'So do you think . . . I mean, they went off to settle in Canada? And he never got there? Why not?'

'I can try to find out,' said Laura. 'If you want me to.'

'Of course I want you to! I want to know about this guy! Where did he get to? Did he desert her when they got to Montreal? Did he maybe ditch her even before they set sail, and she didn't know what else to do but go? I mean, she couldn't go back to Sir What's-his-name. What d'you think happened?'

Laura said gently, 'One thing is pretty well accepted. In those days, Neil, a young mother very often called herself a widow because she couldn't stand the shame of being cast out by society. All we know is that she was alone in Quebec with her child and chose to call herself Mrs Crandel.'

There was a thoughtful pause. 'Yeah,' said Neil with a sigh. 'You mean my great-great-great-grandpa was a dubious blessing to her. Well, I guess I can stand having a blot on my escutcheon. So let's go on.'

Four

Sunday brought a very fine day with pleasantly warm breezes. That meant that the brunch at Kim's place could be out of doors. Although the gardens at Yalcote had been allowed to deteriorate, Kim had had a patio laid out as almost the first item of improvement. Sheltered from the west wind by a clump of straggling viburnums, it was a pleasant spot; since the food and drink were always excellent, you could just ignore the weeds and tangled shrubs. Kim had had an array of breads and salads laid out, several little tables had been arranged, the barbecue was lit, and at noon there were already four or five guests sampling the charcoal-roasted chicken.

Laura and her father came to the party straight from church. Kim waved at them as they were shown through the back door by Mrs Stevens, the daily help. From a respectable distance she was supervising the cooking, being done for her by a devoted lad from the village. She was clad in designer jeans of the palest blue and a knitted silk sweater that exactly matched – certainly not the clothes to wear for standing close and tending a barbecue. Her black hair had streaks of mahogany red today, which gave her an air of mystery, as if some hidden fires were burning inside that slender body.

Laura sighed inwardly. She too was in jeans and sweater, but the jeans were from a high street chain store and the sweater had been bought at a church handicraft fair. Moreover, she knew she was there only because it was Kim's way of paying off her social obligations. Really important people got invited to dinner; local bigwigs were given lunch. And about once a month those who'd been useful, or might prove so, were invited to the Sunday get-together.

Ronald hurried to Kim's side. Laura made her way to one

of the tables to greet neighbours. Mrs Stevens intercepted her with a tray of drinks.

'Chablis from an end-of-bin sale,' she confided as she offered her wares. 'It's not bad.'

'I'll stick to orange juice, thanks. I'm the driver.'

'Huh,' said the waitress. 'That doesn't bother some.' She was the wife of a farmer who'd got out of the business after twenty or so very stressful years. Now he ran a local taxi service while his wife did domestic chores for those who needed her.

Because of their work, they tended to know everything that was going on in Brinbank. One of Mrs Stevens's pleasures was to give out little hints of her knowledge. Laura took her drink and was about to move on when the waitress deterred her.

'They had a row about the church flowers yesterday,' she confided. 'Those lilies at the font? Mr Astell paid for those, it's his grandson's christening this afternoon. Miss Granger didn't like them, said they were obtrusive.' And so on, snatches of gossip that meant very little. About to turn back to her duties with the drinks tray, she paused. 'Is that right that your dad wouldn't have a church service if he got married again?'

'Married again?' Laura echoed, startled.

'You don't think so?'

'What makes you say my father's thinking of getting married again?'

'That's what they're saying down the Fox and Hare.'

Laura had recovered from the shock. 'What gave them that mad idea?' she said with a shrug.

'He did, as I heard it. Couple of weeks ago, when he was there after the parish meeting.'

This wasn't pleasant to hear. She drew in a breath to give her time to think. 'I'm sure if he had something like that in mind he'd have spoken to me about it, Mrs Stevens.'

The other woman gave her a sympathetic smile. 'I wouldn't worry about it too much, dear. It's not likely to happen. A wedding needs a bride, and that particular bride-to-be would want someone with a bit more of a say in the financial world, eh?'

Having caused as much of a stir as she wanted to, Mrs Stevens went off with her tray. Laura buried her nose in her glass to hide her mortification. She knew the whole neighbourhood was aware of her father's infatuation with Kim. But that he should have been prattling about marriage in the local pub . . .

Surely he must know that Kim Groves would never think of him as a possible husband? Kim was a bright light in a firm of solicitors in Oxford, an expert in corporate law consulted by the colleges when they had problems over land rights. This wasn't to say that she was any cleverer than Ronald, who had a first-class brain when he chose to use it. But where their earnings were concerned, Kim eclipsed him in every way.

Moreover, she was very shrewd when it came to managing money. She'd bought Yalcote at auction for a song, and, although it had taken her two years or more, had restored the interior to its former late-Victorian glory so that now the house was worth something over a million. Laura rather thought she would sell up by and by, and couldn't help hoping it would be soon so that she would move to somewhere far away. Whereupon her father might recover from his foolishness . . .

But that couldn't be until Yalcote's gardens were brought back to good order. It seemed to Laura that there was at least another year's work to be done in the grounds, unless Kim chose to call in a firm of specialists. But of course she wouldn't do that while a gang of besotted male friends were willing to do the work for nothing.

Another guest arrived and was shown to the patio. Joining him, Laura went to sit at one of the tables. They chatted about local affairs until Kim came up to invite them to choose something from the replenishments now ready on the grill. As they strolled across to the barbecue Kim remarked, 'That rhododendron seems to have reacted to the treatment suggested by Ron's chum – you know, the tree man.'

'Neil Crandel.'

'Oh yes. I half thought of inviting him today but it slipped my mind.'

'He'll be here tomorrow,' Laura said. 'Papa inveigled him into helping with some of the congested plants.'

'He did? Well, whatever congested plants are, I dare say they need attention. I'd have the whole lot ploughed up by one of those machines—'

'A cultivator.'

'Yes, one of those, but I got a quote for laying a lawn and it just seemed silly to spend that sort of money. After all, Ronald says there actually are some good plants hidden in that tangle.'

'Yes, a herbaceous border. I read about it when I was doing some research. In the twenties they used to open the grounds to the public for things like the church fête.'

'Hmph,' murmured Kim. 'I'm not opening this place to the public once it's up to scratch again. But I do want it to look good because a handsome garden increases the value of the whole thing. This Crandel chap – perhaps he'd take a look at the orchard? It's not very big, you know, but if it isn't going to provide any fruit I'd just as soon have the trees pulled up.'

Having got her message across about the work she wanted done, Kim turned her attention to other arriving guests. In all there would prove to be about ten or a dozen, coming as and when their Sunday morning got going. Laura chose some non-fattening salad then went to sit with acquaintances. Conversation ranged from local politics to what they'd been watching on television. She played her part, but was glad when people began to leave. She signalled to her father that she too wanted to go, and watched him reluctantly leave a group that had Kim at its centre.

'It's a bit early to be leaving,' he complained. 'Kim was just telling us about an interesting case she's involved in.'

'I want to get back to put something in the oven for this evening.'

'You go, then. I'll walk home.'

She left him to return to his enchantress. She knew he might stay there until the last guest was leaving, taking little part in the chat but happy to be near the woman whose life he felt impelled to share, however slightly.

She'd said she wanted to put something in the oven for that evening's meal, but that wasn't quite true. She'd simply wanted to get away. However, she spent the time making some special little cakes for tomorrow's afternoon tea, in the expectation that after their session in the garden wrestling with recalcitrant roots Ronald would bring Neil home with him.

In that she was wrong. Her father turned up on his own.

'Why didn't you bring Neil with you for a cup of tea?'

43

'Oh, he wanted to get back to the hotel to have a bath and change. He's going up to London this evening. Had something to do there tomorrow.'

'An appointment with his physio?'

He shrugged. 'I think he said he was going to see a show.'

'A show?' It took her aback, but after all, why not? The West End was full at the moment with blockbusting musicals. Hotels could always get tickets for guests, even for most sold-out performances.

She put it from her mind. She started on preparations for dinner. After all, what Neil chose to do was none of her business.

'That business about dividing plants is hard work,' said Ronald in a complaining voice. 'Neil says there must have been a really special herbaceous border there, but everything is tangled up with weeds – thistles, you wouldn't believe what a forest of dead thistles there is lying there – and ragwort is beginning to sprout in among the good stuff; it's really a mess.' He drank from his mug of tea. 'And those apple trees – I don't know if Kim mentioned it to you? She wanted Neil's opinion on them.'

'What did he say?'

'Absolutely refused to take them on. He told me they're very old, some of them are dying, but there might be historic varieties from times long past, and they need a specialist to decide whether they should be saved.'

She began to think that perhaps Neil had gone to London as an escape from the demands being made on him. If that was so, she couldn't blame him.

She busied herself for the next few days with work for various clients, including Neil's research. By Friday evening she thought she had some news that would interest him. so rang him at his hotel in the evening.

'Mr Crandel doesn't reply, madam,' said the receptionist.

'Oh. Perhaps he's in the dining room?'

'That's possible. I can have him paged, if you like.'

'N-no.' After all, it wasn't urgent. News that had been derived from a century and a half ago . . . 'I'd like to leave a message. I'm Ms Wainwright.' She spelled it out. 'Would you say that I have some information for him?'

'Certainly.'

She expected him to call back later that evening but there was no response. The next day went by. She began to feel worried. Had something happened? Had he seen the orthopaedic surgeon in London and been kept for treatment? She rang the Sceptre Hotel again.

'I left a message for Mr Crandel on Friday. Could you just check that he got it?'

'Er . . . Let me see . . . It was on his room phone, madam, and it's been cancelled, so he got it.'

'Oh. When was that – Thursday evening?'

'Our message system doesn't show that information, madam. Just that the phone message has been received and cancelled.'

'So what does that mean? His phone was blinking and he was told the desk had a message for him?'

'Quite so, yes. There would have been a note for him at the desk.'

'And he came to the desk and got the message.'

A hesitation. 'Er . . . no . . . I believe it was read to him over the telephone.'

An inspiration came to her. 'He rang from London?'

'I don't know where he rang from, madam,' the receptionist said briskly.

'But Mr Crandel isn't actually staying in the hotel at the moment?'

'I'm not permitted to disclose information about our guests, madam,' was the icy response. 'But if you care to leave a message I will signal it for Mr Crandel.'

'Thank you. Will you say that Ms Wainwright called again. That's all.'

At first she was quite hurt. But then she reproved herself. What right had she to be hurt or resentful because he didn't keep her informed of his movements? And, besides, it was perfectly natural that he should go to London for a few days. See his consultant, take in a show or two, do some shopping – why not? That's what most visitors from abroad would do.

Saturday morning she was supervising the window cleaner's activities as he teetered on his ladder outside the oddly shaped cottage windows. She heard a car come through the gateway. She turned. It was Neil's Honda.

45

'Hello there,' he called.

'Well, hello!'

He parked neatly then there was a pause. Laura had time to lament that she wasn't looking her best, with her hair tied up out of the way for a morning's housework and her torso veiled by an old shirt stained with paint. And not a lick of make-up.

When Neil got out he was using a different walking stick, a rather more surgical-looking affair. 'Spring cleaning?' he enquired. 'I gather spring cleaning is a big affair in England – there are notices all over the supermarkets about cheap cleaners and things.'

'No, the window cleaner comes regularly. You can see all the panes of glass are funny shapes and moreover you need a ladder to get at the outside properly. Come in, it's time for coffee.'

He followed her through the cottage to the kitchen. While she began on the coffee, he looked out of the open back door to the garden. 'Your plum tree's come out.'

'Yes, nice, isn't it?'

'The Chinese thought that plum-tree blossom had a special message – something to do with immortality or something.'

'Papa was saying you didn't think Kim's apple trees looked exactly immortal.'

'No, it's a rotten shame! Poor old gals! Neglected for years and years.'

'Well, the house was empty for a long time before Kim bought it. I believe the village kids got in and used it as a den, and of course probably played cops and robbers in the grounds.'

'Well, I'm not going to take the responsibility for grubbing the trees out. I hear that's what Kim Groves wants to do. But she ought to engage an expert.'

Laura brought out the cakes she'd made for Monday – reduced in number because her father had made inroads into them. 'Keep an eye on the kettle,' she said to Neil. 'If it boils, fill up the cafetière. I'll just go and call Papa. He's upstairs using his personal computer.'

She had to go upstairs because her father wasn't wearing his hearing aids. He nodded that he'd be down in a minute. When she came back the coffee was made and Neil had taken one of the remaining four ginger cakes.

'This is good. It's so nice to be a pal of someone that does home baking!'

She began to pour the coffee. 'I gather you've been up in London?'

'Yeah, what a place that is! I used to be impressed by Edmonton and Toronto, but London seems to spread for miles in every direction.'

'Papa said you were going to see a show? What did you go to, *Miss Saigon? Chicago?*'

He chuckled. 'Not that kind of show! I went to the Royal Horticultural Society's event – flowers, not really my kind of thing, but I met a few guys and bought some books.'

Ronald came in, running a hand through his thinning hair and looking cross. 'Something's wrong with that Heirloom program, Laura. I want you to take a look at it.' He nodded at Neil. 'Hello, how's it going?'

'Not bad. How's the wilderness?'

'Haven't been back since Monday. It's too much on my own. I've arranged to drop in at Yalcote this evening to have a word with Kim about those apple trees. Perhaps you'd like to come too, if you're free?'

Neil was accepting a mug of coffee from Laura and didn't reply at once. Ronald said, 'Oh, my ginger cakes – is that all that's left?'

'I've just stolen one. I didn't know you had exclusive rights, Ron.'

'They're my favourites. She puts little bits of real ginger in, you know, that stuff you get in syrup.' He picked one up and broke it open to show the ginger. 'I love that stuff. Wouldn't mind having a ginger tree.'

'Ginger's not from a tree, you ignoramus, it's a reed.'

'Oh, what a tale! I've seen the stuff on sale in greengrocers – reeds are tall straight things, ginger's all twisty.'

'That's the *root*. I don't know where you were educated.' Neil shook his head. 'Next time I go to London for a gardening show, I'll have to take you with me and give you a few pointers.'

'Oh, that's where you were? How was it, did you enjoy it?'

'Yeah, great. And I went to see the Changing of the Guard – that was something!'

'You mean you've been behaving like a tourist.'

47

'That's what I am, pal, that's what I am. A real hick from the backwoods with a Davey Crockett hat in my backpack. And now that I've admitted it, can I have another ginger cake?'

The last two cakes disappeared, the coffee was drunk, then Neil said, 'I got your message about having some news?'

'Yes, shall we go and sit down in comfort? I'll fetch it down from the study.'

What she had to show was a sheaf of printouts. He took them as she began her narration but after a moment said, 'Why don't you just lay it out for me? I can see some of this would need a bit of explaining.'

'All right. It's about David Crandel—'

'David? Is that who he was?'

She nodded, watching the interest and appreciation light up his eyes. 'David Crandel, a joiner and cabinet maker of Ramhurst village in Buckinghamshire. In 1860 David Crandel answered an advertisement in a newspaper for carpenters and joiners to work in Philadelphia. He apparently went to London to see an agent of the construction firm and was accepted – the firm was going to do some work for the Philadelphia town council, a public building of some sort.'

'My word. Important stuff.'

'Yes, it made the newspapers in his home ground. Look at the item in that printout of a column from the *Buckingham Reporter* of the summer of 1860 – that's the plastic sleeve labelled three.' She waited while he found it. She saw him raise his eyebrows at the florid style of newspaper reporting in those days but he nodded and looked up attentively.

'I've looked, and David doesn't appear in either the 1851 census for the area nor ten years later in the 1861, which I take to mean that he came to Ramhurst as an apprentice some time after 1851 and had left by 1861. Let's say he took up the apprenticeship when he was fourteen and began it in – let's choose a date – 1853 ... By 1860, when he applied for the work in Philadelphia, he'd be twenty-one. Please note – he was still there in 1860 but had gone by 1861.'

'I see.'

'And Marianne was seventeen.'

'Yes?'

'If you look at the page labelled four, you'll see that Sir

John Higston had panelling put into his drawing room and dining room in 1860. The firm he employed was Pelliter & Son of Ramhurst. That's their receipt for the cost of doing the panelling. The work was started the month after Marianne was married.'

'Yes.'

'I think we could surmise that David Crandel met Lady Higston while he was doing that work as a carpenter from the firm of Pelliter & Son.'

Ronald gave a snort. 'Here we go. One of Laura's fairy tales.'

'I'm not against fairy tales, Ron,' Neil said. 'Often they tell you things that are true.'

Laura smiled. 'Well, my fairy tale goes on like this. Lady Higston and David Crandel fell in love. Sir John was in London for parliamentary business. I've looked it up, he was Member of Parliament for the constituency of Ramhurst and Peridal. Somewhere before the end of that year, Marianne finds out she's pregnant and it probably isn't Sir John's child because he's been off at his London club drinking and gambling for months, or perhaps wheeling and dealing with his parliamentary cronies.'

'But why doesn't she just pass the baby off as Sir John's?' her father objected. 'Parliamentary sessions weren't long in those days. Sir John could have come home for the Christmas break, say. She could have fudged the dates a bit.'

She made no reply for a moment. Then she said, 'She was in love.'

'I vote for that!' Neil said.

'And, besides, I looked through some of the society gossip columns. Sir J. H. is mentioned quite a bit. He was a well-known drunkard. There's a report of him brawling and beating up a beggar or something in Pall Mall – got off with a caution. Later on, after she disappeared, there's some chatter about how he'd treated his wife. We'll come to that in a minute. I printed it out, the extracts are in that plastic folder labelled six.'

'"Treated his wife" – what d'you mean by that? You mean he was unkind to her?'

She let that go for the present. 'Lady Higston disappears.

49

The gossipmongers get interested. Look at the plastic sleeve labelled five. They're wondering where she's got to and laughing at Sir J. H. for not being able to keep her under control. Then around New Year 1861 they're being told that Her Ladyship has gone to stay with a sister of Sir John in Devon "for her health".'

'Oh yes. For her health,' Ronald scoffed. 'That's nonsense. No one who was suffering from ill-health would undertake a long carriage journey in winter conditions. That's a bit of a misunderstanding.'

'No, it was an actual lie. One of the newspapers takes the trouble to find out if she's there and she isn't.' She felt some satisfaction at foiling her father's derision. He always played devil's advocate to her theories, and of course that was necessary, but this morning she felt that it was important to Neil that she be treated with respect.

She went on. 'Now we come to folder six, Neil. You'll see the first one, dated February 11th: "Our missing lady has been sent to Devon where her bruises may be healed and her manners improved."'

'What a rotten thing to say!' Neil exclaimed.

'Well, gossip is often malicious. And that was the view taken in those days – she had to do what she was told or be punished. But look at the printout from the issue of the 21st March. "We learn that the capricious Lady H. is not in safe-keeping in Devon but is either missing again or *still* missing."'

'But nobody ever puts her together with David Crandel,' her father pointed out. 'You still haven't proved—'

'Hang on, there's more to come. Look at the plastic folder labelled seven, Neil.'

He singled it out. There were several documents in it. He opened it and began to take them out.

'The first piece of paper is part of the passenger list of the vessel *Starshine*, sailing from Liverpool on November 18th 1860. It's in alphabetical order. Do you see it?'

'Mr and Mrs David Crandel, of Ramhurst in Buckinghamshire,' he read out.

'I couldn't find a record of any marriage of a David Crandel anywhere in Buckinghamshire. It is just possible that he married someone from a different county and the marriage took place there. But I don't think so. I think the "Mrs Crandel" who sailed with him on the *Starshine* for Philadelphia was our Marianne.' She looked at him with anxiety, uncertain whether he would accept this.

'Yes,' said Neil.

'There's no proof of that,' her father protested.

'No. But it looks extremely likely. Lady Higston disappears. David Crandel's so-called wife sails with him to Philadelphia—'

'But according to your theory she turns up in Quebec!'

'Yes, Papa, and now I'll tell you how. Neil, look at the printout with the newspaper clipping on it.'

He sorted it out and began to read. Then he gave a stifled gasp. 'The ship went down?' Already he'd begun to think of these two people as part of his close family. She saw that he looked appalled.

'Lost during a gale in the North Atlantic, having been seen and noted in the log of another ship, the *Mercury*,' she explained. 'The *Mercury* reported the sighting when it docked in Liverpool in December. It gives the latitude and longitude. Now—' she held up a finger for attention. – 'the *Starshine* does seem to have been a lot further north than you'd expect if it was heading for Philadelphia. But, you see, the war between the North and the South was just about to begin.'

'What's that got to do with it?' Neil asked, at a loss.

'Well, Britain was supporting the cause of the Union. The ships from the southern states were apt to be aggressive towards merchant vessels from British ports. It seems the leaders of what would be the Confederacy were already thinking that Britain was sending useful supplies to a government that was their enemy. So the captain of the *Starshine* may have taken a more northerly course to avoid an encounter with some hostile-looking vessel, and so got caught in a tremendous gale and lost his ship. He went down with her. Almost no one was saved.'

'Well . . .' grumbled Ronald. 'Now you're going to say that all the same some survivors came ashore at Quebec.'

'A few were picked up by fishing vessels. Look at the copy of the clipping from the Quebec *Journal d'Annonces*.'

'It's in French,' said Neil. 'Hang on a minute. It says . . .

51

"Two females and three males, the males all under the age of twelve. Picked up from a lifeboat some fifty miles off the Great Bank and brought to the boat's home harbour of Gaspe."'

'Women and children first,' Ronald quoted, nodding.

'Then if you look at the document dated 8th December 1861? It's an extract from the town records of Gaspe.' It was a hand-written document but stamped with an official stamp, awarding a small sum in francs for the board and lodgings of two females, Miss Angelina Mulroyd, a schoolteacher, and Mrs David Crandel, a widow, 'under the auspices of the Sisters of Mercy at the convent of the Sacred Heart.'

'So Mrs David Crandel survived the wreck, but her husband drowned.'

'There you are, Ron! I knew he didn't ditch her!' cried Neil. 'I knew he couldn't have just walked out on her!'

Five

Despite Ronald's urging, Neil declined the invitation to join him at Kim's house that evening.

'I'd really be no use over the orchard thing,' he explained. 'I don't know anything about ancient varieties of apples.'

'Well, neither do I!'

'Then persuade her to get hold of somebody who does. She could contact Kew, or someone at the Royal Horticultural Society. They're in the phone book.'

'Would it cost a lot?'

'How do I know?' Neil said with some exasperation. 'Have a heart, Ronnie. Just because I grow trees at the other side of the world, that doesn't mean I know the cost of identifying what's wrong with some poor old things in Oxfordshire.'

'Besides,' Laura put in, 'it's not fair to ask him to turn up somewhere this evening.' She appealed to Neil. 'Did you come from London this morning?'

'Well . . . yeah . . .'

'So you must have caught a very early train, which means you've been up since the crack of dawn.'

'Oh . . . if you put it that way . . .' muttered her father.

She was gathering up the papers and documents for Neil to take with him. 'I expect you'd like some time to read through all this.'

'Sure would. But on just a first glance, it's great! Well, no, it's not great, because poor old Great-great-great-grandpa got drowned.' He shivered. 'I can't imagine anything worse – and at only twenty years old. His whole life before him . . . And Marianne, left all alone in a strange land with her baby on the way . . . They were just a couple of kids! Took a lot of guts, didn't it – shucking off the world they knew, doing something that all their kin would think disgraceful, starting out with practically nothing? Well, I'm proud of them.'

He turned to the kitchen door, picking up his new walking stick on the way. Laura would have liked to ask about the change, but he looked as if his mind was on something more momentous than the treatment to his injured ankle.

She saw him out. As he folded himself into his car he said, 'I'll be in touch, okay?'

'Of course, any time.'

He drove off and she waved him goodbye. Now, she thought to herself, he'll read through all that stuff, he'll contact me to say thank you and ask for the bill, and I'll never see him again.

Grumbling, her father went up to his computer. Laura paid the window cleaner and started on preparations for lunch. That done, she went upstairs to see if she could help over the problem with the search programme. She was no expert on technology but she was more patient than Ronald, so that, in the end, she got the screen to fill up with the sort of information he was after.

She then went to her own tasks. The spare room had been converted into a shared workroom but she often found her father a restless work companion. So she had a laptop in her bedroom, where she spent the next couple of hours catching up with the filing.

Lunch went by, and she had a relatively free afternoon before her. Should she go shopping in the village, or drive into Oxford for the big stores? Or give some attention to the garden? Nothing appealed to her. There was an unaccountable flatness about the day, although the April sun was shining on a world becoming green and cheerful.

In the end she settled down on the garden bench with the history book she'd got from the library. She was deep in the convolutions of the act of 1802 for the protection of labour in factories when she heard the house phone ring.

Knowing her father wouldn't hear it, she put her bookmark in place then went indoors. It was about four o'clock. Ronald would be wanting tea soon. Sighing inwardly at the meagreness of this Saturday programme, she picked up the receiver.

'Lauron Family Research, how can I help you?'

'Laura, it's Neil. Listen, your dad's going to be out this evening, right?'

'Yes, at Kim's'

'And you'd be at a loose end – no dinner to cook, or anything?'

'That's true.' All at once the day seemed brighter.

'I wondered if you'd like to come and have dinner with me. I think the restaurant here is pretty good, if you could put up with that.'

'Oh yes, the Sceptre gets a good write-up for its food every now and again.'

'So how about it? Can I tempt you – that is, unless you've got something else planned.'

'To tell you the truth, I was planning to spend the evening with *British Labour Laws of the 19th Century.*'

'Good lord! What on earth for?'

'Well, if you're going to do family research you have to know where people worked and what they might earn.'

'Is it urgent, this expedition to the nineteenth century?'

'No, it's just background stuff.'

'So would you like to come to dinner?'

'I'd love it.'

'Eight o'clock?'

'Fine.' She could drop Ronald at Kim's house then drive straight on to Oxford. And she'd have plenty of time to do something with her hair, and of course there was that little black number she'd bought at the January sales – or would that be too dressy? But, still, the Sceptre . . . She couldn't go to dinner at the Sceptre in slacks and an old shirt.

She hurried upstairs to start on the transformation. The dress, on examination, looked quite demure and when she tried it on she found to her delight that it fitted better than it had in January. She'd actually lost some weight!

Ronald came down for tea quite unaware of what had been going on. He found his daughter in a housecoat with her hair newly washed and her face made up. It took him a moment to realize she was getting ready to go out.

'What's all this?' he demanded.

'I'm going out to dinner at the Sceptre.'

'You are! When did this happen?'

'Neil rang about an hour ago. Listen, Papa, Kim *is* going to give you a meal, isn't she?'

'Well, if we have anything to discuss of an evening she generally has pizza or something delivered.'

'So you'll be all right.'

'Good heavens, girl, I'm not incapable. If Kim doesn't give me supper I can make myself a sandwich.'

'Well, there's a jar of soup in the fridge, and plenty of cold salmon for a sandwich, and if you need pudding there's chocolate brownies in the tin.'

He was nodding and waving all that away. 'Why's Neil asking you to the hotel? I bet it's to go through all that fol-de-rol you gave him this morning.'

'It's not fol-de-rol, Papa. I really believe it happened more or less like that.'

'You'd never make any of it stand up in a court of law.'

She said nothing to that, but instead went upstairs to finish dressing. At around seven she came down, to find her father waiting to be driven to Kim's house.

She could tell he was put out to find other cars already in Yalcote's drive. He'd hoped for a tête-à-tête with Kim but this must be one of her 'Come for a little drink' evenings. For her part, Laura was relieved. At least when he was with others he wouldn't have a chance to get romantic. If he really was getting romantic, for all she had as evidence was local gossip.

She went in for a moment to say hello. Kim's dark eyebrows went up at the sight of Laura in an evening frock. 'You're looking smart,' she commented, uncertain whether Laura considered herself as one of the guests for the 'little drink'.

'Having dinner in Oxford,' she explained.

'Oh, rather nice! Well, have fun.' She turned away to give orders to Mrs Stevens, who favoured Laura with a wink before carrying her tray of drinks and nibbles into the drawing room.

At the Sceptre, a young man in a fawn uniform jacket took charge of the Wainwrights' second-hand Land Rover. Trying not to feel out-classed, Laura made her way into the hall lit by lamps that cast an amber glow over the faux-marble floor. Neil was waiting, leaning against a table and flicking through a brochure that offered suggestions for outings. He pushed himself erect and came to greet her.

'Now aren't you a picture! I ought to have put on my Savile Row suit in honour of the evening.'

She was confused and delighted by his approval, but managed to pass it off with a laugh. 'You haven't been in the country long enough to get a Savile Row suit!'

'Yes I have, first thing I did after I got off the plane. Well, almost. Now come along, I thought we could have a drink and look at the menu, so that if you fancy anything special we can order it in advance.' He led her into the bar, which was more dimly lit than the hall and abuzz with conversation. 'Sorry about the crush. I didn't know there was a rugby match today.'

Despite the crowd he found them a little corner to sit. He caught the barman's eye and signalled. It seemed he was known, for the man came at once to take the order and present menus. Laura had no great demands to make on it; she was happy with items that her conscience allowed: melon as a starter and then grilled sole. Wine, of course, was forbidden – both on account of the diet and because she was driving home. She was at present drinking Perrier.

'Oh, I thought you'd go for this special thing, duck and all the accoutrements – I'm going to have that, just to see what it all amounts to. So let's settle down for a bit of a chat while they put it together for me.'

He enquired after her father. 'Did I gather he's talking to Kim this evening about hiring a consultant? If those trees are going to be pulled out, it's better if the job's done soon –

before they get heavy with leaves. They'll have to be lopped first, you know, and if the branches are leafy it's a dickens of a weight to cart away.'

'Really? Well, it's up to Kim. So far Papa's done everything more or less on his own—'

'No, no, don't let him tackle those apple trees.'

She laughed and shrugged. 'I don't have much influence on him really. But I'll tell him what you say – he has a high opinion of your expertise.'

'Ha! I'm just beginning to get some idea of the onset of spring in England. Some expert I am!'

'How do you like England, now that April's there?'

'Now that's from a poem. I had to read that at school. It's great, you know, what a lot of poems and things there are about the weather in England. 'Fair pledges of a fruitful tree, Why do you fall so fast?' That's about apple blossom. I always used to like that one – it's so accurate, you see. Some old guy back in the seventeenth century sees the same thing we see today but he gets all philosophical about it. Me, I'd be worrying about the crop, he's worrying about life and death.'

'Well, Herrick was a clergyman. I suppose he had to think about life and death quite a lot.'

'Herrick? Is that who wrote it? I guess I should've known that. One thing I've found out since I've been here, I'm only half educated—'

'Nonsense!' But a signal from the head waiter of the restaurant interrupted this survey of comparative learning. They were led to their table, and after that a discussion with the wine waiter kept them busy. He was disappointed in them when they ordered mineral water.

Once the first course was brought, Neil began on a different subject. 'This afternoon I went for a drive and found a nice sort of pond, where I sat and thought a lot about what you told me this morning.'

'Yes?'

'I was really impressed. You made it all come alive for me.'

'Ha!' she said. 'My father says that none of what I suggested would stand up in court.'

'I'm not thinking of taking it to court. But I did get a feeling that it would be nice to know more. Crandel, for instance.

He's a guy I could sort of relate to – a craftsman, but not high on the social ladder in those days – am I right?'

'Quite right.'

'So it took a helluva lot of courage to set out with Marianne and head for the New World. What I mean is, he was kind of equipped to deal with the life they'd meet there, but Marianne? She'd been brought up to expect quite a lot from life, hadn't she?'

'Of course. Daughter of a successful manufacturer—'

'Manufacturer? You know that for a fact? What did he manufacture?'

'Silk. He was from a Huguenot family.'

He studied her. 'What does that mean? I don't think I ever heard of it.'

'Huguenot – members of a French Protestant group who had to leave France in 1685 because their lives were in danger. A lot of them were weavers, so they brought their skills with them to Britain and on the whole they did well. George Etian Dallancy came from a family originally called de Lancy.'

'Well, if that doesn't beat all! You know all about him!'

'No, no, I just did a little bit of research because I had this feeling that his middle name came from the French name Etienne. It was perhaps traditional in his family.'

'So he came from a family of French weavers and by 1860 owned a factory.'

'Yes, in Simmingford. He was a well-regarded man. He bought the estate of Peridal as his country seat – it was quite a few miles outside Simmingford in those days and Sir John Higston's land ran alongside it. So I think that's the reason Sir John wanted Marianne's hand – to enlarge his property. The land was Marianne's dowry.'

'You're saying he didn't marry for love?' The question was half humorous.

'I'd say Sir John was practically incapable of love in the sense of really caring for anyone. He's mentioned quite a lot in the gossip columns of the day, and almost never with approval.'

'Poor kid. Poor Marianne.'

She nodded. 'I found out a lot less about David Crandel. He's from much humbler origins. The family seems to have belonged to the county of Cheshire, and he's simply mentioned in the parish register as having been born in a cottage in a small village called Prieslet. He must have left home in his early teens to take up the apprenticeship in Ramhurst.'

'And so he goes to do some work in Sir John's house and falls for the lady.'

'Right. His relatives in Prieslet probably never heard from him again. There's no particular record of them after about 1880 – I expect they moved to one of the industrial towns, and – not to be doomy about it – but the death rate in the industrial towns was pretty bad. It might well be that Marian Crandel of Alberta is the one who's kept the name in being.'

'If that don't beat all! That's keen, that's really keen.' He paused while plates were removed and the next course was served. 'So the next point is . . . How about the Dallancy lot? Are there any of them around? You see, Dad's brother – the one I told you about, who wouldn't come to the funeral – he and I are the only ones that I know of with the name of Crandel. But there might be Dallancy folk around. It would be kind of nice to find them, to have some relations besides Uncle Matt.'

'I could take a look, if you like,' she said. 'It's a fairly unusual name. I can't promise anything, you know, but I'll see what I can turn up.'

'You're so great!' he declared. 'You don't get fazed when I ask you to delve about among all this dusty stuff. Of course,' he added with a grin, 'you get paid for it. Which reminds me, would you like me to settle up my bill so far?'

'No, no, that's not necessary. We'll do the accounts when I've done the work.' The longer she could put off the final bill, the longer she would be able to maintain contact with him.

'You mean you trust me.'

'Well, I know your address,' she riposted, glancing about the hotel dining room.

'But how d'you know I won't slither off back to Canada without settling up?'

'I don't think you're the slithering kind.'

Now he laughed outright. 'So far I haven't studied up much on the art of slithering. But it seems to run in the family because that sourpuss Uncle Matt slithered out of coming for Dad's funeral.' His laughter died away. 'I thought that was rotten of him. After all, so far as I'd been told, we were the only kin left of that poor young kid who trekked all the way across the prairies with her little boy.'

'But perhaps he doesn't know that.'

He sat back in his chair, surprised. 'D'you know, I never thought of that!'

'It might not mean much to him even if you told him,' she warned. 'There are a lot of people who aren't interested in family ties. But if you ever feel like contacting Uncle Matt again, you might mention to him that you and he are the only two left – unless he's got children?'

'No, as far as I can make out he's been married to two or three bikini babes who weren't the kind to want to rock the cradle.'

'Oh dear.' She decided to change the subject. She was thinking of inviting him to Brinbank for Sunday lunch. For him she'd put on one of her more glamorous menus, even if it meant departing disastrously from her diet.

But no, he had an engagement tomorrow with an Internet friend, to look at some woodland in the Cotswolds. The conversation turned to plans for looking at other picturesque parts of the country. Scotland? Had he been to the Highlands, home of the Scots pine? He asked her advice about places to stay in Scotland but she had to admit she was no expert on that.

'Never mind, the hotel will be able to give me some ideas. Thanks a lot, that's a good thought, but it's for a bit in the future, I suppose. Until this darned ankle sorts itself out, I can't do much rough walking.'

'How is that going?'

'It's a bore,' he said.

So they didn't discuss that. Instead he asked her about the 'awful book' she was reading, which led on to a discussion about work conditions of the nineteenth century in Britain and in the lands formerly thought of as 'the colonies'. Life in Canada had been very hard for the pioneers, and only a little less hard for their descendants until the twentieth century

'But we've got ourselves more or less sorted out now,' he told her. 'So we should, we've got some of the best resources in the world. We've got miles and miles of forest – we turn out masses of wood pulp and paper – and of course there's the prairies, you know. And my part of the country – Alberta – it's got oil and coal . . .' He paused, embarrassed. 'I'm sorry. You don't need a pep talk about my homeland.'

'No, no, it's interesting. You know, our firm gets quite a lot of enquiries from families abroad, whose forebears were emigrants in the first place. I think I can say you're the first client we've had from Alberta, though, so of course I'm interested. I knew that – fairly recently, I think – lots of discoveries were made of oil and so forth.'

'Oh yeah. Big business.' He shook his head, as if he didn't entirely approve, but said no more.

When she left he went with her to the hall and stayed until the parking valet brought her car up from the garage. 'So you'll take a look around the neighbourhood to see if you can find any present-day Dallancys?' he reminded her.

'I certainly will.'

'And you'll be in touch? If I've gone off on one of my tree-study trips, just leave a message. I'll check in from time to time and if it sounds interesting I'll get back to you.'

'That's fine.' Greatly pleased with how things had turned out, she drove home, noting that the cars had gone from Yalcote as she passed.

Her father had walked home after the drinks party and was in a very bad mood. 'That salmon you left had no flavour at all,' he complained. 'I had to put oceans of mayonnaise on it.'

'But, Papa, we had it for lunch yesterday and you liked it.'

'Well, it had gone off, or something – I should have phoned for a takeaway.'

'Did you get a chance to talk to Kim about the apple trees?'

'One of my confounded hearing aids went dead on me. I hate those things! I couldn't make out half of what was being said. I bet they all thought I was an idiot.'

This was a refrain that she'd heard all too often during his period of serious depression. It was like a warning flag to her. Any time things went wrong in his life, he tended to blame it on his deafness.

'I'll ring the technician tomorrow,' she said. But experience suggested it was probably just a dead battery that had caused the trouble.

* * *

61

Early next morning, urged by the feeling that she'd been unobservant recently, she went into the workroom they shared. She stood just inside the doorway, gazing around. Ronald's desk was a mess. Cardboard files were heaped on one corner. Papers were strewn about. Letters were tucked into opened envelopes and left.

When she went closer she could see the correspondence had none of the usual notes scribbled upon it. Usually, her father made decisions as he read, scribbling 'File' or 'Urgent' or some other clue at the top of the letter. To have tucked them back without clues was a bad sign.

She found the communication from the Donovan family at the bottom of the pile of mail. He'd done nothing about it since they'd discussed it over a week ago. As she recalled, he'd said he would contact the parish priest, but there was no sign he'd done so. In other words, the Donovan enquiries were getting nowhere.

She glanced at her watch. By this time Ronald was usually up and about. The fact that he was still asleep was also a bad sign. During the time when he'd been treated for depression he'd taken refuge from life in staying abed so as not to face the new day.

She woke him by banging about in the office and made sure he stayed awake by putting on the radio rather loud. He came downstairs unwillingly, went to church and sat next to her without ever making any of the responses or singing the hymns. He took a dislike to the venison pie she'd made for lunch. In the afternoon he went out for a walk by himself. Since Laura was busy with the washing machine, she didn't notice his departure otherwise she'd have gone with him just to keep an eye on him.

Next day, Monday, was the same. He didn't waken at his usual time. She roused him by talking loudly with Mrs Stevens, who came in twice a week to help with the housework. Mrs Stevens was full of tittle-tattle about Saturday's drinks party at Yalcote.

'Stuff that was a sort of caviar . . . looked horrible. And little twists of pastry – I tried one but it hadn't any taste to my mind.'

'Cheese straws?'

'Might have been. All sent in by the caterers. Can't understand why folk want to eat things like that when they could stay at home and have a proper dinner.'

'Well, they get a chance to chat and, as they say these days, network.'

'I s'pose so. Anyway, I can tell you Miss Groves was tickled to death with herself when it was all over. "Went very well," she said, and I think that's because she spent a lot of time shmoozing with a man who's thinking of putting in a golf course at Norman's Gate. Good long legal wrangles there, I'd imagine.'

Laura nodded, wanting to get to the telephone to contact the technician about the hearing aids. Her father came downstairs, looking dejected. He grunted a greeting at Mrs Stevens, then wandered into the kitchen for his morning coffee. Mrs Stevens said to Laura, 'He didn't enjoy himself much at the party, I'm afraid. He looked thoroughly fed up.'

'His hearing aids let him down.'

'Oh, they did? Perhaps that was what was wrong.' Having passed on news and received some, she went to fetch the vacuum cleaner.

Laura made an appointment with Fred, the hearing aid mechanic, then spent the morning catching up with correspondence that Ronald had neglected. She knew he'd be angry if he thought she was 'meddling', but she found the Donovan case left practically in limbo. When she'd inconspicuously done what she could, she went to her own desk. She decided not to work on her laptop in her bedroom; when he was in low spirits, it was best to keep Ronald company.

But it was a bad start to the week. Nor did it improve after the visit of Fred in the afternoon. Her father hated these interludes because they reminded him of his failings, so he was grumpy and uncooperative with Fred, grumpy and silent with his daughter, and went out to the Fox and Hare immediately after dinner. She knew he'd sit there, morose and taciturn over one drink, until closing time.

Fred had told Laura he could find nothing wrong with the hearing aids. 'If you want my opinion, it's some sort of nervous block he puts up if he feels at a loss. Party Saturday night, was there?'

'Yes, but only a little informal affair.'

'Seems he didn't enjoy himself. I couldn't get him to open up about it but is there a lady in the case?'

'Well, yes . . . there is.'

'Um-m. Well, I've overhauled everything and he should get perfect service when he puts the instruments in his ears. He's talking about going elsewhere and trying a new supplier but those are state-of-the-art equipment. So don't let him go wasting money on new stuff.'

She nodded agreement and watched him drive away with misgiving. She could foresee a long period during which Ronald would be difficult to live with, and she could see no chance for improvement if he kept on believing he was in love with Kim.

She was proved right. For the rest of the week her father was gloomy and disinclined to work. She made no comment but instead dealt with all the things that should have been done from his desk. But then came Saturday, and another of Kim's gatherings was known to be taking place.

By all the rules of social interplay in Brinbank, it wasn't the turn of the Wainwrights to be invited again. Yet Ronald fretted and worried, hovering by the telephone in hopes of a call, afraid that if he left the room he wouldn't hear it ring. He disliked using a mobile because he'd never been able to find one that he could listen to with ease, and so it was the landline on which he depended. But the phone in the living room refused to ring.

'We still haven't discussed how to deal with those apple trees,' he muttered. 'She'll be thinking of having me to the house this evening.'

'But she'd have let you know by now, Papa,' Laura said gently.

'No, no, she's always got a lot on her mind. She lives her life at a different level from us, you know.'

'Well, if you're concerned about the trees, why don't you ring her? You could discuss it all by phone, surely.'

'That wouldn't be the same. I need to be there, to point out which trees to save and which have got to go.'

'Neil says it ought to be done soon, Papa – before the trees get their leaves on and become a bigger job to handle.'

'I know that. He told me. You needn't think you're the only one he talks to.'

She'd have said, 'Of course I don't think that,' but she knew her father was spoiling for a fight. She wanted at all costs to keep things calm, because it took him days and days to recover after a confrontation. He would never apologize, and she for her part seldom knew exactly what it was that had gone wrong. In this case, she understood that it was disappointment over Kim's attitude that was causing his misery. He wanted to be seen as a suitor, a lover, but common sense should have told him it was impossible.

'And let me tell you,' he surged on since she made no reply, 'getting yourself all dolled up in a new frock won't do you any good! Just because he invites you to dinner, that's no reason to think he's interested. It was only because he wanted to discuss that yarn you spun to him, about how Marianne and the Crandel fellow got together – absolute moonshine, the whole story! I hope you had the decency to tell him you were making it all up.'

'Papa, there's no need to talk like that—'

'Yes, there is a need! You take it for granted that you know how to handle clients, but most of what you tell them isn't founded on anything solid. Documentary evidence, that's what counts—'

'I know that, Papa, but—'

'And another thing, I don't want you poking about among the things on my desk! We have an understanding: you handle your clients and I handle mine. I don't want you "tidying up". Don't think I haven't noticed how you'd shuffled about among my papers.'

'But I felt I had to move the Donovans' case a bit further—'

'Who asked you to? Have they complained?'

'No, but—'

'There you go again, you see? You imagine they're getting worried but the fact is, they have full confidence in me—'

'Of course they have, but, after all, the longer things hang on, the more it's likely to cost them—'

'Not at all, not at all. Are you saying I would charge them for time I hadn't spent on their work?'

'I didn't mean that, but it's expensive to call from Buenos Aires and you know they don't like email so if they wanted to enquire it would be by telephone—'

'Stop babbling, child! The Donovans are perfectly happy and everything is being handled. Just keep out of my work and I'll keep out of yours – unless I see you ready to make a fool of yourself over a bit of common politeness from a client! It's just this overheated imagination of yours; it's a bad thing in business but in personal matters it could lead you to make an utter fool of yourself.'

With that he stamped out of the living room. Laura sank into a chair. This wasn't good. When Ronald got to the stage of personal abuse, it meant he was trying to defend himself against criticism by attacking first. He ought to see his doctor, and, more effectively, his psychiatric counsellor.

But now wasn't the time to suggest it. She had to let him cool down first, and then bring it into the conversation as mildly as possible. In the past, when his marriage was breaking up, Ronald had eventually been brought to accept the facts. But at present the facts were difficult to be sure of. He thought he had a chance with Kim Groves – but that was only an opinion, a fantasy perhaps.

The trouble was that anything she said about Kim was taken by her father as envy. That made it very hard to suggest to him that Kim was extremely unlikely to be interested in him as any kind of partner in her life.

The day passed; he received no invitation to come to any of Kim's weekend gatherings. Giving in at last, he rang about four in the afternoon, only to be greeted by her answering machine. No personal response, no invitation, no interest of any kind. He retired to the Fox and Hare in the evening. Sunday he decided to go for a walk rather than attend church.

And so it went on, well into the following week.

On Thursday Neil rang to ask if he could come for 'that dinky afternoon tea you put on'. She agreed at once; she had information for him. When he arrived he was walking better, so she wanted to know how the treatment for his ankle was coming along. He shrugged it off. They were just about to start on her news of the Dallancy family when Ronald came in from a lonesome walk around the local woods.

He looked terrible. Wan, weary, unshaven, untidy, he took one look at the placid scene in the living room then with a snort of annoyance turned and stamped out of the room and upstairs.

'Good lord! What's wrong?' Neil exclaimed, utterly taken aback.

'It's . . . things have been difficult . . . He's not too well . . . He gets these episodes, gets very depressed . . .'

'How long has he been in that state?'

'Over a week now. It's . . . He's got these feelings for Kim . . .' She shook her head. 'I shouldn't be telling you this!'

'It's all right. I went through the same kind of stuff with my dad.' He shook his head. 'What about his doctor?'

'I can't even mention the idea of going to see him. He gets very upset.'

Neil rose from his armchair. 'Let me talk to him.'

'No, really – Neil! He won't listen to anybody.'

'Let me have a try. Just hang in there, Laura – I think I can help.'

With that he went out and she heard his footsteps on the stairs. She sat there in anxiety, but thinking that perhaps he was after all the right person to help. It needed someone less close to Ronald, someone he might see as impartial. A man, perhaps, rather than a woman. No one could accuse Neil of having any dislike or envy of Kim, since he scarcely knew her.

From upstairs she heard a loud voice – her father exclaiming at Neil's appearance in the office. Then a more subdued sound, conversational though not exactly friendly. She caught herself up in reproof – what was she doing, sitting here being a kind of eavesdropper? She went out into the garden to take out a few weeds.

After about fifteen minutes she thought of the tea in the pot, getting cold and stale. She went in, emptied it, and started the kettle to boil for a fresh brew. As she was wondering whether to pour the boiling water on the tea leaves, she heard Neil and her father coming downstairs.

Neil put his head in at the kitchen door. 'Where's this fancy spread I was promised?'

She gave him a questioning glance. He replied with a slight nod and the sketch of a smile. Then he withdrew to keep Ronald company in the sitting room.

When she went in with the freshly made tea she saw to her

pleasure that her father had been persuaded to tidy himself up a bit. He hadn't shaved, but he'd washed and changed his shirt. The grey tinge to his skin was somehow ameliorated.

They sat down as if nothing had happened. Neil said, 'Milk in first, yes?'

'Right. And home-made shortbread to go with it.'

He accepted his cup, set it down on the little table by his elbow. 'I came to hear how you'd got on with the Dallancys,' he said. 'Anything on the burner?'

'As a matter of fact, yes.' She paused to hand tea to Ronald and offer him a shortbread biscuit. To her surprise he took one; in the last few days he'd eaten almost nothing, and what he had accepted he'd found fault with.

'Well, go on! Don't leave me hanging from the cliff by my fingertips.'

'There's a family called Dallancy living in Simmingford.'

'Simmingford?'

'Oh, that's a grimy little industrial town about sixty miles away,' Ronald said, with something of his habitual disparagement.

'Now, Ron, them's my folks you're talking about,' Neil remarked. 'Grimy, indeed. I bet the Dallancys wouldn't live anywhere grimy.'

'You'd lose your bet,' Laura said. 'I'm afraid Simmingford is grimy. Though I believe they were doing some . . . what's it called . . . regeneration in the town centre a while ago.'

'There you go! That's a good word. Anywhere my folks are living, that's a good place.' He hesitated. 'So . . . Can I get in touch?'

'If you want to.'

'Sure I want to. That was the whole point.'

'Steady on,' warned Ronald. 'It can be a dodgy business, contacting long-lost relatives.'

'Dodgy. Meaning difficult? Meaning they may not want to know me?'

'That's possible.'

'Who wouldn't want to know me? I'm harmless and well-meaning.'

'In the first place, people often think it's some sort of confidence trick. And in the second, they sometimes think

68

even if it's genuine that it's a way of getting something from them – money or heirlooms or something.'

'Gee, Ronnie, you do see the sunny side of things! Let's suppose they're waiting for me with open arms. How do I go about it?'

'The best thing is to telephone first.'

'Telephone? But do we know their number?'

'Yes, I've got it here,' said Laura, offering a sheet of paper with the necessary details.

'Now how on earth did you get their number?'

'I looked them up in the phone book.' She couldn't help a smile of amusement.

'Well, there you are. It pays to bring in an expert. So . . . Should I give them a bell?'

Laura exchanged a glance with her father. For once, he gave her an approving look then shook his head at Neil.

'Not just at this moment, Neil.'

'Why not? What's wrong with now?'

'It's the middle of the afternoon. If anyone's at home, it's likely to be a woman – the husband or partner is likely to be at work. Women don't like to receive telephone calls from complete strangers. Especially men.'

'Oh.' He couldn't hide his disappointment. 'So . . . What's a good time?'

'Some time in the evening. Not too early because they might be having their evening meal. Let's say eight o'clock or half past.'

'But that's five hours!'

'Patience, Neil, patience. You learn that in the genealogy world.'

'So what am I supposed to do in the meantime? I'll die of suspense!'

'First of all you should drink your tea and eat your short-bread,' Laura prescribed. 'Then you should have dinner later – let's say about seven thirty. And then when it gets to about eight fifteen you can dial the number and see what they say.'

'If I live that long.'

'Come on, it's only a few hours. I tell you what, lad, why don't you stay on with us and have dinner? Then we can hold your hand until it's crunch time.'

69

Laura was amazed. Her father seldom invited anyone for a meal, and when he did it was always with some forethought. This spontaneous offer was wonderful. It meant that somehow Neil had unlocked the prison of misery in which Ronald had closed himself for the last two weeks.

And as she turned to him she could see that he knew this was so. He gave her a little grin then said, 'If it's okay with the lady of the house, I'd be glad to stay. And *you* can dial the number for me.'

Six

They sat in the living room with their after-dinner coffee. Nobody was actually gazing at the telephone, but their attention was concentrated there, despite the attempts at conversation.

Finally Ronald said, 'Well, I make it eight ten. Let's do it.'

It had been agreed that Laura should make the first contact because a woman's voice was less alarming than a man's. She pressed the buttons for the number then sat listening to it ring. She had a horrible suspicion that no one would be at home.

After quite a wait, an answering machine clicked on. The message was: 'Speak after the tone.'

She responded with: 'This is Laura Wainwright of Lauron Family Research. I'm calling on behalf of a client who is trying to find relatives of the Dallancy family. Please pick up if you're there, but if not, this is our number.'

She waited once more, but no one responded. She replaced the receiver. 'All we can do now is wait to see if they listen to their messages regularly.'

'Probably out at the pub,' suggested her father.

'Or watching television.'

'Or they may think it's some sort of a hoax,' Neil said with a sigh. 'I know back home we were plagued with folk trying to sell us new kitchens or replacement windows. But Laura doesn't sound like that gang.'

Laura poured more coffee and offered chocolate mints. Time went by while they talked about sightseeing in Scotland, pine trees both in Britain and Canada, and Kim Groves's derelict orchard.

At almost exactly eight thirty the phone rang. Despite the fact that she'd been listening for it, Laura was so startled she almost spilled her coffee. She picked up.

'This is Norman Dallancy ringing Lauron Something-or-other, the tape's a bit fuzzy. Make it quick because I want to watch Coronation Street.'

'This is Laura Wainwright of Lauron Family Research,' she said with careful diction. 'I have a client who is interested in finding any descendants of the Dallancy family. Your family name is Dallancy?'

'What if it is?'

'Would you be willing to speak to our client?'

'Who is he, if you don't mind? Is he some nut?'

'Not at all. He has come from Canada in hopes of finding some relatives on the maternal side—'

'You what?'

'We believe that among his great-grandparents there was a Marianne Dallancy, from Peridal in Bedfordshire—'

'Is this a joke?'

'Not at all.' She looked over the receiver at Neil. 'Not very receptive.'

'Should I speak to him?'

She said into the receiver, 'I have our client with me now. Would you let me put him on?'

'Well, I . . . Who is he?'

'I'll let him speak for himself.' She handed over to Neil, who took her place in the chair by the telephone.

'Hello there,' he said. 'My name's Neil Crandel and I believe my great-great-great-grandmother was a Dallancy—'

The loud chortle was clearly audible to Laura and Ronald. Neil frowned and shook his head. She gave a little shrug but wouldn't give up hope yet.

'Don't laugh,' Neil said. 'I've come all the way from Wenaskowa in Alberta to find some kinfolk. You're name's

71

Dallancy, right? What? Oh, Norman Dallancy, I get it, yeah, thanks.' He was making waving motions at Laura, who rightly interpreted this as the need for a pen and notepad. 'Yeah, yeah, got that. So, listen, could we meet? Yeah, Simmingford, I know you live in Simmingford, Laura got that out of the phone book. Laura – you just spoke to her.'

He held up what he had written on the pad so that she could read it. 'Wife and daughter, father Ernest D.' She nodded. She already knew that from her research.

'How about a drink? Somewhere in Simmingford. No, I don't know Simmingford. Well, sure, I'll find it. Let's say lunch-time tomorrow. No? Well, evening then. Evening, say eight? What? Oh, okay then, how about nine?' He looked at the Wainwrights, mouthing, 'Television.'

Laura sighed inwardly. Norman Dallancy's original greeting had warned her that he was likely to put other things second to his television programmes. She heard the rest of Neil's conversation, which ended with: 'Okay, tomorrow evening, the Old Falcon at Simmingford. How will we know each other? Yes . . . Okay . . . See you then.'

As he hung up he said to the others, 'He says *he*'ll know *me* because I won't be a regular at the Old Falcon.'

'First contact!' cried Ronald. 'Voyager has landed on Planet Dallancy.'

'Hm-m,' Neil said. 'The natives didn't seem all that friendly.'

'People are often wary at the first introduction,' Laura soothed. 'He'll warm up, I'm sure.'

'Wife and daughter . . . Wonder whether *they*'ll be more interested.'

'I'm sure of it,' Ronald said, with a little smile that had some scorn in it. 'Women are always more welcoming to any notion of drama or a family get-together. Did you get their names?'

'No, I didn't think to ask, and besides he wasn't eager to go on talking – I was keeping him from his TV programme.' He sounded downcast, and Laura experienced a great desire to take his hand and tell him it would probably work out fine.

'I'll ask at the Sceptre how to get to Simmingford. Probably they could get me a street map. Norman said the Old Falcon is in the old town centre. The Old Falcon – I bet it's some old place with beams and an open fire and all that.'

'Nonsense, lad! Simmingford is, or was, a little industrial town. Most of it was probably built when the factories were booming – late nineteenth century.'

'Well, that's old! Or it sounds old to me.'

'Laura's infecting you with her romantic notions. It'll be a run-of-the-mill pub with a big TV screen for watching cricket and football.'

'I'll go for that, if it hands me a family of kinfolk like my dad was trying to find. Say, Ronnie, would you come with me to help break the ice?'

Ronald was taken aback. 'Me? Well, I'm . . . I'm not much good at the personal contact thing. That's more Laura's line.'

'So would you come, Laura?' Neil asked.

She was delighted to be asked. In general, clients preferred to make these contacts on their own, fearful of a public rebuff, so in fact she had very little experience of how to manage a first meeting. But her view was that if she said little she could scarcely go wrong.

Her father's cheerful mood seemed to be lasting. As Neil was making his farewells he said, 'Give me a lift to Kim's? I think it's time she and I really got to grips over those trees.'

'Sure thing.'

Ronald went upstairs to fetch a jacket. Laura said to Neil, 'You seem to have done him a world of good. Thank you.'

'Don't mention it.'

'I can't think how you managed it.'

'Well, it isn't black magic or anything like that. He needed to talk to somebody about this Kim character. She seems to hold a big place in his affections.'

'Yes, she's become more and more important since she first came here a couple of years ago. Not just to Papa, of course – she's become our local celebrity.' She checked herself, knowing her tone was cool. 'Sorry. That sounds carping.'

'No, it sounds worried. I only met Kim that once, for a few minutes, so I can't judge. This evening I may get a chance to see them together, see if there's anything in it.' He hesitated and added, 'Because if there is – I mean if he's really serious about her and she's indifferent – things could be difficult.'

She was about to say more but Ronald's footsteps could be

73

heard on the oak staircase. She said, 'About tomorrow. When and where should we meet?'

'Oh, I'll come and fetch you—'

'Nonsense,' said her father as he joined them. 'She can take the train from Brinbank Junction to Simmingford – you can meet her there.'

'But perhaps Laura would rather—'

'Nonsense, nonsense, you'd have to bring her home and that would involve you in an awful lot of driving around at night and after all you don't know the roads all that well.'

This was undeniable and so Laura said, 'Yes, that's best, I'll drive to the junction and get the train there. No problem.'

'So I meet you at Simmingford station?'

'Yes, and as we're seeing Mr Dallancy around nine, I'd better take the eight fifteen from the junction. I don't go to Simmingford much but I imagine that'll get me in at about eight forty-five. Okay?'

'Sounds fine. I'll poke around and find the Old Falcon beforehand.'

'Right. Simmingford station at a quarter to nine, then.'

'It's a date.'

Ronald had to walk back from Yalcote. Laura waited with apprehension. But when he came in he was still on an even keel. Laura was so accustomed to wide swings of mood when he was depressed that she almost hugged him in relief.

'How did things go about Kim's trees?'

'Neil's going to come back in a day or two and look at them in daylight.'

'Oh. You mean you all went out to inspect them?' She'd rather thought it would be a doorstep hello and goodbye.

'No sense in having him there and not getting him to explain things to Kim. Glad I did, because she seemed more inclined to listen to him than to me. Of course, I've always insisted that I'm no expert. But she could see Neil knew what he was talking about.'

'So when is he going back?' She sighed inwardly. He was about to be recruited to Kim's band of faithful followers.

But her father had decided it was time for a nightcap and bed. He walked away from her without answering her question.

Next day was busy, with two new clients making long phone

calls and a lot of research answers arriving by email. She and her father had dinner rather early. She was at Brinbank Junction in good time for the train. It was only then that she remembered she'd always thought railway stations were gloomy at night, but the train chuntered in and she boarded.

Neil was waiting for her on the platform. She noticed that he wasn't using his stick, although when they began to make their way out she saw that he was still limping. Perhaps he thought walking with a stick would make a poor impression on his new-found relation. 'Gee, what a downbeat sort of a place this is!' he remarked as they went into the tunnel that would lead them to the exit. 'Until the train came in I thought it was closed.'

'Country stations are never exactly full of life, even in the daytime. Still, I got here on time. Have you had a look at the pub?'

'Yeah, I'm a bit let down about that. It's got no oak beams or anything. Still, we don't need oak beams.' He offered his arm, and they set off out of the quiet station and into the town.

Ronald Wainwright's description of the place had been more or less accurate. Industry had left it, so that now the town centre was almost deserted. The one-time shopping area had been replaced with a pedestrian area and some fountains and flower beds. Traffic signs directed cars toward Simmingford New Town.

'Oh, it's been redeveloped. I seem to remember that – some complaints about taking up green sites for a shopping mall.'

'Shopping malls are everywhere,' Neil agreed. 'Even Oxford's got that sort of thing, I must say it surprised me – city of dreaming spires, you know, I expected cobbled streets.' He chuckled. 'And Simmingford has every right to a shopping mall if it wants one, I suppose. What was the industry that's folded its tents?'

'Oh, textiles. George Etian Dallancy had a factory here for making silk. But that's completely gone now, I looked it up.'

'So I can't even gaze at the building and tell myself it was owned by my great-great-however-many grandfather.'

They took a side road off what must have once been a main street but now bordered a boating pool using water from the old industrial canal. A few yards along a sign hung above a doorway, with an idealized falcon perched on a twig. The place was 'old' – that's to say it had been there for a hundred years or so. But the interior had no beams and no open fire. Instead a widescreen television showed a rugby game. Perhaps half a dozen men were watching, most of them standing at the bar.

A man at a table rose at their entry. 'Mr Crandel?'

'That's me. And you're Norman – I'm going to call you Norman because you're my cousin. And I'm Neil, and this is Laura Wainwright, who rang you last night.'

'How d'you do,' said Norman Dallancy, shaking hands with less enthusiasm than Neil. There was wariness hidden behind his polite expression.

He was rather short, rather pale, with a little too much flesh around his chin. Laura guessed he had a sedentary occupation. His clothes were casual style, not by any means new.

'Well, now, this calls for a celebration, doesn't it?' said Neil. 'What will you have, Norman?'

'Er . . . Half of bitter, please.' Laura, whose ear was acute, caught the undertone. Norman was thinking, If I have to buy the next round, I'm making sure it's inexpensive.

'What about you, Laura? Champagne?'

Norman looked alarmed, but Laura laughed. 'No, no, sparkling mineral water, please. I have to drive home later.'

'Okey-doke, I'll be back in a minute.'

The others sat at the table. Norman said, 'What's it exactly, this business you're in?'

'We research for people who want to find out about their origins. My father and I are in partnership – he used to teach history at Rillford School so he's very good at it.' She told him this to reassure him. She sensed he expected some sort of scam.

'And people do that? Hire you to find out things?'

'Yes, it's grown very popular. We get a lot of enquiries from overseas, because you know people left this country in the last century to settle in Canada and Australia and all over the place.'

'Oh yes. So he's from Canada, did you say yesterday?'

'Yes, Alberta. He and his father—'

Neil returned with the drinks. 'You're talking about me, I can feel my ears burning,' he said. 'Here you are, Norman. I'd like to try that, but I've got this wonky ankle and have to take medication so I'm not allowed alcohol for the moment. Cheers.' He sipped his mineral water and Norman, a little more cheerful, took a mouthful of beer.

'I bet you wonder what on earth brought me here looking for you,' Neil began. 'My dad and I ran this tree nursery—'

'What?'

'Tree nursery – we grew trees for gardens and parks. It was great, we really did well, but Dad died last winter and he'd started this research – you know, who was the first Crandel to come to Canada and that sort of stuff. So I thought I'd carry on, as a sort of mark of respect, but it's got really interesting, and it seems like you and I are related.'

'Fancy that!'

'Laura could tell you all the details – not that I suppose it would interest you a helluva lot – but the main point is that a girl called Marianne Dallancy went to Canada in 1860 or thereabouts with a guy called David Crandel, and she's a grandmother half a dozen times removed, and she's a relative of yours, too.' He looked at Laura, who took it up.

'George Etian Dallancy was the father of Marianne. His brother, Martin Dallancy, inherited when George died. He owned a silk mill here in Simmingford for some years but artificial silk and then other man-made fabrics seem to have ruined the business. I think Martin was your great-great-great-grandfather.'

'Well I never!'

'So Neil's right to say you're cousins, although at some distance.'

'I never would have thought it!'

'So I wanted to meet you, Norman, and say hello, and ask if there are any other Dallancys that you could introduce me to.'

'I . . . er . . . I never got to hear of any. But then I . . . you know . . . I'm not into all that.'

'You were an only child?' Laura prompted.

'Yes, quite right.' He looked uncomfortable. He clearly didn't relish the idea that she knew things about his family that he himself did not. 'Er . . . I think there was some bunch in Carlisle or Newcastle or somewhere . . . An uncle . . . We used to get Christmas cards from his widow . . . Eileen would know.'

'Eileen is . . . ?' Neil queried.

'My wife. Eileen. Yes, and I've got a daughter, Shelley . . . She's seventeen, just left school more or less . . . She didn't want to work in the shop so she's in an office in the New Town.'

'The shop? You've got a shop?' Neil asked, interested.

'Yes, not far from here. We live above it. Newsagent and sweets and lottery – used to be a real little goldmine until they moved everything out to the New Town.'

'Oh, something went wrong?' said Neil.

'You bet it did! No passing trade any more. Used to do a lot, first with folk on their way to work – ciggies for the day, you see, and then magazines and sweets when the shoppers came out, and the evening paper on the way home. But the town planners got all the big shops moved out to the new mall, and the tobacco trade's gone down the drain more or less now that there's all these smoking bans and everything. Of course, we've still got a few regulars, families that live around the neighbourhood, and I do a morning delivery now cos Eileen can handle the shop trade by herself, it having gone down so much. But honestly, it's just a shadow of itself, the business we do now.'

This speech seemed to relieve Norman's feelings. It was clearly something he liked to declaim about, and moreover in the present situation he perhaps felt he was warding off any appeal for funds or investment from this new-found cousin from the colonies.

Neil looked sympathetic. 'That's really tough. You didn't think of taking a shop in the new set-up?'

'You're joking! At those rents? Besides, who wants to buy their newspapers and lottery tickets in a shopping mall? You want it to be somewhere you pass by on your way to the bus, and though there were a few shops to let on the new streets they laid out, you had to be quick off the mark to get one and Eileen and I just missed out on it.'

'So you've decided to stay put where you are?' Laura asked. The unasked question was, Will you survive?

'We're thinking of selling up and going to Spain.'

'Spain?'

'Yes, open a bar or a beach shop or something. Shelley

78

fancies that. Question is whether we'd raise enough to make a fresh start. There's some folk seem quite keen on buying up old premises and tarting them up as places to live – I'm looking into it.'

'Sounds as if I got here just in time to have the chance of meeting you. And of course, Norm, now I've met you I'd like to meet the rest of your family. How do you feel about that?'

'We-ell . . . There's nothing against it, I suppose.'

'How about another drink? What's it called in your lingo – the other half?'

'Thank you, yes, that would be nice.'

While Neil made his careful way to the bar Norman Dallancy frowned and seemed to search for words. 'You haven't known him long, I take it?'

'Just a few weeks.'

'He contacted you from Canada?'

'No, he was in England, staying in Oxford. He's still staying there, though he goes around a lot – to London, and to look at trees—'

'Look at trees?'

'Yes, he mentioned that, he and his father grew trees on a sort of farm.'

'Sounds weird.'

'No, when you come to think of it, somebody must raise the trees we buy for our gardens, mustn't they?'

'Never thought about it. The wife and I have never had a garden.'

'Well, I've never actually bought a tree, but you know, if the local council decide to plant ginkgos along the roads, they have to get them from somewhere.'

'What's a ginkgo?'

Neil, arriving with two little bottles of mineral water and a glass of beer, set them down and said, '*Ginkgo biloba*, native to China, also known as the maidenhair tree, fan-shaped leaves, been around since Jurassic times. Shall I go on?'

'No, that's more than enough,' Laura said, laughing. She gave a glance that included Norman in the joke. 'He likes to show off about trees. The first thing he did after we met him, my father and I, was to save a tree in a neighbour's garden that my poor papa was going to cut down with a saw.'

'Your father's a gardener? I thought you said he was into this family research lark.'

'Oh, he's helping a neighbour with her garden in his spare time, that's all.'

'Never mind Laura's neighbour and all her problems. What about that rendezvous with your family, Norman? Would you like to make a date or something?'

'Well, but where would we meet?' was the hesitant reply. 'We only have the flat above the shop and I don't know if Eileen would . . .'

'I thought I might invite you all to have lunch with me. On Sunday, say.'

'What, here? Eileen's not much in favour of pubs.'

'No, I thought where I'm staying in Oxford. The Sceptre, do you know it?'

'Never been to Oxford.'

'It's nice, Norman,' urged Laura. 'I had dinner there last week. The restaurant's got stars and things for its food.'

'Oh, yeah, it's not a bad place – a bit fancy, with a wine waiter in a fancy jacket and that sort of thing, but it's highly respectable if Eileen's worried about that. So how about it, Norm? Would you see what your wife thinks?'

'Well, I could ask her . . .'

'Okay, then you talk to her about it and give me a ring. Here's one of the hotel's cards with the number, and I'm in room 18. Might be out, of course, but the desk will take a message.'

'Well, all right.'

And that was how it was left.

As they made their way to the station, Neil said to Laura, 'That wasn't exactly a roaring success.'

'No,' she sighed. 'I suppose it happens like that sometimes. Families aren't always like doves in a dovecote.'

'He thought I was going to ask him for money.'

'Oh . . .' She couldn't exactly deny it. She'd seen the wariness in Norman Dallancy.

'And there was I thinking it would be the other way round – the poor folks at home hoping for a long-lost cousin who'd found a goldmine.'

'Oh, you'd be smoking a big cigar if you'd found a goldmine.' Then after a moment she added, more seriously, 'I think maybe he's had a bad time these last two or three years. You know, when town planners start hovering around it probably makes you feel insecure, and it seems clear he's lost out all along the line.'

'I guess so. Poor little guy . . . But I can't say I took to him any more than he took to me.'

'He'll be better when he's having a nice relaxed lunch. And wife Eileen and daughter Shirley will be kinder.'

'Shelley. Her name's Shelley.' He gave a little chuckle. 'I couldn't help thinking they didn't seem the type to name their daughter after a poet.'

'Well . . . I don't think it's anything to do with poetry. Names go in fashions. There are a lot of Dwaynes and Madonnas around these days.'

They reached the station. It seemed even gloomier than it had earlier. There was no sign of anyone else – no station staff, no passengers.

'You sure there's a train?' Neil asked. 'Looks dead to me.'

'There's supposed to be a ten fifteen.'

He glanced about then took her by the elbow. 'This is ridiculous! Come on, I'll drive you home.'

'No, no, I left the Land Rover at Brinbank Junction—'

'I'll drive you to your car, then. Come on—'

'But you don't know the roads—'

'Listen, Laura, I didn't argue about all that yesterday because when somebody's down in the dumps the way your dad is I think it's best to save any quarrels for the bigger issues. But I'm capable of driving around a few twisty lanes in the dark without getting lost.'

'Yes. Sorry.'

'It's okay. In any case,' he said with amusement, 'if I lose my way you can tell me where to turn and go back.'

'Yes, but when you drive back to Oxford from Brinbank Junction who's going to keep you on the right road?' she parried.

'That's enough of that. Here we are.' He had left his Honda in the station car park. He unlocked and helped her in, then went round to the driving seat. 'Forward into the unknown!' he declaimed as they nosed their way out.

The journey by car was longer than by train. He had no trouble finding his way, only once waiting at a fork road for instructions. At the car park he walked with her to the Land Rover. When she'd unlocked, he stood hesitating.

'Say . . . Laura, would you come to this lunch on Sunday?'

'Oh, but— It's for you to get to know Eileen and Shelley . . .'

'Yeah, and think how awkward it was with their dad! I could do with some support. Would you come? Unless you've got something else on.'

'No, no, nothing. Of course, if you think I—'

'That's great! And bring your dad, too, if he'd like to.'

Her spirits, which had soared a little at being invited, sank to normal again at having to include Ronald in the party. But she said, 'I'll ask him and let you know.'

'Perfect. You're the best, Laura.' He gave her a little kiss on the tip of her nose. 'Night, then!' He helped her in, closed the door on her, and waved her off.

She drove away smiling in delight.

Seven

To Laura's surprise, her father was quite willing to be included in the lunch party for next day. She'd half expected him to say he wanted to wait in case Kim invited them, but then learned in passing that Kim was already away at a weekend legal conference.

Ronald listened with enjoyment to her description of Norman Dallancy. 'I suppose he doesn't even know he's got French blood in him somewhere.'

'No, and I didn't go into any of that. In fact, Neil did the family background bit. Did it very well, just enough to explain the connection.'

'And there's only a daughter, you say. So the great Dallancy name ends up at a little shopkeeper. Well, truth to tell, it wasn't ever very great, only weavers if you come to look at it squarely.'

'Neil never expected any blue blood, Papa. He just—'

'You don't know what he was expecting. Don't run away with the idea you have any special rapport with him, girl. Well, so he's meeting the whole menagerie tomorrow. I don't mind going along since he's invited me.'

He himself rang the Sceptre to accept. Laura heard him chatting jovially to Neil, and was thankful. It occurred to her he might be viewing Neil as the son he would rather have had. The fact that his wife had only produced a daughter and didn't want to try again was one of the reasons for their discord

Sunday dawned cloudy and cool. Laura felt justified in wearing a new cashmere sweater that she'd bought as a bargain in a spring sale a year ago but had put aside because she felt it showed off her curves too well. Today, her curves seemed less bountiful – her months of self-denial were really having an effect. So with the addition of a silk scarf that matched the sky-blue of the cashmere, and bootleg jeans, she felt she could meet the head waiter's eye at the Sceptre.

Even Ronald spruced himself up; he put on what Laura thought of as his 'country-gentleman's outfit' – well-tailored grey slacks, sports jacket of genuine Harris tweed, and a grey shirt with a faint white stripe. He drove the Land Rover and was good humoured with the parking valet although he'd often said to Laura that he thought them an unnecessary nuisance. When they got to the hotel foyer they found the Dallancys already there.

'Good morning, glad to see you,' Laura said, making introductions quickly. She thought they looked perplexed, sitting in luxuriously deep armchairs in the foyer. Eileen Dallancy in particular – short, plump, unable to be comfortable in the big leather chair, she had turned sideways so that her feet could touch the ground. Her daughter, Shelley, had solved the problem by sitting on the cushiony arm.

'Where's Neil? Seeing to the menu or what?'

'I dunno exactly, Mr Wainwright. He's not around.'

'You haven't asked?' Ronald said, surprised.

'Well, I . . . er . . .' It was clear Norman was unaccustomed to splendours such as the Sceptre.

Laura quietly went to the desk to ask for Neil. The receptionist picked up a phone and called him. 'He'll be right down, madam.'

She conveyed this message to the others, and Shelley exclaimed, 'Told you, Dad! We should've asked.'

'Oh, well, you know . . . We were early, it seemed sort of . . . well, anyhow, here he is.'

Neil came out of the lift. He was using his stick. Laura thought to herself that walking around without it on Friday evening had not been a good idea. Her father made the introductions, Mrs Dallancy shaking hands weakly and Shelley offering a nod of greeting. She looked older than the seventeen years Norman had mentioned, taller than either of her parents, slender, showing off long legs in very tight jeans and spiky shoes. Her hair was short and fair, dressed with gel into a spiky cap. If not exactly pretty, she had her own style.

'Shall we go straight in?' Neil suggested. 'We can have drinks at the table, if that would be okay.'

As if by magic the head waiter appeared when they entered the dining room to conduct them to their table. The wine waiter fussed up to them. Norman said he'd have lager, Eileen asked for sherry, and Shelley enquired whether the bar could supply a Marbella Moonshine.

'Of course, madam,' murmured the wine waiter. 'Mineral water for you, sir? And madam?'

Neil and Laura agreed. Ronald asked for the same since he was in charge of the Land Rover. He said he'd allow himself one glass of wine with the meal, so Neil ordered Chablis after politely consulting the Dallancys. They, clearly at a loss, agreed with the suggestion at once.

Laura longed for the drinks to come and soften the atmosphere. Norman Dallancy was on edge from some sense that he had to safeguard his womenfolk, Eileen Dallancy was peeping sideways at everything for clues on how to behave, and Shelley was determined to be nonchalant.

'So you drove to Oxford?' she enquired of Ronald.

'Oh, absolutely – Sunday trains, you know . . .'

'What car do you drive, Norm?' Neil asked. 'I've got a Honda on hire.'

'Oh you have? Nippy cars, I hear. From Nippon, you see.' Everyone smiled obediently at this joke. 'Mine's a Vauxhall. Family car, a good old thing.'

Ronald joined in with a report of the value of the Land Rover for country-dwellers, then the drinks came and everything became easier as the menfolk went on about their cars. Laura asked Eileen whether she drove.

'Oh yes, I do sometimes but I'm not good in traffic.'

'I just passed my test,' Shelley reported with pride. 'Passed first time I tried!'

'Oh, let's drink to that,' cried Neil, raising his mineral water in salute.

Shelley rewarded him with a smile. Her features somehow softer, the I-don't-care attitude vanished. He asked how much driving she'd done; she told him she borrowed the car almost every evening, she liked clubbing, did he like disco? She became more relaxed as the ingredients of the cocktail had their effect.

'Now, Shell,' said her mother, 'that's enough about all that.' She glanced at the others. 'Can't keep her at home in the evenings! Doesn't get enough sleep, that's what I say – her boss will give her the push if she keeps getting in late. And driving home after being at a disco – she swears she only drinks one real drink but I always think the police are so anxious to catch people out . . .' And so on in a motherly drone that somehow lost its emphasis as she spoke.

'I suppose you don't get out and about much, do you, Miss Wainwright? Living out in the wilds so to speak.' This was Norman, unwilling to let his wife criticize his daughter.

'Oh, please call me Laura, we agreed that the other night, didn't we?'

'The other night. That was a right gobsmack. Relatives in Canada, the other side of the world! The missus couldn't take it in, could you, Eileen?'

'It's exciting in a way, Dad. I just think it's so sort of strong and determined. Coming all this way just to find us.' This was Shelley, twinkling at Neil.

'Oh, well, to be completely honest, that wasn't the only reason. But I've got to say it's a great pleasure to have so much success. I've got Laura to thank for that.'

'I'm sure I don't know how she's done it,' Eileen said. 'I think I read somewhere about this family research business but I certainly never dreamed anyone would do any on *my* family—'

'Well, it isn't *your* family, Mum, it's Dad's—'

'Now now, Shell, that's enough,' her father reproved.

The waiter arrived to take their order, and the usual delays ensued while they studied the menu. When everything was settled, Shelley said to Neil, 'I suppose you get to the States a lot, living just over the border. It's a great dance scene there, from what I've heard.'

Laura could see Neil smother a grin. 'No, I was only in Seattle for part of my university course. And I didn't have much time for the party scene—'

'But why on earth not? Seattle's quite a place, isn't it?'

'Well, I was out at agricultural sites, you see. On campus, or under canvas sometimes. Studying the vegetation – trees in particular.'

'Oh, the great outdoors.'

'Something like that.'

'Yes, Dad told us you were into trees.' She looked mystified.

'He's a fund of knowledge about them,' Ronald said. 'Absolutely great. Although, you know, Neil, I never gathered you'd studied at university.'

Neil shrugged. 'Anyone want something more to drink? Another lager, Norm?'

The meal continued. The Dallancys relaxed under the influence of wine and lager. Norman launched out on a long tirade against the town-planners who had wrecked his business, Eileen provided a chorus of agreement, Shelley became flirtatious. Roland Wainwright described the glories of Kim Groves's house and his admiration for her taste and ability without gaining much of an audience.

''S all right for them that's got a lot of money,' Norman Dallancy grunted. 'New house, new garden, change everything to suit yourself – you've got to have the cash for stuff like that and that's what I complain of – not a penny in compensation did I get!'

'That's right, dear,' agreed Eileen.

'If I had a lot of money I wouldn't waste it on an old place

86

in the country,' Shelley said. 'London, me. You like London, Neil?'

'It's okay. But I prefer the country.'

'Oh, I can see that in a way. I'd go along with that for a lovely new house and a swimming pool and all that. Somewhere warm. Spain, f'r instance. I bet you've been to Spain, Neil, haven't you?'

'Not so far. Can't leave the business and expect trees to grow themselves, you know.'

Shelley shook her head so that the sunlight glinted on the spikes of fair hair. 'But you're not always going to be growing trees, are you?'

'Why not?'

'Well . . . I dunno . . . doesn't sound like much fun. I like a life that's got something going for it. That's why I'd like us to go to Spain if Dad gets rid of the shop.' She sighed and pushed her dessert around on its plate. 'But we're stuck here for a while, I s'pose. Not much success in the shop-selling line. Spain – salsa music and long warm nights . . .'

Hiding a smile, Neil said, 'There are some interesting tree species in Spain.'

'Oh, get real! Tree species! Listen, Neil, you come with me one night and even in stuffy old Simmingford I'll show you a bit of life!'

'Neil and I are a bit too old for the swinging scene, Shelley,' sighed Ronald.

Laura was about to protest at that but Shelley forestalled her. 'Well . . . yeah . . . but Neil's, like, an American. I mean, he's Canadian, of course, but if you don't tell, he *sounds* American.'

'And that makes a difference?' Neil asked.

'I should say so! I mean, the States is where it's at! The dancing, the *sound*—'

Eileen gave her daughter a little pat on the hand in reproof. 'Really, Shell, not everybody wants to spend the night dancing to that noise.'

'Oh, Mum, you're dead old-fashioned.'

'It's not healthy, that's what I say. You don't get enough sleep, Shell. I always say,' Norman declared, 'you've got to look after your health.' He looked round owlishly for approval.

'I mean, here's poor old Neil, walking with a stick, got the arthritis or whatever, and I bet that's being out in all weathers doing stuff to his trees. Hard graft, isn't it, mate? If I were you I'd change to something else when you go home cos it can't be doing you any good, and of course there's maybe a bit of money in it but not enough to make up for ruining your health. That's what I say.'

At last the meal ended and it was time to break up. With great thankfulness Laura shook hands and lied about being pleased to have met the Dallancys. They had talked almost exclusively about their own interests and without any offer of hospitality or companionship to Neil.

They all went out to the exit, where they chatted as they waited for their Vauxhall. The guests ignored this last opportunity to suggest another meeting. Despite Shelley's remarks about clubbing, she made no move. Their car was brought round, they got in, and Mrs Dallancy, who had drunk the least, reluctantly took the wheel. The others waved them off.

'What a bunch,' snorted Ronald as he and Laura waited for their car. 'I bet you wish you hadn't wasted money on finding them, Neil!'

Neil was leaning rather heavily on his stick. 'It was kind of nice that they were sorry about my supposed arthritis,' he said in rueful tones. He drew in a breath and let it out slowly. 'Well, there you go,' he said. 'I often think I prefer trees to people.'

The Land Rover came, and the Wainwrights were about to get in. 'Say,' Neil began. 'Is that it? Is that all we can find out about the Dallancys?'

Ronald was surprised, but Laura felt a lifting of the heart. This wasn't, after all, a final goodbye.

'Well . . .' Was there anything she could ethically suggest? 'I don't think there are any other living relatives,' she began with a falter in her voice. 'You recall that Norman mentioned some people in the Newcastle area. There is a widow of William Dallancy, very elderly now I believe, and of course she isn't a blood relative. They had a daughter but she died – I rather think of meningitis but I didn't look up her death certificate – in childhood.'

'Ah.' Neil made patters on the concrete with his stick and looked downcast.

'But of course if I went back and looked at some other aspects . . . the wills, for instance. You can often tell a lot from how money was bequeathed. Illegitimate children, you know.'

'You mean, little mistakes besides the one by poor little Marianne?'

'Well . . . you know . . . I'm not saying there are any but I could look.'

'Would you?'

'Come on, Neil,' Laura's father said in irritation. 'If there are any they probably don't bear the Dallancy name. It's a waste of money to try to find them, even if they exist. What's the point?'

Neil waited a moment before replying. Then he said, 'I came a long way, Ron. I just want to make sure I do everything I can.'

'I could look,' Laura said. 'But it might be a waste, as Papa says.'

'Oh, him,' laughed Neil. 'He always looks on the bright side, doesn't he?'

Ronald had the grace to look ashamed and give a little laugh of apology. Neil went on. 'Well, something else. Do you want to send me some kind of a bill for the work done so far? I guess it's mounting up.'

'Oh, that's all right,' she returned, flustered. 'And in any case, if I'm going to do more . . .'

'Have a look-see, Laura. I'd appreciate it. Unless you've got more important work on hand.'

'Leave it to me,' she said. 'I'll ferret around and let you have a report.'

'Great.' He nodded at her with approval. 'Thanks for coming today. You too, Ron. I'd hate to think what it would have been like to be alone with that little bunch. So long for now. Drive safe.'

She drove off. Her father said, 'More money than sense.'

'Would you like him to break off the search and vanish from the scene?' she parried. 'Who'd look after Kim's dodgy trees if he went away?'

'Oh. Well. That's true. Yes,' he said, deciding to agree with her for once. 'And he's a decent sort, after all.'

That being agreed, they went home.

* * *

After the year 1858, wills became available to be read at the Principal Probate Registry. Laura began her research with enquiries at Kew for the wills of George Etian Dallancy and his brother Martin, and also the will of Sir John Higston.

Photocopies gave an almost exact representation of the beautiful penmanship of the days before typewriters but, nevertheless, they presented difficulties. Country lawyers in particular could be tricky to decipher, since, though the writing was often fine, the sense of what they were saying wasn't always obvious.

Laura threw herself into the task with enthusiasm. She looked into the local archives to examine the day books and household accounts of the manor at Peridal, a building long since vanished. She was surprised to discover that George Etian Dallancy had had extensive business dealings concerning land and property, had been a charitable man leaving many donations to the poor, and had had many a haggle with his neighbours over boundaries and ditches.

In the meantime, her father continued in fairly good spirits. He went back to work in Kim's garden. Laura heard reports of Neil's inspection of the old orchard. The grubbing out of some of the trees was organized under his supervision. He then left for London and was gone some days. He was beyond Laura's range of vision but he was *there*, and just to know he hadn't gone back to the other side of the world was a comfort.

I'm an idiot, she frequently told herself. Yet she was happy. Sometime in the near future she would see Neil again, which would be great. She preferred not to examine the reasons. There was a saying by some French sage – Pascal, perhaps – to the effect that the heart had reasons that reason itself wouldn't acknowledge. Good old Pascal, she thought, how right you were.

She was surprised to receive a phone call from Shelley Dallancy. 'I just thought I'd ask – what's our pal Neil doing these days?'

It took Laura moment or two to think how to respond to this. 'I'm not sure . . .'

'I mean, is he around? I've given him a ring at his hotel a couple of times but they keep saying he's out and would I like to leave a message.'

'And did you?'

'Well, no . . . I just thought I'd have a chat and see if he wanted to – you know – go anywhere and do anything.'

'He's in London, I think. Or he might be with some friend who's showing him some woodland or an estate with interesting—'

'Trees,' Shelley supplied. 'That's sort of weird, but men do have sort of funny hobbies, don't they.'

'But it's not a hobby for Neil—'

'Well, that aside, he's sort of different, you know, and I thought it'd be fun to introduce him around because none of my chums have got anybody sort of different, if you know what I mean, and I wondered if you knew if he was going to be around or if he's planning to go off home or anything.'

'Not that I know of, although I suppose eventually—'

'So if he's gone to London, do you know when he's coming back to his Oxford hotel or anything?'

'I'm afraid not.'

'He's just a business acquaintance, then?'

'Yes, that's right.'

'Oh, I sort of . . . I mean, I thought you might be – but he just brought you to that lunch thing because you knew about the family history?'

'Exactly.'

'Oh, well then . . . I mean . . . if he gets in touch would you . . . No, I'll ring the Sceptre again and I'll . . . I could leave a message, just to say I'd called . . . After all, we are sort of family, aren't we?'

'That's true.' Laura knew she wasn't being sympathetic but Shelley's questions had taken her so much aback that she didn't know how to react. It was dawning on her that some sense of attraction towards Neil had spurred the call. Perhaps even after the alcohol had worn off she'd felt he was worth cultivating. Or, Laura seemed to recall from friends of her own teenage, there was a tendency for girls to fall for older men.

Or something.

At any rate, she didn't feel qualified to help Shelley nor had she any information to offer about Neil's activities. It was perfectly true, she had only a business acquaintance with him – well, perhaps more than acquaintance. She couldn't categorize it. At the moment all she could do for Shelley was say yes and no and perhaps.

'Well, righto then, thanks, nice to speak to you, Miss Wainwright.'

'Any time. Bye for now.'

She decided not to mention the call, not to her father nor even to Neil when she saw him again. It was for Shelley to pursue the matter if she felt like it. She couldn't help wondering what his reaction might be if Shelley actually got in touch – but that was none of her business.

It was the turn of the Wainwrights to be invited to one of Kim's Sunday gatherings. This time it wasn't brunch but a strawberry tea, for it was May with a spell of unexpectedly hot weather. Local growers had an early harvest they were happy to sell.

The garden at the back of Yalcote looked undeniably better for the efforts of Ronald Wainwright. Although the lawn was still rather patchy and there were some bushes that needed attention, the flower beds on the whole were pretty. Laura suspected that pots of flowers had been brought in and planted by her uncomplaining father. Once again little tables and chairs were set about. Both Mrs Stevens and her husband had been called in to pour tea and hand around freshly delivered scones, fresh butter, strawberries and double cream, or yoghurt for those with a cholesterol problem.

Ronald of course made a beeline for Kim Groves. She was sitting in the shade of a maple, in a group with three or four others. As Laura followed her father to join them, she nearly exclaimed in astonishment. Neil Crandel rose from a chair to greet her.

'Hello,' she faltered as he gave her a warm handshake. 'I thought you were still in London . . .'

'Got back last night. Didn't want to miss my first English strawberry feast.'

'Oh, how did you . . . er . . . you had an invitation?'

'Sure thing, the hotel sent it on to me. So, how're you? Found anything in your archives and things?'

'We-ell . . . There is a sort of something. But I want to read through the Married Women's Property Act before I make any deductions.'

'Married Women's what?'

'Property Act. Came in in 1882. Before that married women couldn't own things in their own right.'

'I don't get you.'

'Anything a married woman owned belonged to her husband.'

'You're joking!'

'Not at all. Unless there had been prenuptial agreements signed and sealed before the ceremony, she had nothing.'

'Sort of, what's mine's my own and what's yours is mine too, from the husband's side.'

'Exactly.'

'Unbelievable!' He was shaking his brown head. 'And what's this got to do with—'

'Now, now,' scolded Kim, coming up behind them, 'no business talk during a party, that's the rule. Off you go, Neil, you ought to have a second helping of strawberries and cream to keep your strength up.'

With a smile of amusement he obediently sauntered off.

Kim was wearing what seemed to be a Punjabi suit in raw blue silk. Laura, in a cotton voile dress that had seen two or three hot summers, felt like a dull moth beside a sparkling dragonfly. Kim put a hand on Laura's shoulder with unexpected camaraderie. 'Now, my dear, this is the first time you've seen the lawn since Ronald took the mower over it. What do you think?'

'Certainly an improvement on a field full of weeds.'

'Aha, are you saying you can still see patches of dandelion leaves? Ronald's looking up gardening books to deal with those. Now, come along, darling, let's have a cosy little chat about how things are going in your world.'

She put a hand under Laura's elbow to lead her off to the edge of the flower border, as if to admire it. Laura was astonished. Generally she and Kim had little to say to each other, and to imagine that Kim cared a jot about 'her world' was absurd. But Kim leaned towards her so that they were almost head to head. 'Listen, duckie, I didn't realize this man from the backwoods knew important people.'

'What makes you think he does?' Laura asked, intrigued.

'His specialist in Harley Street, my dear – Sir Donald McClaridon! Very impressive!'

'How do you know?'

'Well, it came up when Mrs Stevens asked in her nosy-parkering way today if his ankle was better, and he said McClaridon seemed to have done the trick. Now that's a big name in orthopaedics, darling. B-i-g!'

'But that's outside your—'

'Outside my field, you were going to say. But I've seen his name in legal reports – he gives evidence in important compensation cases – he's Harley Street and all that. Seems to me our chum Neil must have good contacts to get attention from Sir Donald, if you see what I mean – he doesn't take just anybody. So it seems he's not just some hick farmer after all.'

Laura nodded, but in agreement with something she was thinking. 'I noticed he didn't seem to have his stick with him today.'

'Oh, he was using a stick, of course, I remember that now. My dear, I didn't really pay much attention to him at first, but he's rather sweet, isn't he?'

Laura's heart sank. The term 'rather sweet' usually meant that Kim had added a new member to her coterie.

'Do you think he *is* anybody?' Kim enquired, coming at last to the real point of her conversation.

'Well, he's Neil Crandel from Wenaskowa in Alberta, and he's got a tree nursery there, and from the research I've been doing for him he's got Victorian family connections here-abouts—'

'Oh, big stuff? Connected to dukes or earls or anybody?'

Laura thought of the newsagent from Simmingford and his family. She shrugged. 'It's confidential, Kim, you know that. But I don't think there are any coronets or anything.'

'Too bad.' Kim frowned then smiled. 'Still, he's good at gardens.'

Someone was waving at Laura from the other side of the lawn. 'Excuse me, there's Mrs Bleyburn trying to attract my attention. I must just have a word . . .' With that she escaped from Kim and her investigative process.

After a word with Mrs Bleyburn about the forthcoming school sports day, she wandered off to the tea table set in the shelter of a great rectangular umbrella. So far she'd had no strawberries and cream, not even a cup of tea. There was a gathering there, in earnest conversation about the best variety for garden cultivation. Neil was listening with interest.

'Royal Sovereign—'

'Oh, there are better varieties now—'

'Keeping the slugs off, that's the problem—'

'Polythene—'

'The best thing is to grow them under glass—'

Neil saw her on the outskirts of the group and went to her side. 'Tea?' he enquired, taking on the duties from Mrs Stevens. 'Now milk in first, yes? Oh, there's a silver strainer! Now isn't that just dinky! Now I guess that's for the tealeaves. This is really classy. Is that about right, Laura?'

'Looks fine to me. No sugar, thanks.'

'You hang on there and I'll get you some strawberries. Now let me get it right. I bring a dish with the fruit, and the sugar shaker for you to put on your own.'

'No sugar, thanks,' she said again. 'But I'd like a little cream.'

'How about you find a seat? I'll be with you in a moment, madam,' he said, adopting a waiter-like attitude and looking about for a tray.

She sat on an Edwardian garden bench in the old apple orchard to drink her tea. She was thirsty – the day was warm and she'd been standing about in the sun. The apple trees, now beginning to lose their blossom and push out leaves, gave blessed shade. In a moment Neil arrived with strawberries in two china dishes together with spoons and napkins on a little silver tray.

'I could get addicted to these,' he remarked as he settled beside her. 'What d'you think of our handiwork?' He nodded at the apple trees.

'Nice. It's a sort of alley.'

'Yeah, some of them are mebbe not in perfect spirits yet, but with good treatment the dear old gals will perk up and there may even be fruit in a year or two.'

'Oh, of course, trees that produce blossom are girls.'

'Right. Though if you want to argue that half the trees in any species have got to be female, that's okay by me.'

She laughed. 'So – you're walking without your stick today.'

'Yes, great, isn't it? Still some peculiar clicks and clanks, but it's all come together pretty well. Good thing, too, because next week I'm going to Abbotsbury. That'll mean quite a bit of trudging about.'

'You're interested in Scott?'

'Who?'

'Sir Walter Scott. His house is – oh, no, that's Abbotsford.'

'Hang on a minute – you've lost me. I'm going to Abbotsbury Sub-tropical Gardens, in Dorset.'

'Right. I've never heard of it but it sounds interesting.'

'You don't surf the right websites. Those of us who know what's what, we know about the great stuff they've got at Abbotsbury, and if like me you come from the cold northland you want to see things like tree ferns and palms and such when you get the chance.'

'I've seen tree ferns. There's quite a fashion for them at the moment, in people's gardens. They're a bit dwarfish, aren't they?'

'Dwarfish? Take care what you say, missy – that's prejudice against the vertically challenged! Anyway, *Dicksonia antarctica* can get as high as twenty feet. Though so far I've never seen one that big. We grew them, you know – under protection, of course.' He paused so as to eat a spoonful of strawberries and cream.

She said, greatly daring, 'Could I come with you some time to find out about things like that?'

He was dabbing at lips with a napkin. 'Good idea,' he said.

'I beg your pardon?'

He took away the napkin so as to enunciate clearly. 'Good idea. Why don't you come to Abbotsbury?'

She was sure she'd misunderstood him. 'But – but – that's in Dorset, you said.'

'Have car, will travel. Couple of days, mebbe three. That's if you can get away from the job?'

'Oh . . . Oh, of course . . . Why not?'

'Well, good, that's a date. Next week, Abbotsbury – I think it's near a town called Weymouth. I'll get the hotel desk to sort out a place to stay. Um . . . What day shall we go? Do you need time to clear stuff off your desk?'

'Well . . . I've got requests out for a few things . . . It would be nice to get answers . . . A day or two . . .'

'Shall we say next Thursday?'

'Yes . . . Oh, well . . . Yes, Thursday.' She was breathless.

'Right. Thursday morning, bright and early. I have to go to Norfolk tomorrow but I'll get the desk working on it this evening and I'll be in touch – let's say, well, day after tomorrow. That okay?'

'Yes. Okay.'

When she told her father she was going to Dorset on Thursday with Neil, he at first thought she was joking. 'Ho, yes, I believe you. And one of our clients will turn out to be the Duke of Plaza-Toro.'

'No, I mean it, Papa. We're going to look at tree ferns in a place called Abbotsbury.'

'That's in Scotland, not Dorset.'

'No, you're thinking of Abbotsford. This is a garden near Weymouth.'

'Tree ferns?'

'You know – those sort of short trees with fronds growing out the top.'

'Since when have you been interested in tree ferns?'

She coloured up. 'Papa, it's just a sort of break from routine – a trip to look at something that interests Neil.'

He went silent. She could tell he was vexed. He thought of Neil as *his* friend. But it seemed he couldn't think of anything to say that would sound reasonable. She was afraid he'd go into one of his long gloomy spells, but luckily Kim summoned him to confer about the dandelion roots in her lawn.

Neil made all the arrangements. A country hotel upstream on the banks of the Wey and, she learned as soon as he reported the arrangements, separate rooms.

She was both relieved and disappointed. Too much to expect, she told herself, that he was asking her away for a romantic interlude. Who did she think she was, Mata Hari? She surveyed herself in the long mirror in the hall and shook her head.

True, she was slimmer than she had been, and wearing her hair longer but put up in a French plait was rather fetching. But when she compared herself with . . . well, with Kim, or even with Shelley Dallancy . . . Kim was so svelte and had so much charm. And Shelley was so *young*, with all the appeal of naïveté.

Whereas she herself was so ordinary. And not exactly a newly opened flower bud. And . . . and . . .

But she wouldn't let any of that spoil the delight of going away with him.

When he drove up on Thursday morning in his hired Honda she thought of it as a golden carriage more treasured than the Coronation coach. He gave her a little kiss of greeting before he handed her into the car. Her father, still in his dressing-gown, waved from the front window.

'Here we go!' Neil said, waving back through the wind-screen.

Here we go, she thought. Towards three days in his company. Towards seventh heaven.

Eight

Neil gave his attention to his driving until they'd cleared the network of country lanes and were en route to the motorway. Then he said, 'Less than joyous support from your father as he waved you off.'

'What? Oh well . . . He doesn't like having to cater for himself.'

'Doesn't like to cook?'

'No, but he won't have to. I left plenty of things in the fridge for him, and Mrs Stevens is coming in every day to peel vegetables and stuff like that.'

'Every day! You make it sound like you'll be gone for decades! We'll be back in three days.'

'Yes, I know, but still . . .'

'You never go on holiday?'

'Oh, of course we do. But mainly to conferences or sympo-siums on genealogy.'

'You mean you go together.'

'Yes.'

'Hm . . .' He was silent for a few minutes then said, 'You know, when Ma died Dad went to pieces for quite a while, but I think your dad is worse. He doesn't seem to admit that he has to get over things and live life like everybody else in the end.'

'He was really ill for quite a while, Neil,' she protested.

'So I gather. But he always seems to want barriers between himself and the rest of the world. He's finding excuses not to move on. And you're part of that barrier. Or, at any rate, that's what I think.'

'You think I'm preventing him from moving on?' She was hurt and shocked.

'Not consciously, Laura. Of course not. But you're protective – you do things for him that he should do for himself.'

'You mean, protective like leaving meals ready for him in the fridge?' She managed a little laugh.

'Listen, angel, a grown man ought to be able to look after himself for at least a day or two. He could go out and eat at that village pub. He could drive to Oxford and have a super three-course meal. But by dutifully leaving things all ready for him, you encourage him to hang around at home – and probably dangle after Kim all the more.'

'Oh! That's very critical.'

He gave a snort of agreement. 'Yeah, you're right, so tell me to shut up. I'm supposed to be drinking in the English countryside. Tell me the names of these wild flowers we're passing. What's that filmy white stuff?'

Grateful for the purposeful change of subject, she said, 'That's Queen Anne's Lace, or, to give it its low-class name, cow parsley. Unless you mean that taller thing at the back of the ditch, which I think is hemlock, and it's poisonous.'

'That's nuts. Hemlock is a tree.'

'No it isn't, it's a weed that grows about on river banks and places.'

'It's a tree, grows in eastern Canada – *Tsuga canadensis*, has pretty-ish new shoots in spring. So that white thing can't be hemlock.'

'But I'm almost sure . . . I'm no expert on wild flowers . . . Perhaps it was something else . . .'

He laughed. 'Yes, of course, that was probably hemlock. I'm only joking. You said it was poisonous – that was the stuff poor old Socrates had to drink in something or other BC, wasn't it? Whereas the Canadian hemlock's only been known to civilization since about the mid-nineteenth century.'

'Why one earth should anybody call a newly discovered tree after a poisonous weed?'

'I think it had to do with the smell of the leaves of the tree. I can't say for sure because I wasn't around then. What's that one?' he asked, pointing to a patch of yellow blossoms.

'Oh, that's ragwort! Absolutely awful! It gets everywhere. If you've got a tree called that in Canada, you're welcome to it.'

'You're a ha-a-rd woman, Laura Wainwright,' he said, laughing. 'First one's poisonous and the next one's invasive. They look like pretty flowers to me.'

'Huh! Deceptive, that's what it is. You must have things like that in Alberta?'

'Oh, sure. Where I live, plenty of moss!'

She could see he was teasing, but didn't challenge him as he negotiated their way past the outskirts of Reading and on to the motorway.

He settled in to the business of steady driving. She knew better than to distract him with chatter. After a few moments he said, 'If you'd like some music, switch on the radio. There's a CD-player but I don't have any discs, they're all back in Wenaskowa.'

She tried the tuner until she found a station playing gentle jazz with a piano as the lead instrument. The tune they were playing was unknown to her but it was melodious, not harsh or strident.

'Hey, that's Tord Gustavsen,' Neil exclaimed.

She was astonished. 'You know him?'

'He and his two pals were at the FIJM about a year ago.'

'The what?'

'The Festival International de Jazz à Montreal. Good stuff!'

'You were there?'

'No-o,' he replied with a shrug. 'Too busy at work. But it was on radio. I went round the nursery with earphones all the while.'

'I didn't know you were a jazz fan!'

'Sure am. Some of it doesn't sound so good to me – some of the guys out in California were making funny noises a while ago. What I really like best is the old stuff, from the early days in New Orleans. What about you?'

She shook her head. 'I'm no jazz enthusiast. I like classical music.'

'Big symphony orchestra crashing about like elephants?'

'Oh, come on! A symphony orchestra can be like a tiger prowling or a lark soaring.' She hesitated then went on, 'Do you like the kind of music they play in clubs – the sort of places Shelley Dallancy goes to?'

'Oh, her,' he said with a grin. 'She rang me, you know.'

'She did?'

'Surprised me. I dunno what exactly she was trying to convey. But it ended up with saying she wouldn't mind being shown round Oxford – by me, you understand! Been there a couple of months and she thinks I could be a tour guide.' He shook his head.

'So did you take it on?'

'I thought of suggesting she should join a group that goes round the colleges with a lecturer. But it ended with a faint promise to call her some time.'

'And will you?' She was ashamed of herself for prying so far, but she couldn't help herself.

He laughed and concentrated on passing a huge pantechnicon. She knew better than to take up the subject again, because that would be making too much of it. But she was comforted. He hadn't felt any great desire to see Shelley again, she thought.

Without further conversation, and to the cool tones of the piano, they tooled steadily along the M3 until the signposts began to mention Southampton. 'Don't want to go there,' he murmured. 'Let's get off on to some quieter route.' Before she could comment, he was off at the next exit going west, and soon the signs began to mention Wareham. 'Wareham,' he muttered. 'Didn't I read in some guide book that there's an old castle thereabouts?'

'Corfe Castle.'

'Battlements? Dungeons? Stuff like that?'

'I think it's pretty much a ruin,' she ventured.

'But a genuine ruin? Really old?'

'Oh, I think so. I think it was important during the Civil War.'

'Um . . . Civil War? 1861?'

'That was the American Civil War! No, the one we had here was the 1640s and ended with King Charles getting his head cut off.'

'Oh . . . Yes . . . That does ring a faint bell. He got his head cut off at Corfe Castle?'

'No, no—' But she broke off as she saw that he was grinning. He had a way of taking her into a little snare that she found very intriguing.

'Let's go there,' he said. 'It's on the way. And I'd like to see a genuine castle. I went to Windsor, but it was kind of pretentious, if you know what I mean.'

Corfe Castle was unpretentious. It stood up on its hill like the remains of jagged teeth. A booklet gave the information that Neil wanted. 'Gee,' he said in some disappointment, 'I thought it mebbe got knocked down during a battle but it says here the Parliamentarians did all that afterwards.'

'I think they do reenactments here sometimes – dress up, you know, Cavaliers and Roundheads.'

He nodded. 'They do that sometimes around Wenaskowa. Heritage stuff. The meeting of the pioneers with the local native tribes. Ma used to be into that, got herself into a long frock with frills on the hem and she'd wear that piece of lace . . . what's it called – the bertha.' He sighed at the memory. 'But we don't attract many tourists up there – the weather's kind of tricky because of the mountains. So it was mainly us locals that supported it, so it was no big deal. And it's going to die out soon anyway.' He led the way down the path to the main gate. 'Come on, it's coffee time.'

There was locally made cake on sale at the tea house. Laura contented herself with a nibble of Neil's portion. By the time they set off again, the sun was beaming down so that the interior of the car was too warm at first. Laura peeled off her sweater. Under it she was wearing a soft shirt of blue-sprigged cotton to go with her well-worn blue jeans. Neil was in Dockers and a shirt that looked like a lumberjack check except that it was fine poplin. They were both wearing good walking shoes for the expected excursions to Abbotsbury.

They wended their way along the A351, and at the sign for Dorchester Neil turned off. 'Hey,' Laura said. 'I thought we were going to Weymouth?'

'Sure, but there's no hurry, eh? Dorchester, I've seen that on TV, haven't I? *The Mayor of Casterbridge,* that guy who sells off his wife. How about looking at the place? It seemed pretty neat on the TV screen.'

She began to laugh. 'You're a sightseer! I never thought it of you! Where's your video camera and your guidebook?'

'They're on the back seat,' he said, gesturing with his thumb over his shoulder. And, sure enough, there was a row of books there and what might have been a camera in a case. But the titles on the book spines were about trees and plants.

'Those are textbooks. Where have you hidden the folding strip of postcards about Buckingham Palace and the Changing of the Guard?'

'You can laugh, but I'm trying to tidy up the holes in my education. I'm an ignoramus, you see. Trees, yes, I know a lot about trees. But at McGill I didn't pay attention to much else, so now I'm soaking up everything I can. That's so I can boast to the folks at home when I get back.'

Those last words sent a chill through her. She said nothing more, and it took all Neil's delight at the crooked roofs and Tudor timbers of Dorchester to warm the chill away. They walked around, Neil insisting he should see the window from which the Mayor of Casterbridge first saw Susan again.

'You liked that TV series a lot,' Laura suggested.

'Not an awful lot. It was real melancholy, wasn't it? It's just that it's so great to look at places where a writer like that one – Hardy, wasn't it – got his ideas.' He smiled at his own enthusiasm. 'See, around Wenaskowa nothing much happened in the past. Oh, I mean folk struggled to get there, and to make a settlement, and build up a community – don't get me wrong, there's history there, I'm not belittling all that. But for a place to be sort of an inspiration to a writer . . . And then there's all the other things you've got here, castles and so on. I don't think there are any castles in Alberta!'

She laughed, and they went in search of lunch, which they

found in an ancient inn. There were brochures lying about advertising local places of interest. 'Maiden Castle!' Neil exclaimed. 'There's a castle just down the road! We've got to see that after we've eaten.'

'It's not a castle,' she protested. 'Not really. It's an earthwork.'

'An earthwork. You mean for mining?'

'No, no, it's a big wall made of earth with grass growing over it – at least I think so.'

'So what's it for?'

'Who knows? They say here–' she was reading – 'it dates back to 2000 BC.' She met his questioning glance. 'Sorry I can't be more helpful. Documentary evidence, that's what I specialize in. I don't know anything about people who didn't write things down.'

He insisted on inspecting Maiden Castle, and once there set off round the rampart. She felt he was testing his ability to walk. She trudged along with him, rather afraid she would have to fetch help if his ankle let him down and glad when they turned back after a reasonable distance. She was even happier for herself when they reached the car and could sit down. The day was very warm, and they'd been very active.

After a little misdirection they got to the Roseworth Hotel by late afternoon. The first thing Laura did on taking over her room was to fill the kettle for a quick cup of tea. Then she took a long cool shower, lay down on the bed for a rest, and almost dozed off.

She roused herself, guilty at being lazy. But it was difficult to be full of vigour. First there had been the anxiety of advance preparations for her father's comfort during her absence. Then there was the stress of not knowing exactly what the relationship was between herself and Neil. The physical activity had been greater than she had expected and she thanked heaven for the good walking shoes she'd put on that morning. And now she had to dress for dinner, whereas to tell the truth she was more in the mood for a quiet snack in her dressing-gown.

All the same, she swung herself off the bed and set about unpacking. There was an after-six dress, which she hung up by the open window to air in case there were any creases. It was a linen sheath, never put on all last summer because it had grown too tight. But on surveying her wardrobe for this trip, she'd found the dress folded on a shelf and, not expecting good results, tried it on. To her surprise the crisp tailored lines had fallen about her body with ease. It was a sort of slate blue, with a square neck. The faint tan she'd achieved by ordinary life in the sun looked good.

Now she put up her hair in its French plait and applied a little make-up. She was too tired to go through any long beauty routine. She put on the dress, zipped it up, and surveyed herself.

Not bad. She wasn't exactly sparkling with energy, but she wouldn't disgrace her escort even in this rather up-market country-house setting. With a sigh she pushed her weary feet into elegant sandals and went out.

They'd agreed to meet by the lift to go down to the dining room together. Laura got there first, and pressed the indicator. While she waited, her mobile phone rang in her handbag. She knew whose voice she'd hear before she switched on.

'Laura,' demanded her father, 'did you do anything with those brochures I got from the garden centre about dandelions and things?'

'No, of course not. You know I never interfere with your personal stuff.'

'Well, I can't find them. They were in the living room. You must have put them away somewhere.'

'No, really, Papa—'

'Then it must be that confounded Stevens woman! She's always "tidying" things she shouldn't touch!'

'Well, I'm sorry—'

'Why we have to have her here I don't know! She's nothing but a nuisance. And you know she says things about people behind their backs—'

'But we've got to have help in the house, Papa. And who else is there?'

'I don't know why you say we've *got* to have help. We don't make all that much of a mess—'

'Papa, the house is two hundred years old and full of nooks and crannies. You're busy with your work and your other interests, I'm busy with my work and—'

'And flitting off for a trip to some idiotic garden that you never heard of before in your life. I don't understand you, Laura!'

'Well, I'm sorry, but—' Out of the corner of her eye she saw Neil coming round a corner in the corridor. He raised his eyebrows, and she mouthed, 'My father.' He came alongside, so that he was able to hear the complaining voice of Ronald Wainwright tinnily issuing from her phone.

'And I want those brochures so as to talk to Kim about them tonight—'

To Laura's astonishment Neil took the phone out of her hand. 'Hey there, Ron,' he said. 'What's up?' He listened while Ronald seemed to recover from the astonishment of hearing him, then resumed in a jovial voice. 'Listen, Ronnie, Laura and I are just going down to dinner. I'm tired and she's tired after a long day. What say you look all this stuff up on the Internet when you get to Kim's, eh? She's online, I take it? Yes? Well, then you can sit down with her and look at the information together. How's that?' He stood nodding and smiling at the response from the other end then with a cheery, 'So long then,' he disconnected.

Laura held out her hand for the phone. He shook his head, switched it off, and put it in the pocket of the blazer he'd donned for the dining room.

'Neil!' she protested.

'Silence is golden, especially while we're having a meal. I'll give it back after dinner.'

'That's hijacking,' she told him. But he refused to look guilty and the lift came at that moment.

'And that was bribery,' she went on as they entered it. 'Telling him he could sit alongside Kim.'

'His call was emotional blackmail, wasn't it?' he replied with something of a frown. 'You know that, of course.'

'Yes,' she sighed. 'I do.'

They were met at the door of the dining room by the head-waiter. They were conducted to a table alongside an old sash window giving a view of the lawn sloping down to the river, which gleamed in the dusk like a silver ribbon. The scent of mock-orange blossom drifted in, and the sound of a blackbird singing his last song of the evening.

The dining room was well patronized, the food was excellent. Laura at first declined the suggestions of the wine waiter but in the end accepted a spritzer of white wine and elder flower. Unexpectedly delicious. Neil said he thought he'd celebrate the occasion with a glass of Chardonnay.

'No more painkillers then?' she asked.

'Only if I need them. The ankle's behaving well, and so it should after all the attention that's been showered on it these last few months.'

'How did it happen?'

'Oh, some machinery capsized on a hillside. Weather conditions were difficult – ice and snow, that sort of thing. Which is why I have this obsession with things that grow in warm climates.'

He then began to speak about what they might see next day at Abbotsbury, and it occurred to Laura that he had turned the subject quite adroitly. She realized that he almost never spoke about himself. It wasn't that he was secretive, he just seemed not to want to discuss his own affairs.

'Are you thinking of moving somewhere warmer? So you can grow things like that?' she enquired.

'Well, not in the near future. There's stuff waiting for me back home. Might not be bad, one day, to start a specialist nursery for things like *Ensete ventricosum*, for instance.'

'What on earth is that?'

'It's a kind of banana but you can't eat the fruit—'

'So what's the point of growing it?'

'Man doesn't live by fruit alone. The leaves are great – about twenty feet long – you'll love it when you see it.'

'I don't know if I can quite summon up enthusiasm for another of your interests at the moment,' she said, taking a long sip of the spritzer. 'If today's anything to go by, we'll be dashing about all over the place in this garden of strange plants. Do you think they'll have little golf buggies to take us around?'

'I've no idea. If you get too tired I promise to carry you.'

She could imagine nothing more enchanting. But she said, 'Think what you're saying. I'm no lightweight, you know.'

'Oh, I know you keep worrying about not eating and drinking the wrong things but you worry too much. My dad used to have an expression about a girl – "A nice armful", he'd say. That's what he'd say if he'd met you.'

She gave her attention to her food so as to hide her delight.

Later coffee was brought, and she drank two cups so as not to get drowsy after such an excellent meal. It was only about ten o'clock, they might sit and talk for hours yet.

They went out into the scented night. The atmosphere was heavy with the perfume of honeysuckle and roses although there was a coolness now in the breeze.

'We could walk down to the river,' Neil suggested.

'You could walk, I could totter.'

He laughed. 'Right, then let's just sit and enjoy the moon.' There was indeed a moon, waning, but filling the sky with an opal glow. They sat in silence.

I'll never forget this moment, thought Laura. When he's gone back to Alberta and forgotten me, I'll still remember. He's been so lovely to me and I know he's my friend, so even if he doesn't feel the same as I do, I have a lot to treasure. And I will treasure it, even when he's far away.

By and by they went back into the hotel and took the lift to their floor. He took her card-key at the door of her room and opened it for her.

'Goodnight, then,' he said, and dropped a kiss on her cheek.

It was as if some spark flamed up inside her. She put her arms around his neck and kissed him on the lips. 'Don't go,' she said. 'Don't go.' She clung to him, her head tilted back, gazing into brown eyes that filled with a delighted wonder.

The door behind her swung a little further open. She pulled him with her, into the room. She let the door close behind them.

Nine

It was a long time since Laura had woken in the morning with a man at her side.

His arm was around her, her head was on his chest. She

could feel the steady rise and fall of his breathing. She gently looked up, wanting to know if it was still night-time, but met his eyes.

'Good morning, sleepyhead,' he said. 'I thought you'd never wake up.'

'Mm-m . . . Is it late?'

'No, it's just after six.'

'And you call me sleepyhead? It's the crack of dawn!'

'Us tree-growers are always awake and aware early. But it's not tree-growing I'm thinking of at the moment.'

'What are you thinking of?'

'This.' He leaned over her to kiss her. 'And of course this too.' His arm about her drew her closer so that they were in total contact, skin to skin.

They made love, and this was for the second time. Last night, at first, they'd kissed and embraced in a slow, leisurely way because they were both physically tired, and in fact they'd fallen asleep in each other's arms on top of the bedspread until the discomfort of clothes awoke them. That was somewhere around midnight.

Then had come the pleasure of undressing, of kissing each curve and hollow revealed in the pale moonlight that still glimmered in the room. Shadow and the sheen of skin, warmth and the shiver of expectation, they came together in a miracle of harmony.

They lay together afterwards, murmuring endearments, exchanging random thoughts. 'I thought you were so businesslike . . . I was afraid to try . . . A man can easily think he's making the grade with a woman when she's just being friendly . . .'

'I felt I was making a fool of myself . . . I couldn't quite guess how you'd feel about it . . . but it just seemed right, at that moment . . .'

'Think what we might have missed!'

They'd fallen asleep again, wound about each other in the aftermath of passion. And now here was another day, and she was in his arms as if it was her natural place in this world.

Around them the daylight grew stronger yet they were unwilling to go forward into the everyday world. They lay together watching the sunshine creep across the ceiling, until at last Neil said, 'I have a terrible confession to make.'

'What?' she asked, not in the least alarmed because there was laughter in his voice.

'I'm hungry.'

'Scandalous! Thinking of food at a time like this.'

'Yeah, it's pretty unforgivable. But you wouldn't want me to fade away into a skeleton, now would you.'

'That isn't likely.' She kissed the muscles of his chest, pulled his willing arms around her, felt the weight of his big body against her. After a moment she said, her voice muffled against his neck, 'Do you mean you want to get up and get dressed – and leave all this?'

'Now that presents a dilemma. And I have just the right solution.'

'What's that?'

'We'll have breakfast sent up.'

She imagined herself opening the door to the waiter with Neil still in bed behind her. She began to giggle. 'There goes my reputation,' she said.

'Oh, pooh, if it means all that much to you, I'll sneak into the bathroom while the food's brought in.'

She tried to give him a reproachful shake. 'You've done this before!'

'Sure, dozens of times. A girl in every garden centre. But how about it, shall I call room service?'

The food was brought, Laura opened the door for it and after the waitress had gone hung the Don't Disturb sign on the outer handle. She was in her dressing-gown, Neil had put on shirt and slacks. They sat across from each other over the little table to drink coffee and eat croissants. They put on the bedside radio for some music, could find only a station playing golden oldies and settled for that.

'My dad used to sing this,' Neil remarked. The tune was 'Lady of Spain'. 'I think it's a paso doble or something. He and Ma used to go ballroom dancing, that's how they first met, at a ballroom in Edmonton. He used to say to her, "One day I'll take you to Spain, Ella, and we'll dance to a real Spanish band."' He sighed.

'Did they go?'

'No, never made it. Dad used to talk about going on his own now and again – he was the one that gave me this interest in things that grow in Mediterranean or tropical places.'

'Perhaps you'll go one day.'

He shrugged. 'But there's still a lot waiting back there in Wenaskowa.'

She made no response, and when the tune ended the disc jockey put on 'The Sunny Side of the Street'. She sighed inwardly. Her street would not be sunny when Neil went home.

But she mustn't think of that. He was here now, and they were together, and that was enough.

'Should we get dressed and start the day?' she wondered.

'What's your hurry?'

'Well . . . I thought you wanted to go to this special garden.'

'It'll still be there this afternoon,' he pointed out.

And so they went back to bed. It wasn't until Neil groaned that he really needed a shave and he'd better go and have one that they relinquished their private world. After he was gone she picked up the pillow from his side of the bed and hugged it to her. It smelled of him, the soap he used, that individual scent that made her feel warm and yielding.

They set off for the gardens in the early afternoon. It was a day of warm weather and in the sheltered valley the atmosphere was almost sultry. Hand in hand, they strolled among the plants, Laura in such a haze of happiness that she took almost nothing in. Life seemed so good. There was nothing in the world to ask for – except that he would never go back to his homeland.

She was standing in the shade of a tree whose name plate proclaimed it to be a *Hoheria glabrata* when her mobile rang. Neil had restored it to her when he had collected his belongings before going to change; it had been in his blazer pocket all night. He glanced back at the sound, but returned to the picture he was taking of another variety of *Hoheria*.

Sighing, she answered.

'Laura, what am I supposed to be having for my evening meal? There's a casserole in the fridge with a note saying "Heat for twenty minutes on mark 4" but it's much too warm to switch on the oven, and I don't really fancy a hot stew.'

'There's some cold duck in the freezer. If you get it out now it should be defrosted by the time you want to eat.'

'But what am I supposed to eat with it? Mrs Stevens did vegetables this morning but that means putting them on to boil and that sounds hot and sticky.'

'Do them in the microwave, Papa.'

'The microwave! You know I don't know anything about the microwave!'

'Then have some salad instead.'

'Salad?'

'Lettuce and tomatoes. They're in the bottom shelf in a plastic container.'

'The bottom shelf of what?'

She lost her patience. 'Oh, come on, Dad, you know very well they're in the fridge.'

'That's your side of the housekeeping. *I* don't know where you keep things.'

'Why are you behaving like this? You've made yourself a salad sandwich a million times, you know where the salad things are kept. And if it's all so much trouble to you, why don't you go and eat at the Fox and Hare?'

'What?'

'They do quite good food, so Mrs Stevens says. And not expensive—'

'Mrs Stevens! I wouldn't take her word on anything. It'll be a day in the next millennium before I take her advice on anything!'

'Papa, I can't waste any more time on this. I'm looking at *hoherias.*'

'What?' said her father faintly.

'Bye for now,' she said, and disconnected.

It was the first time since her father's long bout of depression that she'd ever gainsaid him. She felt strange, as if she'd taken a great risk and only just survived it. She then thought that perhaps she wouldn't survive it, because argument was one of the things that made Ronald distressed. If she'd brought on one of his bouts of dark stagnation, life would be dismal.

Come on, she said to herself, we just had a disagreement about lettuce and tomatoes. Surely a thing as trivial as that wasn't going to cause a setback.

Neil didn't ask about the phone call.

She stayed close to him for the rest of the afternoon. It was as if merely having him take her arm was a shield against adversity. They stayed until the gardens closed then drove to Weymouth, which she explained was a typical old British seaside resort. A cooling sea breeze refreshed them. They stood for a long time with their arms round each other's waists, watching the sea birds and listening to the soft rhythm of the waves on the shore.

When the first star began to twinkle in the dusk, they found a comfortable old-fashioned café for supper. They ate a huge meal, for they'd had nothing since breakfast in the bedroom. It was quite late when they drove back to the Roseworth Hotel.

This time they didn't start to say goodnight at her door. Instead they went inside together, to find again the magical hours of shared passion.

Next morning they returned to Abbotsbury 'just for a final check-up', as Neil put it. The afternoon was spent at Kingston Lacey, which was nearly as big a hit with him as Abbotsbury. The parkland and the woods were full of trees to enthuse about and to photograph. When they followed the guidebook and found Badbury Rings he was speechless.

'Everywhere you go,' he exclaimed, 'there's something where somebody's lived and worked centuries ago. And then these rich guys in the seventeenth century – was it the seventeenth?'

'Yes, seventeenth and eighteenth. The ascendancy of the country mansion. There are lots of documents about how much they spent, who they employed, what they bought and from whom. They sent out scouts to find plants on other continents—'

'Yeah, sure, I got that bit at college. But somehow when you actually see the results . . .'

'Rich men abroad were doing the same thing. If you ever get to Spain – or France. France particularly, although their gardens were much more formal.'

'Well, someday, maybe. But there's too much other stuff needing my attention.'

On Sunday they had to head for home. They spent the morning looking at Thomas Hardy's cottage and then went on to Dorchester. They found themselves at last in a thick traffic stream going north. As they made their rather slow way, Laura had time to think that her father hadn't called her again since she'd told him to stop being silly and go out to eat. She felt guilty. Had she hurt his feelings too much? Was he sitting up in his room, listless, sullen?

When Neil drove into their driveway she was apprehensive. But her father appeared at the door as they drew up. 'Well,' he said, 'had a good time?'

'Saw a lot of trees,' said Neil. 'My kind of good time. So, how you been?'

'Perfectly fine, thank you.' Ronald now saw fit to acknowledge his daughter. 'Mrs Stevens said to tell you you've run out of potatoes.'

'Righto.' Laura was gathering up the various goodies she'd bought en route during the trip – farmhouse cheese, home-made jam, biscuits named after villages to give them some heritage value and appeal to tourists. Neil took her travel bag into the hall.

'I'll push off now, shall I?'

'Oh . . .'

'Stay and have a cup of tea,' Ronald put in. 'I bet you need it, after that trip – the radio said the traffic was bad.'

'Okay, then, tea it is. Any scones?' He looked around hopefully.

Ronald laughed. 'That's Laura's department, I don't bake.'

'Oh, Papa, there are some in the freezer, it'll only take a moment to heat them up. And I've brought some clotted cream to have with them.'

'This is another tradition, I guess?' Neil enquired. 'Like cream with the strawberries?'

They sorted themselves out – Ronald led Neil into the living room while Laura went to the kitchen. It seemed smaller to her than when she left it. In a way she almost resented having to settle into it again. Her world had changed.

But then she thought, Not for long – he'll go home by and by.

While she was making tea, her father put his head round the door. 'There's some mail for you. I put it on the hall table, didn't know which would be business and which would be personal.'

She nodded her thanks and while the scones were defrosting in the microwave she went out to pick up the mail. One thick packet she opened immediately. It was something she'd been waiting for: a copy of a Victorian map of the countryside around the house of George Etian Dallancy.

She spread it out on the kitchen table. Then after some study of it she straightened, staring up at the ceiling for a moment or two in a mixture of satisfaction and hopeful expectation. She took it into the living room.

Gentlemen,' she said, 'I have an important announcement to make.'

Her father stared at her. Neil chuckled. 'The scones got burned. Like King What's-it.'

'More important than that. Mr Crandel, I have to inform you that you are probably the owner of a piece of land about sixty miles from here.'

Ten

There was a stunned silence.

'What?' Neil said

'The maps!' her father exclaimed.

'Maps? What maps? What are you talking about?'

'The maps that arrived while Laura was away. What did you see, girl?'

'A plot of land called Tansy Field. It looks to be about ten acres, perhaps a bit more because maps of that era aren't totally accurate.'

'Tansy Field?' Neil echoed, baffled.

'George Etian Dallancy left it in his will.'

'Not to me! He didn't know I existed!'

'He left it to his daughter Marianne—'

'Laura, I told you, you can't prove—'

'Hang on, hang on – left it to Marianne? I thought she'd

disappeared off his horizon in the middle of a scandal. You can't tell me he left her anything – and besides, didn't everything she owned go to her husband? Didn't you tell me that a few days ago?'

'Yes,' said Ronald, 'anything left to Marianne would pass to the awful Sir John Higston.'

Laura laughed. 'Shall I tell you the story?'

'Oh, one of your imaginary biographies,' he scoffed. 'Mind what you're saying, child! There's tangible profit involved in this fairy tale.'

He was, as usual, critical of her attitude to research. Yet now there was normality in his manner. When he'd spoken to her on her arrival there had been a compression of his lips, a certain tinge to his expression, that spoke of disapproval. He'd guessed what had happened between them, and wanted her to know he thought her a hussy.

But now that was forgotten. The excitement of what she might have discovered had conquered his distaste.

She said, 'Let me fetch the tea and we'll get settled first. Because it's going to take a while to explain.'

When she returned with the tea things they had the map spread out on a coffee table and had found Tansy Field. Neil looked up and cleared the map away so she could put down her tray.

'So I'm not a duke or an earl, am I?' he enquired.

'No, but I think it entitles you to the rank of "gentleman".'

'There you go! Success at last.'

She poured tea and handed round the scones. They busied themselves for a few minutes with that, Ronald complaining after his first bite, 'I never think things taste as good once they've been frozen, you know.'

'They seem good to me,' Neil said, finishing his first scone in two bites. 'Well, now, come on, kiddo – explain how I come to be the owner of Tansyland.'

'Tansy Field. Well, I've pieced this together from newspapers of the time, some of them local and a couple of them national—'

'National?' Ronald cried.

'Oh yes. It was quite a big happening. But not at the beginning.'

'The beginning of what? That's what I'm in doubt about.'

116

'Papa, if you'll just let me get started, you can knock me down afterwards.' She held up a finger for attention. 'Now. Marianne Dallancy left her husband to run off with David Crandel. It caused quite a lot of gossip—'

'Well – gossip – that's nothing—'

'Papa!' He fell silent, and she began again. 'There had been a contract between Mr Dallancy and Sir John that Marianne's dowry should consist of some land running alongside Sir John's estate, which would then become his property. That land now belonged incontestably to him even if his wife had gone.'

'Well, we know that, Laura—'

'From some hints in the local newspapers there was great ill-feeling between Mr Dallancy and Sir John afterwards. That's only natural. For instance, Sir John wouldn't let Mr Dallancy shoot over his land, that kind of thing. A few years went by. Then Sir John wanted to marry again, so as to father an heir to his estate. So he—'

'Brought an action for divorce?' Ronald cut in. 'My word!'

'What?' demanded Neil. 'What's so big about that?'

'Neil, in those days divorce was a terrible disgrace. You can't imagine how awful it was to be named in a divorce case. Usually, it was only men who took such action – women probably cringed at the mere idea, and in fact very few divorces took place. So Sir John's divorce suit was big news, and the two national newspapers carried reports.'

'He brought suit on the grounds of desertion, I take it.'

'Quite right, Papa. And the necessary number of years having gone by, he won his case. So Marianne was not merely a runaway wife, she was a divorcée. There was quite a lot of glee in the gossip columns about it.'

'Poor little soul,' murmured Neil.

'Yes, it would have been a bad time for her if she'd been there to know of it. But of course she was off in the wilds of Canada.'

'Well, that's interesting, but it makes it even less likely that any of Dallancy's property comes down to Neil,' said Ronald. 'The Dallancy brother inherited, and Sir John had the bit he'd always wanted, as I recall your groundwork.'

'George Etian brooded over it, in my view, until towards

the end of his life he added a codicil to his will. You know I said to you that wills often revealed things like illegitimate children and so on?' she added, turning to Neil.

'Sure. Go on.'

'Well, Marianne's father bequeathed Tansy Field to "my dear daughter Marianne and to her heirs in perpetuity". In other words he'd come to terms with the idea that his daughter had run off with someone and probably had illegitimate children.'

'But Laura!' cried Ronald. 'Everything she owned belonged to Sir John Higston, you *know* that.'

'Not at all.' She waited until her father's full attention was on her. Neil was gazing at her with wonderment.

'Divorce was very, very rare in those days. Marianne's father got it into his head he could retrieve her dowry from Sir John, since the marriage had been ended. There are a few letters in the Dallancy archive, obviously replies from solicitors he'd tried to hire to deal with this project over the years.'

'Well, it sounds logical—'

'But he was advised there wasn't a case to bring. I have a feeling the poor old soul got obsessed about it – he wanted to hit back at Sir John for disgracing the family. And I think he wanted to get back the land so as to make provision for Marianne in case she ever came back, or got in touch.'

Ronald nodded, looking thoughtful. 'When you come to think of it,' he murmured, 'having a daughter disappear – that's awful.'

'The Married Women's Property Act came into being in 1882. There'd been a previous Act in 1870 but that only gave partial control to the wife. This gave total right to own money and property – and *that* was when Dallancy added the codicil to his will.'

Neil clasped his hands together and threw them above his head. 'Good for George Etian Dallancy!'

'Yes, rather splendid, isn't it? And he wrote a sniffy letter to Sir John telling him all about it. The papers belonging to the mansion at Ramhurst are preserved as an archive and that letter is there – with of course no reply from Sir John.'

'Great! Great! George Etian for President!'

Even Ronald was laughing.

'So you see, Neil, Tansy Field is yours. "In perpetuity" means—'

'For ever!'

'Exactly. You're Marianne's descendant. You'll notice that there's no nonsense in the bequest about male heirs or anything like that – no conditions – it just says to Marianne and her heirs in perpetuity. So Tansy Field belongs to you.'

'And this is it?' he asked, putting his finger on a roughly rectangular patch on the old map.

'That's it. The will describes the whereabouts of the land – "running alongside the Fordall road", it says. I'll give you photocopies so you'll have it word for word. I couldn't tell you about it, you know, until I got the map. For all I knew, it wouldn't appear, and in that case it would have been difficult to be sure what Mr Dallancy meant. But it's there, exactly as he describes it.'

'Well, that's really neat. Neil Crandel, Gentleman, of Tansy Field. I wish it had been Tansy Mansion or Tansy Castle, but you can't have everything. Could I grow something on it? Plant trees?'

'Hold on, hold on,' cried Ronald, holding up both hands as a warning. 'I hate to throw cold water on all this enthusiasm, but I repeat what I've been saying from the very first. You can't prove any of this.'

'Oh, come on, Ronnie! It's in the will and on the map—'

'Yes, yes, the land exists and old Dallancy made the bequest – I'm not arguing with any of that. *But you can't prove you're the heir.*'

'Papa, it all matches, 'Laura insisted. 'The names on the ship's passenger list, the arrival of Marianne in Quebec—'

'That's not evidence. That's supposition. There's no marriage licence giving her married name and her maiden name – no signed declaration that Marian Crandel and Marianne Dallancy are one and the same—'

'The lace,' Neil suggested. 'The lace collar—'

'It would be laughed out of court.'

There was a pause, while the bluntness of this remark sank home. Then Laura took up the challenge.

'How can you explain a piece of lace turning up in the

119

possession of a Canadian family, a piece that was made in Buckinghamshire and owned by a lady of the Dallancy family?'

'We've been through this, Laura. I don't argue against the idea that the lace collar can be identified by an expert as originating in Buckinghamshire, but even if we accept that Marianne owned it, she could have sold it, or have given it to somebody to pay for something, or had it stolen from her.'

'Yeah,' Neil said slowly. 'That's all true.'

Laura studied his face. He didn't look too grieved at the thought.

'But I want you to have Tansy Field,' she mourned. 'I really believe it belongs to you.'

'My dear girl, do you really believe that whoever owns Tansy Field at this moment is going to give it up to some visitor from the other side of the world?' cried Ronald in irritation.

'Well . . . I hadn't thought that far . . .'

'You hadn't thought beyond the thrill of discovery, that's what.'

'Spoilsport,' said Neil, aiming a mock fist at him. 'I was really getting quite keen on being a "gentleman".'

'Who does actually own it at the moment?' Laura wondered. 'I only got so far on that point.'

'We need a modern map,' suggested her father. 'Let's see. My maps are in the garage. Hang on and I'll fetch something. Let me see . . . the Allford road . . . No, it's the Fordall road.' He was leaning over the reproduction map of the Victorian landscape. 'Never heard of the Fordall road but it looks as if it runs towards the river – oh, of course, Ford-for-all, no ferry needed, no tolls – that's where it gets its name. So I want a map that shows the route alongside what was the Dallancy estate heading towards Simmingford. Right, I'm sure I've got one that will do.'

He hurried off, and at his going Neil and Laura exchanged a smile. 'I thought he might have been a bit . . . you know . . . huffy,' Neil said, 'because I kind of choked him off on the phone the other night.'

'Me too.' She thought back to her response to his call while she was at the gardens. She smiled and sighed. 'But he's all taken up with proving or disproving the bequest. Mainly disproving, I'm afraid.'

'That's okay. It's no big deal.'

'You don't mind how he's putting us down?'

'Nah,' he said inelegantly, turning his attention to the scones, 'I never thought I was going to inherit anything when I started this gig. I just wanted to follow up on Dad's investigation, tie up the loose ends.' He swallowed a bite of scone then went on. 'You've done marvels, Laura. You really are so *bright*.'

She felt herself blushing with pleasure. 'And you're really not disappointed at the way it's turning out?'

'It's turned out great. Even if we can't prove it, we know I'm the legal owner of Tansy Field, and that old George Etian didn't go to his grave condemning his daughter.' He sighed. 'Poor little Marianne. Never knew her father had forgiven her, I suppose.'

'No, I'm afraid not. The way communications were in those days . . .'

Ronald came bustling in. 'Here we are, this one should show us. I'm afraid it's not very up to date. Let's see – edition's about fifteen years old . . . Still, it'll give us an idea.'

In order to study the maps side by side, they had to lay them on the floor. Laura knelt down, Neil took up a squatting position, Ronald sat forward on a low stool.

It took some time to find what might once have been the Fordall road. It was now a lane, its name having changed to Fordinall. It threaded its way for a short time through the country from the south-west, along the edge of some open land dotted with buildings. It then joined a main road leading to the town of Simmingford.

'I think that must be it,' Laura said, putting her finger on an area called Tansfield Park. 'Tansfield – Tansy Field – yes?'

'I think you're right.'

'Tansfield Park. Public Recreation Ground,' read Neil from the map. 'So mebbe it's got trees on it after all!'

They all straightened and exchanged smiles of self-congratulation. They traced the outlines of the park, noted the fact that it had a boating lake, and a bowling green, and were for the moment delighted.

Then Neil said, 'Hold on a minute. I don't want to appear grasping, but if I own that piece of land, how come Simmingford Town Council could turn it into a park?'

'Yes indeed, daughter dear,' said Ronald. 'Explain that.'

121

'That's one of the things I had to solve,' said Laura. 'I had to get the will of Sir John Higston before I worked it out. You see, when he and Marianne got married there had been an agreement that he should become sole owner of the land that might have been regarded as Marianne's dowry. It matched alongside his estate and he'd always wanted it – tried to buy it from Mr Dallancy more than once.'

'Right. I'm with you so far.'

'Then Mr Dallancy added a codicil to his will leaving Tansy Field to Marianne. But as far as I can gather he didn't spread the word about that – the only person he seems to have informed was Sir John Higston. He died, his brother Martin inherited most of the property, there were a few bequests to servants and old friends. Tansy Field was a separate issue and after some squabbling it was left in abeyance. But Marianne never turned up to claim it, and apparently Martin never took it to Chancery. So I think it just sat there for years. Martin didn't do anything about it; it wasn't any of his business – he probably forgot it existed.'

'Now, my dear daughter, that's pure supposition,' her father intervened. 'For all you know, Martin may have fought tooth and nail to claim that field.'

'There's no documentary evidence of that. And judging by how inept he was in coping with the new manmade fabrics that came in—'

'Manmade? You mean like nylon or something?'

'No, no, it was called artificial silk. Or art silk, as most of the shops seemed to call it. That was to mislead people into thinking it was "artistic silk", whereas it was something completely different – and cheaper, of course. So Martin lost out at his factory of real silk and was too busy to think about Tansy Field.'

'Makes sense,' Neil acknowledged, although Ronald was frowning and shaking his head.

'So Martin forgets about the land, and Sir John Higston dies. And somehow the land gets included in his estate, I think, because of course lawyers thought it came under the conditions before the Married Women's Property Act.'

'What date are you giving for Sir John's death?' Ronald demanded.

'He died eighteen years after his second marriage, having produced two daughters, who couldn't inherit the title or the estate. The necessary male heir was a child who died unmarried in one of the battles of the First World War. So the title lapsed and the estate got dispersed. That happened a lot after the end of that war, as we well know, Papa.'

He could only agree. The First World War was like a great chasm in the landscape of family history. Young men died, the survivors were often left with scars, mental and physical, that precluded marriage. Families and estates long established withered away.

'Anyhow,' Laura resumed, 'Tansy Field was listed as part of his estate at first, just after Sir John died. As I've explained, I tried to track it down and got as far as the early twenties. It changed hands a few times but nothing much was done with it. That's as far as I'd got; I gave up for a while at that point.'

'You mean to say you've been lazy and slack?'

She laughed. 'I tried my best, sir!'

'It's all very well to joke about it,' Ronald reproved, 'but you started off by saying you thought Neil owned that land. Now it seems as if his claim is a non-starter—'

'If Neil wanted to spend the time and the money, I think a case could be made out—'

'I still want to know how it became a park,' Neil said.

'Oh, sorry, well, in the 1920s Simmingford was flourishing because cotton textiles and other industries were picking up again. You know, there was a bit of a recovery from the war. Simmingford Council were expanding so that piece of land became a sort of suburb. They bought the land from the supposed owner of that date – I think that was 1924. Then came the Depression, and their plans for whatever they were going to do fell by the wayside. So it became known as Tansfield Common, just a piece of open land where people could perhaps go for walks and fly kites and so on. That's the last bit of my research, though I meant to go on with it by and by.'

'It must have been turned into a park with a boating lake later on, when times improved. Perhaps after World War Two, when there was a determined effort by a lot of town councils to improve things, so I gather.' This was Ronald, thinking it

123

through. 'Not a bad bit of work. No wonder you've been rooted to your chair in front of the computer. But I still say you shouldn't have told Neil he owns the land. "Possession is nine points of the law" – and he doesn't possess it.'

She agreed with a sigh. 'I just thought it would give him a thrill to think he had a claim to a piece of English countryside.'

'A short-lived thrill. Common sense tells us that he's never going to stand on it and say, "This is mine."'

'At least it's doing some good,' said the legatee. 'A park. That's neat.'

'We might be able to get its name changed,' Laura suggested. 'Crandel Park – how does that sound?'

'Don't be ridiculous,' said Ronald with indignation. 'Why on earth should Simmingford Council agree to a name change when the place has been Tansfield for years? It would cost them *money*! Signboards, street names – they'd laugh at the idea.'

'Hey, come on, lighten up, Ron,' said Neil. 'It was just a passing thought. In any case,' he added, 'I'd want it to be changed to Marianne Dallancy Crandel Park. How does that grab you?'

Ronald had the grace to look a little ashamed of his last rebuke. He shrugged. 'Well . . . Of course I didn't mean to sound didactic about it . . . I must say I'm quite impressed with what's been found out so far.'

Neil raised his teacup in a toast. 'I hereby declare my legacy to be well and truly handed over to Simmingford town with the blessing of the Crandel family, particularly Marian Crandel, formerly of that parish.'

'Hear, hear!' cried Laura.

He smiled at her, and Ronald was tempted into a nod of appreciation.

Laura reflected how different it might have been. Had Neil been a different kind of man – grasping, self-seeking – her disclosure of the bequest by George Dallancy might have caused trouble. Ronald's view of the legal position might have been a source of resentment. Now, as far as she could tell, Neil was simply pleased at the proof that his ancestor had forgiven his wayward daughter. He had no ambitions about owning property here.

Although if he'd been able to claim it, he might have stayed in England . . .

They settled down to finish the home-made scones. Laura made fresh tea. Ronald remembered to ask if Neil had seen the trees he was interested in.

'Oh, sure, particularly the *Cymbidium*.'

Ronald looked lost. Laura said, 'It's sort of a tree fern, Papa. Beautiful light green frondy top. And another thing that was interesting. Did you know palm trees have flowers?'

'Flowers?'

'Yes, up at the top, just under the leaves – big bunches of white blossom, though not all that blossomy, really. But I'd never realized that before.'

'So I suppose you thought dates or bananas grew on trees without ever having a blossom that could be fertilized?' Neil enquired, with a pretence of scorn.

'What?' said Ronald, trying to catch up.

'Don't bother, Papa, he's just showing off.'

Ronald felt obliged out of politeness to go on for a little about trees, then inevitably diverged off into Kim's problems with her garden. Neil nodded and shook his head but kept saying that he didn't really know anything about lawns, or starting a vegetable plot.

'Stay for dinner,' Ronald invited, with a gesture towards the sky as it darkened towards evening. 'You can whip something up, can't you, Laura?'

'No, no,' Neil said quickly. 'Laura's probably tired—'

'Nonsense, she's got things in the freezer – haven't you, my dear?'

'But even so,' persisted Neil, 'I'd like to get back to the hotel, to run the pics I've taken through one of their computers and see which I could use.'

'Use? For what?'

'Well, I want to email some of them back home.'

Ronald looked perplexed. 'Somebody there is interested?' he asked, without much tact.

'Sure thing. The Northwest Alberta Arboriculture Group, otherwise known as NAAG, which is what we do, mainly, nag, I mean. We nag the government about trees. Not that I'm going to nag them about *Cymbidiums* or *Dicksonias*. But everybody was interested when I said I was going to look at sub-tropicals, and I promised to write an article for the magazine.'

Laura smiled at her father's amazement. The fact was, Ronald kept underestimating Neil. True, it was news to her about the article for the society's magazine, yet it didn't surprise her. There was an awful lot they didn't know about Neil, actually.

'Well . . . well . . . if you really feel you must go . . .'

'I really must. But thanks for the thought, Ron.'

'Some other time, perhaps?'

'Yeah, sure.'

They began their goodbyes. Laura went out with him to his car. He gave her a kiss and a fierce hug in parting. 'Thanks for the scones,' he whispered. 'And everything else.'

'Shall I see you soon?'

'Ah. Well, not for a day or two. I have to go up to London.'

'To the physiotherapist?'

'That, and other matters. But I'll call you.'

She returned to the house in a mixture of pleasure and uncertainty. The feeling of a few minutes ago returned. There was so much that she didn't know about Neil. What else could be taking him to London besides treatment for his ankle? They had joked about his visits, she'd teased him about acting like a tourist – surely it wasn't sightseeing that took him to London so often?

Well, if you fell in love with a stranger, that was one of the drawbacks. You didn't know much about him at first.

And she was in love; she acknowledged that to herself. For the first time since her student days, her happiness depended on being loved in return. Does he love me? That was the question that rose up before her now.

Yes, he loved her. That's to say, he desired her. Their physical pleasure was proof of that, the perfection of their joining together. But did he feel, as she did, that she couldn't live without him?

She shook her head. Of course not. Because he could speak quite casually of going back to Alberta.

The thought of his leaving was like death to her. What would she do without him?

126

She hugged herself with her arms and tried to banish the thought. He was still here. There were moments of supreme happiness still to come. She would treasure those moments, as a rampart against the loneliness of the future.

Eleven

Back to work. She had correspondence to catch up with, and of course the family histories of other clients to pursue.

On the following Thursday her father sat back in satisfaction from a very good home-cooked dinner to say, as if struck by a new thought, 'Does it seem about time to have a dinner party again, Laura?'

Now and then they paid off social obligations with a party. Not on the scale of Kim Groves, of course, yet they were pleasant affairs.

'I suppose so,' Laura agreed. 'Whom should we invite this time?'

'Well, Kim, naturally, we owe her for about eight or nine invitations. And the Feltons, for that lunch at Easter – and Neil, of course.'

'Yes,' Laura nodded. 'And Mary Lindell, and her young man.'

'Right, that makes it eight and you always say you can't cope with more than eight.'

'We can't seat more than eight round our dining table, you mean. We could have more if we had the meal in the kitchen—'

'No, no, cottage dining is all right for family, but we can't really lower our standards for guests. Right, that's settled. You start planning menus and I'll ring round with the invitations.'

'When is this to be?' she enquired.

'Well, it can't be a weekend because Kim has company then, but I thought next Monday?'

Local entertaining was usually informal so it wasn't short notice for their friends. She agreed, getting out paper and pencil to start thinking what to shop for.

Later in the evening, after a session on the telephone, Ronald said, 'Everybody's invited except I can't get in touch with Neil. I left a message at the Sceptre.'

'He's in London, I think.' She didn't say that he'd rung her from there.

Around ten, he came through on her mobile. 'The receptionist at the Sceptre tells me you've left a message?' he said.

'Not me, it was Papa. He wants to invite you to dinner.'

'What, a formal invitation, you mean? When's this?'

'Next Monday. Can you make it? Will you be back?'

'Oh, sure,' he said, and the easy tone made her think he could probably come back any time he wanted to.

So why was he so far away from her?

'Dinner, eh? Does this mean I should hire a tuxedo?'

She laughed. 'Of course. Or even white tie and tails.'

'Who else is going to be there, if I may ask?'

'Oh, a few people, neighbours, you know. And Kim Groves.'

'Aha!'

'What do you mean, aha?'

'Is this some ploy of your father's? Let her view what he has to offer – a beautiful little country cottage in exchange for her Victorian domain?'

'Don't, Neil. Even as a joke. You've met her, you must know she'd never pair up with a man like Papa.'

'Can't argue with that. A real high-flyer. So it's just catching up with social obligations, is it?'

'I imagine so. You'll come?'

'Yes, it's a date. I was thinking about getting back to Oxford anyhow.'

'Finished in London?'

'I'm actually in Amsterdam at the moment.'

'Amsterdam! What are you doing in Amsterdam?'

'Oh, just a little side trip, you know. What about you? What are you doing?'

'Sitting in my bedroom watching the sunset.' But now her mind was attending to something more important. Why on earth was he in Amsterdam? Then she recalled that the

Netherlands was a great centre of horticulture. That must be the reason.

'Speaking of bedrooms,' he said, his tone easy and light, 'why not join me in London some time?'

'Oh!' The thought took her breath away. She had been wondering if she would ever have his arms round her again; if it had all been a fanciful dream she'd had.

'We could go to Kew,' he said, 'and Wisley. In the daytime, I mean.'

'More trees?'

'Ha! Do I gather you'd rather spend your time in Sloane Street and Selfridges?'

'I was only joking, darling. Of course we'll go to Kew, and anywhere else you want to go.'

'We'll talk about it when I see you. Next Monday, then? About what time?'

'Eight o'clock. And you needn't wear your frock coat. Collar and tie is all I demand.'

She reported Neil's acceptance to her father, who grunted in recognition of the fact that she was likely to be in closer contact with Neil than he was. Next day she set about planning the menu in earnest, because she didn't want to let herself down in front of her guests – particularly Kim, who had expensive caterers for her parties.

Gazpacho, she thought, a nice cold soup to start with. Then a hot dish. Duck? Venison? Fish? If they had fish it would mean ordering it from a special firm. She rang them, was told they had everything she could desire including fresh tuna and North Atlantic sea bass, and would deliver as always on the day she specified. She settled for the sea bass, which would be grilled and served with special dill sauce. Pudding would be a cold open fruit flan, suitably decorated with flourishes of cream.

All this was making a big dent in the housekeeping money. It caused her some shame because she knew it was all to impress Kim. Nevertheless, she was pleased with the plan, and spent the Sunday evening before the event preparing everything that could be prepared in advance.

That left the matter of her appearance. It was late June, sultry and thundery. She had very few clothes that would meet

129

the circumstances – comfortable because she was going to be trotting back and forth between the kitchen and the dining room, flimsy because it would be warm indoors though they would have the windows wide open to the garden, dressy because . . . well, because.

She settled for a gauzy cotton voile she'd bought in Torquay when at a conference there a couple of years ago. She'd bought it as a sundress, but it was simple and – well, she hoped it had a certain sophistication. As for her hair, she booked an appointment with the hairdresser in Brinbank, no great name but a sympathetic girl. She emerged at four o'clock on Monday afternoon with her hair in a simple top knot held by a bow that matched the apricot tones of her dress.

She was swathed in an apron when Neil arrived. He laughed when he saw her. 'You look as if you're about to feed the five thousand!' He dropped a kiss on the newly achieved top knot. 'I thought you'd do this the way Kim does – all the stuff brought in.'

'I'm showing off. One of my few talents is that I can cook.'

'Well, I knew that. You make great scones. I know some of your other talents too.'

She leaned against him for a moment to let him know she understood exactly what he meant, but Ronald came bustling in. 'Ah, it was you that just came in. Good, good. Come and help me with the wine. You can drink wine now, can't you?'

'But only one glass cos I'm driving. Are we having something special?'

'It's an '86 white Burgundy to go with the fish. There's a Frascati as well, a bit lighter, you know, and to eke out.'

'Oh, you're a connoisseur? I didn't know that.'

'Huh,' chuckled Ronald, 'I asked Kim. She knows all about wine.' He bore Neil away to the dining room, quite forgetting that he'd promised to welcome the guests as they appeared.

But everyone knew they could just walk in, so the party soon assembled in an amiable group, accepting 'the usual' from Ronald; these were people they saw on an almost daily basis so their tastes were well known. Kim, the last to arrive, who always asked for white wine, said she would try out the Frascati.

'How is it?' Ronald asked anxiously, hovering.

'Soft, you know, but it's nice and cold.'

He looked as if he didn't know whether this was a compliment or not, but when she smiled at him over the glass, he relaxed.

She was looking exceptionally striking this evening in well-cut jeans and a bright blue satin shirt, severely styled but left unbuttoned over a simple T-shirt. Her hair, no doubt cut and styled by a well-known hairdresser, clung to her skull like a black cap. She looked as if she were ready to strike out on some exciting safari, except that a handsome sapphire sparkled on her right hand.

Outclassed. That was Laura's feeling. But she had to put that aside to look after her guests. She shepherded them into the dining room and was comforted when the women gave a cry of delight at the table flowers. These were garden roses, one at each place in a holder of damp moss. Laura couldn't help feeling a certain pride. Years of helping out with the church flowers had taught her a lot. She'd sometimes felt it was a mumsy-ish kind of thing to be doing, but tonight it earned its reward.

Everything went well, the food was enjoyed and complimented, conversation ranged from local events to Neil's trip to the Netherlands. He gave them a description of his visit to a famous plant market. They all said they must definitely go there one day. Coffee and liqueurs followed in the living room. Those who lived locally drank a little too much because they were walking home and didn't need to be under the driving limit. They soon became sleepy after this unaccustomed feast of good food and wine so took their leave. By ten thirty the only guests remaining were Kim Groves and Neil.

Kim leaned back to study Neil over her little glass of Cointreau. 'Ronald was telling me a rather interesting thing about your family research, Neil. He says you might have some rights to a piece of land.'

Laura stifled a gasp. She stared in reproach at her father. It was forbidden to discuss the family affairs of a client with an outsider.

Ronald looked shamefaced but said nothing in his own defence. He knew that his daughter though he had misbehaved; he also knew that she guessed his reasons. He wanted to appear interesting to Kim. His work, perhaps rather dull, had

131

never roused any enthusiasm in her. To be able to say that he and Laura had perhaps helped to find a missing heir was – well, it was different, intriguing, perhaps even romantic.

Neil, unperturbed, gave a nod and a shrug. 'Something like ten acres,' he said. 'No big deal.'

'But it all depends where they are.'

'Oh, we know that. It's a little park in that town where Norman Dallancy lives – Simmingford. I met him, did Ron tell you? A Dallancy descendant.'

'Never mind him – Ronald mentioned him, but *he*'s not the heir.'

'No, I am, and I've got to tell you I was really thrilled to think the old guy – old George Dallancy – had come up smiling about Marianne. Rounds it all off nicely, I think.'

'Rounds it off. You're not thinking of leaving it there, are you?'

'Sure. What else?'

'Well, that piece of land you inherited is extremely valuable.'

'What, a little park with a paddling pool and a bowling green?'

Kim put down her glass, got to her feet, and stood so that she could hold his attention totally. 'That map you looked at was about fifteen years out of date. I looked it up on the latest Ordnance Survey, and the ten acres you inherited are slap bang in the middle of a fairly new housing estate.'

'What?' The cry of surprise came from both Neil and Laura.

'Extremely valuable real estate. There are several blocks of flats on the land—'

'Blocks of flats?'

'And the financial value would be significant.'

'Who to?' he countered. 'The guy that built them must be the owner—'

'But the *ground* belongs to you. Don't you understand? You could claim that the structures were put up without your permission and have—'

'Have them pulled down? Is that what you were going to say? Talk sense, Kim! If Ronnie's been talking to you about all this, he must have told you he doesn't think the case would stand up in court. I can't prove that the Marianne Dallancy, who was supposed to inherit, is the same woman as my great-great-however-many-grandmother.'

Kim threw up her hands in a little gesture of dismissal and laughed. 'You don't have to! You could bring a case and provide what evidence you have—'

'But that consists of a lace collar.'

'There's a passenger list, isn't there? With her name on it? Well, whatever,' she said. 'We could do some heavy research and put up a claim. It might take—'

'Listen, Kim, thanks and all that. I can see where you're coming from – to you it's an interesting piece of legal manoeuvring. But it would just be a waste of time and money—'

'Not at all. It would take time, I grant you that, but it could be very profitable.'

'But I don't want to own blocks of flats! That's not for me, Kim.'

'Oh, I don't think you'd end up owning anything concrete. But you'd make a lot of money.'

Ronald was nodding in agreement. Clearly he'd already been through all this with Kim.

Laura was very angry with him. She understood now why he'd wanted this dinner party – simply so that Kim could start this conversation and show off her expertise.

Neil was looking perplexed and unwilling. 'What are you suggesting?' he asked. 'Is it some sort of scam you've got in mind?'

'Not at all. Perfectly legal. You put in your protest about the use of your land, you threaten a lawsuit, it all gets settled out of court. The nuisance value alone would cause the town council to come to terms.'

'The town council?' he echoed, completely baffled.

Laura caught on almost immediately. 'It's a council housing estate!' she exclaimed.

'Exactly.' Kim smiled in triumph.

There was a lull in the conversation. Neil was frowning at the carpet; Ronald was watching Kim with appreciation; Laura was appalled at what was going on.

Neil said; 'You're suggesting I should sort of blackmail Simmingford Town Council.'

'I'm proposing that you should exert your rights of ownership.'

'Listen to me, Kim. I came thousands of miles to this country

133

to see if I could find my ancestors. I didn't come to trick a local government out of its property.'

'But it's not their property! You know in your heart you think that Marianne Dallancy and Marian Crandel were one and the same person. You do, don't you?'

"Ye-es.'

'And that her father left her this piece of land to take care of her if she were ever to come back—'

'But she never did—'

'That's not the point. The bequest was instituted, she never claimed it, so it falls to her heirs in perpetuity. *In perpetuity.* You're her heir. The land belongs to you. You have a right to—'

'I don't have any right to hold anybody to ransom over it. You're a really bright lady, Kim, but you'll never persuade me to—'

'Think about it. Don't say no to it right now. There could be big money involved, you know, Neil. Simmingford Council would probably settle for a substantial sum to avoid the cost of a long court case.'

'Absolutely not,' said Neil, and walked out.

Twelve

By the time Laura caught up with him he was getting into the Honda.

'Wait! she cried, and he left the door open as she ran up. 'Neil, I'm so sorry! I had no idea that was going to happen!'

He shrugged, gazing through the windscreen at the clematis clinging to the walls of Old Brin House. 'She's a real go-getter. Somebody tells her about a thing like this, she's got to take it on.' There was a reluctant admiration in his voice.

'Papa had no right to tell her—'

'Oh, I see how it came to happen. He thought it would

134

interest her because it's her field, isn't it – that's the kind of law she's into, property law. I'm not blaming Ron, because he's all the time trying to catch her attention. And not Kim, either – she just couldn't resist the challenge. But I mean it, Laura. I'm not going to cheat some poor little town council into parting with money from its citizens – that would be a ratty kind of thing to do.'

'I think she understood that, Neil.'

'You do?' He looked relieved. 'I couldn't think how to argue against her. I was all shook up. But you do see, don't you, that it would be a mean sort of thing?'

'Yes, I do. I'm with you.'

He smiled. 'Good to know.'

'I apologize on behalf of my father, and of Lauron Family Research. All the work we do is supposed to be in strictest confidence.'

'You mean I could sue you too?' He reached up a hand, caught her by the shoulder, pulled her down and kissed her. 'Let's call it a day, huh? I'll call you.'

He let her go, she stood back, he closed the car door and drove out of the driveway. With a final wave as he turned into the lane, he was gone. She stood for a moment, wishing she could have said more. She understood his way of thinking. He wasn't the kind of man who'd go rushing into a legal battle unless he thought he had just cause. He was too much of a straight shooter to do a thing like that.

Kim and Ronald were in close conversation when she re-entered the living room. She said at once, before her courage failed her, 'I thought that was a disgraceful performance, and if I'd known what you were up to I'd never have agreed to the dinner party.'

'Oh, please,' Kim murmured in a bored voice, 'we've had enough uprightness for one evening, if you don't mind.'

'Kim only wanted to let him see what a good position he was in—'

'Don't try to talk me into accepting any of it. You know you had absolutely no right—'

'But we only wanted to do him some good, Laura.'

'He's from a very simple sort of background, I imagine,' Kim remarked. 'Not accustomed to thinking in terms of

135

legalities. It's such an attractive case – so much leeway in the argument—'

'You're talking as if everybody involved in it would be some sort of puppet!' Laura cried. 'How dare you? Just because it would give you a chance to show off and manipulate people—'

'Now, Laura, that's no way to speak. Kim is our guest—'

'Kim is *your* guest. *You* can look after her. I'm going to bed.'

With that she stalked out, upstairs to the sanctuary of her room. She left the dishes, the clearing up, all the chores she usually attended to. It was for her a conscious rebellion. Let Ronald see, for once, that he had offended and hurt her. Let him acknowledge that he was in the wrong. Let him suffer . . . even if it was only to the extent that she'd shown him open and outright disapproval.

It was a long time before she fell asleep, although she was physically very tired. Her mind was in a whirl. She tossed and turned, trying to see her way through the problem. Not the problem of a lawsuit over Neil's property – because he himself had put a total embargo on that. No, it was the scene with her father and Kim that troubled her. For the very first time she'd let him know that she hated the way he carried on about Kim. She thought it was belittling, foolish, likely to cause him hurt in the end. He had learned what she felt. But perhaps more than that: she'd let him know her opinion of Kim.

He idolized her. She was clever, beautiful, full of ambition and energy. She had taken up a position as some sort of ruler of the community, arbiter of what was important and who. It had happened almost unremarked.

Everyone in Brinbank agreed that Kim was the leader. To be invited to one of her parties was the final accolade. To be thought of as a man she liked – might even have affection for – that was important to Ronald. He was quite unaware that some of the inhabitants of the village saw him as absurd.

If that thought now occurred to him – because of what she'd said tonight – it could be a disaster.

Next morning she came downstairs to find her father sheepishly attempting to stack the dishwasher. She was so astonished she could only stare at him.

''Morning. Did you sleep well?' he muttered.

'Ah . . . No . . . You're up early?'

'Thought I'd lend a hand.'

'Thank you.'

She glanced at the open dishwasher and knew that the moment he went out of the kitchen she'd have to take it all out and re-stack it. But she wasn't going to say so. Any move on his part to help with the domestic chores was very new and very welcome.

She set about making the coffee. While she waited for the kettle to boil she opened doors and windows. The morning was still fresh, but the sun already had strength. Once she'd aired the house she must pull down the blinds to keep out the heat. She sighed inwardly. She found this kind of weather very enervating. If you're going to have a family quarrel, she thought with some ironic amusement, you should do it in the winter.

She poured the hot water over the coffee, then made toast. When they had settled at the kitchen table Ronald said in a subdued voice, 'I'll ring Neil later.'

'To apologize?' She wanted an open acknowledgement.

'Er . . . yes.' He swallowed a strengthening gulp of coffee so as to be able to go on. 'I see now that . . . er . . . perhaps I put my foot in it . . . meant it for the best, of course . . .'

She occupied herself with scraping the minimum of low-fat spread on her toast.

'Come on, Laura, don't behave like this. I've never seen you so cross before.'

'Cross?' She was astonished at the word. Was that how he saw it? That he'd committed some minor gaffe and she was 'cross'? 'I'm furious! You played a trick on me,' she accused, her indignation getting the better of her. 'You set things up so that Kim could play *her* tricks, and you made me ashamed—'

'Ashamed?'

'Yes, *ashamed*. In the first place you had no right to tell Kim any of Neil's business. In the second place, how could you be so weak and silly.'

'Weak?' The word was a faint echo, full of reproach and surprise.

'You don't think it was weak to invite Neil here so that your lady-friend could try out her wiles on him?'

'Oh, now come on, child! Wiles? All it was . . . It was simply a business proposition.'

'Rubbish! She thought it would give her a chance to shine – to champion the cause of this poor hick from the backwoods. And let me tell you, she underestimates Neil and so do you!'

'Laura, Laura, for heaven's sake . . . I'm sorry . . . I've said I'll apologize to him . . . What more can I do?'

'You can try to get out of the habit of toadying to Kim.'

'Toadying?' He stood up, jarring the table so that his coffee spilled. 'Now that's enough—'

But she overrode him. 'I should have said this months ago. You don't want to hear it, but it's time it was said.' She stood up so that she was facing him. 'Answer me this. Would you have talked about Neil's bequest to anyone else but Kim?'

He'd been about to stalk out of the room but her challenge stopped him. He frowned, hesitated. 'Well . . .'

'No, of course you wouldn't. And why did you talk to her about it? Because you thought it would make your work seem more entertaining, more glitzy. You're afraid she thinks you're a dull old stick, so this story about Neil gave you a chance to amuse her.'

'No—'

'But she took it seriously, saw it as an opportunity for herself – and by then you'd talked yourself into thinking it would be a good thing if she got involved.'

'But it *would* be a good thing—'

'Only if he wants to do it – only if he thought of it himself – and you surely know after all this that he's not the kind of man who's out for money at all costs.'

'But that land is really his—'

'Oh, *you've* changed your tune! A few days ago it was, "Don't be silly, Laura, it would never stand up in court."'

'But it wouldn't get to court.'

'No, and you know why? Because Neil wants nothing to do with it. Are we clear on that?'

'Well, yes, and I've said – I'll ring him and apologize. What more can I say?' He was totally at a loss. Not since the great long quarrels with Laura's mother had he had to listen to accusations like this.

'Oh, sit down and eat your breakfast,' she said with a sigh.

138

She hadn't the energy to go on and, besides, she was un-accustomed to taking him to task.

For years now her first care had been not to upset her father, not to bring on one of his dismal moods. It had taken the anger roused by last night to make her face him with her disapproval.

Ronald slowly subsided into his chair. His coffee had grown cool. He took a sip, made a face, but apparently thought it best not to complain.

Luckily at that moment the delivery boy came up the drive on his scooter, so Ronald was able to escape to the front door to accept the morning paper. He and Laura were glad enough to escape from the confrontation. He opened the pages and pretended to be immersed.

So a fragile calm came over Old Brin House and Laura set about clearing up after last night's party. Later she heard Ronald on the office telephone but she didn't ask if he'd got through to Neil nor what had been said.

The house restored to order, she went up to the office for the day's work. Later she went out to the post. In the village post office she came across Mrs Stevens buying a lottery ticket. Mrs Stevens had helped with some of the chores in preparation for the dinner party – moving furniture, looking out the best tablecloth, things like that.

'Everything go all right last night?' she asked as she tucked her lottery tag away.

'Oh yes, thank you.'

'Dill sauce turn out right?' Mrs Stevens had actually provided the dill for the sauce.

'Yes, fine.'

They went out together and on the pavement Mrs Stevens put a hand on Laura's arm. 'Is that true what I heard, that your friend Mr Crandel owns a big chunk of Simmingford?'

'What?' gasped Laura.

'What a turn-up, eh! When my Joe told me, I thought he must have got it wrong, but he swears it's true.'

'But how did he – I mean, how could—'

'Oh, Her Ladyhip herself – who else?'

'You mean Miss Groves? She told your husband?'

'Well, not exactly – Joe was up Yalcote early, to mow the

back lawn before it got hot, but the mower wouldn't start so he was pottering with it. And there she was having breakfast on the patio with her mobile, chatting to some chap she works with, saying for the moment it was no go, but Mr Crandel would probably see by and by what a good thing it would be to claim his rights and all that.'

'You mean all this is just some garbled stuff Joe overheard!'

'No, no, she saw he'd heard and said he was to keep it to himself and he asked if it was right, then, that Mr Crandel really owned this big patch of Simmingford, and she smiled and said not to let on to anyone. Which means it's true, of course.'

'Mrs Stevens,' groaned Laura, 'You haven't been telling all this to anyone else?'

'Of course not. Miss Groves said not to. But being as you're such a friend of his, I thought you'd be in the know.'

'Please don't talk about this to anyone.'

'Of course not, dear.'

Which meant, Laura knew, that within the week most of Brinbank would have heard the news.

Did that matter? The village . . . a community of about five or six hundred adults . . . And yet some of those commuted to London and Oxford. If they heard the story, would they gossip about it? Tell it to their friends on the train? After all, it could turn out to have tremendous effects on property values, should Neil take action.

She felt she couldn't chance leaving him in the dark. She didn't have her mobile with her so she hurried home. But when she rang the Sceptre it was to hear that Mr Crandel was out.

'We're expecting him back, madam,' the receptionist told her. 'He's ordered afternoon tea for himself and a friend.'

A friend?

'Would you ask him to ring me?' she requested. 'Tell him it's rather urgent.'

'I could put you on the recording machine, madam – would you prefer that?'

'Thank you, yes.' When she heard the tone she began, all in a fluster. 'Neil, the story about your inheritance has got out. The village gossip's got hold of it. It may not come to anything, but all the same . . . I felt you had to know at once.'

That done, she sighed in a mixture of relief and apprehension.

Her father was at work in the office. She didn't know what to say to him. Should she reproach him, challenge him? But after all he wasn't responsible for Kim's carelessness.

She went downstairs to make preparations for lunch. As she worked, she was thinking – a friend? Not Kim. No, of course not. But suppose she'd followed up on last night's disclosure? Asked to come and have a quiet discussion with him?

Kim was sure to see Neil as much more interesting now. He could turn out to be a *someone* – a source of profit but also of good publicity. What could be more alluring to the general public? The long-lost heir turning up to claim his inheritance . . .

Ronald came down about half an hour later, in search of a long cooling drink. He took that into the living room. When she called him to the meal he obeyed in silence. He was clearly very chastened by her rebuke at breakfast time.

She was still trying to think what to say to him about local gossip when he seemed to summon himself up and enquired with great politeness, 'You went into the village earlier?'

'Yes, to the post office. Papa, I met Mrs Stevens there. She'd heard about Neil's legacy.'

He stopped with his fork halfway to his mouth, then put it down with a clatter. 'Great heavens! How on earth—'

'Joe Stevens overheard Kim on the telephone this morning.'

'Overheard? You mean he was eavesdropping!'

She had to agree that that might well be true. Mrs Stevens had a tendency to lurk where she would hear conversations, and it was possible her husband had caught the infection. In summer weather, with doors and windows open, it was easy to 'happen to overhear' what other people were saying.

'Whatever,' she said with a sigh. 'The point is that Mrs Stevens knows and it's almost certain she'll pass it on. I asked her not to and she promised, but that doesn't mean much.'

Her father pushed the food about on his plate. He didn't look at his daughter. After a long pause he said, 'How did it happen? Who was Kim talking to?'

'A colleague at her office, I gather.'

He nodded. 'She told me a couple of days ago – when I first mentioned it to her – she said she'd have a word with one of the partners. He's a bit of an expert on inheritance.'

'Well, I think perhaps she was telling him that they wouldn't be pursuing it.'

'Well . . . That's all right then.'

'I hope so. I tried to ring Neil to warn him but he was out.'

Nothing more was said. Then Ronald got up, shrugged, and went out of the kitchen. She heard him leave by the back door. He was going for a walk to one of his favourite spots, a knoll where there was a view of fields and a curve of the little River Brin.

She cleared away his half-finished meal then made coffee for herself. By and by she went up to the office. She'd been at work for an hour or so when the office phone rang. 'Lauron Family Research, how can I help you?'

'That sounds familiar. You left a message?'

'Neil! Yes, I felt you had to know. I'm sorry.'

'Gee, don't sound so upset about it! Folk gossip in Wenaskowa, you know.'

'But it's *our* fault that it got out.'

'So who squealed on us?'

'Well, Joe Stevens . . . that's our local taxi and odd-job man . . . He overheard . . . someone . . .'

'Was it Ron?'

'No, Papa didn't . . . It wasn't Papa.'

'And it wasn't you – I'm sure of that. It only leaves Kim.'

She made no reply to that and he was silent for a moment. Then he said, 'Well, worse things happen in a storm in the backwoods. Let's just say that it's not about footballers or pop stars so most folk won't pay much heed.'

'I hope so, Neil.'

'Okay, so that's that. Do you know that I've ordered the full malarkey for afternoon tea? Scones and cream and fresh strawberry tartlets – the menu gets positively poetic about it now that summer's really here. So what say you come and enjoy the feast?'

'Oh . . . But . . . The desk clerk said you were having a friend to tea.'

'Friend? An expert in greenhouse heating! He's the guy who supplied the set-up we used for the tender plants at the nursery.'

She felt a wave of relief, but also of some shame. How could she have been so silly as to leap to conclusions about

142

Kim? 'Oh, I wouldn't want to intrude if you're going to have a discussion with an expert—'

'I'm just being polite and paying a debt, Laura. Tell the truth, he's probably going to want to talk about cricket. You'd be doing me a favour.'

'Oh, well, in that case . . . Not that I know anything about cricket.'

'Great. If the two of us show how dumb we are, maybe he'll cut it short. Come on, Laura. Help me out here.'

She laughed and agreed to go. When she'd disconnected she went at once to her bedroom to decide what to wear. She certainly wasn't going to the Sceptre in jeans and a T-shirt, even if the guest for the strawberry tea was only a business friend.

She used the park-and-ride system, taking a bus from the parking area to the Sceptre. Neil and his guest were in the shaded conservatory at a wicker table, talking earnestly over a brochure. They rose as she approached and the guest, a rotund man in his mid-fifties, was introduced as Peter. 'He and I have been Internet friends for years,' Neil explained.

Tea and the summer treats were brought at once. The conversation never once veered towards cricket, though it dwelled long and earnestly on temperature control and humidity. After an hour or so Peter glanced at his watch and said he had a train to catch. They said goodbye.

When he had gone Neil said, 'How shall we spend the rest of the evening?'

'Oh, but—' She felt a little thrill of anticipation. 'I thought I was only coming to tea.'

'Think again.'

'But Papa will be expecting me home.'

'Never mind him.'

'But he didn't eat lunch. He'll want a decent evening meal.'

'Ring him. Tell him to go to the local pub.'

'Oh, I . . . Well . . . It would be a good thing to stay out of each other's way,' she acknowledged. 'We're not on good terms at the moment.'

'There you go. Helps out all round. Come on, you can ring him from my room.'

They went upstairs. His room was cool and quiet. He

143

gestured to the bedside phone. She went to it, picked it up, dialled her home number. It rang for the prescribed half-dozen rings then she heard the answering machine. She said over her shoulder to Neil, 'He's out.'

He had taken a seat on the bed behind her. As she left a message she could feel his fingers gently nudging at the zip of her dress. Her breathing turned shallow and fast. She said hastily into the phone, 'Shan't be home for dinner, there's food in the fridge. Bye.'

Then she turned into his arms, and the everyday world went away.

Thirteen

It was very late when she reached home. Her father had gone to bed. Inspection of the fridge and the dishwasher led her to think he had gone out for his evening meal. She recollected with a feeling of guilt that she'd deprived him of transport had he wanted to go further than the village.

Yet she was too happy to let it matter.

Next morning she was late getting up. Ronald was in the kitchen already, making toast. She nodded good morning then set about making the coffee. They were rather silent during breakfast, conversation limited to 'Please pass the marmalade' and 'More coffee?'

Hard at work all morning, they were ready for a break by midday. Laura was in the middle of preparing one of her special salads, as a gesture of reconciliation, when the office phone rang.

She heard her father pick up. Then a short interval before he came clattering downstairs. His normally pale face was even paler.

'That was the *Simmingford Messenger*,' he said. 'They wanted to know if it was true we'd found the heir to a big property in the town.'

'Oh!'

'I didn't know what to say. I put the phone down.'

They stood looking at each other, not knowing how to deal with this. The phone rang again upstairs.

'You go,' urged Ronald.

She hurried up the staircase but the phone had fallen silent by the time she reached the landing. She hesitated, turned to go down, and the phone rang again.

A determined caller.

She picked up. 'Lauron Family Research, how may I help you?'

'Who am I speaking to?'

'This is Laura Wainwright. And you are?'

'This is the *Simmingford Messenger*. I was cut off before.'

'Yes?'

'I was enquiring about a news item we want to use. Is it a fact that your firm has found the heir to an unclaimed piece of land in Simmingford?'

'I'm afraid I can't comment on anything to do with the firm's work. We offer complete confidentiality.'

'Oh you do, huh? Why's that?'

'Because research on behalf of a client turns up facts to do with family matters, which by common consent are private matters.'

'Is a Mr Neil Crandel a client of yours?'

'I can't comment on that.'

'Why not? Surely it's not a secret?'

'People who come to us wouldn't want publicity.'

'But what harm can it do to tell me if he's hired you to work for him?'

'Our rule is that our client list is not available to the public.'

'But the public – the public of Simmingford – are entitled to know if someone's turned up out of the blue and is claiming something they thought was theirs.'

'Has someone turned up to claim something?' she asked with great coolness.

'Well . . . I hear he's going to.'

'From whom do you hear that?'

'Oh, a journalist never reveals his sources.'

She allowed herself a little ironic laugh. 'So confidentiality is important in journalism?'

The reporter on the other end was silent a moment. Then he said, 'The fact that you're so cagey makes me think there's something in this story.'

'*Stories* are usually fiction, are they not? Goodbye.'

She hung up, and as she turned to go the phone rang again. She picked it up, laid it on the desk, and walked out of the office.

When she reached the hall, the phone in the living room began to ring. With a little gasp of irritation she went in. 'Hello?' she said.

'Miss Wainwright? Something's gone wrong with your business phone. I hadn't finished what I wanted to say. Where can I—'

She put the receiver down on the bureau and left the living room. Before it could ring, she reached for the mobile in her handbag to switch it off. She was fairly sure he wouldn't have her mobile number, but better safe than sorry.

Ronald Wainwright was sitting at the kitchen table, shoulders hunched as if to protect himself from an onslaught. Laura went to the worktop to resume lunch preparations. Any appetite she might have had was gone, but it was something to do.

'They'll give up,' her father said.

She made no reply.

'They'll give up, won't they? If we just say nothing?'

'I've no idea, Papa.'

'What did Neil say? That's where you were last night, isn't it? You told him?

'Yes, of course. He shrugged it off.'

'He wasn't annoyed?'

'He said people gossip in Wenaskowa too.'

'Oh, that's good. That's a sensible way to look at it.'

She made no response to that. Having completed the salad, she put the bowl on the table then turned to get bread rolls from the oven. The larder provided a variety of cheeses, and there was home-made pickle to go with it. None of it had the least appeal for her.

'Lunch is ready.'

He simply shrugged and walked out.

After a few minutes she cleared away everything she'd prepared. Then she got her mobile out of her bag to ring the Sceptre. She didn't think she'd reach Neil, because he'd told her he was going to Stratford on a simple sightseeing trip, and indeed the receptionist said he was out. She left a message that she needed to get in touch urgently.

Then, after a moment's thought, she looked up the number and rang Kim at her office in Oxford.

'I'm sorry, Ms Groves has gone to lunch.'

'This is Laura Wainwright. Will you tell Ms Groves to ring me urgently?' She gave her mobile number. 'Please tell her it's urgent.'

'Certainly, Ms Wainwright.'

Next she tried her father on his mobile. But either he hadn't taken it with him, which was quite common, or he didn't hear it because he didn't have his hearing aids in. She might have gone out to find him and ask him for Kim's mobile number but she didn't know which direction he'd taken. And she wasn't going to run all over the countryside looking for him. She wanted to sit quietly and think.

She was pretty sure that soon the story of Neil's legacy was going to come out. A keen reporter would soon find ways. He already had Neil's name; simply by asking around at hotels in the area, he'd soon find out where Neil was staying.

She had no idea how Neil would react to questions from the press, but once anything appeared in the *Messenger* it was only a matter of time before someone rang the paper to say, 'I know about Neil Crandel.' Mrs Stevens, for example. She'd take a bet that Mrs Stevens had been the original source from which the reporter had begun his enquiries.

However, all Mrs Stevens and her fellow gossips could say was that Neil Crandel was a client of Lauron Family Research, and that the research connected him with a piece of land. What the land was, how great an extent it covered – all that was unknown to them. At least she hoped so. She was reasonably sure that Kim had said as little as possible to Joe Stevens once she had realized he'd heard her phone conversation.

The question was, would the editor of the paper want to take it any further?

She thought he would. It concerned Simmingford, and

anything that concerned Simmingford was the concern of the *Simmingford Messenger*. Small-town newspapers got little enough chance to publish anything really attractive. The story of a stranger inheriting a plot of land must surely hold the editor's attention. He'd want to know where and why.

The afternoon was going by. Kim had still not returned her call. A very long lunch break, Laura thought with some irritation. She was about to try her again when there was a knock at the front door.

A stranger, obviously. Friends and neighbours usually walked in.

Without thinking what she was doing, she went to the door.

'Ms Wainwright?'

'Yes?'

'Just a few questions. Whereabouts in Simmingford is this piece of land that Mr Crandel has inherited?'

Astonishment held her frozen for a moment. Then she stepped back and closed the door.

'Ms Wainwright? Ms Wainwright? Can you just tell me if Crandel is going to challenge Simmingford Council for this land?'

'Go away!'

'Ms Wainwright, the citizens of Simmingford have a right to know! Ms Wainwright! Let's just talk about this—'

She shot the bolt on the front door and retreated to the living room. From its window she was able to see the reporter standing on the doorstep, knocking. Unfortunately she could also see her father coming up the driveway.

The reporter turned to greet him. 'Good afternoon, sir? You are . . . ?'

'Who are you?' Ronald replied, perplexed.

'Pete Pelman, of the *Simmingford Messenger*. Are you connected with the firm of Lauron Family Research, sir?'

'What's it got to do with you?'

'I'm investigating this story that one of your clients is making a claim against Simmingford Council about the ownership of a piece of land.'

'It's the first I've heard of it!' Ronald said.

'He's not going to claim the land?'

'Not as far as I know.'

148

'But Mr Crandel is a client of yours?'

Too late, Ronald understood he was talking too much. 'Excuse me,' he said, brushing past Pelman, 'I have work to do.'

'Jut one more thing, sir—'

'Go away,' Ronald said over his shoulder. 'You're trespassing.'

Laura hurried to the door to slide back the bolt, opened it, and ensured the gap was just sufficient for him to slip through.

'Mr Wainwright! Mr Wainwright!' shouted Pelman from the other side.

'That's the reporter who was on the telephone,' Ronald groaned.

'Yes, and he's not going to give up.'

'Mr Wainwright, could you fix up an interview with Mr Crandel?'

Ronald was about to reply but Laura put her hand on his arm. 'Don't,' she murmured. 'Anything you say will be reported in the paper and made to sound as if it's a big drama.'

'But perhaps if he spoke to Neil and heard from him that he's not interested in the land—'

'Listen, Papa, I told him *nothing*, yet he was telling you he'd heard Neil was making a claim.'

'Well, I told him he wasn't. That should put him off, surely?'

The reporter was knocking on the thick oak door of Old Brin House. 'Does it sound as if you've put him off?' Laura asked.

They retreated to the kitchen, furthest away from the front door. Ronald sank down on a chair. Laura picked up her mobile phone and offered it to him. 'Ring Kim,' she said.

He took it with reluctance. He pressed a memory key. There was quite a delay but at last he got a response. 'Kim, this is Ronald. We need to talk.' He listened for a moment then put his hand over the mike to say to Laura, 'She's with a client.'

'Say it's urgent.'

'It's urgent, Kim, it's about Neil. There's a reporter outside our front door.' There was panic in his voice, which seemed to have an effect because after a moment he nodded then disconnected. 'She says she'll call back as soon as she can.'

The knocking had ceased. Laura went to the living room to look out. The reporter had left the doorstep but was sitting in his car in the drive.

Better put the landline back, she thought. She'd read somewhere that it was easy to listen in to mobile calls. Perhaps she was being unduly cautious but she thought it best.

She was making tea in the kitchen when Kim rang back. She used Ronald's mobile number but hung up and waited for him to call back on the fixed line. He said to Laura, 'All this hush-hush stuff . . . She sounds put out.'

'Too bad for her.' Her tone was hard, and Ronald gave her a startled glance.

Once they were in touch again he explained what had happened. Laura stood near to hear her replies.

'That confounded Joe Stevens! He should be run out of Brinbank!'

'Kim, it's no use going back to that. What are we going to do now? Neil could be very angry at all this.'

'You haven't told him?'

'We can't get in touch. Laura says he was going to Stratford for the day.'

'Good Lord, what a time to go sightseeing! If he—'

Laura cut in. 'Kim, don't start blaming Neil. This is all your fault and you know it. What we have to do now is decide how to cope.'

'Why should I do anything?' Kim replied, very crisp and cool. 'He's not my client. He refused my advice—'

'You didn't offer advice, at least not as to alternatives. You just urged him to enter a claim—'

'All right, put it that way if you want to. But I don't see what the problem is, Laura. All he has to do is say no every time they ask about his claim and they'll let it drop eventually.'

'Kim!' groaned Ronald. He wanted her to do something clever, to rescue them from this unwanted publicity. He wanted her to *shine*.

'Well, they will,' came her voice from the receiver. 'Newspapers are always quick to go on to the next big item—'

'Not a little newspaper like the *Messenger*,' objected Laura. 'For them this is big news.'

'I don't know what you expect me to do,' Kim said, turning

150

huffy. 'I gave him my view and he ignored me. I admit I shouldn't have been discussing it with Joe Stevens hanging around nearby but good heavens, are we all going to have to use carrier pigeons if we want to keep our affairs secret?'

'Couldn't we at least discuss all this with Neil?' Ronald pleaded. 'I do feel we've let him down badly, Kim, I really do.'

Her sigh was clearly audible. Then after a pause she said in a more conciliatory tone, 'All right. This evening? Any time after seven thirty – I can't get away any earlier.'

'Not at our house. The reporter might still be here.'

She sighed again. 'All right, my place. Will you tell Neil?'

'Soon as we can. I left a message at the Sceptre,' Laura said.

Ronald hung up. Almost immediately the phone rang. He picked it up and said a wary, 'Hello?' Then he put the receiver down too energetically. 'It's him again.'

Laura glanced out of the window. 'He's sitting there in his car using his mobile.'

The phone on the bureau rang again. Laura picked it up, said nothing, and placed it gently down on the desk.

The rest of the afternoon passed in restless attempts to do something useful. They tried to do some work in the office, they had a cup of tea, Laura sent some emails, her father tried to read. From time to time Pete Pelman came to knock at the door.

Laura was in the kitchen considering what to do about an evening meal when Ronald came in. 'He's gone,' he reported.

'Really?'

'He drove off about ten minutes ago. I waited to see if he'd come back again but he didn't. At least, not so far.'

She nodded at the wall clock. 'Probably got hungry.'

She had her mobile in the pocket of her jeans. It rang and she got it out in haste. For a dreadful moment she thought Pete Pelman might have got the number but the voice that spoke was Neil's.

'Something urgent? The Sceptre tell me you tried to get in touch around lunch-time.'

'Neil, we've had a reporter here in the drive all afternoon. He's got hold of the story about the property in Simmingford in some form or other and he's been very determined, stayed on the job all afternoon. He just left about ten minutes ago.'

'Ouch,' said Neil.

'We've been in touch with Kim to warn her, in case they track the rumour back to her.'

'Is there some way they could?'

'We-ell, I imagine it was one of the Stevens family who gave the tip-off. And as Joe Stevens got it from Kim in the first place . . .' She could imagine Joe excitedly calling the newspaper to say he'd heard the local legal star talking about Neil Crandel and accepting a very welcome fifty pounds reward for the tip.

'Uh-huh.' Neil accepted her opinion without demur.

'She's suggested we meet at her house this evening. Can you be there?'

'Sure, why not. What time?'

'Any time after half past seven.'

'Just gives me time to shower and change. This sightseeing business isn't for cream puffs, you know. I'll have a sandwich sent up.'

'I'm sorry to visit this on you when you've had a long day—'

'No problem. Let's say I'll get to Kim's some time around eight?'

'Papa and I will meet you there.'

She put her head round the door of the living room to say they should head for Yalcote around eight. 'In the meantime, we ought to eat. What would you like, Papa?'

'I'm not hungry.'

'But we ought to have something.'

'No, I couldn't eat.'

She knew him in this mood. When the world around him seemed dark or unfriendly, he would retreat from normality, losing his appetite, refusing to be coaxed. She said, 'Well, we'll probably get drinks at Kim's. You shouldn't drink on any empty stomach—'

'I'll look after myself, if you don't mind.'

'But you don't want to get fuddled or sleepy while we're there.'

The thought of making himself look foolish in front of his

beloved made Ronald reconsider. 'Well, perhaps we should have just a bite.'

'Okay then, you go up and change – you've got dried mud on your trousers – and I'll call you when it's ready.'

She already had the salad she'd prepared at lunch-time. She whipped up a large omelette for them to share. When the meal was over she hurried upstairs to change out of her jeans and shirt. She knew she wouldn't be able to outshine their hostess but at least she wanted to look presentable. She put on a blue linen skirt and a thin blue shirt, tied her hair on top with a dark blue bow, and thought that might do.

Neil's car was already there when they got to Yalcote. They had to ring to be let in – Kim didn't subscribe to the easy-come, easy-go attitude of Brinbank. One glance told Laura she'd wasted her time in prettying up. Kim was wearing a lemon yellow leisure suit – slim jeans and loose sleeveless top of knitted silk. Against her black hair and olive skin, it looked gorgeous.

Neil was sitting at ease with a long cool drink. He got up as they entered the drawing room, and to Laura's eyes it was clear he'd rather overdone things at Stratford. He was favouring his injured ankle as he stood.

'Sit, sit,' urged Kim. 'What will you have to drink?' She glanced at Ronald. 'I've got that Japanese beer you like.'

He agreed to it. Laura asked for what was in the big thermos jug, which turned out to be Pimm's with lemonade. They settled in rather lush armchairs round a low table.

'How did you elude the reporter who was doorstepping you?' Kim enquired.

'He left around six thirty. But just in case, we went out of the back door and came on foot.'

'So . . . What did he actually ask you?'

Ronald answered first. 'He phoned and asked if it was true that we'd found the heir to a big property.'

'And you said?'

'I – I didn't say anything, Kim. I put the phone down. I was so startled!'

'So what happened next?'

'He kept ringing. Laura answered.'

153

'He tried to get me to accept that Neil had inherited a big spread and that he was to claim it. I asked where he'd heard that and he said he couldn't reveal his sources. So that was my way to end the conversation. I said we never divulged anything about our client list and hung up. He kept ringing so we just left the receiver lying on the desk.'

'But that can't go on,' Ronald said in a very rattled tone, 'because we can't run a business like that – the office phone number appears on our letter heading and our advertisements.'

'I see that.' She nodded at Neil. 'He says that so far no one has tried to contact him at the hotel.'

'When I got back from Stratford there were only two messages – one from Laura and one from a London contact, nothing to do with Simmingford.' Neil spoke in a relaxed manner, very much in contrast with Ronald's nervy tone. He raised his glass towards Ronald as he went on. 'It's no big deal. Kim thinks it will all die away.'

'I said I *hope* it will die away. If something more important happens in the Simmingford area, the editor could decide not to pursue it.'

'Yeah, the more especially if nothing comes of the tale that I'm bringing a legal claim for the land.'

'However, that in itself might rouse a lot of curiosity, Neil.'

He frowned. 'How come?'

'Well, if anyone tracks back on the research Laura has done—'

'But they couldn't do that.'

'I believe they could.' Kim turned to her. 'You went to well-known sources, yes? Looked up archives, went to libraries?'

'Well . . . yes . . . of course . . .'

There was a little pause.

Kim resumed. 'A good reporter knows how to do research or could hire someone to do it. I think in a day or two, if someone cares to look, they'll know that the place in Simmingford you were researching is the Tansfield Estate. And that is a *very* interesting proposition for a local paper. The town council believe they own it but who really does? What will happen to the tenants on the estate if there's a court case? Those are the things that will be a drama in Simmingford.'

Ronald groaned. Neil said, 'But I stick to my point. If I don't make a claim, why should it be news?'

'But why don't you make a claim, Neil? Any newsman would want to know why. It will seem very strange to him. And to tell the truth, my friend, it seems strange to me too.'

Laura gasped in indignation at this remark, which seemed to her to be a slur of some kind. Her father frowned, looking from one to the other. Neil sipped his drink, then set it down.

He turned Kim's question into a question of his own. 'You think it's strange that I don't want to take on the expense of a court case for a place I never heard of until a few days ago?'

'If it's the cost that's bothering you, my firm would gladly take it on a no-win no-fee basis.'

Ronald made a startled little movement. His daughter frowned in consternation. Kim wasn't given to making generous gestures.

'Uh-huh,' said Neil. 'In the hopes of making a profit, I imagine. Is that ethical?'

'It's not unheard of. If we believe it's justified.'

'That's very big-hearted. But I don't think I'll take you up on it.'

'So the question remains. Why do you shy away from it?' Kim persisted, a glint of battle in the dark eyes.

'Let's just say that I don't want to be in the limelight.'

'Why not?'

'Limelight isn't good for my complexion.'

She rose, to stand gazing down at him as he sat at ease in his armchair. Although she was by no means tall, she dominated by sheer force of personality. 'Have you some particular reason for wanting to stay incognito?' she challenged.

He smiled up at her. He seemed unaffected by her manner, in which there was something like antagonism. He shook his head. 'You thinking of being a trial lawyer? You're good at the cross-questioning angle.'

'I'd just like to know what's behind all this. I was surprised at the outset, when you didn't want to follow up on the Tansfield Estate,' Kim declared. '*Nobody* turns down rich pickings without a good reason. I mean, you didn't even want to *see* the place. I call that very odd indeed.'

'I'd guess you really want the claim to go forward because

it would be good for your career,' he suggested. 'Get you in the public eye, make your name for you. Is that it?'

She shrugged, but he had clearly hit the mark. For the moment she couldn't think of a response.

'And if I don't go along with it, you're not going to be exactly unwelcoming to the press. You wouldn't mind a bit of helpful publicity.'

'There's no reason for me to be reticent. You're not my client.'

'No-o, I'm not. But if I were, you'd take my instructions? Keep things quiet? If I said I wanted to stay out of it, you'd protect my privacy?'

'Of course. Normal client–solicitor relationship.'

He looked up at the ornate Victorian ceiling as if in thought. Laura, who had listened and watched in growing stupefaction, tried to guess what was going through his mind. Some kind of fencing match had been going on, which she didn't understand.

At length he looked back at Kim.

'Okay, then,' he said. 'You're hired.'

Fourteen

Kim wasn't shy about wanting the Wainwrights to leave. 'Neil and I need to have a serious talk,' she said, 'but finish your drinks, there's no hurry.'

So of course Laura and her father took two more swallows and said their goodbyes.

'It's business,' Ronald commented as they walked out of the gateway. 'Business has to come first.'

'Oh yes, business. Never mind good manners.'

'But Laura, it *was* a business meeting. To sort out what to do.'

'Did you understand what just happened?' she demanded.

'Well . . . She set things out for Neil and he . . . he decided to engage her as his solicitor.'

They strolled on out of Brinbank, the sun sending their shadows in long silhouette ahead of them. The scent of hay was in the air. Rooks were flying home to tall trees.

'Why does Neil need a solicitor?' she asked.

'He . . . er . . . he doesn't want to be badgered by the press.'

'Neither do we. But have we hired a solicitor?'

'No, but then we're not the ones who're claiming a bit of Simmingford.'

'Neil is not claiming a bit of Simmingford. He most definitely is not. So he doesn't need Kim for that.' She paused, holding up a hand to emphasize her words. 'He hired her so he could stay out of sight.'

'Yes, that's understood.'

'But it's why he wants to stay out of sight that's so bewildering. It's very important to him.'

'He's got a right to privacy—'

'And using that, she blackmailed him into engaging her as his solicitor.'

'Laura!' Ronald was appalled. 'What a word to use! Blackmail?'

'What else was it? She wanted to have him as a client. She wants to make something out of it for herself – be interviewed, get her face on television—'

'Now that's enough,' her father said. 'I've known for a while that you have something against Kim, but now I see it's just plain envy! She's clever and ambitious and you resent that!'

She was hurt by the accusation yet had to ask herself whether what he said was true. Was it simply envy that made her so unhappy about what had just happened?

She realized that from now on Kim could be closer to Neil. Laura's usefulness was at an end because she'd done all she could by way of research into his family. That had ended with this astounding possibility that he might have claims on part of Simmingford. From the business point of view, she belonged to his past.

Yet she'd taken it for granted that she meant a lot more to him. She'd thought he loved her.

She was silent as they walked on, deep in the throes of an

internal argument. Did he care for her as more than just a physical partner? Were the feelings that she had for him mirrored in his heart? In some ways he was difficult to read. Easy-going, good-natured . . . Shallow?

Had she thrown herself away on a man who took her too lightly?

Her father had been following his own train of thought. 'You know, Laura, I thought you and Neil were – you know – I thought you were what they call an "item".'

'Seems we were both wrong.'

'You really don't know why he's so shy of publicity?'

She shook her head.

'If you come to think about it,' he went on, 'we don't really know anything about him.'

He waited, but she could only shrug.

'He contacts us out of the blue, says he wants to look up this family, Dallancy—'

'No, Papa, *we* found the Dallancy family.'

'But perhaps he knew there was some sort of legacy – not where it came from but perhaps back home there was the tradition that they had had rich relations—'

'So he came all the way from the other side of Canada to see what he could inherit – is that what you're suggesting? It might have been a gold watch, a family painting.'

'No, but he wanted to see this special orthopaedic surgeon—'

'There are good medical facilities in Canada, Papa. I can't believe he came on the assumption it was going to bring him a fortune. I truly think he just wanted to carry on what his father had begun, the search for the family's origins.'

'Humph. Well . . . yes . . . And now of course he finds the origins bring him a parcel of land that he could make a fortune with. And yet he doesn't want it.'

'He said, at first . . . He said he didn't want to make money out of some poor little town council.'

Ronald found a twig on the path and picked it up, to run it along the top of the hedge as they walked. 'Kim will talk him round.'

'You mean you think he should pretend to sue the council? Oh, Papa . . . Don't you think that's a bit mean-spirited?'

'But if it's his by right?'

'But you were always the one that said it couldn't be proved.'

'But, remember, Kim says he doesn't have to prove it.'

'We're going round in circles. My head's spinning. I can't talk about it any more.' To her own dismay, her voice trembled. She was on the verge of tears.

They walked in through their own gate in silence. Ronald went into the house, into the living room, and switched on the television set as a sign of agreement that they shouldn't talk any more. Laura went into the kitchen, to stand by the window and stare out at the garden. The sun was low behind the trees now, tingeing them with amber. Clouds were gathering from the west. Perhaps she wouldn't need to water the garden tomorrow.

It wasn't yet ten o'clock. She had no desire to go to bed. She got out ingredients to bake a cake, then sat at the table reading the labels on the spice jars. Cinnamon from Sri Lanka, caraway seeds from Tunisia . . .

A teardrop fell on the jar she was holding. She set it down, folded her arms on the table-top, rested her head on them, and wept.

By next morning, her mood had changed. Get a grip, she told herself as she sat doing her hair in front of her dressing-table mirror. What did you think? That he was making a life-long commitment? You *knew* he'd be going home before long. To him it's just what's called a 'holiday romance'.

She looked back and admitted that she'd made all the running. She'd thrown herself at him. And why should he turn down an offer like that? She was passably good looking, he'd said she was bright, he was all on his own in a strange country – why shouldn't he take up what was being proposed?

Angry at herself, she brushed hard at her hair, tied it up in an elastic band on top of her head, and went downstairs without a scrap of make-up. Punishing herself.

As for him, she thought. As for him . . . She'd been wrong about him. She'd begun to think a lot of him because he'd come to her father's aid, handled him so well, made a difference to his day-to-day life. He was someone she'd felt she could rely on for help, whereas in the past there had only been

159

herself and the psychotherapist to whom Ronald had finally refused to go.

Yes, well, that was a point in his favour. There was no getting away from the fact that he'd been really nice to Ronald, had shown insight, had been a help to Laura herself in changing her perspective a little.

All the same, that didn't change the fact that he was shifty, that he was hiding something. What? What could it be? She was sure it wasn't to do with the Dallancy family. Her discoveries in that area had been a complete surprise to him. She remembered the delighted sympathy with which he'd greeted her story about Marianne's bequest. He'd been so pleased that Marianne's father had forgiven her.

And his quiet disappointment with Norman Dallancy and his family. He'd been hoping – hadn't he? – to find people who would embrace him, who would treat him as kinfolk. That had been genuine. He'd judged them as she herself thought they should be judged – self-centred, unwelcoming.

It was only after the news about the bequest leaked out that he changed. And the change came about because for some reason he didn't want to be in the public eye. It wasn't just the usual reluctance to talk about personal matters in public. At first, when it was only gossip in the village, he'd been unconcerned. It was when the newspapers began to take notice that he shied away.

Although his reasons for wanting to remain incognito might seem strange, it was his reaction to Kim's challenge that grated on her most.

He'd given in. He must have seen that Kim was up to no good yet he'd submitted. It had been weak, almost cowardly. It wasn't what she'd expected of him. He'd let her down – yes, he'd made her ashamed. A man who could be manipulated by someone as self-seeking and artful as Kim Groves . . .

She sighed to herself and shook her head. He wasn't the only one. Half the male population of Brinbank was in the same state. Her father, for instance. Last night, coming away from Yalcote, he'd been seeking ways to excuse Kim's behaviour: 'It's business. Business has to come first.' Ronald didn't seem to consider that in this instance 'business' could mean 'sharp practice'.

No use grieving over spilled milk. And speaking of milk,

she ought to go down and take the milk off the doorstep and start getting breakfast. She glanced about as she did so. No sign of the reporter, thank heavens.

Ronald didn't come down for breakfast. She left everything ready for him then went up to the office. She was starting on a new case, looking for the forebears of a West Indian client. She knew it was going to be intricate and time-consuming: the slave trade was tricky because there was so much denied guilt. Time ticked by and still Ronald didn't get up.

It was a bad sign. She switched on the radio in her bedroom at a high volume so as to rouse him and at last, about eleven, he surfaced from the deep sleep that was his refuge in bad times.

She hurried downstairs to start fresh coffee. When he came into the kitchen he looked downcast. He'd shaved unevenly, he'd buttoned his shirt up wrong, he hadn't put in his hearing aids. *Very* bad signs.

She knew it was because he couldn't acquit Kim of chicanery. He couldn't bear to think she was less than perfect, because he saw her through the eyes of love, of devoted acceptance. Laura had a fellow-feeling with him, perhaps for the first time, because she too had been under a delusion. She'd thought Neil was wonderful. It hurt to find out it was all foolishness. She half wished she, too, could find escape in deep slumber, in self-deception.

But instead she got on with making the coffee. Ronald accepted it eagerly, drank his first cup in two gulps, and asked for more. She poured. 'What about toast? Cereal?'

'I'll wait till lunch-time.'

She'd put the newspaper by his plate but he paid it no heed. 'Any phone calls?' She heard hope in his voice. He wanted Kim to have rung and explained herself.

She shook her head. She'd replaced the receivers after the reporter left last night. Her mobile was switched on, but where Ronald's was, who could say? Perhaps in the pocket of his jacket in the hall.

'What are you working on?' he enquired.

'The Johnsons.'

'Oh yes.' If he wanted to, Ronald could be a great help in that matter. His knowledge of history extended to understanding

161

who had owned which island of the West Indies at what time and for how long. But he offered no advice so she busied herself with little kitchen chores until he'd finished his coffee and gone droopingly out to the garden.

She thought she might as well begin preparations for lunch, and since Ronald seemed to be in such a dismal mood she decided to cook something that he particularly liked. She was engaged in making a complicated pasta sauce when he came in again.

'I think I'll go for a drive,' he remarked, shaking the car keys at her. 'Might get a bite somewhere.'

'Oh. Okay, then.'

When he'd gone she surveyed her handiwork, took it into the pantry, then sat down with a sandwich for herself. After that she went back to the office and worked consistently until late afternoon. She heard her father come in, so rose willingly to make afternoon tea.

She found him awaiting her in the hall, a newspaper in his hand. 'Look.'

She took it. It was the *Simmingford Messenger* and its head-line ran: 'DOES HE OWN YOUR HOUSE?'

Alongside this was a blurred photograph which might have been of Neil. The background looked like the entrance to the Sceptre Hotel. The lead-in was: 'Neil Crandel may own a substantial section of housing in Simmingford,' followed by a paragraph stating that a family research firm had established his right to ownership in consequence of an ancient legacy. No specific area was mentioned nor was there anything about making a claim. The report went on to say that Simmingford Town Council had no such information and regarded the whole thing as speculation.

'Where did you get this?' Laura asked.

'In Oxford.' Seeing her frown, he went on. 'I wanted to speak to her. Just a word, you know. I thought we might go out for a drink and a sandwich. But she was busy, and I was going along Broad Street when I saw this kiosk with all the local papers for the area so I saw the headline and bought it.'

She turned towards the living room. 'We must ring Neil—'

'He's gone.'

'What?'

162

'He's gone. I drove to the Sceptre because I wanted to show him the paper but the man at the desk said he'd gone.'

'You mean, gone away? Left Oxford?'

'I don't know where he's gone. They wouldn't tell me – or at least they said they didn't know.'

'We'll ring Kim—'

'I tried that. I had my mobile. Their receptionist said she was in a meeting. I left a message for her to ring me but she hasn't.'

'Is your mobile switched on?'

He gave her an angry glare. 'Of course it is.' He couldn't always make a statement like that with confidence but on this occasion she was sure it was true, because he'd used it to ring Kim. She was sorry she'd asked. It only exacerbated his mood.

The telephone in the living room began to ring. She exchanged a hopeful glance with Ronald. Kim was ringing back. He hurried to the phone but as she came in after him he was groaning and shaking his head.

'Who is it?'

'Norman Dallancy.' But he only mouthed the name and she didn't catch it. He gave a helpless wave, offering her the phone. He'd wanted so much for it to be Kim.

'This is Laura Wainwright. I—'

'Oh, your Dad too busy? Never mind, love, I just wanted to say hooray for you!'

'What?'

'Saw the *Messenger*. Great, you've done really well. I tried the hotel for Neil but they tell me he's left and I don't blame him. This is *really* going to set the cat among the pigeons, isn't it!'

'I'm sorry, I don't—'

'Give them a taste of their own medicine, eh? They took my livelihood away from me, told me my case was invalid, couldn't claim any compensation – well, now they're going to find out what it's like! I hope he sues them for every penny in the council's coffers.'

'But Mr Dallancy, I don't think Neil is going to—'

'How big a piece of property is it? Of course, it would be best if it was a lot but even a patch of land could be a real pain for them. Does he own a whole street?'

'Mr Dallancy, I can't discuss—'

'Oh, I understand – keeping it under your hat, is that it? Well, I understand, you're in business, you don't want to do anything you shouldn't, but when I rang the paper they were ever so pleased. They've offered me quite a decent sum for my story, but the real point is they know now about the Dallancy tie-up so they'll soon find out what it is he owns. They've got the facilities to find out all that sort of thing.'

'You rang the *Messenger*?' she asked faintly.

'Sure thing! I rang them right away, when the van delivered the papers. This is own-back time, love. They made me suffer, the rotten gypsters, so now I'm going to help put them through the mill!'

Fifteen

Norman spent five more minutes enthusing over the situation. At last he came to an end by asking for Neil's telephone number.

'I don't have it,' Laura said.

'Oh, he's only just left Oxford, then? Not settled elsewhere. When you get his number will you let us know? We're really chuffed about all this, the wife and I. Want to give him all our help.

'I understand.'

'Bye for now. All the best.'

She looked so disturbed as she turned away from the bureau that her father actually noticed. 'What?' he demanded.

'Norman wants to be a big help to Neil in his fight with Simmingford Council. He's been talking to the *Simmingford Messenger*.'

'And saying what?' Ronald asked, beginning to be alarmed himself.

'Nothing so far. It appears he's been offered money but I gather the interview hasn't actually taken place.'

'Oh, Lord.'

'It's the last thing Neil would want.'

'Humph.'

'Try Kim's mobile again,' she suggested. He did so but shook his head. 'She's switched off.'

'Okay, then we'll have to ring the office and say it's urgent.' She didn't have Kim's office number but Ronald immediately pressed a memory button on his mobile. In a moment he was answered by the office receptionist.

'This is Ronald Wainwright. Will you please tell Ms Groves that, quite against the wishes of her client Mr Crandel, someone is chattering to the *Simmingford Messenger*.' He spelled out the name of the newspaper so that there wouldn't be any mistake. 'She has our number,' he added.

They sat down. They looked at the telephone. About ten minutes later it rang. Ronald picked it up. 'Hello? Oh – yes, it really *is* important . . . Norman Dallancy . . . You remember, I told you Neil had a couple of meetings with him in Simmingford . . . Well, he actually *lives* there . . . He saw today's copy of the *Simmingford Messenger* . . . It's got a bit about Neil . . . You haven't seen it?'

There was a long pause while Kim apparently went on another line to give instructions for the immediate purchase of a copy. While he waited Ronald said to his daughter, 'She knew nothing about it. Can't blame her, of course, why should she bother to look at a newspaper from another town?'

Laura had to acknowledge that Kim wasn't at all to blame, but she only nodded in response to her father's eager defence. At last Ronald was engaged in further conversation with her. 'Well, I don't think we should talk about it on the phone. I'm on my mobile and I read somewhere that . . . Yes, can be easily overheard. Well, it may well be true, Kim. I'd rather not discuss . . . Well, why don't we meet and talk it over?'

He wanted to speak to Kim face to face. That had been his aim ever since he drove off in the car at midday, although matters had turned out to be dramatically different from how he had expected. For once Laura quite agreed with him. This was something that needed concerted effort from herself and her father They had met Norman Dallancy: they had to convey to Kim how keenly he was looking forward to punishing Simmingford Town Council.

Ronald was nodding agreement. 'Yes. Right. Yes, of course. So long.' He disconnected. 'She's going to drop in on her way home. That'll be about seven-ish.'

'We'll be eating dinner—'

'Nonsense, that's not important. In any case, I'm not hungry.'

'But, Papa, you've eaten nothing all day.'

'Oh, stop fussing.'

'But really—'

'All right, all right, if it will keep you quiet, I'll have a sandwich now. We usually have afternoon tea about now, don't we?' He glanced at his watch. It seemed to surprise him that it was late afternoon.

Laura made a substantial sandwich with trimmings of salad. When she called him to the kitchen for the snack he was unconcerned, yet she was glad to see he ate what she'd prepared. She herself had some salad and a glass of milk. She was still, she found, sticking to her diet – thought now the incentive had gone because the man she loved had deserted her. But, more than that, she too had lost her appetite because of recent events.

Neither of them could settle to work. Ronald put on the television to watch a cricket match. Laura busied herself by bringing out the best wineglasses, last used at the dinner party, washing them and then polishing them to brilliance. This was so that Kim wouldn't be able to find any fault in them. Idiotic, really. Why should she care if her housekeeping standards weren't equal to Kim's? Kim had all kinds of outside help whereas she . . . Oh well, I don't care, she insisted to herself.

Ronald was pretending to listen to the seven o'clock news when Kim's car nosed into the drive. He was at the door in an instant, unashamed of his longing to see her.

She came in, trim and smart in a patterned silk blouse and skirt of dark blue linen. Today her hair had chestnut glints and was worn back from her forehead in a new style. Laura, who'd changed hurriedly into a print dress and sandals, felt at once like a country mouse. So much for the 'I don't care' attitude.

'You'd like a drink, I know,' she offered hospitably. 'White wine?'

'Is it anything good?'

'Australian Chardonnay.'

'Oh, well. Yes, thank you.'

Ronald busied himself at the drinks tray. He too had smartened himself up a little since the morning. His chin still had a few little tufts of grey hair but he'd changed his shirt and put in his hearing aids. Even to have Kim in the same room had lightened his mood.

'Tell me what the problem is with this Norman Dallancy,' she demanded.

Ronald burst into speech. He covered the main points but in so much of a hurry to be of use to his darling that he wasn't quite comprehensible. Laura added a few helpful comments. Kim listened with pursed lips.

'He sounds a bit of a loose cannon.'

'Well, he's got a score to settle with Simmingford Council and now's his chance.'

'What can he actually tell them?'

'Er . . . That Neil is from Alberta, that he's here on an extended visit, that he believes he's descended from the Dallancys.'

'What does he know about the bequest?'

'Nothing. I only found out about the bequest after we'd met him and his family for lunch and Neil asked me to find out a bit more,' Laura explained. 'I think he was so disappointed in Norman's crew that he hoped for someone else in his background, someone a bit more likeable. We've not been in touch with the Dallancys since the lunch. Except,' Laura added, 'that the daughter, Shelley, rang me in hopes of getting together with Neil. But nothing came of that, I imagine.'

'Mmm. So this Norman person can't really do any damage.'

Laura had been thinking about it. 'He can tell the *Messenger* where Neil comes from. Whether he bothered to pay attention to the conversation when we first met – that was in a pub in Simmingford – I don't know. I thought he was too full of himself to listen to Neil.'

'So what?'

'Kim, isn't it obvious?' Laura exclaimed. 'The newspaper could make enquiries in Wenaskowa, if Norman recollects the name.'

'And find out what? That he and his father own a tree nursery? Big deal.'

They thought about that for a moment. Laura had no idea whether there was anything to be 'found out'. All she knew was that Neil was unwilling to have his private life talked about.

It seemed that Kim had the same thought, for she remarked, 'I ought to speak to this Norman character.'

'Yes.'

'Warn him off.'

'But how? He's all agog – he wants to get into the news-papers so he can air his grudge against the council—'

'I can tell him I'll take him to court.'

'You mean get a court order – an injunction – to prevent him from—?'

'Exactly.'

'But Kim, wouldn't that be making a mountain out of a molehill?'

'It isn't a molehill from Neil's point of view. He's adamant that he doesn't want to be talked about in the press.'

'Have you been in touch with him?' Ronald asked, which was what Laura was longing to know but would never have asked.

'No, I don't seem able to get him on the phone at the moment but I'll talk to him this evening.'

'Try now,' Ronald suggested, nodding towards their tele-phone.

She gave it a moment's thought then rose to pick up the receiver. She pressed buttons. She stood listening for a time then said in a businesslike manner, 'This is Kim. Something important has come up. Please ring me at home.'

'No luck?' For she'd clearly been leaving a message.

'It doesn't matter. He'll be in touch later. We arranged that he'd ring me when he was settled.'

'Settled where?' asked Ronald, once more asking what Laura could not.

'That's privileged information, Ronald.' She finished her drink still standing by the bureau then put the glass down on it. 'Well, I'll push off home. I've a load of work to do this evening. Thanks for the drink.'

'Wait a minute, Kim. What are we to say if Norman Dallancy gets in touch again?'

'As little as possible.'

'But what reason are we to give?' Ronald asked, intent on keeping Kim as long as he could.

'You don't have to give a reason. Just say you don't know anything.'

'Which is true,' Laura pointed out.

'All the better, then. You'll be convincing.'

'But why all the mystery, Kim?' Ronald wondered. 'Isn't it all a bit over the top? If he's just a visitor from Canada looking into his roots, why all the hush-hush stuff?'

'My client's wishes are confidential, Ronald. I'm afraid I can't discuss it.'

Rebuffed, he fell silent. She picked up her handbag and made her way to the hall. Ronald, anxious for a friendlier farewell, went with her to see her off. As soon as they'd left the room Laura sprang up to go to the telephone.

Guiltily she pressed the redial button. The phone rang out. She waited, but there was no reply. A machine began its instructions. 'The owner of this telephone isn't available at present. Please leave your—' It wasn't Neil's voice.

She'd replaced the receiver and was picking up Kim's used wineglass when her father came back looking reasonably happy. Apparently Kim had bestowed a smile or two upon him while saying goodbye.

Laura too was happy. She had the phone number of the place that Neil had moved to. So long as no one dialled another number on that phone, she could call back. And perhaps speak to him.

At that thought her pride took over. No, she wasn't going to ring him. He'd disappointed her, let himself be caught in Kim's trap, and he'd disappeared without a word. He was behaving all wrong. Hiding, sneaking about . . .

So with that thought she resolutely pressed buttons for the number of one of her Brinbank friends, thereby eliminating Neil's.

There. She'd done the right thing. She should be proud of herself. So why was it that when Joan answered she found her voice breaking?

Around midday next day Norman Dallancy rang again. 'What's going on?' he cried. 'I got a snooty phone call from some solicitor type first thing this morning threatening me with a summons if I talked to the *Messenger* about Crandel.'

'You did?'

'Yes, I did, and what I want to know is how did she find out I was doing an interview with the *Messenger*? Did you tell her?'

'Well, I—'

'Because you're the only person I told, except of course Eileen and Shell, and *they* wouldn't tell anyone, because they knew the *Messenger* was going to put it out as an exclusive—'

'Mr Dallancy—'

'And I could've used that money because the shop takings aren't getting any better, and now I've had to tell the *Messenger* I can't do it, and I don't understand what's going on!'

'I don't really understand either, Mr Dallancy. The main point is, Mr Crandel doesn't want any mentions in the newspapers—'

'Well, good luck!' grunted Norman. 'Cos it's all over the *Comet* this morning.'

'What?'

'Mini-headline, halfway down the front page. "Mystery heir dodges press". Making a big thing of it, human interest, they love that kind of thing. It'll be in the Sundays, you can bet on it. And I'll tell you this – I've got a call in to the *Comet*, and if they offer me anything to talk about him, I'm going to give 'em an earful cos that snooty woman only said I couldn't talk to the *Messenger*!'

'But, Mr Dallancy—'

'So you tell whoever it was you got on to at this legal outfit, you tell 'em I'm no jelly baby. Said I was banned from talking to the *Messenger* but nothing about the others – and she'll have to be quick off the mark to stop me and the *Comet* coming to a deal, cos I'm waiting for them to call back now.'

'But, Mr Dallancy, you don't know anything about Neil! What could you tell them?'

'That's for me to know and for you to read in the tabloids, missy.' With a clash he hung up.

170

At once Laura put in a call to Kim. 'Tell her it's about Norman Dallancy,' she told the receptionist.

With unexpected speed Kim returned the call. 'What about Norman Dallancy? I warned him off with the prospect of an injunction—'

'He's furious. He's contacting the *Comet*—'

'The *Comet*?'

'He said the story's in this morning's *Comet* and he's going to give them more – which can only be about Neil being a relation of his and how he came to meet him. The family story, you know. Once you get into the *Comet*, it seems to make you a celebrity.'

The national tabloid took pride in crusading for 'us ordinary folk', as its advertising claimed. It took up the cause of pensioners who felt they'd been cheated by shopkeepers, landlords or cowboy tradesmen. It campaigned against traffic wardens. This was enough to alarm even Kim Groves.

'But what on earth have the *Comet* got? How did they get it?'

Laura had had time to think about it. 'I'd imagine the *Messenger* sold the story on to them, don't you think? I believe local papers try to do that, increase their income, you know. Nationals probably pay quite well for something they can use. "Poor little householders in Simmingford threatened with eviction", that sort of thing. From the adverts I see on TV, that's the *Comet*'s big appeal.'

'Nobody's threatening to evict anybody!' Kim protested.

'I'm just guessing. I haven't seen the paper. To get one I'd have to drive into the village.'

'I'll send out for one. Ring you back.'

But she didn't ring back, and after a wait Laura drove to the village stores to buy one. They were sold out. Not on account of the coverage of the Neil Crandel story, but because they only ordered enough copies to service their regulars.

Outside the shop there was a little crowd patiently awaiting the arrival of the bakery van. So far as she could see, they weren't huddled over copies of the *Comet* and exclaiming about Neil Crandel.

Mrs Stevens would have a copy of the *Comet*. Laura walked to the converted shop from which the couple ran their domestic

171

and taxi service, and knocked. Ten to one Mrs Stevens was out cleaning someone else's kitchen.

No, she came to the door with a shady hat on her head and sunglasses in her hand. 'Oh, Miss Wainwright, dear – I was just going to drop by and show you this.' From the cluttered desk just inside the door she picked up a copy of the *Comet*.

'What a funny thing to say about him,' she complained. 'He seemed such a nice man, why should he be dodging them?'

Laura took the paper, unfolding it so as to read the headline on the lower half of the front page. Sure enough: MYSTERY HEIR DODGES PRESS. Then in smaller type: 'Thought to have inherited homes in Simmingford, Northants, Neil Crandel (*see page 2*).' She obeyed. The upper right-hand half-column was taken up with the rest of the story, so-called. It said nothing overtly libellous. Neil was likely to claim the properties but was lying low to avoid any protests from homeowners who might be dispossessed, that was the gist of it.

It wasn't as bad as she'd expected. She found herself breathing a sigh of relief.

'I suppose you never really know how people will behave,' said Mrs Stevens, taking the paper from Laura and setting it back on the desk. 'I'd never have thought he'd be the type to turn anybody out of their home, myself.' She came out, closing her door behind her. 'But you never know, do you? Money matters . . . Some people can act funny.' She moved away from her door, causing Laura to go with her. 'Now I've shown that to you, I want to get on. I'm just going round to the shop. This is Mr Patel's day for getting fresh doughnuts in.'

On doughnut day, there was usually a gathering. Villagers liked to have fresh doughnuts for tea and arrived in good time for the van. However, Laura knew that Mrs Stevens was going there to enjoy a good chinwag about Neil Crandel. She knew him, had served food to him, had chatted with him. His celebrity would confer distinction upon her.

Laura felt she ought to do something to prevent any damage that might come of it. So she said, 'I can tell you categorically that Neil has no intention of claiming any property.'

'So it's true he's inherited something, like my Joe told me?'

'I didn't say that, Mrs Stevens. I'm just telling you that the

172

last time I saw Neil he was saying he had no interest in that sort of thing.'

'So why's he scarpered, then?'

'That's only what the *Comet* is saying. It only means they can't get in touch with him.'

'Well, why not?'

'He probably doesn't want to talk to them.'

'Can't see why he shouldn't.'

'Would *you* like to have a newspaper prying into your private affairs?'

'Nothing to pry about,' snorted Mrs Stevens. 'Seems to me if somebody makes themselves scarce there's something funny going on.' She put on her sunglasses and stepped out more smartly into the sunshine of the main street. It was clear she thought she was wasting her time with Laura.

Laura made her way to the little village car park. She wondered whether she'd done more harm than good. She decided that from now on she'd say nothing to anyone about Neil, because it never seemed to do any good.

Quite late into the evening Kim at last telephoned. 'I think it would be a good idea of we all had a chat about how to handle the bequest problem,' she announced.

'Okay,' said Laura, who had answered. 'Do you want us to come to you or will you come to us?'

'Neither. It will have to be somewhere secluded because I want Neil to be there.'

Laura's heart gave a great thud. 'Neil?'

'Well, it's his problem, after all; we have to settle how to carry on so as to meet his wishes.'

'Which are what?'

'That's what we're going to find out. He's considerably put out about the way things are going.'

I don't blame him, thought Laura. You held out the prospect of 'no publicity' when he hired you and you've totally let him down.

'So are you on for a meeting about all this?'

'Oh yes, certainly. So where and when – you said not at Old Brin House and not at Yalcote, so where could it be? He's left the Sceptre . . .'

'We'll have to go to London. And it should be tomorrow.'

173

Laura drew in a sharp breath. After a moment she said, 'I see.'

'I take it Ronald is willing to come too? He needs to be kept in the loop.'

Ronald, who had decided not to answer the phone because it was never Kim who was calling, sat watching his daughter and listening to her replies. She covered the receiver to say, 'Kim wants us to go to London for a discussion to include Neil. You agree on that?'

He nodded with vigour. To have a few hours in Kim's company he would have gone to Mars.

'Right. Shall we meet there? Wait till I get a pencil to write down the address.'

'Don't bother,' Kim said curtly. 'I'll pick you up tomorrow and we'll all go in my car. I'm not telling you the address.'

Sixteen

'**O**h.' Taken aback, it took Laura a moment to say, 'Whatever you like.'

Kim seemed to be carrying confidentiality to extremes. 'You'd think Neil was a fugitive from the law, rather than a man who doesn't want to feature in a newspaper,' Laura muttered to herself. 'And what's more, you're enjoying all this. Like a kid who gets to dress up as the Fairy Queen.'

She didn't point out that they might just as well follow Kim in their own car; the arrangement suited her because she didn't much want to take the Land Rover into London. Nor did she mention that once they'd been to the meeting place they'd know the address. No, wait – it dawned on her almost at once they couldn't be going to where Neil was staying.

So many precautions. And all, in her opinion, rather too late, although in belated justice to Kim she had to acknowledge that no one could have foreseen the *Comet* playing a part in Neil's affairs.

Ronald was delighted at the prospect of the outing. So much so that he was up early next day, coming downstairs in what Laura thought of as his summer fête garb: pale blue shirt, neat grey trousers, and a cream linen jacket. She herself had taken some care with her appearance. She was in a new denim dress tricked out with a white-and-blue neckerchief, and navy sandals. Perhaps due to the fact that she'd eaten very little and been restlessly busy for almost a week, she looked slim and svelte.

Kim drove up as they were clearing away the breakfast things. Her Volvo was, as always, gleamingly spotless, the interior cool. Laura knew her father would want to sit in the front passenger seat and had the good sense not to oppose it. The journey to London wouldn't be a long one, although Saturday shopping traffic would slow them down.

They wound their way through some residential roads in North London. Laura thought they were in an area south of Edgware. They drew up at last in front of a new block of flats, postmodern, expensive looking. Kim had made a call to Neil on her mobile as they entered the neighbourhood so that the concierge, expecting them, let them in at once. They went up in the lift to the fourth floor, where Neil was waiting.

He smiled in greeting, shaking hands with Ronald and giving Laura a quick hug. 'Good to see you,' he said. But she felt it was comradely rather than loving.

To her eyes he looked not worried, but harassed. 'This way,' he said, and led the way along the corridor past steel-framed mirrors and Rothko prints. A door was standing ajar. He led them into a hallway graced by a tall jar full of curly hazel twigs – the sign of the hand of an expensive professional decorator, Laura thought. The living room confirmed that view. It had a pale wooden floor, very low cantilevered armchairs, glass tables, and reed blinds at the tall windows. One thing she was certain of – Neil Crandel had never chosen these furnishings.

He ushered them to the sitting area, grouped around one of the glass tables. 'Drinks? Something cool, or coffee, or what?'

'Coffee if you have it,' said Kim. They all nodded.

175

To Laura's astonishment Neil went to the door of the room and called, 'Lisa?'

A middle-aged woman appeared – the London equivalent of Mrs Stevens. 'Coffee for four, then, Lisa.'

'Somesing to eat?' asked the maid in an accent Laura thought might be Romanian.

They all declined. Neil said, 'I've got lunch arranged for later, if that's okay.'

'You're living here?' Roland asked in some awe.

'Gee whiz, no! This sort of place scares me to death. What if you spilled something? No, I've got a few contacts in London; a guy loaned it to me for today while he's visiting his dear old ma in Kent – the apartment plus all the facilities including the maid.' He grinned as he explained. It was clearly as unusual for him as it was for them.

The coffee came, in a fine plain silver pot and accompanied by plain white beakers of eggshell china. The maid offered to pour but withdrew when Kim at once took it on.

'So,' said Neil, 'did you have a good journey?'

'A bit slow.'

'Hot weather for driving.'

'Yes, but Kim's got good air conditioning,' said Ronald. And so on until they'd taken a few sips and settled themselves in the rather comfortless chairs.

'Let's get down to business,' Kim began, always a take-charge type. 'First I'll tell you what I've decided. I didn't ask for an injunction to prevent the *Comet* or other newspapers from pursuing the story. I thought that would only attract greater attention.'

'Oh, right,' said Neil, looking uncertain.

'Our tactic must be to say nothing. Nothing to anyone. "No comment".'

'That always seems to me to mean "I know a lot but I'm not going to tell you,"' said Laura.

'Well, choose some other set of words. The main thing is not to say *anything*, because they'll twist it to make it seem like news.'

This was the conclusion Laura had come to herself, and she nodded agreement. Ronald looked his assent, proud of Kim's wisdom.

'My opinion is that the press will get tired in a few days, the more especially if some other story takes the interest of the tabloids. Something about a celeb or a footballer.'

'I can go along with that,' said Neil, in hopeful tones.

'The main stumbling block is the awful Norman Dallancy. Why didn't you warn me what he was like?' Kim said with some indignation.

'Well, gee, we didn't know what he was like,' he returned. 'We only met him twice. The first time he was on his own and he went on and on about his grudge against the council. Tell the truth, I thought he might ask me for money, but he didn't. Then next time he brought his family. I thought that might make him seem more of a welcoming guy but . . . Well . . . There you go. I didn't realize he'd try to use the bequest to get even with the town council.'

'He isn't likely to go quiet very easily,' Laura remarked. 'He was spitting fire over your threat about an injunction, Kim.'

'He's a boor,' sighed Kim. 'How does it come about that he's descended from the Dallancys? I thought they were a well-regarded family.'

'Just bad luck, I guess. Laura said the brother who got the silk mills made a hash of it and perhaps everything slid downhill after that. And the result is poor old Norm and his family.'

'Don't you think the best way to quiet him down would be if you were to make a statement about not asserting your rights to the estate?' Laura ventured. She wanted him to agree, and from there to go on to explain himself.

But he shook his head. 'That's not an option, Laura.' Seeing her frown he added, 'What would be the point? Until a couple of weeks ago I'd never heard of the place. I don't *want* it; if other people would only mind their own business there wouldn't *be* a problem.'

'How do you know you don't want it?' Kim put in. 'You've never even seen it.'

He shrugged. 'It doesn't really belong to me. It belongs to Marianne Dallancy, and she died about a hundred years ago, so why bother?'

'George Etian Dallancy left it to Marianne *and her heirs*. You're her heir.'

'Who says? Ronnie says none of it stands up. That's why I think this whole thing should just be left to die of its own accord.'

'Well, that's what I'm working towards, even though I don't understand your reasoning,' Kim said in an authoritative tone and with some rancour. 'But I feel it's terribly ill-judged. Tansfield Towers is worth a bit of consideration. Old Mr Dallancy didn't make the bequest just to have it ignored on a whim—'

'A whim?' The word startled Neil.

'It's not good sense, in my view. You've taken up a position that I simply can't understand.' She set down her coffee cup so as to concentrate on what she was saying with all the force of her considerable character. 'I'm not pressing you to do something against your will, but it seems to me it would show respect to at least take a look at the property. Otherwise it's almost an insult to your forefather and to the daughter he wanted to safeguard.'

'She's right, Neil,' urged Ronald. 'The bequest wasn't made lightly. It's a duty to your great-great-great-grandfather to see what he left her and what's become of it.'

Whether Ronald really believed what he was saying was debatable. Laura felt he was simply backing up Kim because he thought it would please her.

'Well . . .' said Neil. He seemed rather perplexed by the weight of their words.

At that point the maid came in to say that "Lonch will be sairved in heff an hour." Neil offered pre-lunch drinks, so there was a stir while he poured them. 'The food's coming from the restaurant attached to the building,' he explained. 'Don't know if you noticed, it's off to one side. Can't tell you what it's like because for me this is all just a one-day stand.'

Laura longed to ask where he was really staying but couldn't bring herself to do it. Kim was greatly impressed with the status of the place and its facilities. 'Your friend's really found the perfect answer to "having it all". I suppose he's a big career man, too busy to want to bother with housekeeping. And what a blessing to have catering on hand! I've got people coming this evening and the food's got to come from Oxford – it's quite worrisome, being away this afternoon but Mrs Stevens is there to take it in.'

Ronald hid his chagrin. Kim was having one of her 'gatherings' but he wasn't invited. But then he and Laura were usually included in the more informal Sunday affairs. 'It's good of you to give up your Saturday to our problems,' he remarked, anxiously including himself in Kim's circle.

'Absolutely necessary,' she returned, with a smile that accepted his allegiance. 'Though I spent half the evening contacting people to say they should come at eight, not seven. We must be back in Brinbank by then, of course.'

'Dear me, what a life you lead! And I suppose you've got something going on tomorrow too?' he asked, half hoping she'd say, 'Yes, and you must come too.'

'Croquet,' she said, laughing. 'I've invited a few friends for a croquet match.'

'But the lawn isn't good enough yet for croquet, surely?'

'Oh, I don't know, Ronald, it isn't bad, and, anyhow, none of us knows anything about croquet, it's just for fun.' She turned a regretful glance on Neil. 'We'll miss you in the garden. You were our *Ground Force* team.'

The reference meant nothing to him since the TV programme hadn't been shown in Canada, but he didn't object to being included in her band of helpers. Ronald, always eager to emphasize his importance to her, talked for while about what he had achieved in her garden on his own recently, though there wasn't much to tell. He didn't mention that he'd lacked energy due to a spell of dejection.

Lunch was served in the dining room. This continued the theme of the living room – glass dining table with brushed steel legs, black leather chairs, a sideboard that bore quite a resemblance to an office filing cabinet.

The food too was somewhat spare. The hors d'oeuvre took up less than a third of its plate, though it was beautifully presented. The main course was a lamb fillet encased in filo pastry and surrounded by a narrow border of vegetables. To Laura it had the appearance of a small parcel whose string had unravelled. She smiled at the thought. Neil caught her eye and they both began to laugh.

'What?' demanded Kim.

'You could always stop for a hamburger on the way back,' Neil suggested.

'Hamburger?' said Kim.

'No, we've still got our packets of sandwiches in our back-packs,' chuckled Laura.

'What on earth are you talking about?'

'Pay them no heed,' Ronald advised. 'They're just being silly. Laura has rather old-fashioned ideas about food.'

'If this is new-fashioned, I'll take Laura's view any day,' said Neil. 'Tell you what – I'll ask for double helpings of dessert to be sent up.'

Kim continued to be baffled. When the dessert actually came – peach compote with raspberry sorbet – they turned to business matters.

'Which day shall we set for the visit to Simmingford?' Kim enquired. 'Not Monday, I wouldn't have time to get a surveyor by then.'

'Surveyor?'

'Of course, Neil. You want some idea of the value of the property, don't you? How about Tuesday.'

'Can't do Tuesday, I'm busy that day. Wednesday would be good for me.'

Wednesday was agreed. Ronald remarked on a questioning note, 'I'd rather like to see the place?' He was thinking that here was another chance to be with Kim.

'Come with us, then,' said Neil. 'You too, Laura. You were the one who uncovered the bequest. You've got as much right as I have to give it a going over.'

'Well . . . that would be nice.' She sighed at herself. Her father wanted to be with Kim. She wanted to be with Neil. What a pair, she mourned inwardly.

When they left, the time and the meeting point had been arranged. The drive home was worse than the outward journey, clogged traffic heading out of London for the weekend. But Laura, left to her own thoughts in the back seat, didn't mind the slow progress. She would see him again on Wednesday. And there had been something comforting about their shared laughter over the food. Surely if she understood him so easily over a thing like that she ought to be able to understand his motives over the Dallancy bequest. But it was still a mystery to her. A mystery and a disappointment.

One day he would explain it. One day she would realize she'd been wrong to doubt him. But perhaps that day would

180

come after he'd flown away to his home in north-west Alberta.

Kim dropped them at Old Brin House, promising to be in touch soon about arrangements for Wednesday. Consequently Ronald Wainwright was in a good mood when they got indoors. He busied himself pouring reviving drinks for them both, bringing them into the kitchen where Laura was making preparations for dinner.

'That was a marvellous place Neil had borrowed,' he remarked. 'Can't say I liked it but my word! Think of the money it must have cost. That furniture – you couldn't buy that in high street shops, now could you?'

'I think it was all what you'd call designer furniture.'

'Yes, and the food! I'm not knocking it, you understand, because it was all very good to eat. But that's the kind of thing you get in trendy restaurants.'

'Very much so. And quite beyond my catering abilities.' She laughed. 'So I'm going to do salmon fillets for dinner – is that okay?'

'Of course, anything you like. I wonder who the fellow was – the man who owns that flat?'

'Oh, Neil's got all sorts of friends in England,' she rejoined, thinking back on what he'd told her in the past. 'He's got connections with people everywhere, it seems – on the Internet. Mostly about trees, I think.'

'Mm-m . . .' Ronald sipped his lemon-and-lime. 'There's more money in "trees" than I thought, then, if all that decor came from growing them.'

Laura herself had wondered at the affluence displayed by the home of Neil's friend. He'd mentioned people but they were usually connected with horticulture or the orthopaedic clinic. Could a hospital consultant earn the kind of income that would fund that flat and its contents? Could the growing and cultivation of trees produce the money to buy chairs by Breuer, limited-edition Rothko prints?

Ronald went off in pursuit of the point that he really wanted to make. 'You see now, Laura, don't you – Kim was giving Neil good advice when she wanted him to take a look at the place in Simmingford. He's had time to think it over and now he sees it's a good idea.'

'Yes.'

'You're pleased, aren't you? You wanted him not to turn his back on the bequest.'

'It's really nothing to do with us, Papa. We did the research, we provided him with the possibilities. What he did with the information was none of our concern.' Nor Kim's, she said to herself. She still thought her father had been irresponsible in telling her about it. But she'd regretted her outburst of open criticism. His equilibrium was so uncertain where Kim was concerned that it was best to keep quiet.

On Tuesday Kim dropped by on her way home. 'Everything's fixed up for tomorrow. I've got Tyler to come along so as to give a few thoughts on the value of the property.'

'Tyler?'

'David Tyler, he's a partner in a firm of surveyors. I thought we'd all meet at Simmingford station, if that suits you – there's parking there for the car and—'

'Of course, of course,' Ronald hastened to say. 'Handy for us – Laura and I can come by train from Brinbank Junction—'

'That's fine because Neil's coming by train too, from London. I'll have the Volvo and Tyler will have his car, so we'll have enough transport. He and I agreed it would be best to take a look at the place and get some thoughts from Tyler, and then we can all go for a bite to eat – there's a rather good restaurant about a couple of miles out of the town so I've booked a table there.'

'Yes, fine.'

'So that's agreed, then.'

'Yes, and it's very good of you to take all this trouble.'

Kim gave him a flashing smile. 'Darling Ronald, it all goes on the bill in the end. When it comes to the balance sheet, Simmingford Council are going to pay for it.'

'Only if Neil brings a case against them,' Laura said.

'Well . . . I feel that in the air, don't you?'

Laura shook her head. 'I don't think he's after money, Kim.'

She laughed. 'We'll see, we'll see. Right then, meet you in Simmingford tomorrow – about eleven, okay?'

'That's a date,' Ronald said, basking in the sunshine of Kim's good humour.

* * *

182

July had come, with sultry weather and sudden thundery showers. Laura put on jeans and a loose cotton shirt from Gap for coolness, and stowed an umbrella in the car before setting out. Ronald was in well-pressed chinos and lightweight jacket; he'd taken the trouble to put fresh batteries in his hearing aids, which meant that he was looking forward to the day.

And so was Laura, because every chance to meet with Neil was precious now. She had the feeling that very soon he might be leaving England; there had been an impression, a sort of feeling in the air, when they parted on Saturday.

They were in good time for the train at Brinbank Junction. Outside in the Simmingford car park Kim was standing at her car talking to a burly middle-aged man in slacks and an Aquascutum rain jacket. Ronald hurried to join them, positioning himself on the other side of Kim, who was in a business suit minus its jacket, and wearing sensible but fashionable walking shoes.

She and the surveyor had a map spread out on the roof of his car. As Laura came up he was saying, '. . . the building plans of eight years ago. You can see that the base of the foundations is somewhat below the surrounding area. I'd say that long ago that hollow was perhaps a sheep fold or something of that sort, a communal safe-keeping place for stock in winter weather. Didn't matter much when it was a park – I think they ran a drain into the pond – there was a pond, I'm pretty certain. But it brought problems to the builders, I expect – the run-off for rainwater probably hasn't been dealt with too well.'

He paused as Laura stopped beside them. Kim performed speedy introductions. 'Neil's coming on the London train, it's due in about ten minutes,' she informed her, glancing at her watch. 'Mr Tyler is saying that the housing estate isn't exactly prime land.'

'I gather you're a research team,' he said, with polite nods at father and daughter. 'I expect you know a lot about what I'm telling Ms Groves.'

'No, no, we only did research on the family and documents concerning inheritance,' Ronald said, claiming credit for the work of the partnership. 'To tell the truth, I think we just stopped short once we'd identified the fact of the bequest.'

'Well, if he should ever take possession of this layout,' Tyler said, 'I'd advise him to pull the whole thing down, raise the elevation by about a metre, and invest in industrial warehousing.'

'That's not the intention at all, David,' Kim told him with a shake of her head. 'All we want is to have some idea of the problems it would pose to the council if Neil claimed it.'

'Huh! It may not be Millionaire's Row, but it's home to – let me see – four towers, each six storeys, four flats to each floor, that's close to a hundred families. They could make a tremendous row if they thought they were going to be evicted. I don't envy the man who's representing them on the town council if that ever becomes an issue. They'd make his life hell.'

Laura was only half listening. She was watching the station entrance for Neil, and now here he came, walking well, broad shoulders in a cotton pullover, nylon rain jacket over his arm, brown hair ruffled by a passing gust that brought yet another thunder cloud. There was a smile of recognition and a wave as he descried them among the parked cars.

'Hi! You look busy,' he called as he approached.

'David was just giving us some useful info about the terrain,' Kim said. 'I'll fill you in in a minute. How was your journey?'

'Oh, I loved it. I love the railroad. I'm not used to travelling in trains, you know. How are you?' he enquired, taking in the Wainwrights.

David Tyler shook hands then said at once, 'Shall we get going? I think there's going to be a thunderstorm any minute now.'

They bundled themselves into the cars. Neil took the passenger seat in Kim's before Ronald could assert any right to it, so he got in the back. Mr Tyler politely opened his passenger seat door for Laura so she had no option but to get in.

Anyway, she scolded herself, it makes no difference. Neil's entire attention is on Kim.

And it was so. As they followed Kim out of the car park she could see that Kim was talking with emphasis, and that Neil was turned towards her attentively. It was impossible to make out his expression.

'You had a lot of work finding out about this legacy of Mr Crandel's?' the surveyor queried.

'Yes, for my sins.'

'You don't think it's a good thing?'

'I thought it was a good thing to tell him what I'd found out, because I felt it would set his mind at rest about an event in the family history. I'd no idea it would lead to ... to an expedition like this.'

'An expedition! All we're doing is looking at a piece of housing property.'

'With the intention of causing trouble.'

Tyler looked faintly puzzled but shrugged. 'You can't get away from the fact that you discovered a legal document giving Mr Crandel rights in that land. The council is at fault. Their legal department didn't go far enough back or weren't diligent enough. It might well turn out they had no right to build there.'

Laura said nothing to this. Instead she look out through the windscreen at Simmingford as they drove through it. They skirted what had once been the main square, with the Town Hall's tower peeping out above the other buildings. These had been textile factories, some now converted into spaces for loft living. The square had been furbished with flower beds and pedestrian paths along the canalside, as Norman Dallancy had complained.

Next came narrow streets, once the home of household shopping – butchers, bakers, ironmongers. Some of these were still open for trade but now they were boutiques, offering candles, herbal medicine, wedding clothes. The big stores had gone to the mall, which gleamed some three hundred yards further on, on the main road leading out of the town.

After that came furniture warehouses, do-it-yourself emporiums, a business park. There were some old houses, the remains of the once-opulent homes of the wealthy factory owners, converted into flats some years ago, their gardens parking areas. Churches, a fifties housing estate, owner-occupied and pleasant enough, two or three big car showrooms.

'Tansfield Estate seems a long way out?' Laura ventured.

'A little over a mile and a half from the town centre – or I should say roughly two kilometres, which is the official version these days.'

'You'd wonder why they put family housing so far away from the town.'

185

'Well, they have problems over low-rent housing. Factories near the old town centre can be converted but it costs a lot and only people with money can afford them. It's a conundrum lots of old industrial towns have to face. Those grand old textile mills are worth preserving but it's a big investment. And, you see, as people move out looking for new work opportunities elsewhere, the town's income shrinks.'

'Yes, I see.' Economics, except in history, weren't her strong point.

Kim was signalling a turn to the left. They followed her up a minor road where, sure enough, four housing blocks stood surrounded by what might once have been lawn. By city standards the buildings hardly justified their name of Tansfield Towers, but in this out-of-town situation six storeys seemed high. There was a low cement wall, brick paths between the blocks, one or two open areas with shabby iron benches, and a road leading round to one-storey garages at the back.

A notice board topped with a shield and the name 'Tansfield' offered a cracked glass compartment for announcements. As they passed Laura glimpsed a flyer for a Buddy Holly tribute at a pub, and a more sedate notice about church services. Both were being dampened by the rain seeping through the damaged glass.

Kim drove round to the back, where the garages could be seen. There was ample space here for tradesmen's vehicles servicing the blocks, and here she parked. Tyler followed suit, first leaning over to the back seat for a big golf umbrella. This he opened protectively over Laura when they got out. Ronald had the Wainwright umbrella, which he opened over Kim. Neil unfolded his nylon raincoat, put it on, and stood looking around.

'So this is my ancestral home?'

Kim laughed. 'All yours, if you want to take it.'

'Don't they do any maintenance?' A little flick of his hand indicated their surroundings.

Graffiti was everywhere, those strange unreadable names of artists, or of gangs, or mere fame-seekers, in that strange script that seems to spring from comic book pages into gaudy colour on walls throughout the Western world. Weeds flourished in the cracks of the brick paving. Some of the roll-down doors of the garages were stuck askew. Sodden plastic bags lay about, blue and green and with supermarket names half visible.

'Looks bad because of the rain,' Tyler suggested. He moved away on a tour of the perimeter. They followed. He elected himself as conductor of the survey. 'My understanding is that about nine years ago they intended to have six towers. Then they had to alter the plans for financial reasons, so they used part of the area for garages. Not every resident owns a car but those that do pay an extra charge for garaging.'

'Not every family owns a car? How do they get about?' Neil enquired. 'I mean . . . if I remember rightly, we didn't pass much in the way of shops or facilities. Is there a shopping strip further on?'

'No, if you drive on westwards on the main road you come to an industrial park and then there's nursery gardens – glasshouses, that sort of thing.'

'So where do the residents get their bread and milk and stuff like that?'

'Milk's still delivered, I believe. There may be a bread van too. As to the rest, I think they'd have to go to Chespinhall – where there's that big red-brick church on a corner, did you notice it? There's a decent row of shops up that road, a mini-market, that sort of thing.'

'But if they don't have a car?'

'They go by bus, I suppose.'

Neil was shaking his head in wonderment. 'What about schools?'

'I'm not au fait with that, Mr Crandel. Did you do any background work, Kim?'

She shook her head. 'It didn't strike me as necessary. We're only here to let you see what old Mr Dallancy bequeathed to you, Neil, not work out how the citizens live.'

'I guess so.' He fell silent.

The rain became heavier. It dripped off the edges of their umbrellas.

'Let's walk all round, just to get a final impression. Then I think we should head for lunch,' Kim suggested.

She strolled away. They followed. It was noticeable that big puddles were forming not only on the neglected lawn but at every dip in the brick paving. Drains had pools around their

187

gratings. Laura said to Tyler, 'You were right about the rain-water.'

'They should have put in better footings.'

'Does it mean there's a damp problem with the buildings?'

'Only the ground floors, I expect. I bet cars in the garages develop a rust problem, though.'

Their final inspection did nothing to raise Laura's spirits. She would have been interested to hear what Neil thought, but he was listening to Kim as they made their slow way round the estate.

As they reached their cars Laura heard the thud of a football against stone and a lad appeared, rain-hood up against the shower and trainers aiming a ball in a low curve at the garage walls. His attention was on his footwork but he paused as he became aware of them.

'Nice car,' he remarked as he surveyed Kim's Volvo.

'You live here?' asked Neil.

'What if I do?'

'You like it?'

'What?' A startled expression on the chubby face. No one had ever asked that before, clearly.

'Living here – is it nice?'

'Oh, marvy. Central Park Avenue, this is.' Quick witted, he'd caught Neil's accent. Here was someone from across the Atlantic, where everything was 'marvy'. He flicked the football up with a little kick, tucked it under his arm to get a look into the Volvo. 'You got a nice CD player. Good sound?'

'Whereabouts in the block do you live?' Neil persisted.

'What's it to you?' Now he was wary.

'I'm just interested.'

'If you're interested cos you're thinking of buying anything, I'll give you some free advice. You wouldn't like it. Charlie Aimes bought *his* flat from the council, allowed to cos he lived there permanent, an' he does nothin' but moan. Lift doesn't work, window frames are corroded, his neighbour's stereo drives 'im up the wall cos the soundproof is rubbish. He's put it up for sale, but he gets no takers.' He bounced his football once or twice, as if to emphasize his point.

'And is your apartment like that too?'

'Apartment, eh? Our *apartment*'s on the top floor an' my mum's sick and tired of luggin' the shopping up all them stairs. Other than that, chum, it's heaven.'

'You go to school?'

He was quite offended at this slur on his seniority. 'Nah, left last year. Why? Goin' to offer me a job?'

'Sorry, no can do. I just wondered, where is the school?'

The boy jerked his head towards the main road by which they'd come. 'Woodley Comprehensive. Eton and Harrow, eat your heart out.'

'Is it far?'

'Half an hour's walk. Less on a bike. Why? You got kids? Send 'em somewhere else.' He was determined to hold his own against any interfering stranger.

'How long on the bus?'

'What bus? You're a stranger around here, pardner,' he said in scorn. 'No buses unless you walk to Chespinhall Road. But *you* don't need to worry, you got your Volvo an' all.' Tired of standing in the rain, he gave them a shrug of farewell and trotted away, his football inches ahead of his trainer as he guided it through the puddles.

'Not a favourable report,' Mr Tyler observed.

'But we're not thinking of living here, David.'

'No, that's true.'

'I'd like you to give me an idea – just an educated guess – at what the value of this place would be to Simmingford Council.'

'Well now, Kim . . . I'd like a minute to think about that . . .'

'Okay, lunch-time,' she ordered, and the cars chirped acknowledgement as their doors were unlocked. They piled in, and minutes later they were driving on to the main road and on out towards the industrial estate and the nursery gardens and then what appeared to be an arts and crafts centre, Kim acting as guide.

Mr Tyler kept up a friendly conversation with his passenger about her work as a researcher. He himself sometimes had to do research on land and buildings, so he compared methods and discussed websites. Soon they were entering the gates of a country mansion whose old blond sandstone façade was glittering now in sunshine. The thunderstorm was over. Laura remarked to herself that Tansfield Towers would have looked better in sunshine – though perhaps not much.

The mansion had been converted into a handsome restaurant. There were already several customers enjoying a first course in what had once been the ballroom. Kim's party was expected; they were shown to a table in a bay with long sash windows giving a view of a knot garden.

Drinks were ordered, menus were supplied, a period of study followed while they tried to decide if they really wanted any of the substantial dishes offered by a restaurant specializing in British food made with local ingredients. When they had ordered, they had drinks to sip, and the gathering relaxed.

Kim had clearly decided to abide by the old custom of saving business until the end of the meal. She and David Tyler, with some help from Ronald, maintained a conversation about generalities until they reached the pudding course. Laura played her part yet felt somehow on the outskirts of it all. Tansfield Towers had depressed her. She even felt rather sorry she'd ever unearthed the bequest because all it had done was cause trouble. Poor Neil, badgered into viewing the place. The intention of old Mr Dallancy had been to leave something to his wayward daughter as a comfort, as a message of forgiveness. Now it was an unlovely, rather miserable setting for people who would probably rather live somewhere else.

'Well, now, David, what about your assessment of value?' Kim said as coffee was poured into her cup.

David Tyler's broad face broke into a tentative smile. 'It's a teaser, isn't it? If the estate were offered for sale no one would want it as a going concern. It needs too much doing to it.'

'Why don't the council do the work?' Neil enquired, with a little shake of the head that seemed to denote bewilderment. 'It can't be to their advantage to let the place get run down like that.'

'Local councils are all in trouble, Mr Crandel. You're not au fait with British politics, I imagine, but central government has powers to restrict the spending of local councils, so money is tight. The first thing to suffer is usually parks and public grounds – little decorative touches such as flower beds at traffic roundabouts, upkeep of pavements, that sort of thing. Then when things get tighter they have to lower standards on housing estate maintenance – and so on and so on. Tansfield, being a bit out of the town, probably fares badly. Out of sight, out of mind.'

'Nobody's envisaging putting the place up for sale to the average property buyer, David. We all saw that it would need a lot of work to generate income from renting the flats. But look at it from the point of view of development. To someone who thought of pulling it down and building afresh on that site – what do you think?'

'You mean, for instance, as an industrial site? Business park? Even a big storage facility – that sort of thing?'

Kim shrugged. 'Just make a big guess at the price in a no-strings-attached sale.'

'We-ell . . . It's something like four hectares in area. There's pros and cons . . . access would have to be improved . . . you'd have to take the drainage problem into consideration . . . but it's really not far out of a town with rail links . . . Someone might want to build high-value apartments . . .' He took a breath and ended, 'I'd say four-and-a-half. Perhaps five.'

Ronald looked from Tyler to Kim Groves. 'Five what?' he ventured. 'Not thousands?'

'Millions, of course.'

No one spoke. Kim was smiling rather proudly; Ronald Wainwright was looking dazed; David Tyler was eyeing them all with satisfaction at his thunderbolt.

'Pounds,' he added after a moment, in case Neil were thinking in terms of Canadian dollars.

'That's the sort of money it's worth,' commented Kim. 'So if we approached the town council and told them it belonged to Neil Crandel, they'd be worried.'

'I'd imagine so.'

'So we could offer them an out-of-court settlement for . . . let me see . . .' She gave it some thought. 'Three million, perhaps.'

Laura was listening to it all in disbelief. That shabby set of buildings on a boggy piece of land was worth three million? Now she understood why Kim had been so eager to carry the matter forward. The litigation involved would bring enormous fees to the law firm and make the name of the solicitor who handled it. It was bound to attract great public attention.

'Three million for that deplorable excuse for a place to live?' Neil asked.

'I think so, Mr Crandel.'

'You see, Neil?' urged Kim. 'You can't turn your back on money like that.'

He frowned and there was a silence. Everyone was gazing at him in expectation.

After staring at the tablecloth for a moment or two he looked up and nodded. 'Right. *Do it!* Tell 'em we're going to take them for every cent they own.'

Seventeen

On the train to Brinbank Junction, the Wainwrights were not talkative. Laura was too distressed for conversation.

The luncheon party had broken up quickly. Kim wanted to whisk Neil away to her office for a discussion on how to attack the town council. Laura had moved off and was waiting by Mr Tyler's car when it came to leave-taking. Neil said a word to Kim then appeared to be heading Laura's way, but rather than speak to him she got into the back seat of the car. In the fuss of closing the door and buckling up, she managed to avoid any contact. Her father, in front for the lift to Simmingford station, had an approving chat about Kim most of the way there, in which Laura didn't join.

The day's events had put an end to the last of her hopeful dreams about Neil. She'd tried to give him the benefit of every doubt but today had proved him to be nothing but a money-grabber after all.

It seemed that, in order to force every penny out of the council, he was willing to put the inhabitants of Tansfield Towers through months of misery. They'd be afraid they were going to be turned out of their homes. Much though the buildings lacked, they were at least affordable shelter guaranteed until now by the town's housing department. Who could tell what provision could be made for them if Tansfield changed hands?

As the train clacked its way towards the Junction, she knew that her father was silent for different reasons. He was in a state of secret delight at the thought of seeing quite a lot of Kim in the next few days. She would want to consult them over the historical evidence on which Neil's claim was based – and Roland would put himself forward as the expert on that. She saw him smile and nod to himself now and again as he pictured these meetings – himself for once on an almost equal footing with Kim, the authority on family research and the authenticity of the documents.

As for Laura, she was determined not to take part if it could be avoided. She did in fact believe that Neil had a lawful claim to the land, but she couldn't approve of what was going to happen. She might have been more or less indifferent if it was someone else making the demand, a client with whom she'd had very little contact. But having got to know Neil – or believing she had – her sense of disappointment was like a thorn in her heart.

When they reached home it was late afternoon. Ronald leaped out of the Land Rover as they drew up. Over his shoulder he said, 'If you're going to make tea, bring me up a cup. I wanted to get started on printing out the documentation.'

She was going to say, 'But I haven't collated the evidence yet,' but he was unlocking the front door. All at once she was loath to be in the house with him. He'd be 'busy', keen to do everything he could to help Kim. She found she couldn't bear to have him praising what she thought was a totally wrong enterprise.

She stayed in the Land Rover. He turned in surprise as she failed to follow him. 'Aren't you coming?'

'We need to fill up with petrol,' she said. Which was quite true, but not urgent.

'Oh. Okay then. What about tea?'

She waved then drove round the turning circle and left the drive. Let him for once make his own tea, find the teabags in the old Victorian tin on its familiar shelf, look for biscuits or scones in containers that ought to be familiar to him. Let him mange for himself. Let the whole household grind to a standstill. What did she care?

An hour later she was sitting in the car in a parking area

alongside the River Brin, watching the rain cascade down the windscreen. The brown water of the stream was dappled by raindrops, the leaves dripped and shook in the rough west wind. Blow, winds, and crack your cheeks, she quoted to herself with irony. Ye cataracts and hurricanoes, spout! The pathetic fallacy, that Nature sympathized with your mood.

She began trying to make a plan for her future. First of all, she must forget about Neil. He'd never been a stable figure in her future, because he was always due to return to his homeland.

In a happier situation she might have dreamed of going with him, but that had never really been on the cards. Though for this afternoon she'd abandoned her father, she could never leave him. That was totally out of the question. His mental well-being depended on a steady, durable environment. He'd been thrown off balance by the desertion of her mother, a fact which made it impossible for Laura to desert him too, even for a new life with Neil.

She had faced the fact that Neil had never suggested any kind of permanent commitment. She'd never really had any hopes for their relationship beyond the period of his stay in England. But now she had to face the fact that he was a man she couldn't have lived with even had he wanted to. She'd mistaken him entirely. It was her own fault.

What a fool. And while she was accepting that, she might as well admit that she was wrong to be so critical of Kim Groves. She was resentful of her success, of her independence. She was envious of her good looks, of her sense of style, of her capability. She scolded herself: Grow up, stop disliking her because she's cleverer and prettier than you.

Very good advice. And she was going to try to take it, along with other homilies from her conscience. She was going to be more tolerant of her father's moods. She was going to make a long-term plan for Lauron Family Research so that they might be able to take on another researcher, and thus have more free time. She was even going to try out an idea she'd had for new software, which might be marketable and bring in extra income.

Her father was very cross indeed when she got home. 'Where have you been? It's getting quite late and you haven't even begun on the preparations for dinner! And there've been a couple of phone calls who I think were clients but I couldn't make out a word they were saying. It's too bad of you!'

She apologized then apologized again. By and by he was settled down in his armchair with a drink, ready to watch one of the twenty-four-hour news channels. She put on an apron and set about the making of the evening meal, reflecting that it would be less luscious than their lunch.

But she wasn't going to think about the lunch. She had resigned herself to the fact that she wouldn't be seeing Neil again. Or, as she tried to see it, she'd decided to rule him out of her life.

On Friday morning, while she was filling the kettle for breakfast coffee, she heard the phone ring in the living room. It was very early for telephone calls. She hurried to answer, and was astonished to hear Mrs Stevens on the other end.

'Miss Wainwright, dear, I thought you ought to know – what d'you think? It's all in the *Comet* this morning! Our Mr Crandel and all that about inheriting that place in Simmingford – it's on the front page!'

She'd half expected it but all the same she was struck dumb.

'Miss Wainwright, are you there? What do you think?'

'I . . . I haven't seen the *Comet* . . .' She hadn't yet been to the front door to see if their newspaper was there. In any case, it wasn't the *Comet*.

'What it says is, it says Mr Crandel has informed the town council of Simmingford that the land where this housing estate was built is legally his, and it says he wants it back. Wants it back! They're saying in the *Comet* that you'd expect a grabby property developer to go about things in that sort of sneaky way and not face up to the tenants. What d'you think of *that*!'

'Mr Crandel isn't a property developer.'

'And it says our Mr Crandel found out about his inheritance through the work of a family research partnership, and that's you, now isn't it, Miss Wainwright, dear!'

This was a statement, not a question, and there was no sense in trying to deny it. So Laura contented herself with saying, 'I'll just go and see if our paper's arrived yet, Mrs Stevens. Thanks for calling.'

She found it sticking through the letter box, as usual. When

195

she opened it she didn't find the item on the front page, but the table of contents listed 'Ownership problem for Simmingford Council, page 6', so she turned to that. And found the news.

'Solicitors Merks & Trehallis of Oxford have entered a claim with Simmingford Town Council regarding the owner-ship of a plot of land on which a housing estate was built by them some years ago. The claimant, Mr Neil Crandel, bases his case on the discovery of a will made some one hundred and twenty years ago leaving the acreage to Marianne Dallancy, of a family at that time very prominent in the area. Ms Kim Groves of Merks & Trehallis states on behalf of Mr Crandel that Marianne Crandel nee Dallancy was his ancestress, and that the right of ownership therefore descends to him.

'A spokesman for Simmingford Town Council says that they have not as yet had time to study the documents. They deny any wrongful assumption of title on their part.'

Reading this, Laura guessed that some PR official had been approached after the council offices had closed yesterday, and that after hasty consultation with one or two councillors could only come up with a holding statement. Today would be the day when the housing department called in their solicitors and got to grips with the problem.

She thought this was a clever ploy on the part of Kim Groves. It caught the council wrong-footed, it stole a march on them by getting the news into the papers before they could put up any rebuttal, and it mentioned by name the solicitor handling Neil's case.

And no, this wasn't envy speaking. She could see that from the point of view of the coming conflict Kim had done well for her troops even if she herself had also done well out of it.

She went back to her breakfast preparations. Her father came down in good time, meaning that he was still feeling pleased with life. He'd been to see Kim in Oxford on the previous day, taking with him printouts of everything from their investigations that might be relevant. She hadn't ques-tioned him about it, and when he'd described the meeting he'd talked mainly about how clever Kim was, how efficient, how greatly respected by her colleagues in the firm.

No doubt Merks & Trehallis were delighted with her. This would be a high-profile case. Laura knew very little about the legal profession but she imagined they were as glad as any business to be in the public eye and thereby gain new clients. Kim had always been their specialist in land law. Now she was going to earn them golden gains with this unusual story.

Laura left the newspaper by her father's plate while she got on with the toast. She heard him exclaim, and turned to see him reading the page with the news of the Dallancy bequest.

'Ah, so she went straight ahead. Well done!'

Laura poured coffee for him. 'Mrs Stevens says it's on the front page of the *Comet*.'

He looked up at her, frowning a little. He disapproved of tabloid newspapers. He decided to let that go. 'She must have messengered the documents to them after I left. She and her assistant were working out the wording when I came away. I thought it would take longer to put it together but she really is an amazingly capable lawyer.'

'Yes indeed.'

Now he nerved himself to approach the subject of the item in the *Comet*. 'What did Mrs Stevens say?'

'As far as I recall, she said Neil was a grabby property developer.'

'What?'

'Well, you know, a paper like the *Comet* isn't going to look at this in a friendly way, Papa.'

'It's typical,' he snorted. 'They don't know a thing about him, yet after one interview they're calling him names.'

She was shaking her head as she took her place at the table. 'I doubt they've interviewed him at all, Papa. I can't quite remember what Mrs Stevens said but I got the impression that the *Comet* hadn't been able to reach Neil. I think he's still incommunicado.'

'Oh. Well, that's good.'

Why was it good? But she didn't ask it aloud. Could it be that he was perhaps ashamed of what he was doing? But no. He'd put on the cloak of invisibility *before* he decided to claim the property.

After clearing up the breakfast things she went up to the office. Her father had chosen to go out for one of his long rambles. She was deep in a search program when she heard someone knocking on the front door. As she hurried to answer she was half afraid it would be someone from the press, but it was someone even more unwelcome.

On the doorstep was Norman Dallancy, with his daughter, Shelley.

He brandished a copy of the *Comet* at Laura.

'Right then, what's all this?' he barked. '*I'm* not to speak to them but *she* can shoot her mouth off, and she's saying he's inherited something and he's only somebody from nowhere with a different name and *I'm* a Dallancy!'

He was thrusting himself forward as he delivered this tirade so that at the end he was in the hall. His daughter put a hand on his arm. 'Cool it, Dad,' she begged. To Laura she said, 'He's been in a tizz ever since he saw it.'

'In a tizz, am I? We don't know where he is, that solicitor woman won't speak to me, and all this property they're talking about, *he*'s to get it, and where do I come in?'

'Mr Dallancy—'

'And what's more, you should have told me there was money involved! Just meeting his relations, that was his story, but all you were doing was sounding us out to see if we knew there was this Tansfield place—'

'Mr Dallancy, please! Calm down! We can't discuss this if you keep shouting at me—'

'Shouting at you! I'll do more than shout! I'll have the law on you – this Crandel bloke isn't the only one that can hire solicitors, I'll have you all in court for trying to defraud me—'

'Dad, will you *shut up!*' cried Shelley, hitting him forcefully on the arm with her fist. This had the effect of startling him into silence, so that she could turn to say to Laura, 'He's been like this all morning. On the phone trying to get that Ms Groves and ringing the newspapers and getting nowhere. I'm sorry about all this. I've tried to explain to him that it's summer – the silly season – the papers haven't got anything else to make a fuss about—'

'Make a fuss! Who's got more right than me!'

Shelly rolled her eyes heavenwards.

'I came with him to try to calm him down but seems I'm not doing too good.'

'Come in,' Laura said, seizing the chance to normalize events. 'Let's sit down and have a chat.'

Norman was surprised into assent. They went into the living room, where she got them both seated in armchairs. Armchairs were a calming influence, she always felt. It was difficult to wave your arms about in a deep armchair.

'Well, I've a right to be upset,' grunted Norman. 'You've played a trick on me.'

'That's not so, Mr Dallancy. I'm as surprised as you are at how things are going.'

'Huh!' But the reply intrigued him all the same. It gave him pause.

'I've been trying to tell him,' said Shelley. 'You can't rely on what's in the *Comet*. That Mr Crandel seemed too nice to be playing a trick like this on us.'

The sound of Ronald coming downstairs attracted their attention. Laura gave a sigh of relief. Her father had heard the uproar and was coming to investigate. She hoped fervently that he'd paused to put in his hearing aids. She needed an ally.

'Good heavens,' he said as he came in. 'Fancy seeing you, Mr Dallancy. And Shelley too. How nice to meet you again.'

Norman Dallancy was too astonished to respond. He'd come for a fight and it was turning into a social call. Shelley said, 'Nice to see you too, Mr Wainwright. Dad here is on a bit of a rampage about this Tansfield Towers thing. We don't quite get the hang of what's happening.'

Roland was finding himself a seat. He paused to say, 'I suppose it *is* a bit complicated. I say, Laura, how about making us all a cup of coffee so we can be comfortable while we discuss it?'

She was quite glad of the chance to escape. In the kitchen she leaned for a moment against a worktop, getting her breath back. For perhaps the first time in her life she wished Kim were here. Kim would know how to quell this angry man.

Taking the coffee into the living room some ten minutes later, she was in time to hear Norman declare, 'But it's Dallancy property! He's not even a Dallancy!'

Her father shook his head. 'The will doesn't specify the legatee has to have the Dallancy name. It simply states that the descendants of Marianne Dallancy are to inherit.'

'Well, she was a Dallancy. *I'm* a Dallancy—'

'But *you're* descended from the brother of George Etian Dallancy. You're not in the direct line of inheritance.'

'That can't be right! How can it be right that a man who's only just turned up from abroad can claim the property, whereas me, I've been here in this country all my life, playing my part, paying my taxes, and I get nothing?'

Laura offered the coffee. 'Cream? Sugar?' On accepting her cup Shelley raised her eyebrows at her and sighed. It was clear she understood what her father was refusing to acknowledge – that he was completely mistaken.

Ronald said, 'Ms Groves could explain this better than I can—'

'Well, there you have it, she won't talk to me! Her switchboard is either engaged or it keeps telling me she's in a meeting—'

'That's probably true, Dad. I mean, it's in the *Comet*, so you can bet it's in all the other papers too, and they're probably all screaming at her trying to find out more about it, cos it's a human interest story, isn't it?'

'It's time somebody showed some interest in *me*! I've got something to say, haven't I? But that Groves woman choked me off when I tried to tell the press about my argument with the council and now this about the housing estate seems to be taking up everybody's attention, so where do I come in?'

There was a silence. The only answer was 'nowhere' but no one wanted to say it.

'My father has been working with Ms Groves over the documentation,' Laura remarked. 'Perhaps he could ask her to see you and explain the legal position more clearly.'

Norman Dallancy's attention was caught. He looked at Ronald. 'Could you do that? Get her to see me?'

Delighted to be thought of as influential with his idol, Ronald glowed. 'I'll speak to her about it,' he said. 'But you have to understand, Norman, this is an extremely busy time for her. She's just starting this case against the Simmingford Council—'

'I can help her with that!' cried Norman eagerly. 'I can give her chapter and verse about the way they treated me! I tell you, she ought to listen to me, I could say a lot that would put the council right in the soup!'

Her father was about to explain that Kim would have no interest in Norman's complaint but a shake of the head from Laura gave him pause. After a second's thought he said, 'I'll see what I can do, Norman. It may take a day or so.'

'We-ell . . .'

'Drink your coffee before it gets cold,' Laura urged. 'Biscuit? They're home-made.'

He picked up the mug she'd left for him on a table by the armchair. He sipped. 'People take advantage of you,' he grumbled. 'Think you're not worth bothering with if you can't afford big lawyers and all that. If Neil Crandel had explained all about the inheritance to me I could p'raps have lent a hand with it. After all, we're cousins.'

'Neil knew nothing about the inheritance until later, Mr Dallancy,' Laura said.

'And as a matter of fact,' Ronald picked up, 'we're not sure his right to the property can be justified. In law, that is.'

Norman frowned. 'What d'you mean by that? He rang me up and explained he was a Dallancy and we met and he told me all about it. How can they stop him from getting what's his by rights?'

It was all Laura could do not to scream at her father. Why on earth had he brought up the subject of doubt? They had just pacified this unreasonable, self-centred man, and now he might set off on yet another diatribe.

Shelley Dallancy sensed the danger. She said, 'Oh, Lord, Dad, let's save all that for the lawyer lady. I've had enough grand opera for one day.'

'I think that's wise,' agreed Laura. 'My father and I aren't legal people, our business is research. Kim Groves will be able to make it all clear.' And I wish her luck in the doing of it, she added mentally. To Norman she said, 'You've taken time off from the shop, then?'

'Eileen's looking after it. Not much doing after the morning rush, such as it is. Shell and I will be back in time for the evening papers.'

'You're helping in the shop?'

'Just temporary,' said Shelley. 'Got the push from my latest career – an accessories boutique it was. Er . . . Tell me . . . How's Neil getting along in all this hoo-ha?'

Laura shrugged. 'We're not in touch now. Our part in the affair is over, you see.'

'Yes, Ms Groves is handling everything,' her father put in. 'She's a neighbour of ours, you know.'

'You recommended her to Neil, then? According to the *Comet*, she's a bit of a babe.'

'A what?'

'Sexy. Got the goods.'

'Oh . . . well . . . She is very good looking. But clever too, you know,' boasted Ronald. 'Oh yes, Neil's in good hands, excellent hands.'

'So what's his phone number? Be nice to catch up with him,' said Shelley rather wistfully.

'I'm afraid we don't have that.'

'Don't have his phone number. Can't get through to Groves. Is this how to do business?' Norman demanded. 'I'm fed up with it, and that's a fact. I've a good mind to go to that solicitor firm and park on the doorstep until she sees me.'

'No, don't do that,' Ronald said hastily.

'It's all right for you to say that, because you're in cahoots with her. Look here, ring her up now and tell her I want to be included in the bargaining. You probably got her private phone number and all that.'

'I've got her mobile, but she's switched off. I know because I tried her earlier. And you say the office switchboard is jammed—'

'Well, you got anything else? What about the home number? Can you ring there?'

'It would only be the machine at the moment—'

'Right then, ring and leave a message. Tell her I'm part of the fight against Simmingford Council and I want to see her.' And, as Ronald hesitated, 'Go on, it's not a problem, is it?'

'Er . . . No . . . I . . . Very well then, I'll do that.' He went to the fixed-line phone in the living room and pressed buttons. After a pause that signified the answering machine, he said, 'Kim, this is Ronald. Mr Dallancy is here and wants me to say he urgently needs to speak to you about the Dallancy bequest. Will you please ring him? His number is in the Simmingford phone book.'

As he hung up, he looked for approval to Norman. 'Humph,' said Norman. 'That's not how I'd have put it.'

'Dad, not everybody goes at things like a bull in a china shop,' his daughter soothed. 'Come on now, we've done what we came for so let's push off home.'

Laura felt obliged to offer lunch if they cared to stay, but she shook her head. 'Nah, Mum doesn't like being alone in the shop. She's always scared she'll get a customer she can't handle. Thanks all the same. Come on, Dad.'

She urged him into the hall. He went more or less willingly. At the door Shelley lingered a moment while he went to unlock the car. 'Thanks for everything,' she said. 'I know Dad's a bit of a roughneck so it was good of you to put up with all that. And . . . just one more thing . . . if you hear from Neil would you say I'm rooting for him?'

'Of course.'

Laura's father was looking out of the window when she returned to the living room. When he was sure Norman was driving out of the gate he went at once to the telephone. Laura, about to collect up coffee mugs, paused in curiosity.

'Kim, this is Ronald again. I couldn't speak freely before, because Dallancy was more or less standing over me. He's in a very aggressive mood so be careful about agreeing to see him.'

Laura shook her head at him. He defended himself. 'Well, I had to let her know he's a bit of a menace.'

'I agree he's a problem.'

'The whole family's a problem. The mother's a dimwit, the father's a boor, and the daughter's an airhead.'

'Papa!'

'You must see she's got as much intelligence as a cupcake.'

'Oh, I don't know . . . Under all that spiky hair and make-up there might be a nice kid.'

Ronald decided not to pay any heed to that. He went upstairs to carry on with some work. Laura washed up the mugs and put them away. Despite protesting at her father's verdict, she could agree that Norman might become an obstacle to a sensible negotiation. He was so determined to be included, partly because of his long-standing rancour against the council, but partly because he hoped to make some cash out of being part of the family.

In her opinion it would be best if Kim would see him, and somehow bring him on side without promising him too much. It was surely better to have him as an ally than as a discontented meddler.

Kim's view was different. She arrived just after they were

finishing their evening meal. She came stalking in from the hall as Laura was clearing the table.

'Look here, Ronald,' she began, 'what have you been saying to that blockhead about the proceedings? You didn't tell him I'd see him, did you?'

He got up hastily from his chair. 'You got my message? I thought I explained that he forced me to—'

'I know what you said, I called up my messages from the office before I left for home. I came straight here to sort it out in person. I want it clearly understood that I can't have that stupid lout interfering in the negotiations. There's a lot of money involved here, you know, a *lot* of money!'

'Yes, but—'

'I'm not seeing him. Is that clearly understood? He keeps leaving ridiculous threats with the switchboard that make me think he hasn't got all his marbles! He's got to get it through his head that he has no business barging in where he's not wanted. This is a dicey affair; we have to keep the public on our side and if he starts bad-mouthing the Simmingford officials it'll give the press something to snipe at us with.'

'But why should they snipe? I thought they were all taking a sort of romantic view of the "lost heir"—'

'Just give them an inch and they'll take a mile. The *Comet* will dash to the aid of the poor little tenants who might be evicted—'

'But, Kim, eviction's not part of the plan, is it?'

'No, of course not, it's a bargaining point, that's all. But we can't unveil that until we get to stage two, when I offer the council a chance to settle out of court. Until then, I need to keep the media on our side. And dear Norman is likely to put them right off.'

'Kim,' ventured Laura, 'Norman's not very bright, I agree, but don't you think it would be better to make a friend of him?'

'What, offer him a share of the proceeds? If that's what he's after, he's chasing rainbows.'

'I meant, just treat him with—'

'Don't say respect! I haven't time to bother with crazy fools who think they can elbow into someone else's lawsuit with something totally extraneous. You don't understand legal argument, Laura. To use a very old metaphor, you can't chase two hares at once. Norman Dallancy is a secondary hare, and a mad one at that.'

'But he could go to the press whether you befriend him or not, couldn't he?'

'Not him. He's tried and got the brush off, now hasn't he?'

'I don't know that he has. You stopped him with the threat of an injunction last time.'

'Oh, don't be so simple minded, Laura! At the press conference this morning somebody – I think it was from the *Comet* – mentioned him and I explained him away in two sentences. He's a nobody – the reporters understand that.'

'But he's a nobody who happens to be a Dallancy.'

'Now, Laura, you're just being annoying,' her father reproved. 'Kim knows what she's doing. And, anyway, we're keeping her from getting home and winding down after a hectic day. I bet you're worn out, aren't you, Kim?'

Kim agreed it had been very frenzied. 'Newsmen are so persistent,' she sighed. 'And those television cameras are so intrusive. And I had to keep going over and over the same ground. And of course they were *desperate* to get Neil's address out of me.' She nodded in appreciation. 'You know, at first I thought his absence would be a tremendous drawback but of course it all adds to the drama of the thing. "Mystery heir" – they love that.'

'So there will be more about the case in the news?'

'Of course. The more the merrier.'

'You welcome all this brouhaha?' Laura asked in disbelief.

'It puts pressure on the council. One thing town councillors hate is being in the limelight unless it's for something that will win votes, like opening a fête.'

She stifled a yawn, stretched, then got up to leave. As usual, Ronald saw her out to her car. Laura went back to clearing the table. When at length they settled down in the living room her father eagerly went through the television channels trying to get something about Kim. Somewhere around eight he found her on a news summary between programmes.

She was leaning against the jamb of the heavy outer door of the Oxford offices. Mid-morning sunlight lit up the dark gleam of her hair and the tint of her olive skin. Part of a prepared statement was read out but the shot was then changed to a question and answer session.

'He won't come forward to face his critics?'

'I am empowered to speak for him—'

'But why is he staying out of sight? Is he afraid of—'

'My client has nothing to be afraid of,' she cut in crisply. 'He has an excellent case and he will pursue it until he gains possession of what is rightfully his.'

The clip ended there. Ronald said, 'Isn't she marvellous? So dedicated! And of course it's brave of her to face such a mob of questioners—'

Laura enquired, 'Why does she have to face them? I'd have thought it was easier all round if she just sent them all an email.'

'But you heard what she said – it puts pressure on the council if there's publicity, and you must admit, my dear, the best publicity is TV.'

There was no denying it. She left her father still making the rounds of the news programmes and went upstairs to get on with some correspondence.

Next day she went out to do the household shopping. When she got back the light was blinking on the office answering machine. She switched it on, expecting it to be one of Lauron's clients.

Instead she heard Neil's voice. 'Sorry not to reach you, Laura. I'll ring again some time. Bye.'

She stood there staring out of her office window at the tree-tops. Despite her good resolutions, the view of the trees dissolved into a misty blur as her eyes filled with tears.

Eighteen

During the next few days the news media kept up their interest in the Dallancy story. Laura drove into Brinbank Junction to buy the newspapers at the railway kiosk. The tabloids were divided in their reactions. Those with a more liberal outlook expressed disgust at the money-grabbing attitude of this mysterious claimant. Those who took a serious view of tradition maintained that a will was a will and if the property had been left to Neil Crandel, then Neil Crandel must be awarded ownership. Those who were somewhere in between began to raise questions: was the claim valid? Had he proved he had a right to Tansfield Towers? Television and radio gave the item only peripheral importance in news reports, though talk-show hosts asked their audience about the case.

The Wainwrights received an official telephone call from the firm of Merks & Trehallis. 'This is Ms Groves's secretary. She is arranging an interview with Mr Norman Dallancy for August fourth; that's next Wednesday. May I ask if it would be convenient for you and your father to attend the meeting?'

Laura was so astonished that she couldn't answer. Her father, from the other side of the office, raised his eyebrows at her. She covered the receiver with her palm. 'It's Kim's secretary. She wants us to go to a meeting with Norman.'

'What?'

'Are you there?' the secretary was asking in Laura's ear.

'One moment. We're having a discussion.'

'I understand.'

'Kim is seeing Norman?' Ronald asked.

'This woman's saying it's being arranged.'

'But why?' he wondered.

'No idea.' Into the phone she said, 'Why is Ms Groves meeting with Mr Dallancy?'

'I'm afraid that's not within my knowledge, Ms Wainwright. I could ask Ms Groves to call you later with that information but for the moment I need to establish that you can be present on the fourth. Am I to tell Ms Groves that you agree?'

'Do we agree to go?' Laura asked her father.

'Oh Lord. Do we have to?'

'No, it's Kim's game. I've no idea why she's inviting us there.'

Ronald had got his wits back. 'It's because she thinks he's a bit of a handful. I suppose she thinks that if we're there we can act as a calming influence because he knows us.'

'Safety in numbers, you mean.'

'Something like that. Besides, my dear, you have a way with people, you always have had.'

'Look here, Papa, I don't know what Kim's up to with this ploy. I don't mind acting as a peacemaker if this is something that will help poor Norman, but—'

'Poor Norman? The man's a menace!'

'But he's so unhappy—'

'Unhappy? The way he goes on, he deserves to be unhappy! And, besides, what business is it of ours?'

'So you don't want to go to this appointment?'

'I didn't say that. I don't care if Norman Dallancy's heart is broken, but for Kim's sake I think we should go.'

'May I say that the engagement is agreed?' the secretary enquired with conspicuous patience.

'Yes, it seems that we'll be able to attend. What time and place?'

'Oh, here at the office, of course. You know the address? 23 Lamb's Lane, Oxford. The time is three p.m., and that's the fourth August, next Wednesday. Do you know Oxford?'

'Yes, I do.'

'Then you know the park-and-ride facility is best if you're coming by car. If you come by train, I should take a taxi because Lamb's Lane is rather difficult to find.'

'Thank you. Will you ask Ms Groves to let us know in advance what the meeting is about?'

'I'll pass on your request. Thank you, Ms Wainwright.'

The weekend came and Kim hadn't contacted them. Laura's father volunteered to go to Yalcote on Saturday afternoon, but didn't return until nearly seven in the evening.

'She was getting ready for one of her important dinner parties,' he explained. 'You know, she really knows how to do things in style. She was having a big canvas awning put up over her patio and the dinner table's been taken out there – al fresco without the danger of getting wet if it rains.' He smiled a happy, admiring smile.

'And what about Wednesday?'

'Oh yes, she apologized for not getting in touch personally but she's been up to her eyes in work and then of course this party—'

'Papa, what did she say about Norman?'

'Yes, of course, Norman ... Er ... We only had a quick word while we were helping to move the chairs ... Kim says she wants to put him in the picture and let him play a part in the proceedings—'

'You're joking!'

'No, that's what she ... I think that's what she said. She wants to let him play a part so he'll be happy and won't keep interfering. She'd keep his role pretty limited but he'd feel he was getting something out of it.'

Laura was amazed, yet relieved. She had thought some confrontation had been planned, something that was quite likely to drive poor Norman into a frenzy. But this seemed sensible and almost kind-hearted. Once again she reproved herself for always thinking the worst of Kim Groves.

Nevertheless, on Sunday, having had time to think it over, she rang the Dallancy household. It was mid-morning, and it was Shelley who answered.

'Oh, good morning, Miss Wainwright. Nice to hear you.'

'Thank you, Shelley. Could I speak to your father?'

'Oh, Dad's at the shop. Sunday papers, you know.'

'Oh, of course! I'm sorry, I didn't think ... Listen, Shelley, you know there's this meeting at Merks & Trehallis?'

'Yeah, Dad's really chuffed.'

'Well, I was wondering ... Do you know what it's about?'

'Only that he's going to get some good out of it, I gather.'

'That's what I hear too. But I was wondering ... is he going to the meeting on his own?'

'You mean he should take his "mouthpiece" with him?' the girl asked with a gurgle of laughter.

'Not exactly, but you know ... He gets upset very easily, and ... you know ...' She stumbled into silence.

'What?' urged Shelley.

'Ms Groves has asked us to be there too.'

'What, you and your dad?'

'Yes, and it struck me that perhaps Ms Groves wants us there to be sort of a buffer ... I don't quite know how to put it into words but I feel there may be some reason she's asked us.'

'You know her,' Shelley said after a momentary hesitation. 'Are you saying she's up to something?'

'No, no, not at all.' Although perhaps she was saying that. 'No, it's not some kind of a trick, if that's what you mean. It's just that I . . . I feel my father and I would not have been invited if Ms Groves were expecting plain sailing.'

'Um . . . And of course the only one likely to cause a rumpus is Dad. So what does that mean? Should he change his mind and not go?'

Laura sighed. 'Do you think he would change his mind?'

'You got me there! He's convinced himself he's going to be invited in as a partner in the lawsuit.'

'Oh no!'

'Well, something like that. But he was telling my mum we could mebbe have a little trip to see where we'd like to move to in Spain if and when we sell the shop.'

'So he thinks he's going to get some money?'

'Money and sort of help. With his own affairs. That was the impression he got.'

'Perhaps I'm all wrong then, Shelley.'

They each paused to consider their opinions.

'Tell you what, I'll tag along with him,' said Norman's daughter. 'I can usually stop him when he's about to go off on one of his toots. If it's money and it isn't a big enough offer, he could get stroppy . . . D'you think I should go?'

It seemed at least some kind of safeguard. Laura agreed that Shelley would probably be a help. They disconnected with the agreement to see each other at the meeting.

She didn't mention this conversation to her father. He had such a poor opinion of Shelley that her presence at the meeting wouldn't impress him one way or the other.

The important day arrived. The Wainwrights went early to Oxford by train, so as to have a leisurely lunch before heading for the solicitors. Ronald wanted to make a good showing at this event and didn't want to be rushed through a meal.

Kim was awaiting them in the conference room. The place was rather heavily furnished and imposing, speaking of stability and financial security. 'The Dallancys are on their way,' she told them. 'Norman phoned in a message to say he was bringing his daughter.'

Ronald shrugged, Laura nodded. The remark was given no importance. Ten minutes later the Dallancys were shown in, with Kim hurrying to the door to greet them. 'You parked outside the city, did you? No problems finding us?'

'No, none, thanks very much, we asked a college gatekeeper and he gave us directions.'

Norman, like Laura's father, had put on a dark suit for the occasion. The two men still looked different, though. Ronald Wainwright looked what he once was, a serious, confident teacher. In his business gear Norman's stocky figure seemed trapped. Hs expression was a mixture of wariness and muted delight.

Shelley, in her role as supporter to her father, had toned down some of the fashion traits. Only one earring in each ear, the bleached-blond hair smoothed down, jeans and top of plain black. For today, recommendations in teenage magazines had been set aside.

Kim, in a trim dark dress, was smiling. 'So shall we sit down? Tea is coming.' She glanced at her watch. 'Or something stronger if you prefer?'

'No, tea'll do me fine. Got to keep a clear head, haven't I?' There was almost a wink accompanying this, as if Norman were warning her that his defences were up.

She smiled and let it go by. A young woman came in pushing a trolley with fine china cups and saucers, a matching teapot, and a plate with German sugar biscuits. She poured tea and set it by each place. She gave responsibility for the cream and sugar to Kim then left. Shelley captured the plate of biscuits and began munching immediately.

'Well now, of course we have business to discuss so we should perhaps get on with it. I expect you have things to do, and I have another client coming in half an hour.'

Norman was a little offended by the time limit but managed to say, 'Suits me.'

'As you'd suppose, it's about the Dallancy bequest.'

'Yeah,' he breathed. This was what he'd come for.

'You've expressed your eagerness to be a part of the proceedings, Mr Dallancy, and it so happens we've reached a stage where I believe you can play a very useful part.'

'Anything I can do.'

'Good. That's what I like to hear. Well, let me go back a little. The negotiations have to go forward in carefully mapped

211

stages, and we've reached a point now where Simmingford Council have expressed doubts about the validity of my client's claim.'

'Yeah, I read that in the papers. Typical,' Norman growled.

'We opened the battle by saying Mr Crandel has a piece of lace that obviously belonged to Marianne Dallancy, but – as we expected – they have said that isn't proof enough of his descent.'

'Kim, dear, I always said you couldn't get anywhere in court with material like that—'

'And you were quite right, Ronald.' She sipped her tea.

'But the will . . . ?' Shelley queried. 'The will's okay, innit?'

'No one challenges the will. It was made by George Etian Dallancy and somehow got lost or disregarded in the selling of various parcels of land. The will states that the property now known as Tansfield Towers is to be inherited by Marianne Dallancy and her heirs, but you must understand that the will in itself is just a legal instruction. To claim the land with any certainty Mr Crandel has to prove that his great-great-great-grandmother was the Marianne Dallancy mentioned in the will.'

'Well, she was, wasn't she?'

'We believe so but we have to prove it. We have to prove that Mr Crandel has the same blood running in his veins that belonged to Marianne Dallancy.'

'You going Gothic?' Norman demanded. 'Going to dig up the old girl back in Alberta?'

'What good would that do, Dad?' Shelley said in irritation. 'It's *Neil* that's got to prove he's a Dallancy.'

'Yes, that's exactly the point, Shelley,' Kim approved. She gave the girl one of her sparkling smiles. 'Now, to set the scene, it so happens that before he left Alberta Mr Crandel and his father were the victims of a very serious accident involving earth-moving equipment. Mr Crandel's father died of his injuries—'

'Oh,' Shelley sighed.

'And Mr Crandel suffered a concussion and very serious damage to various bones. Mr Crandel's father was very badly crushed. So much so that he was barely recognizable. Neil Crandel was on sedatives. The insurance firm was very bloody

212

minded about the whole thing because very large sums of money were involved. They insisted on a total work-up by their own specialists and in doing so they took samples of the blood of both Mr Crandel and his father.'

'Ah,' said Ronald.

'And also DNA samples.'

Laura and Shelley were nodding in comprehension. Norman was looking rather baffled. 'So they got his DNA, right, I get that. So what?'

'If we can prove that his DNA matches a known descendant of the Dallancy family, that will validate his claim to inherit.'

'Huh? I don't see that,' he muttered. He'd been in a totally different mind-set for this meeting, so couldn't cope with the information Kim was offering.

'If his DNA is the same as the DNA of a Dallancy, then he too is a Dallancy. That's accepted as evidence in law.'

He thought this through then nodded. 'I get it. Yeah. So what you want is a certified member of the Dallancy family and that means me, now doesn't it?' Triumphant at working it out, he beamed.

'Exactly, Mr Dallancy,' agreed Kim, pointedly using his name. 'And since you've expressed your desire many times to take part in the claim, I felt it would be an opportunity for you to do so. What do you think?'

'Sure,' said Norman. 'No problem.' He picked up one of the German biscuits and broke it in his fingers. 'So what's in it for me?'

'Well, what you seemed to want. You'll be enabling Neil Crandel to win his case. You've expressed interest in taking part.

'Against that lot at the Town Hall – yes, great, I'm all for that. But I want something in return for doing this favour.'

To Laura it seemed that Kim was expecting this. She said at once, 'Well, you have to understand, there are issues here. We can't actually pay you a fee – some might say that was sharp practice. But if you'd care to go to London to have the sample taken and you choose to put up in a good hotel, and charge us any amount we could reasonably put through as expenses – could you go along with that?'

Norman stared at her for a long moment then gave an angry laugh. 'Lady, you must think I came down in the last rain shower! You sitting there asking me to do this sample DNA thing for peanuts, all out of the kindness of my heart?'

'But Mr Dallancy—'

'Dad—'

Both Kim and Norman's daughter spoke at the same time. Shelley's voice being the louder, she prevailed. 'Come on, Dad, don't be such a dog in the manger. Do it as a good turn and Neil will see you right, I bet.'

'Give me money, you mean. A few hundred for being a decent bloke!' He turned to Kim. 'You've never really listened to anything I was trying to tell you. I don't want a few quid for being a willing helper. I want to get my hands round the throat of the feller in the Town Hall that cheated me out of my livelihood, I want to be recognized as part of the attack on the Town Hall biggies. I want satisfaction for *my* wrongs.'

Kim was beginning to see she'd underestimated her problems. 'But what you're saying is you want to be a litigant of record—'

'Now you've got it! I want to be represented by a posh firm like this –' with a sweep of his hand at the ornate room – 'and have everybody understand that I've been badly treated, and *they're going to pay!*'

She was speechless. It was clear that to her the man was talking utter nonsense, and she didn't know how to answer.

It was left to Laura to say, 'Mr Dallancy, I don't think it's possible to link up Neil Crandel's case with your grievances against the council over the shopping mall.'

'Of course it's possible. I can give Ms Groves and her pals chapter and verse of what they did to me—'

'But don't you see, Norman, they haven't got anything to do with each other. You think the council was unfair to you a couple of years ago over moving to the new mall, and perhaps you're right—'

'Perhaps? That's just what I'd expect! I've got all the letters they sent—'

'But Neil's case is about something that goes back to a legal document dating from over a *hundred years* ago—'

'But we're both Dallancys, aren't we? You can't get round that! And if I give the DNA thing and it matches that would prove it, wouldn't it?'

'Prove what?'

'That he and I have got to fight this thing together and make the Town Hall squirm.'

Laura had done all she could. She looked to Kim, who was somewhat recovering from the shock of Norman's reasoning. Kim now took shelter behind a very cool but reasonable tone.

'Mr Dallancy, I'm afraid what you have in mind is impossible. There is absolutely no relationship between your past difficulties and Mr Crandel's proceedings.'

'Relationship – there you are – you just said it yourself. We're cousins, branches from the same tree, and I'm willing to add my voice to any case he brings. It's got to be a help if they see his relatives are rallying round and adding to the ammunition. I don't know why you're being so stiff-necked about it—'

'Stiff-necked?' cried Kim, her voice rising. 'I'm being rational. Can't you understand the simple premise that your desire for revenge could never be of any help to Neil Crandel?'

'Listen, I know my rights! If I'm asked to help a man having a go at Simmingford Council I'm ready and willing. If you want my help you have to include me. But I'm not interested in a few quid for a scientific gimmick and then a fare-thee-well. I'm in the team for the big push, or I'm not playing.'

'Norman, don't make a big decision like this while you're upset. Think it over,' Laura pleaded.

'Begging your pardon, Ms Wainwright, I'm not taking advice from somebody who thinks a lot of a lawyer who can't see where the advantage lies. *She*'s no great brain, and you're not so clever either if you go along with her.'

'Dad!' his daughter exclaimed in protest.

'Come on, Shell, we're going. When this bunch see some sense they can get in touch.' With that he got up with unnecessary vigour, shaking the table and slopping tea all over its walnut surface. Shelley rose, obedient though reluctant. He stalked before her to the door, opened it, and was gone.

215

Shelley hesitated on the room's threshold. She seemed to be thinking. She hurried back to say in Laura's ear, 'It's okay, he doesn't need to do it, I'll do it instead.'

'What?'

'DNA – mine's as good as his, innit?' Then she was gone.

Nineteen

Into the frozen lull, Ronald spoke. 'I'm sorry, Kim. I should have made it more clear to you. Laura and I went through a scene pretty much like this last week, and I should have . . . I don't know . . . described him—'

'The man's an idiot,' exclaimed Kim. 'An absolute *idiot*! You should have warned me he can't take in simple common-sense—'

'I know, I know, I should have explained that he's obsessive—'

'When you called him aggressive, I thought you meant about money—'

'No, I see that now, I should have—'

'Will you *stop* it!' cried Laura. 'You'll be down on your knees soon, Papa!' She pushed her chair back from the conference table as if to put distance between herself and Kim on the opposite side. 'And as for you, how dare you put the blame on my father? Norman Dallancy has been sending you messages of one kind or another for days and days – he's tried to get you on the telephone, he's probably sent emails – and *you* completely misread him.'

'I—'

'You thought you could throw him some little bone, as if he was a hungry puppy. And when he hit back at you, you *patronized* him.'

'Laura,' begged her father.

'No, it's time someone said it. You treated Norman as if he

216

were a nobody. I *told* you to remember he was a Dallancy. I told you he needed gentle handling—'

'Gentle handling? How can you be gentle with a man who seems to want nothing but revenge?'

'You can try to understand what lies behind it. Norman lost his livelihood when the new shopping mall was opened in Simmingford. I think it's possible the housing staff on the council didn't pay enough attention. Now you come along, seeming to offer the chance to get back at them in a big way – and you shrug off his longing to be part of the attack force.'

'But my dear Laura, that's not the way to conduct negotiations. Don't be silly. I couldn't let him be a co-litigant.'

'Then you should have found a more respectful way of asking for his help. It's your manner that's at fault, Kim, your style. Your attitude to Norman absolutely ensured he'd lose his temper and refuse!'

'Laura, this is no way to speak to—'

'Excuse me, Papa, it's time for a little plain speaking. We were invited here to help her carry the day with Norman, and instead we've witnessed an utter catastrophe.' For the first time since her outburst, Laura paused and tried to think what she was doing. Did she care if Kim made a mess of her dealings with the Dallancys? Did she *want* Neil's claim to go forward? All at once she lost impetus and fell silent.

Kim was angry, but tried to put it aside. 'I still have to look after my client,' she said through stiff lips. 'It's my duty as his legal representative to get that DNA sample—'

At that Laura pulled herself together again. 'Does Neil actually know about that?' she demanded.

'Not as such, but he gave me instructions to pursue the claim up to the point where the council want to discuss an out-of-court settlement – and the next step is to prove his pedigree—'

'My dear,' soothed Ronald, 'I'm sure he'll understand your difficulties. After all, he's met Norman, he knows what a lout he is.'

'Well, luckily there's no need to report this debacle to him at the moment because he's off somewhere on business—'

'Off somewhere?' This was Laura, on the alert to have news of him despite herself.

'He said he had to make a trip back to Canada – something

217

about the property back home. He didn't tell me much.'

Laura was surprised. Her father greeted the information with delight. 'So you can try getting in touch with Norman again and have it all sorted out by the time Neil gets back?'

'You're not thinking of contacting Norman Dallancy again?' cried Laura.

'Well . . .' Kim was aggrieved. 'What else can I do? I've got to convince Simmingford Council that Neil actually is Marianne's descendant.' She paused. 'Now, wait a minute – Laura – you seem to have some sort of rapport with the man. Could I ask you to speak to him?'

'Oh, excellent,' cried Ronald. 'Of course, that's the thing!'

Laura was shaking her head with vehemence. Kim said, 'Look here, I'll forget all that resentful nonsense you were talking a minute ago if you'll just take on this chore—'

'No.'

'But—'

'It isn't necessary to go back to Norman,' she said, glad to have an escape from explaining her relationship with Neil. Moreover, a message had been left with her. 'Shelley will do it instead.'

Both her father and Kim stared at her in amazement. 'How on earth can you say that?' Kim exclaimed.

'Because she just told me so. When she darted back before leaving – she whispered it in my ear. And look – she left this on the table where she was sitting.' She leaned to one side to pick up a little heart-shaped label, the kind of thing a teenage magazine might give away to readers. Printed on it was the message: 'This belongs to . . .' and then written in very small neat print, 'Shelley', and her mobile number.

Recovering from her amazement, Kim held out her hand for it. Laura leaned over the table to hand it to her.

'She left this? On purpose?'

'It seems so. You'd need a way to get in touch.'

'And she said she'd give the DNA sample?'

'Yes.'

Kim gave a loud sigh of relief. 'Oh, great! That's absolutely great! No more fist fights with that awful father of hers! I'm delighted. Of course we'll give the girl a little something for her trouble.'

218

'Wait,' said Laura in a warning tone

'Oh, for Pete's sake, what now?'

'Think about it. If Shelley volunteers to help you, it will drive a wedge right between that family.'

Kim listened to the caution with a crease of irritation between her dark brows. Then she gave an exaggerated sigh and blew out a breath. 'Laura, my concern is not the family of Norman Dallancy. I have to look after the interests of my client. If Shelley Dallancy has volunteered to help, I *must* accept the offer.'

'Her father will never forgive her.'

'Her father . . . How old is Shelley?' Clearly she was thinking that grown-up daughters often had fights with their fathers. Then something more important made her wave a dismissive hand. 'No, don't tell me. As far as I'm concerned, Shelley is a responsible adult, and I accept her offer.'

'And if Norman comes raging into your office afterwards?'

She smiled then shrugged. 'We need not disclose to the public how we were able to justify Neil's claim. The council will be satisfied with the evidence and will be persuaded into an out-of-court settlement – that's all that needs to be made public. Unless Shelley herself tells him, her father need never know.'

'But he'll guess—'

'Do you think so? He doesn't strike me as an intellectual giant. He hardly seems to know how to put two and two together.'

Ronald said, in wonder, 'Why should she do it? It's very strange.'

'Not at all. Shelley likes Neil.'

'What?'

'Yes, she's got quite a lot of feeling for him, I think.'

'You mean she's taken a shine to him?' Kim enquired, laughing in relief and amusement.

Laura pushed her chair back and stood up. She felt her cheeks go hot with anger. She said with all the force of her being, 'I'm not staying here to let you giggle about Shelley. The way you've reacted to her offer does you no credit. She's done you an enormous good turn. You should be *ashamed*.'

And she marched out.

219

Outside, she stood for a moment getting her breath back. It was the first time since university debating days that she'd let her temper get the better of her. After a moment she moved away, to become involved in the home-going commuter tide, though she scarcely noticed it. Feeling the need for physical action to release her pent-up indignation, she walked briskly to the station. At Brinbank Junction she went to the Land Rover but shrank from the idea of sitting inactive until her father joined her. She had no idea how long that might be. He was probably sitting in Kim's office apologizing for his daughter's behaviour.

She took a taxi all the way home. It cost the earth but she told herself with grim amusement that she would add it to the bill for services to Merks & Trehallis as 'expenses incurred in attending meetings, etc.'.

Once indoors, she didn't know what to do with herself. She couldn't sit down to work. Quite soon she ought to start the preparations for dinner, but she was in no mood for that. She changed from city shoes into something more sensible and, taking a book, set out for a favourite spot on the edge of a local copse.

But her attention soon wandered from the novel. She fell into a long reprise of what had happened that afternoon.

She still held to the view that Kim Groves had handled Norman Dallancy with a total lack of understanding. It would have to be agreed that Norman was difficult: not clever, totally self-centred. Perhaps nothing Kim said or did would have satisfied him. But to offer him petty cash in return for his cooperation was a blunder beyond repair.

That she would take up Shelley's offer was, she supposed, inevitable, though she had shied away from the awkward question of whether it was right to involve a minor. Laura thought that as Shelley was only seventeen the consent of the parents ought to be asked. Kim, of course, would do no such thing. She would accept Shelley's proposal. Whether her declaration about keeping it confidential was to be believed, Laura couldn't tell.

But the matter that concerned her most was her own outburst criticizing Kim's behaviour.

She regretted it now. She felt she'd been right in her opinion but she shouldn't have said any of it in front of her father.

Any criticism of his idol always put her father in a bad mood. A 'bad mood' for Ronald could turn into a fit of depression. What was worse in this case was that he might feel some of the criticism was justified. Though he thought little of Shelley Dallancy's intelligence, he would acknowledge that she'd made a generous, unselfish offer. To hear her laughed at might have disturbed him. *Ought* to have disturbed him. His perfect woman ought not to snigger at the romantic feelings of a young girl.

So it was possible that Laura had done her father some harm. She'd drawn his attention to an undeniable fault. He was a decent man, he would surely have to agree that Kim had behaved badly.

She might have harmed him by forcing him to face that. But she'd been so shocked, so hurt on Shelley's behalf . . .

Well. There would be worse to come. He might try to build up some defence for Kim, try to justify her behaviour. If in so doing Laura's father reproached her, asked her to withdraw her censure, what should she do?

She could tell him she was sorry she'd spoken. That was true. She should have held her tongue, she should just have walked out in silence. But if he asked her to apologize she would refuse.

That would be an extraordinary thing to do. No one that she knew ever gainsaid Kim, no one opposed her demands or her wishes. In Brinbank she was regarded as the star of the community – clever, successful, ambitious, rich. In the confrontation in her office, Laura had felt it was time someone told her a plain truth or two. But to have done it in front of Ronald Wainwright was a mistake, and if it harmed him she would have herself to blame.

She walked home in the late evening, the scent of honeysuckle wafting from a wild thicket at the edge of the wood. Her father hadn't yet come home; the Land Rover wasn't in the drive. She was glad, though puzzled. But perhaps he'd stopped at the Fox and Hare for a drink.

It was quite dark when he arrived. When he came in he went straight upstairs, ignoring her greeting. Later she heard the shower running, and doors closing that meant he was in his room. She went up to tap on the door. 'I've made a sandwich for you, Papa.'

His reply was a mere grunt of refusal.

'Well, then . . . Goodnight.'

'G'night.'

Sighing, she turned away. Her father was a little the worse for drink. Drowning his sorrows?

She slept badly and was late getting up. To her astonishment, she found Ronald had had breakfast – made it himself – and had gone out. The Land Rover was gone.

He's avoiding me, she thought. And added, Well, good!

Inevitably, they met at last about mid-afternoon. Laura was going out to gather some herbs for the evening meal, her father was coming in.

'Hello,' she said, casually blocking his way to the inner part of the hall. 'You didn't come in for lunch?'

He bridled a little. 'I don't have to account for my whereabouts.'

'No, of course not. There are some emails on your office computer that need your attention.'

'You haven't been meddling with my computer?'

'No, I just switched it on for messages and there are a couple.'

'There was no need to interfere—'

'Papa, we haven't done any work for two days. I just wanted to check.'

'Humph.'

To get them off dangerous topics she said, 'I was just going to get some basil for the pasta. I'm going to do *alla tonna*. But I'll be back in a minute to make our cup of tea.'

'Humph.' But he went into the kitchen and sat at the kitchen table, which seemed to signify he wanted his afternoon tea as usual.

When she came back she at once set to work so as to give an air of complete normality. She produced her latest batch of home-made biscuits from a tin – ginger snaps, an old and well-loved favourite. She set out plates and mugs while the tea infused, a good strong cup just as he liked it. She saw out of the corner of her eye that he was picking up a biscuit and smiled to herself. That old adage came to mind: the way to a man's heart is through his stomach.

When they were sitting down opposite each other she thought

it was time to try for a little conversation. 'The basil is being eaten by some caterpillar or other,' she remarked.

He crunched his biscuit without replying.

'Or perhaps it's a slug.'

That got his attention. He felt he knew the way to deal with it. 'You should put out those slug traps again.'

These were plastic containers into which the slugs were tempted by milk or beer so that they drowned. She hated having to empty them. She gave a half-shrug of agreement but said nothing, hoping he'd say more on the interesting subject of slugs.

But instead Ronald said, as if reciting something he had rehearsed, 'Everything went very well after you left yesterday. Kim rang Shelley on her mobile and got her while they were on their way home. They couldn't talk then, of course, so she arranged to see her today, and I was there – as an independent observer, you know, to ensure that no pressure was brought to bear.'

Laura nodded.

'All is well. Shelley went to the clinic today and had the DNA sample taken. I gather it takes a couple of weeks for the processing.'

'Yes.'

'So we'll know soon.'

'I see.'

Her father gave a little indulgent smile and added, 'Shelley sent you her love.'

'Oh, how nice. I think she's a nice kid.'

'So you said before . . . and perhaps you were right.'

'Did you ask if she was going to tell her father about the clinic visit?'

'It was all very businesslike. Nothing personal was discussed.'

She pushed the plate of biscuits towards him and he took another. He was relaxing from his stiff manner. 'I'd already explained to Kim that you had a soft spot for Shelley, so she understood why you got so huffy yesterday.'

'Oh, I don't know that I—'

'You thought better of Shelley than the rest of us did.'

'That's true, perhaps.'

223

He frowned and paused. She could tell something very important was coming.

'You and I differ on quite a lot of things, Laura. But I didn't realize until yesterday how judgmental you are of Kim.'

'Am I judgmental?' It was a view of herself she hadn't expected.

'Kim moves in the business world. She has to be a bit . . . steely . . . You do see that?'

'I suppose so.'

'At the moment she's concentrating on this big, important case about the Tansfield Estate. You have to be . . . open minded . . . about the tactics involved.'

Laura didn't point out that giggling at Shelley had nothing to do with tactics. Instead she ventured, 'Did Shelley say anything about her father's state of mind? He was furious when he left the office yesterday.'

'No, we didn't ask anything like that and she didn't volunteer anything. I think she was taken up with seeing herself as a sort of heroine, coming to the aid of the man she admires.'

'Well, she's quite right, she is a bit of a heroine.'

'I won't argue with that. She's done Kim a very good turn, and I think well of her.'

So peace was restored without any need for an apology on Laura's part nor any apparent discord between her and her father. Yet there was a change in the household. Ronald wasn't exactly moody, but he was somehow unsettled. He didn't do any office work. He went out in the evening to the village pub instead of relaxing with favourite programmes on television. He took a renewed interest in their garden, which he'd neglected for over a year while he laboured in Kim's. He'd spend hours out there, trying to kill the nefarious slugs, pulling up weeds that sometimes turned out to be flower shoots.

The relationship between father and daughter was friendly enough. Some subjects seemed to be taboo but they chatted about day-to-day living. If he had been angered by her outburst against Kim he didn't let it show. However, their former practice of sharing out the work of Lauron Family Research was in abeyance; Laura took it all on without complaint. Days went by in a sort of muted accord.

The month of August arrived with a heatwave that made

life indoors very trying. Old Brin House had no air conditioning so she worked with windows open and a fan going. She longed to be outside, by the stream, where it was airy and shady, where the ripple of the brown water spoke of coolness. But they had a rush of work so she was bound indoors.

Her father came into the office looking pleased. He'd said that he would telephone Kim for news, since the time had come for results from the geneticist.

'The DNA sample showed several elements of consanguinity,' he reported in careful repetition of the words he'd just heard. 'Shelley and Neil are deemed to be relations from the same gene string. That means Neil is a Dallancy. Kim got on to the Simmingford people at once.'

'And what was their answer?'

'They've agreed to out-of-court negotiations.'

Laura swung round on her revolving office chair. 'She's pleased, I bet.'

'Of course. Delighted. She's talking in millions, you know. Her firm are delighted with her.'

'Give her my congratulations.'

'Oh, you can do that yourself. She's having Neil over at Yalcote tomorrow evening to discuss strategy and she asked us to come to have a little celebration – you know, a glass of champagne, that sort of thing.'

'I thought Neil had gone to Canada?' she said, ashamed that her voice had a tremor.

'Oh, that was a while ago. I think he got back last week.'

Quite outside her range of vision these days. She had to accept it.

'I said we'd be delighted to be there. Is that all right with you?' In other words, he was asking, do you feel you can be polite to Kim?

'Of course,' she said. Even if she was asked to 'celebrate' something she thought wrong. Anything, if only she could be in the same room with Neil – perhaps for the last time, now that the case was coming to a successful conclusion. Because, of course, he'd go home for good after that.

Twenty

Like the rest of Brinbank village, the Wainwrights were normally invited only to Kim's 'get togethers' – daytime affairs, with many other guests. They did, from time to time, see Kim in the evenings, but only on unplanned visits. To be invited to a celebration, a champagne occasion, was a major change.

Ronald was clearly thrilled by the idea. On the morning of the big day he drove to Brinbank Junction then took a train to a nearby market town now much favoured by the City-commuter types. There he bought a new tie. Unheard of.

At lunch he cleared his throat to ask, 'What are you going to wear for this evening?' Equally unheard of. He had never before in his life enquired as to his daughter's wardrobe.

Laura was amazed, but hid the fact. 'Oh, something neat but not gaudy.'

'Yes, but what, actually? Party frock? Those strappy high-heeled things?'

It crossed her mind that perhaps he was thinking of getting out his elderly dinner jacket. She replied quickly, 'Oh, no, just an after-six sort of thing. And flattish shoes. Because we'll be on foot, won't we? Can't drive after we've been drinking champagne.'

'Ah. Yes, of course.'

Later in the afternoon she heard him pottering around in his bedroom. She pictured him getting clothes out of his wardrobe then holding them up against himself to see the effect in the mirror. When he came down for afternoon tea he looked perplexed, as if he was still having a problem over suitable attire. On the one hand, it was a private little celebration among friends in a country setting. On the other, it was to be a climax point, a champagne evening to look ahead to the harvesting of huge sums of money.

In the event, her father went for the 'country gentleman at a garden fête' look – well-pressed chinos, ivory linen jacket, plain shirt and the new tie, an expensive item of pure silk woven in rainbow colours.

As for herself, Laura had chosen a pencil skirt of plain black, a voile blouse of sedate maroon, and low-heeled black sandals. The whole effect was, as Shakespeare had requested, neat and by no means gaudy, but to her it had an added bonus: she hadn't been able to get into the skirt until recent weeks. Strict adherence to her diet plan and emotional turmoil had brought her dress size down to what it had been in her student days. Something to celebrate, she'd told herself ironically as she dressed.

She was much less thrilled by the coming party than her father. She had agreed to attend, and had dressed so as not to let herself down. Yet even though she would see Neil again after what seemed a very long absence, she was dreading it.

At some point during the event she expected to have to make a protest. She was totally against the reason for their being there: they were to decide how Kim was to carry the battle forward and to estimate how much money they could get from Simmingford Council. Somewhere in the discussion Laura was going to have to say out loud what she felt with profound conviction: 'This is a mean and despicable scheme!'

Having read the will made by George Etian Dallancy all those years ago, she knew he had left the land to his daughter in reparation for his authoritarian decision about her future. He had forced her into a marriage with a libertine, selfish and loose-living, interested only in extending the acreage of his estate. He had wanted to hear Marianne referred to as Her Ladyship without thinking what it meant to her happiness. When she fled her marriage and disappeared for ever, he perhaps blamed her. But when Sir John divorced her, then, too late, he felt remorse.

To ease his conscience he had made the bequest that now was being used by Kim with as much ruthlessness as Marianne's dreadful husband, Sir John Higston, had behaved.

If Kim's plans went ahead the people who now lived on that plot of land would go through a long period of anxiety and apprehension, weeks, months, perhaps as long as a year.

Eventually Kim would accept an offer – but the money would come from funds that were intended for the good of the people of Simmingford, not for the enrichment of a grasping litigant.

The man who made the bequest had surely never intended any such thing. And Laura knew she was going to have to say so at some point.

So it was with trepidation that she set out with Ronald on the walk to Yalcote. It was mid-evening, with sunshine after an afternoon of thunderstorms. The leaves on the trees glistened from the lingering moisture, the scent of refreshed flowers was everywhere. The garden of the old Victorian house greeted them with an emerald glow of well-mowed lawn. The new gravel drive gleamed like a highway of topaz. A peaceful, happy scene.

There was no car to be seen in front of the door; Kim's Volvo was in its garage, and it was Laura's guess that Neil hadn't yet arrived.

She was proved wrong. When Mrs Stevens ushered them into the drawing room Neil was just beyond the French windows examining shiny new bay trees in antique lead pots.

He turned his head at their arrival and came at once into the room. Laura's heart gave a great lurch of joy and trepidation.

Kim, in a little black dress that suggested expensive designer labels, hurried to take her by the hand. 'Laura, sweetie, isn't this great? Makes all our labours worthwhile.'

'Of course, how nice, yes,' she replied, flustered. She knew Kim was sending her a message: 'I'm going to forget that scene in my office and so should you.'

Neil was shaking hands with Ronald. 'Well, old pal, how's things? Been finding any more missing relatives?'

He looked much more casual than everyone else. He was clad in Dockers and an open-necked shirt. Perhaps he hadn't understood that this was to be Kim's victory celebration.

'Glad to see you, Neil. Big achievements as far as you're concerned, old chap. You must be very pleased.'

'Ha! You don't know the half of it. We'll get to that later. Say, I've been looking at the little trees out there, bay trees, Kim says. They're *Lauris nobilis* – the same ones that you use the leaves of in cooking, right?'

'Oh, ask Laura. I don't know about things like that.'

Laura held out her hand. But Neil gave her a great hug and murmured, 'Lordy, it seems like a century since I last saw you!'

Her head reeled, her breath seemed to leave her body. She swayed but was held safe for the critical moment by his arms. As he let her go, Mrs Stevens swam into her view, offering champagne flutes.

She found the edge of a table to lean against and recover her self-possession. Taking two glasses, Neil handed one to her. She held it but knew that if she raised it to her lips her grip would falter. So she stood quietly, trying to take regular, even breaths.

Ronald was taking it upon himself to be leader of the conversation while Kim supervised Mrs Stevens, who was now setting canapés and petits fours on tables here and there. He said, 'How d'you get here, Neil? Didn't see your car.'

'Good Lord, no, the Honda? I handed that in when I had to leave Oxford. And in London you don't really need a car. No, I came on that dinky little train and got off at that little country depot – I love that, you know, it's all so different from Wenaskowa. There's no railroad there. I've got a chauffeur coming to take me back to the station by and by.'

So he wouldn't be staying long. This was enough to restore Laura to normal. She took a sip of her drink.

Kim bustled Mrs Stevens out of the room, much to Mrs Stevens's disappointment. 'That's fine, we'll manage for ourselves now.' Clearly the time had come for business matters. Kim raised her glass. 'Here's to the success of our enterprise.'

'Hear, hear,' responded Ronald. They all raised their glasses.

'I'll give you a short summary of where we've got to,' she went on, with a smiling glance at Neil. 'You left it to me to reach this point and you probably want to know your current position. So ...' She held up a finger for emphasis. 'Simmingford Town Council have accepted the fact that you are the legitimate heir of the land on which Tansfield Towers was built. They accept that the will is valid. They *could* defend their assumption of ownership over the years from 1896 to the present day – they could plead that there was nothing to contradict their belief that the property had passed to others through legitimate sale. You follow?'

'Faint but pursuing,' said Neil in apology. 'Could I have it in simple language, please?'

'Well, the long and the short of it is that though the council could put up a defence, it would cost them a lot in legal fees and might be a very long process. So they've agreed to accept my evidence that you are a Dallancy and they'll begin dealings about reparation for your loss of rights.'

'Ah . . . I think I see . . . That was a good piece of work, then, making them accept that lace collar as convincing evidence.'

Kim paused. The Wainwrights looked at each other. No one said anything. Although it was a point at which Laura might have spoken, she found herself unable to utter a sound.

'What?' asked Neil, looking around in perplexity.

'Well . . . in fact . . . It was DNA evidence that did the trick,' Kim conceded.

He studied her, then frowned. 'How did . . .? Wait, I remember sending you a CV file when you took over this thing . . . I suppose the hospital records had DNA information . . .? Yeah, the insurance firm were kind of picky about everything . . . But hey . . . don't tell me Norman Dallancy . . .' He half shook his head, and there was reluctance when he concluded, 'How much did you have to pay him?'

'Oh, nothing,' Kim said, rather too airily. 'Norman behaved like a raging bull when I suggested it. No, it was the daughter. She volunteered.'

'Shelley?' He seemed too taken aback to speak for a moment then said, 'And he *let* her?'

'Well . . . He doesn't know, actually.' The words were uttered in a very muted tone.

Neil set down his champagne glass. He stared away from Kim, at the view through the open French windows. Ronald cleared his throat. 'I . . . er . . . I was present on the day in question. Shelley signed a voluntary statement saying she wanted to do it. It was all quite fair and honourable.'

Neil turned to Laura. 'Were *you* there?'

'No.' She should have said, 'And I protested,' but the words wouldn't emerge. She knew she was a coward but the tension in the room was like a physical barrier.

A long silence, which Kim broke with more authority, a faint irritation in her manner. 'You did ask me to forward the proceedings up to the point where Simmingford Council agreed to negotiate.'

'Yeah.' He seemed to wait a moment to collect his thoughts. 'It's done, isn't it, and now we're at crunch point. I just don't feel—'

'This is a time for detached consideration, not feelings. As you say, what's done is done, and we now have to make decisions about our target. I've had a long talk with one of the firm's experts on money matters, Neil, and he says we should start high. You may recall that David Tyler – the surveyor I brought in to see the estate? – put a price of about four and a half million on it. But my colleague suggests it's worth nearer five and a half and we should start at three million and settle at somewhere under two million.'

'Jeepers! Listen, Kim—'

'Let me explain.' She overrode his interruption with a determined lift of the chin and a rapid flow of words. 'Leo explained to me that the nuisance value of the claim puts you in a very favourable position. The councillors would probably agree to a significant payment not to have the estate's occupants lining up with banners of protest and complaint outside the council offices—'

'Well, it's my intention to be a nuisance to them so—'

'Excellent, excellent. I thought you'd see the value of that advice. So we'll start at three—'

'Wait a bit there—'

'I've already given them a hint that we intend to stand very firm—'

'Hang on a minute—'

'I've roughed out a statement that I'd like to send tomorrow, by courier, so that they have to sign for it and thus begin evaluation of the lien—'

'The what?'

'Your right to buy and sell property; that's to say, establishing the normal aspect of equity. We must avoid by all means the danger of ending in Chancery—'

'Kim!' Neil said in a loud voice. 'Will you for Pete's sake stop acting the part of the legal eagle and listen to what I'm trying to say?'

She was silenced. Her lips parted in what might have been a voiceless 'Oh!'

She had been standing in a commanding position. Now she looked round as if for the support of a chair, but quickly turned back to say, offended, 'There's no need to raise your voice!'

'Sure there's a need. You're going on and on like the Saskatchewan River without ever letting me get a word in. Listen, I asked you to get to the point where the Simmingford folks were willing to talk to us but I never said I actually wanted to screw them for three million.'

'How much then?' she challenged. There was a glint of anger in her eye. It seemed she resented any suggested change in her agenda

'I don't want money.'

'What?' She momentarily clasped her hands in front of her, as if to make sure this was reality and not a nightmare. It was the first time Laura had ever seen her at a loss.

'I never intended to take any money.'

'But you said – you said – to sue them for every cent they had.'

'Yeah, right, I told you to say that. I wanted to scare the daylights out of them. Great. You've done that. That's where I wanted to get to.'

'But . . . but . . .' And now sheer bewilderment was writ large on her features.

'I can see it's a bit of a shock to you. Just let me explain. I wanted to throw a scare into them – that was Stage One. Now we go to Stage Two. I want you to tell those guys that the negotiations are going to be about improvements they're to make in the estate.'

'No!'

'What d'you mean, no? Those are my instructions.'

'I refuse to do it!'

He let a moment go by while he took that in. 'You're my lawyer, you have to do what I want, right? As long as it's legal.'

'Not if it's nonsense.'

'It's nonsense if you're only thinking about making money. From my point of view it makes perfect sense, so you've no grounds for refusing.'

To Laura this was as much a lightning bolt as it was to Kim. But the effect was different. Her whole world was transformed. A golden warmth wrapped itself around her heart. She'd misjudged him. She'd been a fool, a doubter – she'd been totally and utterly wrong. And she was so happy to acknowledge the fact that she almost broke out into a shout of joy.

Kim, on the other hand, was alight with resentment. 'Of course I've got grounds for refusal. It would make us look a bunch of idiots.'

'Well, I've no objections to looking an idiot—'

'But I have!' she flashed 'I haven't brought the affair along to this point – built up expectations with my senior partners – worked out a set of perfect arguments – What would people say if they heard we'd taken this sort of step? I'm not going to be made fun of in the press for any tomfool notion of yours!'

'They won't make fun. They'll think you're a decent sort of person, trying to do what's best for Tansfield Towers—'

'I never signed on to be a do-gooder for the people in that wretched estate! Did you think that was the sort of thing I do?' she demanded.

He shrugged a little, perhaps defensively. 'Mebbe I didn't give that enough thought. I had a lot on my mind at the time. I just wanted to get the claim moving forward to the point where the housing department would listen to what I wanted to say.'

'But that's not what I understood and you had no *right*—'

'And what I want to say,' he went on, speaking with more conviction and less apology, 'is that old George Etian would be disgusted to see what they've done with the land he left to his daughter. And you're going to help me say it.'

'No I'm not!'

'You won't?'

'No. I was enlisted to play a part in a sensible legal process and it's either that or I withdraw.'

'Okay.'

'What?' She was so completely taken aback that the word was a mere gasp.

'Okay, if you want to walk out, that's okay.'

'But – you have to have a solicitor to negotiate with the council's legal people—'

'Plenty of solicitors around, Kim.' And there was something very cool in his manner. 'One thing I've learned in the year that's just gone by, you can get a lawyer by just holding up your hand and waving.'

'You mean you're . . . you're terminating our agreement?'

'*You're* terminating it. I've given you my instructions and you don't want to carry them out. Fine. I'll get someone else.'

There was an utter and stricken silence. Then Kim said icily, 'Very well. Please send me a letter to say you've ended our association.'

'First thing in the morning,' he agreed amiably.

'And I'd like you to leave my house.'

'Sure.'

He went out, with a farewell nod to Ronald and Laura. Laura, without waiting to excuse herself or explain, followed him immediately.

He was in the hall, with Mrs Stevens opening the door for him. As he stepped into the porch, Laura was at his heels. Mrs Stevens, holding the door handle, mimed 'disaster'– corners of the mouth turned down, eyebrows raised – which told Laura she'd been eavesdropping on the row that had just ended.

She caught up with Neil just outside the entrance. She put her arm through his and drew herself close to him. 'Now,' she said, trying for lightness that might mask the turmoil of feelings within, 'you missed out on your champagne, so you must come home with me and have an ordinary glass of wine. Is that a good idea?'

'That's an offer I can't refuse.' He twined his fingers into hers, and they walked down the drive and out on to the pavement of the village street. After a few paces he said, 'So much for that. And despite what seems like a setback, now for Stage Two.'

'You'll have to find another solicitor.'

'No problem. The guy that owns that glitzy flat – you know?

– he's an attorney, been dealing with something for me over the past year or so.'

'Then why on earth did you take on Kim?' she burst out, in a mixture of confusion and reproof.

'We-ell . . . you see . . . your dad has this thing about her and wanted her to do well. And she was so keen, and at the time I was angry. Angry at what I saw on that crummy housing estate. How bureaucrats can let folk live like that, I'll never understand!'

It had never been about money. She hugged his arm closer to her, trying to convey a thousand meanings by that contact. She asked, 'You always intended to argue about the state of the place?'

'You bet.' He leaned over to drop a little kiss on her temple by way of introduction to his thoughts on the matter. 'My great-great-great-great-granddaddy left that to Marianne as a way of doing good, now didn't he? I wasn't about to let the place go on like that if I could help it. You could tell it was going down the tubes – graffiti not cleaned up, pools of rain-water not draining away – gee, my dad and I kept our tool-shed in better condition than that! But I see now that perhaps I should have made it clear to Kim from the outset . . . Only I had a lot on my mind at the time so mebbe I sort of shrugged it off on to her without thinking of how she'd react. I realize now I didn't really know her well enough to trust her with that sort of thing. But I thought I'd play catch-up when the vital moment arrived, give her an explanation, and it would all be sweetness and light.'

Hurrying footsteps sounded behind them. Pausing, they looked back. Ronald came up to join them. He was pale and distressed. 'I thought I'd stay and . . . comfort . . .' He blinked once or twice. Perhaps there were tears in his eyes. 'She was very rude to me! I . . . never thought . . .'

Laura let go of Neil's arm. They took up position at either side of him and without ostentation helped him as they walked on.

'Laura and I were just saying that perhaps I took her too much by surprise,' Neil remarked. 'I'm sorry you got caught up in it.'

'I tried to say that she should reconsider, because, you

235

know, she could come out of the affair looking good,' he muttered. Then louder and in misery, 'She called me an old fool!'

Laura longed to take him in her arms and comfort him. But her father never welcomed an open show of emotion. Instead she said with great gentleness, 'Never mind what she said. She didn't mean it. She's in a rage at the moment.'

'What I didn't like . . . what worried me . . . she seemed so obsessed with making money!'

Neil said reasonably, 'She's in business to make money. You can't blame her for that.'

'No, I don't blame her. I blame myself. I just . . . couldn't . . . see her as an ordinary human being. I put her on a pedestal.' And then, with bitter amusement, 'And she fell of with a crash.'

Over his head Neil caught Laura's eye. He made a little movement of his head that implied, 'Let's try something else.' Then he said, in a crisper tone, 'Listen, Ron, it's what's called a "mid-life crisis". You've had that now, so you've learned something, eh? You have to look around for somewhere else to park your emotions.'

'You don't understand,' lamented Ronald. 'She was my perfect woman.'

'Well, settle for somebody a bit less perfect next time. Less steel, more heart, if you get my drift. And you don't have to be in a hurry, do you? You could take up something else in the meantime. Golf, mebbe. Or stamp-collecting.'

'It's not funny,' Ronald muttered.

'Who's laughing? But all the same, it's no good going into mourning about it. You made a mistake, but join the human race! – We all fall flat on our faces now and again.'

They were in the lane that led to Old Brin House. Laura hurried ahead to unlock the door. They went into the living room where she switched on a lamp or two to give warmth to the twilit scene. Her father slumped into an armchair and stared at the carpet. She watched him in consternation.

'I was promised a glass of wine,' prompted Neil.

'Yes, we should open a bottle of something nice,' she said thankfully. 'What should it be, Papa?'

'I don't care.'

'That's the spirit,' exclaimed Neil, taking it in exactly the opposite meaning from his host. 'Rise above it. And I'll drink to that! – If I get anything worth drinking.'

'I'll see what we've got,' Laura said. She went through the hall and the kitchen and into the pantry, where the household's small stock of wine was kept. She selected a bottle of Ca' del Bosco because she'd heard her father say it was one of Italy's best, then set wineglasses on a tray. She was looking for something by way of snacks when Neil came in to help.

'He's pretty low,' he sighed.

She nodded agreement. 'He can get very depressed. I'm worried.'

'Don't be. We'll sort it out.' He put an arm about her. She turned her face up to him, and he kissed her.

No matter what else in her world had gone wrong, this was right. She gave herself up to the embrace, sure in the knowledge that, for now at least, they belonged together.

Twenty-One

When they at last returned to the living room with the tray of wine, Ronald was still steeped in gloom. Laura was about to switch on more lights but thought better of it. Perhaps the summer dusk was kinder, and they might be able to get him to talk.

Laura had never been good at this. It had something to do with the fact that, although he would have denied it, she knew he thought of her as an inferior. He had been denied a son, and could never quite forgive either his ex-wife or Laura for the fact that he had only a girl-child.

Yet tonight he was in great need of comfort. And though he had no son to confide in, here was Neil – friend and comrade over the past months, easy-going, sympathetic, and a participant in what had happened.

237

After drinking more than his share of the wine, it seemed that Ronald felt he could talk about the way his world had gone awry. He could talk to Neil. And Laura had the good sense to keep quiet.

'I felt uneasy over the thing with Shelley,' he began in a faltering tone. 'I mean, Kim avoided being told that she was a minor . . . I mean to say, she wouldn't let us say it – that Shelley was only a kid, you know. I think she only left school last year.'

'Yes, she's seventeen.'

'And of course it put us in a terrible position. I mean to say, Neil, you know Laura – she doesn't like that kind of thing. You know? So Laura was really very rude to Kim and then she walked out.' He nodded to himself and took another gulp of wine. 'That's not like Laura. She doesn't say unkind things to people off the top of her head, but she was worried about Shelley. And to tell the truth, so am I.'

'Yeah.'

'Kim said her father needn't know she'd done it. She said . . . she said it was part of a confidential negotiation . . . So it is, of course. But if Norman were to find out . . . You know, he's a bit of a maniac where Simmingford Council is concerned . . . You haven't seen him at his worst but he's . . . Well, I couldn't help feeling that it was wrong to let poor little Shelley get . . . drawn in . . . But Kim . . . Kim didn't seem to *care!*'

'That was bad.'

'Yes, bad . . . it was bad. She did a bad thing. I think it was unethical.' He stumbled over the last word and for a moment fell silent. Yet he had a lot to say and was determined to say it to this undemanding listener.

'So I thought I ought to be there next day when Shelley was to go to the . . . the clinic, I mean the place where they were going to take the DNA sample. She's a spirited little thing, you know. Not the least bit scared of the process, said she'd seen it on TV heaps of times. She signed this disclaimer . . . I'd have gone with her to the place but she said no, no, she was fine on her own . . . To tell the truth, I don't think she took to me. I wanted to be a friend but she probably thought I was just interfering.'

'You did right, Ron,' Neil encouraged.

'Yes, well, I wanted to . . . to . . . I think I was reassuring myself, to tell the abs'lute truth. Because I look back now and I unnerstand I was really shocked . . . *shocked* at Kim getting her involved.'

'Well, that's in the past, Ron. I don't think there's anything to be done about it now.'

'No, cos if we told the council she was underage, I don't think it would invalidate the DNA result. Cos that's a *fact*, isn't it, and facts are facts.'

'You're right.'

'And we don't want to invalidate it anyway, cos you *are* a Dallancy and right's right, you own that land, and then of course there's the matter of the money, you're not doing it for the money, and I couldn't go along with what Kim was saying about that, and I wanted her to . . . to say she was wrong. But she wouldn't ever do that. She wouldn't, would she?'

'I hardly know her, Ronnie. It wouldn't be right for me to judge her. But I have to admit I never entirely took to her.'

Laura smiled to herself at that. It was something she was very glad to hear.

'You didn't?' her father said in wonder. 'But she's so beautiful, and clever. Ev'rybody admires her. Ev'rybody in the village, you know?'

'Yeah, the local wonder-woman. I cottoned on to that.'

Ronald heaved a great sigh. 'They all know I was mad about her. I wanted to marry her! They must have thought I was a cert'fiable lunatic.'

'No, no.'

'They'll have a good laugh when they hear she threw me out.'

'They won't find out.'

'Oh yes they will. Mrs Stevens was there grinning like a Cheshire Cat when she let me out. She'll tell ev'rybody.'

Laura, sitting quiet on the other side of the room, knew this to be more than likely. What a story! The great lady of Yalcote given the brush-off by the heir of Tansfield Towers while her faithful follower is written off as an old fool. It was the kind of thing that would keep Mrs Stevens and her friends happy for weeks.

Neil didn't seem to want to pursue the subject of Mrs

Stevens, whom he scarcely knew. Instead he remarked, 'Seems to me you need to have a rethink. What's important in life – in *your* life? A while ago it was Kim. Now it seems to be Mrs Stevens. Are you going to let other folk control your outlook?'

'You don't unnerstand. Village life . . . tittle-tattle . . .' He had difficulty in saying the words so he paused while he reconsidered. 'All they do is gossip. And I've given 'em a lot to gossip about. I should have listened to Laura. Laura always had sort of second thoughts about Kim.'

Hearing herself discussed made her uncomfortable. She gave a little cough to remind her father she was there across the room. He stared vaguely into the dimness but went on, 'She's a good girl, Laura. A good girl. Put up with me for years and years. One in a million, is Laura.'

'You're right there.'

'I wish I could undo some of the things I've done. What's that saying? Three things you can never recall, the spoken word, the something something, and whatever else it is . . . I've spoken some unkind words to my little girl.' He was beginning to sound lachrymose.

'Well, you can change things now, Ronnie. A new beginning, that's what we have to think of now.'

'Tha's right. A new beginning. Forget about Kim, forget the rose-coloured glasses, look the world straight in the face and ignore wha' they say. 'S easy. I'll just take out my hearing aids.' And he suited the action to the words.

Neil looked at Laura, baffled. She shrugged. No use talking to him any more: he'd refuse to hear, and unless she put on more lights he'd be unable even to see their lips move.

'Okay then,' said Neil. 'That's the end of the amateur counselling session. Come on, old feller, I think it's time for bed.'

He stooped over the armchair, put an arm around Ronald, and helped him to his feet. 'Upsy-daisy,' Ronald said drowsily. He allowed himself to be shepherded out of the room and up the stairs.

Laura sat shaking her head. How many of all these good intentions would he remember in the morning? She got up to collect the wineglasses and tidy the room. She was in the kitchen rinsing things under the tap when Neil came down again.

'I got him into bed,' he said. 'Will he have a hangover?'

'How much did he drink? About four glasses. A little one, perhaps.' She sighed. 'It was so good of you to listen to all that, Neil.'

'Poor guy. It's a bit late for a life-changing experience but he's got to get through it.' He came behind her, put his arms round her waist, and murmured in her ear, 'Say, I hate to seem plebeian but I sure could do with a bite to eat.'

She laughed. The kitchen wall clock showed nearly ten. Late to start on anything elaborate so she said, 'I'll make you a super-sandwich and that will have to do.'

'"A loaf of bread, a jug of wine, and thou—"'

'No more wine,' she objected. 'Besides, if I remember rightly you've got the menu in the wrong order.'

'Well, "thou" is the important part.'

She dried her hands then turned in his arms. 'Let me go. I can't make sandwiches if you hold me like this.'

'Now you're facing me with a terrible dilemma. Do I need food more than I need you?'

He solved his problem by dropping little kisses all over her cheeks and then on her lips. When he let her go he said, 'Refreshments are being served in the interval.'

'The interval of what?'

'The interval between Act One which we've just had, and Act Two, which of course always has to be full of passion and drama.'

'Passion and drama! Promises, promises.'

'You'll see,' he said.

'But listen – wasn't a chauffeur coming to pick you up at Yalcote? What about him?'

'Oh, poor guy, he's probably there now getting the door slammed in his face. I'll call him, tell him he's not wanted.'

Later, as the moon was beginning to gild the clouds with a shimmering silver, they made love with the intensity that comes after a long separation. Laura's bed was narrow, but they clung together as one. Their embrace was their world, joyous and ardent. When the first passion was spent they lay close, murmuring to each other the words of love that had been absent from their lips for so long. When she felt that the bond between them was strong and safe – utterly unbreakable

241

– she ventured to ask him a question that had been troubling her.

'Neil . . . When you went away after the newspapers started being so bothersome about the bequest, I understood that you wanted to avoid all that. But later . . . You never explained why you didn't keep in touch . . . why you left me so much on my own . . .'

He held her close so that he could murmur his reply. 'I guess I should have been a bit more communicative, sweetheart. But I'd been in strange waters for quite a few months, you see. I'd grown super-careful. Big business is scary – you have these clever negotiators trying to find a way to get at you, all the time. And I felt that to let you get involved in any way would be to put you right in the target area.'

'But I wouldn't have minded, Neil. I'd have stayed out of their way, if that was what you wanted—'

'Yeah? Did you manage to stay out of the way of the news-papermen? Sure, after a while the reporters turned their search-lights elsewhere. But the oil company's investigators are a different breed. If they'd got on your track, I felt they might badger you for information about me, something they could use. I felt you'd find it – I don't know how to describe it – invasive, maybe. I was over protective, I guess.' He moved so that his face rubbed against hers, a warm, seductive touch that made her snuggle against him. 'But that's never going to happen again. We're not going to be apart ever again.'

They slept, and then in the early dawn woke to kiss and cling again.

When after a time she heard his deep, even breathing, she told herself that she had to leave paradise behind for a while and return to the mundane world. Morning light was streaming into the room. She rose. Standing by the bedside she looked down at the muscular body, now so familiar and dear. She traced the muscles of his back with the merest whisper of touch, so as not to wake him. She impressed a kiss on a fingertip so as to carry it to the nape of his neck, then with regret turned away.

She put on her dressing-gown and crept downstairs. When she came back with a tray of early morning coffee Neil was still asleep. He had turned over on his back and thrown his forearm over his eyes to keep out the light. She tugged gently at a lock of hair falling over his forehead, then bent to whisper, 'Wake up, sleepyhead.'

He roused, took his arm away, caught her hand and turned it so as to kiss her palm. 'What time is it?' he murmured.

'Nearly eight. It's all right for a man of leisure like you, but I have a business to run. So wake up, drink your coffee, and then we'll start the day.'

'Slave-driver.' But he sat up. 'Take the day off,' he suggested.

'There have been too many days off recently. Besides, Papa won't do much work today. I have to get into the office and do some work.'

'But it's a shame to waste time on the office when I'll be leaving again so soon.'

From the heights of confident affection her heart swooped down into the depths of misery. 'Back to Canada?' Her voice was little more than a whisper.

'Yeah, things to do.'

'But you only just got back from there.'

'True enough, but I had to leave some stuff unfinished. Business stuff, you know.'

She busied herself with the coffee tray, clearing a space for it on her bureau. She poured two mugs full then brought one to him. He sat up, pushing pillows about to lean against. She sat on the edge of the bed. 'Neil, last night . . . What was that you said? Something about an oil company?'

'Yeah . . . I have to go back and finish that up.'

She said nothing. After a moment she felt an arm come about her shoulder. 'What's the matter?'

'Nothing.'

'Come on. Is it because I'll be going away? Don't let it bother you.'

'Oh, darling!' She bit her lip to prevent a moan from escaping. 'You don't know what it's like for me when you go. Everything seems to go dismal and dark.'

'It's business. I can't avoid it, sweetheart.'

'Couldn't you do that on the Internet or something?'

He set down the coffee mug on the bedside table, took hers and did the same, then pulled her closer. 'Come on, don't be so upset. I'll try to explain.'

Blinking away tears, she leaned against him.

243

'This is a bit of a long story, he began. 'I have to go back to before the accident that killed my dad.'

She nodded so that he would know that she was paying attention.

'Our tree nursery is on a hillside near Wenaskowa, Alberta. Alberta is the province of Canada that's got an ocean of oil beneath the ground.'

'Oh yes . . . I think I knew that.'

'A big conglomerate asked for permission to run a prospecting expedition on our land. Dad and I talked it over and refused. We wanted to keep on growing trees. But the company approached everybody else in the district and, though a few were reluctant, they granted exploration rights one by one. Drilling began on a ranch to the south and then there was another team at work and another one. It began to look as if Dad and I would be a little island in a sea of oil.'

There was bitterness in the seemingly easy words. She snuggled against him, to convey the fact that she sympathized.

'Of course in the end we had to give in. The exploration team brought their drilling equipment on to our land, and while they were setting up a big digger slipped down the slope, overturned, and pinned me and my dad underneath.'

'Oh! Neil!' She looked up into his face in horror but he was looking straight ahead, out into the memory of that hideous day.

'Dad died of his injuries. I got a concussion and a collection of broken bones.'

'Of course! I remember! Your ankle . . .'

'Yeah, that was the last thing to get mended. While I was in hospital, *hors de combat*, they found oil – a big lake of it. Now you've got to understand, Laura, I was in a mess. I'd had a concussion, and afterwards, you know, your memory goes for a bit. Days went by and I couldn't remember what had happened. I wasn't fit to sign any documents granting oil rights to anybody, so it all hung fire for a bit.'

She could only shake her head and wish she'd been there to comfort him.

'But the thing that began to loom largest was to do with Dad's death. I had attorneys ringing me in my hospital room, advising me how to sue the drilling company. You can't imagine how weird that is, Laura – being invited to make money out of your father's death.'

'Oh no! That must be horrible.'

'Well, one of the doctors who was taking a bit of an interest in me advised me to sue. He said it was only right. So, although I really felt sickened by the whole idea, I chose a lawyer and he came and talked it all through with me and got medical certificates and so on and so on.' He sighed. 'As a matter of fact, that's some of the stuff I gave to Kim, the medical reports that he arranged. He put up a great show, that guy.'

'What do you mean, a show?'

'I turned everything over to him while I was hobbling around the hospital corridors on crutches. He turned out to be a no-good grifter.'

'Neil!'

He gave a grim laugh. 'Well, I wasn't thinking properly when I chose him, you know. I was trying to come to terms with the fact that Dad was gone. He was just beginning to enjoy life again after Mom's death, and then this oil business came up and nearly drove him out of his mind. So rather than go on trying to live with the constant hassling, we'd given in – and within a few weeks he was gone. The best friend I ever had, and I'd lost him.'

Laura put up a hand to caress his cheek. He caught it and held it tight as he went on. 'So you see I wasn't concentrating on what Quenelle was doing. Peter Quenelle, that was his name. When I caught on, I fired him and got someone else. But in a way I'd done a lot of damage. You see, some pals of mine a couple of miles up the valley hired him too, because they thought that if I trusted him he must be okay. They needed someone to look after an environmental problem. He let them down hard as concrete.'

'I don't know what to say. I had no idea you'd been going through all this misery.' She was reproaching herself. He had come into her life and, selfishly, she had seen him only from her own point of view – as a lover, as the man who could make her life golden and happy. She'd thought him wonderful, then changed her mind and almost despised him because she'd misjudged him. And all the time she should have been comforting him, standing at his side, being his unfailing

245

champion. 'Go on. I can tell these people in the valley are important.'

'You guessed it. I won't go into all their difficulties, because I think it's more or less solved now. They're a community of Nasko Native Indians. Wenaskowa means Valley of the Nasko in their dialect. They've lived on the same tract for years, hunting and fishing, growing a little corn. They've been making out recently by acting as guides to tourists, selling hand-carved toys, taking out hunting parties, that kind of thing.'

She nodded that she understood. She saw that he was frowning at his memories.

'The drilling company's activities were having a bad effect on their livelihood. Tourists don't want to visit areas next door to drilling operations. But, worse still, they were building roads so they could bring in equipment, running water sluices off their fishing river. Quenelle was supposed to get injunctions to prevent all that. But he crossed them up.'

He fell silent. She lay against his side, trying to take in all that he'd told her. 'So it's because of them that you have to go back?'

'Well, there are other aspects. This whole wrangle has as many sides as a geodetic dome. But the main point is that I wanted to do something for them while I was negotiating about other things. The multinational company that Dad and I sold out to is based in Europe. Now, you see, I was advised to come here to consult this orthopaedic specialist who could put my ankle together again. I found a good solicitor here – that's Leo Angrave, the guy who owns that apartment I borrowed. He's the one that's been in action.'

'You mean, for the Nasko community.'

'No, he's been doing stuff for me, too. It's too complicated to go into at the moment but the idea was to incorporate some help for them into his arguments. I'm not saying he was keen on having to bother about them – he kept saying it clouded the issue. But we finally signed off on it all a few weeks ago. It was around the time when Kim took us to look at the housing estate.'

'I remember.'

He sighed. 'I wasn't in a very good mood around then. All

the nit-picking over the contracts, and the clever-clever talk from the executives . . . And then I had a look at Tansfield Towers, and it was just like the Nasko thing all over again – people who didn't have the know-how or the money to protect themselves against being done down by bureaucrats. I lost my cool that day. So that's why I let Kim talk me into bringing a case against the council. I hoped to bring off another score for the underdog.'

She was following with avid interest. Now she said, 'But that doesn't explain why you have to go back to Wenaskowa—'

'Listen, treasure, these folk don't read the *Law Review*. They don't understand legalities. I took Leo with me on my last trip home so he could explain it to them and he just made it worse – they couldn't understand a word he said. They started to worry that he was going to turn out like Quenelle. So I've got to appear at their next community council and explain it in terms they can take in.'

At last he remembered the coffee and picked up his mug. 'Oh, it's gone cold! Sorry, angel – you should have stopped me.'

'No, no, I wanted to hear it all. I wanted to understand. I thought when you disappeared off to London or back to Alberta, it meant you . . . you weren't all that serious . . . Well, no, I mean, I didn't expect you to be bound to me hand and foot but I . . . I . . .' She stammered into silence.

He stretched, sighed, and hugged her again. 'There was a lot of stuff I couldn't talk to you about, Laura. It all had to be kind of hush-hush. These big conglomerates don't like anybody to know what they're up to, and especially if they're having to back away from a project they've been keen on. That's why I didn't want the press on my tail. It must have seemed crazy when I disappeared off the scene, but Leo insisted.'

'I understand now.'

'Leo wasn't at all pleased when your research turned up the bequest and we began to get reporters buzzing around. And Kim was a problem . . .'

'Papa should never have told her about the bequest! It was against all our principles.'

'Well, there you go. He didn't understand there were other

and bigger things involved. But that's turning out okay, I think. Though what Leo's going to say when I tell him I want him to take on the Tansfield Towers thing, I can't imagine.'

'He'll disapprove? Why should he?'

'Oh, he'll grumble and then hand it over to some minion, I expect. Someone about the same level as Kim, on one of the lower rungs of his firm.'

'Neil, I wish I'd known! I wasted such a lot of energy trying to hate you for what I thought you were doing to the Tansfield people! And I thought . . .' She felt herself colouring up. 'I thought perhaps you'd fallen a bit for Kim.'

At that he laughed. 'Sweetheart, nobody in their right mind could fall for Kim. She's too . . . I don't want to say ruthless, but look at how she used Shelley. That was kind of cold blooded.'

Laura nodded. 'I'm a bit worried about Shelley. If that father of hers ever finds out what she did, he'll never forgive her.'

'That's a problem family, no doubt of it. We'll have to give it some thought—'

He was interrupted by the sound of the front door opening and Mrs Stevens's voice fluting up the stairs. 'Good morning! Miss Wainwright, dear, are you there?'

Laura sprang to her feet and, hugging her dressing-gown about her, ran downstairs to face everyday life.

Twenty-Two

Mrs Stevens had picked up the morning paper from the front step. 'A bit late today?' she queried, laying it on the hall table.

'I'm afraid so. Mrs Stevens, you'd better begin on the hall and the living room this morning. I need the kitchen, haven't started breakfast yet.'

'No problem.' She took off her sun hat to hang on the hall-stand. 'Going to be a hot day.' She studied Laura, standing in a cambric dressing-gown. 'Have you taken in the milk? It'll go sour if it's not in the fridge.'

'Er . . . no . . .'

'I'll get it.' She walked past her into the kitchen where she opened the back door, letting in a flood of light already warmed by the sun. Laura followed her to fill the kettle and switch it on for more coffee. Closing the fridge door with a sharp thud, Mrs Stevens went on. 'You know all those cocktail goodies Miss Groves got special from the caterers last night? She threw 'em all on the floor after you left!'

'Oh dear.'

'Upset, she was. I was going to clear up the mess but she ordered me out of the house.'

She now waited for Laura to explain what had brought on this fracas. It seemed that after all she hadn't learned all the facts by eavesdropping.

'I'll be down again in a minute,' said Laura, escaping towards the door.

'The hall first and then the living room?'

'Yes . . . Er . . . no – do the living room first.'

'I bought some of that beeswax polish for the bookcase—'

'Yes, thank you—'

'Mrs Diggory makes it herself. Costs a few pennies more but I think it'll be worth it—'

'Yes, yes, I'll pay for it, don't worry. I must get on, Mrs Stevens.'

In the bathroom it was clear that Neil had already been there for he'd used her father's shaving gear. She took the briefest of showers then threw on whatever clothes came quickest to hand – shirt and jeans from the back of a chair. As she did so she heard Neil on the telephone in the office. She collected up the tray of mugs and was downstairs making a fresh supply of coffee when he came into the kitchen.

'Morning.' He kissed the cheek she offered. 'I used your phone, hope you don't mind. I rang the taxi firm, it'll be here in about fifteen minutes. And I rang Leo, left a message on his office machine to clear a space for me after lunch.

'To talk about taking over the Tansfield thing.'

'You got it. Oh, good, coffee after all. You're an angel.' He hovered near as she poured the water over the ground beans. 'Some time this morning, would you do something for me, Laura?'

'Of course, anything.'

'Can you get in touch with Shelley?'

'Umm . . .' She thought about it. 'I've got the Dallancys' number but I don't think I should ring. I might get Norman, and he'd hang up on me.'

'Does she have a mobile?'

'Yes, but I don't know the number. I had it in my hand a while ago but I gave it to Kim.' She looked back with mixed feelings at that event.

'Well then . . . Could you write? Just a note. I'll give you my London number – wait – have you got a pencil?' She nodded towards the kitchen pad and pencil hanging by the fridge for shopping reminders. While he scribbled she poured the coffee and, with as much satisfaction as Neil, sipped the burning hot liquid.

'Here you are. Ask her to call me.' He pointed. 'That's my address – my real address, not a borrowed hideout. You know, it was Kim that insisted on not giving my real address. She loved all that stuff, keeping me out of reach of the reporters so she could spring her headline story when she was ready.' He shook his head at the memeroy. 'But this is where I'm staying until everything's tied up over the Tansfield thing and I fly back home.'

'I see. Okay, I'll write to her.' Once again she felt that sinking of the heart at hearing him speak of leaving, but this time she hid her dismay, for if she burst into tears Mrs Stevens, in the hall with a duster, would surely hear her.

They sat down at the old pine table. 'I ought to get you something to eat—'

'No, that's okay, I'll get something at Brinbank Junction, I think there's a sandwich bar there. Listen, sweets, I looked in on your dad, he was still out for the count. Are you okay about handling him when he comes to?'

'Of course. I've done it before.'

'But there's the disillusionment-with-Kim factor this time. Is he going to be crying the blues when he comes to?'

250

She shrugged. 'I suppose so. But he's been disappointed before and we've lived through it. He applied for a headmastership once – I thought he'd never get over it when he was rejected. But in the end it passed over.'

'Yeah, but Laura, the village probably didn't know about that. This time he's slipped on the banana peel right in front of all his neighbours. You heard him last night . . .'

'I know. It's not going to be any fun. But we'll manage.'

'Perhaps I should stay on a bit longer—'

'No, no, the world can't come to a halt because Papa's unhappy. You have to speak to your solicitor friend.'

'I could call him on the phone—'

'And that would be easy? I thought you had to explain it to him in person.'

'Well . . . yeah . . . it would be better.'

'You want to do what's best for those families at Tansfield Towers, don't you? That's your job for today. Mine is Papa. I'll deal with it.'

He took her hand across the table. 'That's my girl. Listen, give him that telephone number. If he gets really down in the dumps he might like to call me. Tell him I'm on his side all the way.'

'Yes, I'll tell him.'

'You too – if you feel you need a bit of time out from holding his hand, call me. Don't let him cry on your shoulder for too long. It's not good for you and it's mebbe not good for him.'

'I know, but it's a matter of feeling my way. He's had this problem with depression . . .'

'Sure, I understand, it's no good saying "Snap out of it" like so many folk do. But I think he could pull himself out of this, Laura. He's been through a process, he's been learning that Kim isn't the starry goddess he thought she was. I can see it's hard for him, but he may have turned a corner.'

'I want to believe you're right—'

Mrs Stevens bounced into the room. 'There's a car at the door, dear.'

'Oh! Thank you.' Laura was flustered. She guessed her daily help had been listening to their conversation from the knowing look on her face.

251

Now she had to face the fact that Neil was about to go. Words failed her completely. She followed him into the hall and opened the door as the driver was about to raise the knocker.

'Everything's going to be fine,' he assured her as he took her in his arms for a farewell kiss. 'And don't forget to write to Shelley.'

'I won't. I'll do it in a minute.'

'Call me if you want to. Bye, sweetheart.'

The driver opened the car door for him, he got in, and within seconds he was gone. She went back into the house, her heart as heavy as the old millstone that graced the village crossroads.

Mrs Stevens was waiting for her, pretending to unwind the lead for the vacuum cleaner. 'Miss Groves has missed Mr Crandel's help with her garden,' she remarked. 'Of course he hasn't been around so much recently what with being Mr Mystery Man. He hasn't done any of her garden since June.'

'No, he hasn't.'

'He was looking at those little bay trees of hers last night, said he thought they were potted up in the wrong soil. She paid the earth for them, you know. A pity she didn't get a chance to talk about that, with the party coming to such a sudden end.'

'Oh yes.' Laura was saying to herself, I can't think how I ever thought she was fun. I've got to get rid of her. I can't bear it, the way she snoops and pries . . . But Mrs Stevens was needed for the housework, while she herself was needed in the office; and when her father eventually woke there would be the problem of seeing him through his miseries.

She said abruptly, 'Do what needs to be done on the ground floor as quickly as you can and we'll leave it at that. I've got a lot on my mind today, Mrs Stevens, I need the house to myself.'

'Oh! Well, if you think so . . . Is something wrong, dear? Have you got a headache or something?'

Laura escaped upstairs without a word. She lingered on the upstairs landing until she heard the vacuum cleaner start, then went to the door of her father's bedroom to open it a crack. He was lying with his back towards her, breathing heavily, still deeply asleep. She hoped he'd stay like that until Mrs Stevens had left.

The answering machine on the office phone had several messages in store. She dealt with them, then sat down to look through a collection of correspondence. Mrs Stevens called up to her about mid-morning. 'I'm going now, Miss Wainwright. Is there anything you want me to get at the shop?' A ploy to get her to come downstairs but she called a farewell and that was that.

The exchange seemed to have wakened Ronald. She heard him trudging about, from bedroom to bathroom to bedroom again, heavy footfalls that seemed to denote low vitality. She hurried downstairs to make coffee, enough to help him through whatever hangover he might have and to boost her own morale.

When he appeared in the kitchen he was quite well turned out. He had shaved neatly, his hair was brushed, his shirt was buttoned properly and there was even a faint scent of cologne.

'Good morning,' he said. 'It's very warm, isn't it? Could we have breakfast out on the patio?'

'Of course.' The 'patio' was a small square of paving stones outside the back door, laid by a previous owner for ease of handling such things as dustbins. Laura had tried to transform it by hiding the dustbin behind a trellis and growing a rambler up that. It was a shady spot until late afternoon. She went out to set up the little folding table, and was amazed when Ronald appeared saying, 'I'll do that.'

She turned over the task to him. While he set up the table and folding chairs, she was making coffee. Then she looked for a checked tablecloth to give a festive air to the proceedings. Meanwhile her father amazed her even further by getting out bowls and plates and mugs. True, it took him several tries before he found the right cupboards, but she didn't correct him.

By and by they were settled with fruit and cereal and steaming mugs. Ronald sipped gingerly. He said, 'Much doing in the office?'

'Yes, there are two enquiries from overseas, Malta and, of all places, Rio de Janeiro.'

'Lots of Brits in South America,' he commented.

'Right.'

'I'll take over the Maltese thing, if that's all right. I don't want to have to do any correspondence in Spanish.'

'Portuguese.'

'Oh yes.' He pushed stewed apricot around his bowl for a moment then said, 'I'm turning over a new leaf.'

She debated whether she should say, 'Turning in which direction?' but decided it wasn't the moment for jokes. So she said nothing, merely nodded.

'I've got to do some serious thinking, Laura. It seems to me I've been an absolute blockhead for the last year or so. And bad tempered, too, when I look back.' He waited for her comment, but she merely shook her head and waited for whatever might come next.

'I haven't got very far yet. It's all too . . . It was like being hit over the head with a crowbar last night.'

'I can imagine.'

'But I want to sort it out.' He sighed. 'It could take a while.'

'That's all right.'

'I know you'll put up with it, because you've put up with me all the while and hardly ever even hinted I was being silly. I want to say thank you, Laura. You've been kinder than I deserved. And if you'll help me, I want to make a big change and be a . . . well . . . be a more agreeable person.'

'Well, I don't know that—'

'To start with, I want to be more help with the business. I see now, just taking a quick look back, that I was off doing silly odd-job-man kind of jobs for Kim – slaving over her garden, helping with the paintwork – well, that's all over. You and I are going to divide things up equally from now on.'

'That's good.'

'I don't remember quite what I was going on about last night but I seem to remember telling Neil that the whole village would be laughing at me.' This in a doleful tone.

'Yes, that came up.'

'Well, that's not going to be fun, Laura. I admit I don't know how that's going to go. But I'm going to do my best not to get too het up about it, and if you think I'm being silly I want you to tell me – tell me straight out so that I can look at things and see them in the right way.'

'That's a bargain, Papa.'

She reached a hand over the table and they shook on it, solemnly, like children making a pledge. She smiled, and after a moment he did too. The first smile of the day, the first smile in the After Kim era.

True to his bargain, he went upstairs immediately after the meal to take care of matters that had been waiting now for several days on his PC. Laura thought they'd had enough food to see them through until late afternoon so decided to catch the midday collection with her note to Shelley.

She'd written and rewritten it several times. In the end she had to be satisfied with: 'Dear Shelley, Neil Crandel would like very much if you would ring him at this number. Hope everything is going well at home, Yours, Laura Wainwright.'

She hurried upstairs to change. If by any chance there was any gathering at the village post office, she wanted to look good. Since early morning she'd been wearing what she grabbed at Mrs Stevens's arrival. A glimpse of herself in the mirror made her wonder how any man could have wanted to kiss her.

She put on one of her summer dresses and flat sandals. She took a little care with sun cream and eye shadow. Her hair was tied up on the top of her head for coolness. She walked slowly down the lane in what shade she could find, and arrived at the mail box cool and unhurried. There were only two customers inside the shop, both buying ice-cream. She exchanged friendly nods. Clearly Mrs Stevens hadn't been spreading her news, for they showed only a friendly interest. Relieved, she did some household shopping.

Then she did something to which she'd been nerving herself for some days. Today, it turned out, was D-day. She walked on to the converted shop that was both home and business premises to the Stevenses. She pressed the buzzer, and after quite a delay her household help came to the door. She looked heavy eyed and slow. Clearly she'd been having a siesta.

'Oh . . . it's you, Miss Wainwright. What a surprise.'

'I wanted a word with you, Mrs Stevens—'

'Fancy coming out in all this heat. You could have telephoned, dear.'

'This was something I wanted to say face to face.'

'What?' Mrs Stevens looked puzzled. 'I'm not with you, dear, what d'you mean?'

'May I come in?'

'Of course, of course, in you come, what am I thinking of, keeping you on the doorstep.' But there was something unwelcoming in her tone, and Laura felt she perhaps guessed what was coming.

She stepped into the room used as an office. An electric fan was keeping the air circulating but the old shop window was letting in too much sun though its net curtains. Mrs Stevens waved Laura to a chair and took one by the desk.

'Mrs Stevens, you and I have no written contract but I think it's always been accepted that we could terminate our arrangement with two weeks' notice.'

'You what?'

'I'm afraid I have to give you two weeks' wages in lieu of notice and tell you that I don't require your services from today onwards.'

'Eh? Wait a minute! What's this you're on about? You can't do that!' The other woman had flushed red, anger and astonishment painted on every feature.

'Of course I can, Mrs Stevens.' She was opening her handbag to take out her cheque book. 'If you'll just tell me how much extra I owe for cleaning liquids and things like that special polish—'

'What d'you think you're playing at, Miss Wainwright? If you think you'll get anyone else to take on that stupid old house of yours, you're in for a big surprise—'

'That's not your affair, Mrs Stevens. The matter we're discussing—'

'I'm not discussing it, you're giving out orders! Who do you think you are? I toil and moil, and fetch and carry, and this is all the thanks I get? Let me tell you, if you go to one of them big agencies and hire somebody, that'll take the smile off your face! They'll cost you a fortune—'

'Can we just keep to the point, Mrs Stevens? I've decided that it's no longer suitable to have you come—'

'Suitable? What does that mean, suitable? I'm not good enough for you, is that it? Think you're so special, you and that Kim Groves with her fancy-dancy parties and her "decor" that's only wallpaper after all, spending money like water while me and my Joe have to work all hours of the day and night to keep going. Let me tell you, our farm was a lot better than the useless show she goes in for, and as for you and your pecking-away at that clapped-out computer in your office, *we* produced something that was *useful* . . .'

For the first time, as this tirade flowed round her, Laura understood why Mrs Stevens was such a scandalmonger. Envy and resentment fuelled her need to bring other people down to size. The loss of the farm must have been a dreadful blow, one that Laura had never really been aware of or given any thought to. That was why she stood silent while her former servant berated her, shocking her with the pent-up rancour that now poured out.

'. . . And as for that in-comer that you're so moonstruck over, he's been up to no good all along and he'll let you down, see if he doesn't, and then we'll see who's coming off best!'

Exhausted, scarlet with anger, perspiration standing out on her brow, she sat back in her chair and gasped. Laura seriously thought she might be about to have a heart attack. She rushed to the kitchen for a glass of water and seized a washcloth to run under the tap. Back in the office, she patted Mrs Stevens's brow with the cool damp cloth, wiped away the sweat, and offered her the glass. After shaking her head at it once or twice, she took it and swallowed great gulps.

'Is that better? Have you any cologne or anything that you could dab on? Let me move the fan so that you get the full benefit . . .' Uttering soothing little words, Laura did what she could to help her recover. Her heartfelt wish was to get out of the place as soon as possible but her conscience wouldn't allow her to go until she was sure the other woman was safe.

After some minutes Mrs Stevens let it be known that she felt better. 'Another glass,' she muttered, handing it back. Laura escaped to the kitchen for a refill. When she came back her patient was sitting up straighter, using the damp cloth to cool the skin on her throat and between her breasts. She took the glass of water, sipping it more naturally.

Neither woman said a word. Laura was trying to think how

to bring the encounter to an end but couldn't form a sentence. And to run away without doing what she'd come for would be cowardly. Sick or well, Mrs Stevens was from now on unwelcome at Old Brin House.

Finally she said, 'Are you all right now?'

'Thank you, I'll do. You gave me a shock, Miss Wainwright.'

'So I see.'

A beat of time went by, as if Mrs Stevens were waiting for an apology. When none came she said, in a somewhat cajoling tone, 'I could give you a lower hourly rate if that would suit.'

Laura drew in a deep breath and let it out. 'It's not about the money, Mrs Stevens.'

'I think it's rotten of you to treat me like this after all this time—'

'I'm sorry but the time has come for us to part.' She paused. 'Perhaps you'd like to reckon up how much I owe you and send me a bill.'

'A bill?' There was incredulity in the words.

Of course. Nothing in writing. Nothing to have the taxman on her back. 'But if you'd rather settle it now, I've got my cheque book.' She now produced it, and tried to find the pen at the bottom of her handbag.

'I'd prefer cash as usual,' said Mrs Stevens. Her chin had come up, her mouth was in a mulish set.

'I may have enough cash, if you'll tell me how much.'

Mrs Stevens found a piece of paper and a pencil. After some scribbling she came up with a sum that was a little over what Laura had expected, but she found she had enough to meet it.

'Thank you.' She was throwing the money in a drawer, barely civil.

'So it's goodbye, Mrs Stevens.'

'I'm not to come next Tuesday. Or ever.'

'Exactly.'

'Tell me why, that's what I want to know!' she burst out. 'It's not because I don't do the work, because nobody else could deal with that vacuum cleaner, and I'm into every corner, every cranny! And when I think of how we've had our little chats during the tea break – I thought we were *friends*!'

'I thought so too, Mrs Stevens, but I've changed my mind on that score.'

258

'But why? Why?'

'Friends don't tittle-tattle about each other—'

'Don't pretend you didn't enjoy it when I told you what that Kim Groves was up to—'

'No, I admit I got some laughs from what you told me. I'm not defending myself. But I've got more important things to think about now, and one way and another I've come to the conclusion that it's time to say goodbye.'

'What'll people think?' cried Mrs Stevens. 'Don't you go telling them I've done anything wrong, because I haven't!'

'I'm not going to—'

'And if I did take home a few slices of cake or some frozen cherries, where was the harm? You had plenty—'

'It doesn't matter. I'm going now. Take care.' She went out, shaking her head over the realization that little things she'd missed from the house had gone out in her daily help's shopping basket.

Out of the corner of her eye she saw the net curtains twitch as her former helper watched her go. She didn't hurry. She wasn't retreating in haste. She had made a formal parting and had tried to deal considerately with the outcome.

The afternoon heat beat down upon her. She felt worn out and wished now that she'd used the car for this trip. But as she walked she was saying inwardly, to the rhythm of her footsteps, 'I did my best, I had to do it.' A situation that had become intolerable had been ended; no more spying and eavesdropping from Mrs Stevens.

And other good things were still to come. Her father was aiming at a transformation. If he would take on his proper share of the research and correspondence, she would have time to do some at least of the chores that had been done by the charwoman. With his help, a system could be evolved to run the old house efficiently.

When she got home she found he had gone out. In the office folders were lying open on his desk, papers lay strewn about. His pen had fallen to the floor. He had simply got up and walked out.

So much for the transformation.

Twenty-Three

At mid-morning next day, Neil rang her on the household line. 'How are things going?' he asked.

'You mean with Papa? Fair. He and I had a long heart-to-heart yesterday and he promised to start a new life, more or less. He had a sort of setback halfway through the day but you can't expect miracles.'

'Did he tell you he called me? He seemed in a bit of a fret. But on the whole I think he's going to tough it out from now on. What's he doing at the moment?'

'He's catching up on the work he walked out on yesterday afternoon. I really think he's trying, Neil. How about you? Did you see your big-time lawyer?'

'Yes, and he thinks I'm nuts. A young guy called Charlie Jackson got landed with the job of handling Simmingford, but he seems kind of tickled at the whole thing so I have the feeling he'll do all right. Now, listen, angel, I got a phone call from Shelley.'

'That was quick. Mind you, I put a first class stamp on it.'

'Oh, no expense spared, eh? Well, she's agreed to meet me tomorrow, and as she can't borrow her dad's car in the day and so can't go very far I fixed up to meet her in Salubrious Simmingford. I arranged a lunch date, at that big old-fashioned pub and restaurant near the Town Hall.'

'Yes?'

'We-ell . . . Listen, Laura . . . I don't want to sound idiotic, but I . . . I got the feeling she . . . Well, anyhow, I didn't feel easy about seeing her on my own. I didn't want her to . . . It's difficult to explain . . .'

'I understand,' said Laura. And she did. Shelley had been thrilled at the idea of at last meeting Neil again, and had perhaps shown too much enthusiasm. 'Could I ask why you're meeting her?'

'I feel I owe her something. You know? She went out on a limb for me, going behind her dad's back like that. I want to say thank you and see if there's anything I can do for her.'

'Such as what?'

'Well . . . I can't offer her money, of course. I don't know . . . Something may suggest itself.' A long pause, in which Laura fancied there was embarrassment. 'The poor kid was so shined up because I got in touch that I was a bit taken aback so . . . The long and short of it is, I told her you'd be there too. Is that okay?'

That was very prudent of him. She also felt that it would have been a let-down for Shelley. She said, 'I think that can be arranged. What time?'

'Well, I asked what would suit her and it seems she's got another job so she says she'll come in her lunch hour. That's twelve thirty to one fifteen, so it'll be a bar lunch, okay?'

'That's fine. Remind me where this pub is?'

'It's in the Town Hall square, which I think is called Crainsley after some ancient bigwig, and the pub is the Simmingford Arms. Could you come a bit early so we can catch up on each other?'

'Twelve fifteen.'

'Got you. That's a date then. I've got to go, toots. I'm meeting a climate expert in half an hour.'

'A climate expert?'

'Well, I can't grow trees at Wenaskowa any more because it's planted over with oil wells now, or at least will be soon. So I'm asking this guy to tell me where in my homeland it would be good to move to. He's got charts and diagrams on his laptop to show me. Should be fun.'

'Best of luck,' she said.

'Love you.'

'Love you.' She disconnected. She was divided between joy and misery. In one sentence he asked to see her, in the next he was talking about going away. And the casual sign-off, 'Love you', with no more meaning in it than 'So long' . . .

With a sigh she went back to her work.

Since she was downstairs, she decided to make the mid-morning coffee. Ronald came down, summoned by the aroma of finest Kenyan Mocha. 'That was Neil,' she reported. 'He's meeting Shelley tomorrow and wants me to be there.'

'Meeting Shelley? What on earth for?'

'Wants to find out if everything's okay for her.'

He was morose, yet he'd got up early this morning and had been hard at work on the papers he'd discarded yesterday.

She'd spent all yesterday afternoon worrying about his prolonged absence, rung him on his mobile to which of course there was no response. When he at last reappeared, around eight in the evening, he said merely that he'd walked to the crossroads, taken the bus to the market town of Jessbridge, had eaten and didn't want anything more. He thereupon settled down to watch television. At ten he poured himself a nightcap, drank it, and went to bed. She reckoned she'd had ten words out of him.

Nevertheless, the good intentions had reasserted themselves. So now she said, 'I haven't had a chance to tell you, but I had a word with Mrs Stevens yesterday.'

'Huh!' After a sip of coffee he said, 'I hope the word was "Goodbye".'

'As a matter of fact, it was.'

'What?'

'I . . . er . . . I think the polite phrase is, I dispensed with her services.'

He stared at her for a long moment, and then, to her astonishment, he began to laugh. It was the first time in weeks she'd heard him laugh. After a moment she joined in, although with less merriment because she still had something else to say. Something quite difficult.

'Papa, it means a big difference in how we manage the house. Much though we love it, this is a cranky old place. If we could find someone else to come in and do the hard bits, that would be ideal – but Mrs Stevens is the only one in the village.'

'Ye-es . . . I see that. So what are you going to do – hire somebody from Jessbridge or somewhere?'

'I've looked at the local paper and there are one or two advertisements so I'll try those, but the thing is, Papa, if I get anyone, it's going to cost a lot more.'

'Well, we can afford it, I hope.'

'Yes, but it's not going to be like Mrs Stevens.'

'I hope not!'

'No, I mean, she did everything. Others might have rules. Some cleaning people say they won't do windows—'

'Well, we already get ours done by What's-his-Name—'

'That's the *outsides*, Papa. Mrs Stevens did the insides.'

'Well, What's-his-Name could come in and do the insides—'

'Have you ever looked at the way he sloshes water about? We couldn't let him loose indoors, he'd soak everything in our office. In any case, it's not just window-cleaning I'm talking about. We rather casually let Mrs Stevens into our lives so that she ended up doing all sorts of extra jobs – for which I paid, of course, but all the same, she wasn't an ordinary sort of charwoman to us. I don't think that would happen with anybody else.'

Her father frowned and sighed. 'Now none of that would have occurred to me. You really have a lot of insight, Laura.'

She waved off the compliment. 'It's not insight, it's hindsight. I see now that letting Mrs Stevens get so close to us wasn't a good thing because, as it turns out, she's not a very nice person. But she's not going to be around any more and we have to work out a new regime for handling our household. I have to tell you, quite seriously, that I don't think I can do it all myself. At least, perhaps I could if I slaved at it, but I don't think that would be fair – do you?'

'So we'll hire somebody else and she'll cost us a bit but that's all right, isn't it?'

'It might take a while to find someone.'

'Hm-mm . . . Am I picking up a coded message here? You're not asking me to take on washing the dishes, are you?'

'Papa, we have a dishwasher!' She chuckled. 'That's it there, behind you. And next to it is the washing machine – that washes the clothes. What you do is, you put things in, the machine washes them, and then you take them out.'

'Well, I *know* that.' He paused. 'However, I suspect I'm going to be asked to put things in and take things out.'

'Yes.'

'Hm-mm . . . I think I'd need a course of lessons. But, after all, I learned Norman French so I could follow the history of

William's reign. So I can learn washing-machine. Anything else?'

'You could . . . you could keep your room tidy.'

'Good Lord! That's an echo from my teens! "Keep your room tidy" – you'll be telling me next I should get my hair cut.'

'How you look is your affair. But how the house looks is *ours*. If we could divide up the chores so that they're manageable, I'd feel a lot happier about the post-Stevens era.'

'Never let it be said that we couldn't manage without that confounded woman,' grunted Ronald. 'We'll give it a go.'

'Then there's the garden. If you'd take that on again, and attend to the fruit bushes and the vegetable plot as you used to, that would be a weight off my mind. We missed the cherries this year, Papa – they went ripe and the birds have got them all because we never picked them.'

He coloured up. 'My fault,' he said. 'I'm sorry.'

'It's no big deal. It means none got put in the freezer later in the year. But the late-season raspberries will soon be ready, and it would be a shame to lose them. And some of the garden tools need a bit of attention – the shears need sharpening.'

'I'll see to it.'

'Thank you.' She didn't want to ask for anything more at present. To her surprise he smiled at her and held up a finger for her attention.

'And I've got to do this without leaving you trapped in the office taking on half of my work – right?'

'Oh, I—'

'You don't have to say it. I know it's what I should do. And I'm going to try, my dear, I really am. I admit I went off on a bit of a joyride yesterday, and I can't promise it won't happen again. I get so fed up with myself, you see. I suddenly get the urge to run away from myself. Can you understand that?'

'Only too well.'

'But I'm not a complete fool, after all. I see I've made a mess of things recently and I'm trying to come to terms with it. And if it means washing dishes and sharpening shears, I'll do it, and try to be good-tempered about it. Just give me time, Laura.'

'Oh, Papa, of course!'

*   *   *

264

The first mention of the turn of events concerning Tansfield Towers was on the radio next morning. Laura heard it as she was roused at seven by her radio-alarm.

'City solicitors Garrad-Lome issued a statement yesterday evening about the housing estate in the Midlands town of Simmingford. Tansfield Towers was claimed some weeks ago for a legatee by virtue of a bequest made in the 1890s. The solicitors' statement ends as follows: "An amicable agreement between our client Mr Neil Crandel and Simmingford Town Council is expected in the next few days. No money will be involved in this agreement although the council will guarantee improvements and refurbishments to the buildings over a term of months. Mr Crandel's intention is that the estate should be a credit to the memory of his forebear, Marianne Crandel."'

Later, as she dressed, the news came up as a featured item. The station's legal correspondent was interviewed. 'A bit of a rum do, Ivor. What do you make of it?'

'It's unusual, that's true. But there have been estates in the past where a benefactor has paid serious attention to the conditions in which the inhabitants live. For instance, in London, the Shaftesbury Estate, and then there's the Cadburys—'

'But those were started by industrial tycoons or big landowners, Ivor. This Crandel seems just to be an ordinary chap.'

'We know almost nothing about him, John. He seems to want to stay out of the limelight. Still, good news for Tansfield Towers.'

Next came interviews with one or two of the estate dwellers. Asked for their opinion when they had only just got out of bed, they were for the most part inarticulate but thankful. One old man remarked that there was probably a catch in it but he was relieved at not being turned out of his home.

When she got downstairs to start the day, her father was in the kitchen already, fiddling with the cafetière. 'I shouldn't have put this plunger thing in until I'd poured in the water, should I?'

'No, but never mind. I expect it'll ease itself into the right position.' She saw he'd brought in their newspaper, so while he completed his experiment in coffee-making she picked it up. The list of items on the inside gave an unsensational page

265

five as the home of the item about Tansfield. She turned to it. Two succinct paragraphs, facts only, no comment.

When she got to Brinbank Junction to catch the train to Simmingford, she bought a copy of the *Comet*. The *Comet* was congratulating itself on having forced the elusive Neil Crandel into behaving like a decent human being. 'Result! Our campaign' – what campaign, wondered Laura – 'has saved decent folk from being victimized yet again. You can rely on us to go on fighting for your rights wherever we see injustice!'

She put it in the wastebin before she boarded the train.

The Simmingford Arms had once been an important inn on the coaching route to York. Some echoes of past splendours could still be seen in expanses of panelling and polished brass. The bar, however, was designed to look something like a Mayfair watering-hole, with Art Deco mirrors and pale leather benches. There were a few customers, brought in perhaps by the excellent air conditioning.

Neil was already there, reading a copy of *The Times*. His clothes signalled a relaxed mood, open-necked shirt and jeans. He rose to greet her, taking both hands to draw her close for a kiss. 'You do look nice. That's the dress you wore to one of Kim's garden things.'

'You remember?' she said in amazement.

'I remember everything about you, sweetest. Especially the way your hair escapes in little strands when you tie it atop of your head.'

She put up a hand to pat them back. He laughed and drew her down beside him. When they were settled he signalled a waiter. She ordered a long cool Cinzano. Soft music was issuing from a hidden source, a piano embroidering a gentle tune accompanied by a scarcely perceptible rhythm background.

'What's that?' she asked, smiling.

'That's Oscar Petersen casting his spell from about forty years ago. You like it? I've got that recording in my collection back home.'

She didn't want to talk about 'back home' so she merely nodded then asked, 'Have you seen the *Comet*?'

'Yeah, bought it in London along with the others. Do you get the impression that our case isn't treated as very important?'

266

'I do indeed. It's not headline stuff any more.'

'Thank heaven for that. How was your train journey?'

'Uneventful. You have to realize, darling, I'm quite blasé about trains.'

'I'll miss 'em when I go home. Around Wenaskowa we either had to drive or take a plane. Well, tell me how Ronald is doing.'

'Another session of life-doctoring and promises to do better. I think he's really going to work at it, Neil. By and by I might suggest that he could go to see his counsellor – he had one, you know, during one of his blackest periods.'

'But if he's managing all right without?'

'So far. It's early days.' She sighed. 'Never mind – even if there are ups and downs, I have a feeling it might come out all right this time.'

'Here's something that'll surprise you. My legal buddy, Leo, tells me Kim is talking about leaving her firm.'

'Oh! What does that mean?'

'I think it means she's been given a hard time by her senior partners. But, hey, she's been a good money earner for them up till now, so Leo says – a real star when it comes to land rights. So perhaps it will pass over.'

'I ought to feel sorry for her, I suppose.'

'But you don't.'

'No, alas. If she does up-sticks and go, it would make life easier for Papa.'

'Speaking of moving—' He broke off as Shelley appeared in the doorway of the bar, gazing round in interest at the decor. He waved, and she hurried towards them.

Today the short hair was very blond and arranged with gel in little tweaks. She wore a white tank top and candy pink jeans that clung to her long limbs like a second skin. She was flushed, as if she'd hurried too much in the heat.

Neil rose to offer her a seat. She collapsed on it, waving her hand before her face for air. 'Whoo, it's hot! As hot as Marbella.'

'What will you have to drink? What was that cocktail you had at the hotel restaurant? Marbella Something?'

'No, no, I'm for a long cool glass of lime-and-orange, if you don't mind. Lots of ice.'

The waiter, who was young and keen, surged up to take her order. He was clearly delighted to see someone so stylish and pretty in this sedate setting.

'So what's all this on the news this morning about Tansfield Towers?' she began at once when her drink was ordered. 'Dad nearly went spare when he saw it on GMTV!'

'You mean angry? Surprised?'

'Struck all of a heap, that's what. He called you every name he could think of. You've backed down, haven't you?' Her tone was aggressive.

'In what way?'

'Well, they must have told you to take your claim and run it up a gum tree or you wouldn't have agreed to all this stuff about improvements.' She leaned an elbow on the table, put a finger against her cheek, and studied him as if from a measured distance. 'What are you up to?'

'Shelley!' cried Laura.

'It's okay. She's entitled,' Neil said. 'Listen, Shelley, there's no hidden agenda and there's no backing down. I never went into this to make money. I'm not too fussed about your dad's opinion and if you want to go along with what he thinks, that's your choice.'

That gave her pause. She'd expected to rattle him with her challenge. 'You've got to be making something out of it,' she objected. 'It stands to reason. You can't just ignore money like that . . .'

'Well, you'll have to wait and see, that's all. Anyhow, that's not why I wanted this meet. This is by way of a thank you for helping me out.'

'Yeah, I'm wondering now if helping you out was such a good thing!'

'I wouldn't ever have asked you to do it,' he said. 'That was Kim Groves's idea.'

'Oh, her! Ten out of ten to her, for handling my dad like a piece of dirt. The only thing that made him happy this morning was that she'd been given the push from the case; some other firm was mentioned, high-powered blokes from London, apparently.' She broke off as her drink was put before her. Then she said, 'You know, that day at her posh office . . . Dad was such a pain in the neck that day that I felt I had to sort of put things right. And if it's really true that you . . . that this housing estate . . .' She paused, sipped then went on. 'I've been to see it, you know. What a dump! If you're really making the council do something about it, well . . . p'raps I'm on your side.'

'Thank you, Shelley.'

She shrugged and gazed round after what had been, for her, a painful exchange. Still uncertain, her glance flickered from the bottles on the bar to the other customers. 'Classy place. But I don't think it could ever be my scene.' She sipped again for inspiration, and went on in a jocular tone, 'Dad wouldn't come here either unless it was to lob a brick at the Town Hall across the square.'

'So did your father get over his bad temper this morning?' Laura prompted. 'How is he, in general? Has he had any offers for the shop?'

'I *wish*! I'd give anything if we could pack up and leave Simmingford. No such luck.' Now she was all prudence and earnestness. 'Mum and I want him to give it to an estate agent but he tried that at first and he says the bloke was trying to stitch him up. But sad little ads in newspapers aren't going to find him a buyer, now are they.'

'He was hoping to move to Spain, wasn't he?' Laura observed. 'What was he hoping to do – open a bar?' This, she'd gathered from television life-change programmes, was a popular ambition of émigrés. 'Or a shop?'

'Oh, he sees it clear in his imagination – nice little place on a sea-front somewhere, catering to the English-speaking tourists – cute little mementoes, English newspapers and magazines, bars of Cadbury, that kind of thing.'

'That sounds like a good idea, Shelley.'

'El Dorado, more like – the place that was made out of gold and nobody ever found it. We're never going to make it unless we win the lottery.' With another of her quicksilver changes of mood, she was wistful for a moment then said with briskness, 'Are we gonna eat? I'm due back at work in half an hour.'

'Of course.' At Neil's beckoning the young waiter bustled up and took orders for sandwiches with fancy names. 'A glass of wine?'

'Nah, more of the same, can't go back to the office pissed.'

To the waiter she added, 'And hurry it up, Twinkle-toes, or my boss will chew me up.' He grinned and nodded.

Laura asked after her mother. Shelley replied with a shrug that Mum was fed up. 'Dad's never easy to live with, you know. But ever since he got the story about the Dallancy bequest he's been worse than ever. He keeps grousing that he should have been left something, too, and when Mum tries to point out that . . . Oh, well, he'll have to calm down one day, I suppose.'

'He doesn't know that you took the DNA test?'

'No, and don't ever tell him!' she said in alarm. 'He'd throw me out. Ma doesn't know either, nobody does, except us and Miss Bossyboots in the solicitor's office. You'll keep it that way, won't you?'

'Of course,' Laura promised.

'What I'd like,' Neil ventured, 'is to repay you in some way – give you something worthwhile—'

'What, diamond earrings?' Shelley asked scornfully. 'A tour of the London club scene? How would I explain it to Dad? No, no.' She shook her head. 'Anyway, I didn't do it for . . . for that sort of thing. I wanted to be . . .' She couldn't find the words. She let it go, and the waiter hurried up with her food. She busied herself with spreading her napkin and the moment passed.

She ate quickly. The threat from her boss seemed to be real. She said she'd just go to the ladies' room to wash her hands and then she'd be off. Laura rose with her.

The ladies' room was replica Victorian, with rose-patterned washbasins and crinolined ladies pictured on the wall. Shelley fiddled with the brass taps, head bent. 'I s'pose I was silly to think anything could ever come of it,' she murmured. 'That goofy waiter – he's more my style.'

'I think he liked you a lot,' Laura agreed, smiling.

'I might come back . . . chat him up.'

'That would work.'

She hesitated, then looked up to face Laura squarely. 'But it's what I suspected – Neil's your guy, isn't he?'

'I think he is,' Laura replied. But not for long, she sighed inwardly, not for long.

Twenty-Four

They lingered over coffee. The bar became busier, the gentle jazz on the sound system turned to rock, so they went out to find somewhere less animated. The heat was intense, the open expanse of Crainsley Square was like a baking sheet. There were trees offering shade alongside the canal so they headed for them, but others had had the same idea. They sauntered along among mothers with children, elderly men walking terriers, schoolboys sailing boats.

'Come with me back to London,' Neil said. 'It's nice and cool at my apartment. Have a couple of days of frivolity.'

She sighed. 'I can't, darling. Papa's taken on the evening meal – first attempt at being domesticated. You come home with me and sample his cooking.'

'Can't, angel. Leo Angrave and Charlie Jackson are coming this evening to rough out the conditions we want to put to the Simmingford crowd. Come and add your ideas to mine over that. Ring your dad and tell him to put his cookery effort in the freezer.'

But she was shaking her head. 'That wouldn't be a good idea. Neil. His hold on his new outlook is so fragile. I think he needs a week or two of close support before he's ready to fly completely solo.'

'Yeah . . .' It was a sigh of understanding. 'We've got to work this out, Laura. It needs a bit of study.'

'It does.' She knew what he meant. The days were going by, and in the near future he would have to go home to play his part at the meeting of the Nasko council. The result of this thought was to make her cling more closely against him.

At that moment they reached the shade of a group of willow trees and there, screened by their leaves, they went into each other's arms for a long moment. As they separated Laura felt a new conviction within herself: he loves me, it's not just for

271

now or for a little time, it's for always. Somehow, somewhere, we'll be together.

At last they made their way to the railway station. They would travel together as far as Brinbank Junction, where he would change trains for London. They clung together until the loudspeaker announced the London service. As he let her go he said, 'I'll call. First thing tomorrow, after I've got things sorted out with the legal lads tonight. Wake up early so you'll hear the phone.'

'Yes. I will.'

Then he was gone, sprinting for the underpass that would take him to platform 1.

At home, she saw through the kitchen window that her father was in the back garden, pulling up ingredients for a salad. He came bustling indoors when he saw her wave at him. 'I've got everything ready,' he said proudly. 'It's only ice-cream for dessert, but I got something special from the village.' He opened the freezer to show her the tub, which proved to be one of the most expensive brands. But that he'd actually been shopping for anything as mundane as food was in itself amazing. He hated using carrier bags with shop names, he'd always said in the past that it was demeaning.

Now he set about making the salad. At first he hadn't a clue how to wash the lettuce, but she didn't offer help. When he'd solved that, he couldn't work out how to dry the soaking leaves. She had to show him the salad spinner. 'What a clever idea,' he said in wonder, twirling the lettuce round. She smiled, patted him on the shoulder, and left him to it.

The rest of the afternoon was spent in the office, in a state of determination not to let her mind wander. Two or three search projects had at last turned up results, so she printed the documentation. She sent an email to the client, hoping this would bring this particular case to an end. She brought the computer files up to date. As she ended, it was after six, and Papa was calling that he'd made a nice cool drink.

Thankfully she closed down for the day. Downstairs it was a little fresher, a breeze at last drifting in through the open windows. To her surprise she discovered that her father had set the meal in the dining room, at one end of the old mahogany table. 'I've made the kitchen too hot and steamy with my cookery,' he apologized. 'What do you generally do to keep it cool?'

'Back door and windows open while I cook – and I try to do that well in advance, for instance early morning, so that there's time to cool the room off if it gets sticky.'

'Hmm . . . It's quite an organization problem, isn't it?' He poured liquid into glasses. 'This is a sort of home-made spritzer. Hope you like it.'

It was pleasant enough but she easily identified it as sparkling wine and cranberry juice in frosted glasses. Yet he was looking eagerly at her, waiting for a compliment, so she nodded approval. Likewise during the meal, which turned out to be penne cooked according to the packet instructions then mixed with a jar of stir-in sauce. She was quick to praise it.

She guessed that this cookhouse phase wouldn't last very long. He had no genuine interest in the preparation of food, although he had always liked good things to eat. So quite soon she expected him to turn his attention to other domestic chores and, truth to tell, it was elsewhere in the house that she needed his help. Yet while he was so earnestly trying to turn over a new leaf, she would applaud.

So far he'd been so full of his cooking adventure that he hadn't asked about Shelley Dallancy. When at last it occurred to him, she gave him a quick sketch of the meeting.

'So really there was nothing he could do for her, nothing she wanted?'

'Seems so. And in fact she was right. What could he give her that wouldn't make Norman ask questions?'

Ronald nodded. 'She's not as thick as I thought she was,' he acknowledged. 'I mean, to have worked that out for herself.'

Next morning, in expectation of Neil's call, Laura was up at the crack of dawn. She opened all the downstairs windows and doors to let in air that was considerably more refreshing than that of the last few days. She emptied the dishwasher and put away the contents. She fetched in the milk from the back door, she fetched the newspaper from the hall. She did all the little tasks that started the day. She was sitting down with a glass of orange juice when the sitting room phone rang.

She darted in. 'Hello?'

273

'So you're up and about – that's my girl!'

'Up and about – let me tell you I've done hours of work and solved the crossword puzzle already.'

'Aren't you afraid lightning will strike you when you tell lies like that? Listen, treasure, I've got some stuff to do in London this morning but could I drop in on you this afternoon?'

'Drop in? How'll you get here? I'll meet your train'

'No, no, I'm going to drive. I've got to be in Hampstead for lunch with Charlie – I've got to sign a paper authorizing him to act on my behalf now that we've worked out a plan of campaign. So I'll just drive straight on. Okay by you?'

'Of course!'

'So by around three, half-past three – that's the plan.'

'I'll bake you some scones.'

'Promises, promises. See you, then.'

He sounded upbeat, almost pleased with himself. She smiled as she put down the receiver.

Of course she was unsettled all the rest of the day. First she was in a thrill of delight, next a chill of apprehension. Was he coming to say goodbye? Was he about to go back to meet with the Nasko? But no, he'd sounded as if he was going to bring some good news. Good news about Simmingford? She stared at the screen of her computer, unaware that the screensaver was showing. She'd done no work for quite a space.

She suddenly said to herself, aloud, 'Stop tying yourself in knots, you fool!'

Her father, coming in at the office door, stopped in alarm. 'Who's tying themselves in knots?'

'Nobody. It's just me being stupid.'

'I don't think of you as stupid. What's the matter?'

'Nothing, nothing. It's just . . . it's coming nearer all the time . . .'

'What is, for heaven's sake?'

'The day when he goes home.'

He stared at her. 'Who? . . . Neil?'

She made no reply. At last she saw the empty computer screen and touched a key to bring back text.

'It means that much to you?' Ronald asked. He sounded confused.

She shrugged. She'd never been able to confide in him because he'd never wanted to be her confidant.

He made his slow way to his desk, then paused and turned. 'I'm sorry,' he said. 'I didn't think it was so important.'

'I'll get over it.' She jumped up to make her escape

In her bedroom there was a long moment of struggle with her tears. 'Idiot,' she told herself, and opened the door of her wardrobe. What should she wear? She'd started the day in jeans and T-shirt. Did it matter if she wore something better? No, of course not. All the same, she took out one of her summer dresses and, after putting it on, spent a long time over her hair.

She was in the kitchen when the sound of a car brought her hurrying out to the drive. Neil certainly was not a man for ostentation: the new car rental was a Ford. Before stepping out he reached into the back seat, to appear with a handsome carrier bag from a famous London provision merchant. From it there peeped the glistening cellophane top of a bouquet.

He stood on the threshold holding up the carrier. She went up on tiptoe to kiss him as his free arm went around her.

'Celebrations!' he announced.

She led him indoors. He brought out the bouquet. A great bunch of yellow roses, beautifully arranged and tied with green ribbon. 'Do you like yellow?'

'I love it.' She would have loved anything he gave her.

'And this is for Ronald – I thought we might have it later.' He produced a bottle with the label of a fine château.

Roland was at that moment descending the stairs. He came in, to be greeted with the offering of wine. 'Oh! I say! What's this for?'

'I thought we'd give ourselves a bit of a treat, after I've told you what I've been up to. How's things, Ron?'

'Not too bad. I'm on an even keel . . . so far.'

'Good, great, that's what I want to hear. So now, where's these goodies I was promised? Afternoon tea, the whole performance, please.'

'I'll get it. Just settle down in the living room for a minute, it's all ready.'

She went to fetch the tea things. When she entered the living room Neil and her father was standing by the open window,

275

her father speaking in a low tone and Neil nodding in sympathy. She sat down, moved the crockery around with enough energy to let them know she was there. They came to join her.

'Ron says he's learning how to do the dusting,' Neil explained.

'And I can load the dishwashing machine, don't forget that.'

'Housecraft – that's what my mother used to call it. My dad and I had to do our share, but of course a lot of it was looking after the heating system – that's important where I come from.'

Sighing inwardly at mention of his homeland, Laura offered him tea. They settled down to the pleasant ritual. 'Well, there are things I'd like to tell you about, if you're in the mood to hear it.'

'It's about your meeting with your solicitor friends?'

'You got it. First of all, I want to give you a heads-up about Shelley and her father. Did Laura tell you, Ron, she wouldn't let me offer her anything by way of a thank you for what she did? So I kind of let it rattle around in my head while I was on my way back to London. And I decided that what seemed most important to her was that her dad should sell up and move to this dream-scene in Spain.'

'Oh, that,' said Laura. 'El Dorado.'

'That seemed to be the stand-out thing for them, would you agree, Laura?'

'Yes, she seemed to give it a lot of importance.'

'You're not thinking of trying to help them with that, Neil? I mean, how could you?'

'It wouldn't be hard, Ron. All that it needs is for someone to buy Norman's business.'

'Oh, I *see* . . . You asked your legal advisors to help find them a buyer.'

'Not exactly. I'm going to buy it myself.'

'What?' Ronald was astounded. 'What on earth do you want with a newspaper shop?'

'I don't want it – I'll get the legal boys to sell it on to somebody else.'

'But, Neil, nobody wants it,' protested Laura.

'Right. As a business, it's a dead loss – I bet poor old Norm scarcely makes enough to get by. But we drove past that area

276

on our way to Tansfield, remember? You could see that the actual shops were being used. I think some of them had been converted into living quarters. Anyhow, seems to me Leo and Charlie could arrange all that – they'll hire an estate agent to see to it, they wouldn't waste their time on it themselves.'

'Good heavens, who are they, the firm where the prime minister's wife is involved?' Ronald demanded, sceptical.

'No, but they're heavyweights. So I feel pretty certain they'll get someone to sort things out for Norman, and the Dallancys will be en route to Spain before winter sets in.'

Laura clapped her hands. 'What a good idea!'

Her father, always apt to see the dark side of any idea, was shaking his head. 'You don't know the man, Neil. He's likely to be as miserable in Spain as he is in Simmingford.'

'Can't do anything about his temperament, Ronnie. In any case, it's not for him, it's for Shelley. It's kind of an escape plan for her. I think it could work for her, give her a new way to handle her life.'

'And they're not going to know you were the buyer?' Laura asked.

'Great jumping Jehosaphat, of course not! It would cause all kinds of problems. No, it's all going to be done with smoke and mirrors. What d'you think? It seemed a good idea to me.' He waited rather anxiously for her response.

'It's great,' Laura said. 'It's clever!'

'We-ell . . . yes . . . it's a very kind notion,' Ronald agreed.

'Well, why not,' Neil said. 'After all, they're *family*.' He grinned at the word, then he added, 'Mind you, I'm never going anywhere near the area they settle in!'

Despite himself Ronald laughed, and helped himself to a scone. 'So your big city solicitors are going to tie it up neatly for you.'

'Yeah, but that's not all I wanted to talk about.' He paused. 'Is it okay for me to go on and on about my own affairs like this? I feel it's a load for you to listen to.'

'No, no, old chap, you go ahead,' said Ronald.

'Well, it's about Wenaskowa.'

Laura's heart sank. He was going to say he was leaving.

'Did Laura tell you, Ron? I was doing a bit of legal work for some friends of mine back there, they had problems over their environmental rights.'

'No, I didn't know that.' Her father gave Laura a frown of reproach, as if she ought to have kept him informed. She said nothing in response. She didn't want to take any role in this. It would lead to a final parting, and it was all she could do to nerve herself for what was coming.

'Well, it's complicated, but these pals of mine live in a community north of where Dad and I had our tree nursery. They're – you know – Native Americans by descent and their rights to their terrain aren't written down in the same way as if they'd bought the land with money. So when they were trying to deal with the oil company they had a bad time with a phoney lawyer. Quite a few of my neighbours did, but the Nasko came off worst.'

This was all totally new to Ronald. He frowned and looked attentive.

'Now it happened I was coming to the UK to deal with the headquarters bigwigs in Europe so they asked me to . . . you know . . . do what I could for them.'

'Good heavens. I had no idea.'

'I've more or less sorted it out, but when I was back there a few weeks ago I took Leo with me – Leo Angrave, that's my chief legal eagle. And he just confused them so that they didn't know whether what he was saying was good or bad. You know, deal-making babble, like Kim the other night.' He stopped abruptly, aware he ought not to have mentioned the name.

But Ronald waved him on.

'So they asked me to come back when they'd talked it over among themselves. I reckon they had to consult the ancestral spirits.' He hesitated, waiting for some protest about such a plan, but neither of his listeners said anything. Laura was scared to speak, and Ronald was quite taken with the idea. 'I'm no expert, you know,' Neil went on. 'I think somebody in the tribe has to have a dream that gives guidance in some way.'

'Go on,' Ronald urged.

'Okay, then, see, they've decided that it would be good to have me there for a meeting at the hunters' moon. That's next month, somewhere around the third week. So I'll be going back to Alberta then.'

'Oh.' That was Ronald once more, now beginning to be

278

concerned rather than merely interested. 'We'll be sorry to see you go,' he said.

'Oh, gee, there's no need to say it like that. I'll be coming back, you know. I have to check up on how the deal at Tansfield Towers is going. That's another thing I have to tell you about, and I want your opinion. Last night we talked it through, and I asked Charlie to list about half a dozen specific demands in return for my relinquishing my inheritance. The council is to do a lot of work – clean up the graffiti, deal with the damp problem and the rainwater drainage, lay out a play area for the kids – let me see, what else – oh, extend the bus service from that place the kid mentioned, I think it was Chartenhall Road or something, I'm demanding that the bus goes all the way out to Tansfield.' He broke off. 'I think that's all for the moment. What d'you think? Is there anything else we should ask for?'

Neither Laura nor her father replied. They hadn't thought of themselves as empowered to challenge Simmingford Council.

Laura was buoyed up by a feeling of hope now. Neil would be coming back. She said, 'That seems a good list to me. Is the council responsible for the interior of the flats? Perhaps in a while you could suggest they do some updating.'

'Okay, fine, I'll add that to my list of things to do. Leo and Charlie are going to put all this to the housing department tomorrow – at least, Charlie is, but I've persuaded Leo to take a bit of interest because, you know, he's a high-powered guy, very impressive. He's more or less promised to have some of these things going by the time I get back.'

'How long will you be away?'

'Hard to say. I guess it would be about three weeks – a month, maybe.' He paused. 'I was wondering . . . you know . . . if you'd like to come with me, Laura.'

She felt a stab of amazement. Then she gasped, 'Oh yes. Yes!'

He laughed. 'That's showing a lot of ginger! You don't even know if I'm expecting you to stay in the middle of an oilfield! But that would be cruel. So I'll tell you right away that I've got an apartment in Edmonton. Edmonton's okay, you'll like it.'

Her father got up suddenly and went out, taking with him the bottle of wine that Neil had brought. 'I'll put this away,' he muttered.

The suddenness of his movement and the tone of his voice brought Laura up sharp. 'Oh!'

'What?'

'I . . . I should have thought . . . I can't go . . . I can't leave Papa. He's just . . . you see, he's trying to sort himself out, he's sort of fragile, I couldn't just leave him.'

He got up, pulled her out of her chair, and held her close. 'Nobody's asking you to, sweetheart. He's coming too.'

'What?'

'D'you think I didn't catch on to the state he's in? Of course he couldn't be left here on his own, with his feeling that the village is laughing at him, and Kim Grove less than a mile away. Gee whiz, that would be like sentencing him to the water torture. No, no, he's going to come with us.'

'To Edmonton.'

'Yeah. It's kind of industrial, you know, but there's a university, there's a lot going on, and in the fall it's pretty with the trees going all kinds of colours, and you can get to touristy places, so you'd find quite a lot to do while I'm in the north explaining myself to the Nasko. What d'you think?'

'I should think he . . . well, I don't know, we went once to a conference in the US but never actually holidayed . . .'

'Let's ask him.' With an arm still around her, he urged her out of the living room and into the kitchen. There they found Ronald, at the kitchen sink with a vase full of water, into which he was pushing the roses Neil had brought without much care for their welfare.

He didn't acknowledge their arrival. His back remained stubbornly turned to them.

'Say, Ronnie, have you got any work on hand in the office that you couldn't tidy up by the beginning of September?'

No response.

'Come on, stop playing deaf, I know you've got your hearing aids in. I've got something to ask you, Ron.'

'Stop calling me Ron,' said Ronald, rounding on him. 'I never told you you could call me Ron. Or Ronnie.'

'Okay, okay, I'm sorry. What about all the work on your desk? Anything you can't sort out in the next few weeks?'

'It's none of your business!'

'Papa, Neil is trying to ask you something—'

'What's it got to do with him if I've got a lot of work? Thinks I can't manage yours, too, if you go swanning off to Canada!'

'You know, Ronald, you're really what Ma used to call a sorehead,' Neil said. 'If you don't calm down and do the polite, I might withdraw my invitation.'

'I don't care what you might do or not do—' He broke off. 'What invitation?'

'Aha! That's more like it. I was trying to ask you if you'd like to come to Alberta with Laura and me, buddy.'

'What?'

'Alberta. Forests, rivers, the Rockies . . . That's the tourist bit. Of course there's factories and oilfields, too, but you could ignore those and have a lot of fun. You could keep Laura company in Edmonton while I'm away at the pow-wow.'

Ronald was speechless.

'I don't think you've got anything long-term on your list at the moment, Papa,' Laura urged. 'We wouldn't be leaving until mid-September – that's plenty of time to tie things up.'

'But . . . but . . .' Her father was struggling to make some response. And his first instinct was to conserve his dignity by putting up objections. 'The whole idea is absurd! It would cost a fortune. The airfare first of all, and then there's the loss of business while we're away – and it's all right talking about "the tourist bit" but our finances aren't exactly—'

'Ronald,' said Neil, 'I have a confession to make.'

Ronald stared. Laura was startled. A thousand thoughts whirled in her head. He's ill – he's married – he's done something illegal. It was her father who said, blankly, 'A confession about what?'

Neil smiled and coloured up and looked embarrassed.

'The fact of the matter is . . .' He cleared his throat. 'I'm afraid I have to tell you . . . that I'm a millionaire,' he said.

There was a silence. One of the roses in the vase tilted and fell out with a soft plop. That was the only sound for some seconds. Then Laura said, 'The compensation for that dreadful accident to you and your father . . .?'

'Yeah, sure, that was a biggie in itself. But the rest seems to have passed you by, angel.'

'Well, I admit I . . . You did say you'd had to sell up . . . I remember that.'

'Selling up . . . ! Dad and I entered into a long negotiation and I ended up recently letting go of the oil rights for an enormous sum. You see, we were the last hold-outs in a whole group of drillings. If we didn't give in, it made the whole thing ten times more difficult. But after Dad died the poker game didn't seem so much fun. So I came over here to finalize the deal with Energy Interlock – that's why I've been knocking about here and there, over to the Netherlands; they have their exploration headquarters there but their legal department's in London.'

'A millionaire?' Ronald said in a faint voice.

'I know,' said Neil, with sympathy. 'It seems weird to me, too. But it's true. And after a bit you get more used to it, and one of the things that happens is that you can go places and do things and not have to bother too much about the cost. So if you and Laura would honour me with your company on this trip –' and he paused to smile at the formality – 'I'd be delighted to see to all the financial details. If you'd let me.'

'Well, of course . . . in that case . . .'

'Is that a yes? Great! Because, you see, we could perhaps extend it a bit. After I've seen the Nasko council, you know. We could go looking for a place to start again.'

'I'm sorry?' Ronald said, perplexed.

'Well, I can't grow trees any more at Wenaskowa. So I have to find somewhere else. You could help me do a survey – give me your opinion.'

'You're going to start the tree nursery again?'

'Sure. What else? That's what I am, really. I grow trees.'

Laura, who was standing with his arm around her, pressed herself close against him. She wanted him to know that she was with him in every way. He glanced down at her, smiled, and asked, 'How about it? Would you like to go prospecting for a good site for trees?'

'I don't know anything about trees, Neil,' she protested.

'That's okay. I'll be the tree expert. What I'd like from you and Ron is a view about settling there.'

'Settling?'

'Settling down. Making a home.'

'But . . . but . . .'

'If you're going to say, what about the research business,

282

don't. I've got it all figured out. You don't need to be here in Brinbank, now do you? Most of your work is done on the Internet. You can call up almost anything you need, right?'

'Well . . . yes, but—'

'You remember I told you about old Linus, who did the initial research on the Crandels for Dad? He did it mostly on the Internet. And he did quite well, though he was no expert. When I decided to go on further with it, I could have found your website and got you to do it for me without ever leaving Alberta. Now couldn't I?'

'Yes, but—'

'It happened that I wanted to come to London to dicker with these oil guys. So I decided to contact someone when I got here, someone I could talk to personally. But I needn't have, isn't that so?'

'Yes, but—'

'Stop saying "yes, but" like a recording!' he commanded, laughing. 'I'm right, aren't I, Ron?'

To Laura's amazement her father was smiling broadly. 'I won't say "yes, but",' he remarked. 'All the same, you can't expect us to have a ready reply.'

'Well, let's take it a step at a time, eh? You'll come on my next visit home and look around, see if you like it. Okay?'

'Yes, I think Laura and I agree to that with enthusiasm.'

'Great. So after that we come back, we inspect what Simmingford Council are doing with Tansfield Towers, and you consider whether you could tie up your business and sell the house – and whether you want to do that.'

'That's the big point, Neil. Whether we want to.'

'There's a lot to be said for it. This house, great though it is –' he gestured towards the hall and the rest of the place – 'seems an inefficient setting for a business. Then there's the fact that you've got one or two people in your vicinity that you're not too friendly with. You know?'

Ronald sighed. 'Only too true.'

'And then there's the point that Laura and I want to be together.' He gave her a little hug. 'Right?'

'Yes, we do,' she agreed with fervour. 'I wouldn't want to stay on here, Papa, if it meant being separated from Neil.'

Her father was shaking his head and waving a hand for

attention. 'This is blackmail, you know,' he said, though his tone wasn't hostile.

'It is, kind of,' Neil agreed. 'See here, Ron, you don't have to come on the visit if you don't want to. If you do, I'd like you to think about whether you could make a permanent move. If you say no, we'll give it another look – I could maybe find somewhere in the UK that would suit – though land is kind of scarce here – but there's France, that's not far off. We could give it some thought.'

Ronald nodded. 'Yes, it needs some thought. It's a big change.' He found the rose that had fallen into the sink and made an attempt to put it in the vase. But his attention was elsewhere. 'I think I'll go out,' he said rather abruptly. 'I'll let the notion simmer awhile. I don't think I'll be back for supper, Laura – don't bother doing anything for me.'

With a shrug and a frown he was gone. In a few moments they heard the Land Rover starting. Neil said, rather worried, 'Has he gone off in a huff?'

'I don't think so. In fact, strange though it seems to me, I think he's being tactful.'

'Aha. You mean in leaving us alone together for a couple of hours?'

'Exactly.'

'We should take advantage of it, then, shouldn't we?'

She laughed. They turned towards the door to the hall. She paused, touching him on the arm. 'You know, I never sent you a bill for all the work we did.'

'That's true.' He nodded, pretending to consider it a problem. 'Would it be okay if I settle up by deferred payments?'

'But you just told me you've got lots of money!'

'Yeah, but deferred payments take a long time.'

'You mean you'll be in debt to me for months and months.'

'Years and years, I'd imagine.'

She smiled. 'Sounds good to me.'

He put his arm around her to urge her towards the staircase. 'Let's go upstairs and take a long time over discussing it.'

As they began their slow ascent, it was clear to both of them that they would have very little need for words for the next few hours.